"Lords of the Soil"

You are holding a reproduction of an original work that is in the public domain in the United States of America, and possibly other countries. You may freely copy and distribute this work as no entity (individual or corporate) has a copyright on the body of the work. This book may contain prior copyright references, and library stamps (as most of these works were scanned from library copies). These have been scanned and retained as part of the historical artifact.

This book may have occasional imperfections such as missing or blurred pages, poor pictures, errant marks, etc. that were either part of the original artifact, or were introduced by the scanning process. We believe this work is culturally important, and despite the imperfections, have elected to bring it back into print as part of our continuing commitment to the preservation of printed works worldwide. We appreciate your understanding of the imperfections in the preservation process, and hope you enjoy this valuable book.

"HEATHER FLOWER"

"Lords of the Soil"

A Romance of Indian Life Among the Early English Settlers

BY

LYDIA A. JOCELYN

AND

NATHAN J. CUFFEE

C. M. CLARK PUBLISHING CO., Inc.
BOSTON, MASS., U.S.A.
1905

Copyright, 1905, by
C. M. CLARK PUBLISHING CO., Inc.
BOSTON, MASS., U.S.A.

Entered at
STATIONER'S HALL, LONDON
Foreign Copyrights Secured

All Rights Reserved

To the Memory of
HER HUSBAND
THE "MARTYR MISSIONARY OF THE BLACK HILLS,"
This Work is Affectionately Dedicated

BY

LYDIA A. JOCELYN

Contents

CHAPTERS

		PAGE
I	Poggatticutt's Farewell	1
II	Called by the Great Spirit	11
III	Heather Flower	18
IV	An Indian Shrine	29
V	An Indian Wooing	38
VI	In Constancy	47
VII	For Good or Evil?	55
VIII	An Invocation to Ho-bam-o-ko	64
IX	A Red Esau	72
X	A La Mort	90
XI	A Bow with Two Strings	97
XII	The Warwhoop of the Montauks	108
XIII	The Law of the White Man	118
XIV	Wic-chi-tau-bit	124
XV	Birds of Prey	136
XVI	The Signal Fire	148
XVII	"Noche Trieste"	155
XVIII	"Even to the Half of My Kingdom"	168
XIX	"Unknelled, Uncoffined, and Unknown"	171
XX	An Intricate Webb	178
XXI	True to Birth and Breeding	184

Contents

CHAPTERS

		PAGE
XXII	"Blue Laws"	190
XXIII	On Charge of Witchcraft	199
XXIV	The Majesty of the Law	205
XXV	Ninigret's Captives	213
XXVI	A Parthian Shot	220
XXVII	"'Twixt Love and Duty"	226
XXVIII	An Ancient Family	236
XXIX	"Bull Smith"	246
XXX	Lady Deborah Moody	256
XXXI	Heart Struggles	266
XXXII	Vengeance Conquers Love	276
XXXIII	On All-Hallow Eve	285
XXXIV	The War Party	296
XXXV	Sine-rong-ni-rese	800
XXXVI	A Captive to the Mohawks	307
XXXVII	Viking	321
XXXVIII	After the Moon Went Down	329
XXXIX	An Effective Masquerade	887
XL	The Slave Ship	846
XLI	An Ocean Grave	852

Contents

CHAPTERS

		PAGE
XLII	A Vow Fulfilled	360
XLIII	Cut-was, the Arrow Maker	370
XLIV	Honour for Naught	381
XLV	Reading Between the Lines	391
XLVI	Guy Kingsland's Undoing	397
XLVII	An Indian Torquemada	405
XLVIII	Mah-chon-it-chuge	410
XLIX	The Doppleganger	418
L	Unreturning	425
LI	Taking up the Threads of Fate	430
LII	An Unbidden Guest	437
LIII	Frozen	444
LIV	With Book and Ring	452
LV	Dissolving Views	460

Illustrations

Frontispiece   Heather Flower

	PAGE
"With the quickness of thought Mandush adjusted an arrow to the bow-string"	43
"The traitor's mask had been torn from her false lover"	112
"She was seized and borne shoreward by two powerful warriors"	159
"Slowly, with an interval between each stroke, the cat-o'-nine tails fell"	207
"Colonel Lawrence offered his arm to Elizabeth"	250
"The leader of the band arose and harangued his followers"	299
"She is mine! mine! I will not give her up"	368
"Swift as the lightning's bolt the arrow sped"	403
"The plaintive howl of the hound guided the hunters to the very verge of the fen"	435

LORDS OF THE SOIL

CHAPTER I

POGGATTICUT'S FAREWELL

> "We children of a favoured day
> Inheriting their homes,
> Would guard their history from decay,
> And mark their mouldering tombs."

THE date, a day in the month of May, in the year 1654.

From his wigwam beneath the shadows of the giant oaks, adjacent to Sunset Rock, upon the shore of the lesser Peconic bay, an Indian chieftain emerged, a man of commanding mien, and slow, but stately step. In form he was erect and matchless, although the frosts of a hundred winters had bleached his once raven locks to snowy whiteness, and his eagle eye gazed unblenchingly at the setting sun as he seated himself upon the pinnacle of the rugged rock that for so many years had been his throne.

It was Poggatticut,[1] King of the Manhansetts, who had come forth to take a last look at the setting sun, and to bid farewell to the dying day, for, ere the luminary should again brighten the eastern horizon, the brave soul of the mighty Sachem would be gone to the spirit land.

The last golden beams shot athwart the placid bay, crowning his head with a halo of glory, and turning the crystals of the rough rock to amber and diamond sparks.

[1] *Poggatticut.*—Wise-man.

The sound of a firm, hasty footfall attracted his attention, and along the footpath winding beneath the canopy of forest trees lining the bluff overhanging the green water, a tall, athletic figure was approaching.

The keen glance of the chieftain noted the coming of the white man, but he remained motionless, as though he were a portion of the rock upon which he rested, rather than a conscious being, his gaze fixed upon the white line of foam-wreath lapping the opposite shore; and not a lineament of his grave face changed as the stranger halted within ten paces and stood regarding the noble figure of the aged chieftain with an admiration he could not repress.

"Can my red brother tell me where I may find Poggatticut, the Wise-man of the Manhansetts?" inquired the stranger, addressing the chief in the tongue common to the four tribes who dwelt upon the islands and inhabited the shores of the mainland, which we will translate as far as possible.

The chieftain turned his head and fixed his deep-set, searching eyes upon the speaker, noting in one comprehensive survey every detail of face, form and costume.

"Poggatticut is here," returned the aged King, a glow of half-pride, half-anger in his eyes, which passed like the glimmer of the lightning among the dark clouds, as he laid his hand upon his breast. "I am Poggatticut. What would my white brother with the Sagamore of the Manhansetts?"

"I am called James Farret; and I come with a commission from the Commandant at Saybrook Fort to the Chief of the Manhansetts," replied the stranger, meeting the distrustful gaze bent upon him with a keen eye, a smile curving his finely-cut lips.

The chief rose to his feet with the quiet dignity befitting his station, his features composed; but the gleam in his eyes, playing like sparks of fire in the contracted pupils, warned the visitor that the errand upon which he had come would be likely to prove bootless.

"The wily old Sagamore will prove a thorn in the flesh, if I mistake not the inflexible expression writ on that granite front—I must try the potent power of whiskey. These savages are never proof against the seductions of the bottle," mused Farret, as he glanced furtively at the face of the Indian, then allowed his eyes to wander away across the shining waters, while he waited for the chieftain to speak.

But the lips of Poggatticut were sealed.

In person, the white man was of ordinary size, with perhaps greater breadth of shoulder and depth of chest than the average European; his limbs were well made and muscular to a degree, as revealed beneath the tightly-laced leggings, girded at the knee by breeches of brown corduroy. A serviceable coat of black camlet, with wide cuffs turned back at the wrists to exhibit the sleeves of a white linen shirt; the broad coat-collar rolled low, displaying a silver stock-clasp at the back of the neck, and the whole fashioned with wide pocket-flaps and capacious skirt. A handsomely-embroidered blue waistcoat of heavy silk was opened, revealing the ruffled shirt front to the waist line, which was girdled by a leathern belt. The hilt of his sheathed sword was silver-mounted in elaborate design, matched by the pattern on silver knee-buckles, stock-clasp, and the plate upon the breech of the short gun he carried, which bore the initials "J. F." in old English script. His belt was garnished by a pair of heavy navy-pistols, also silver-mounted, a bullet-pouch and powder-horn completing his warlike equipments. A broad hat rested upon his head, while his hair (after the fashion of the Royalist party during the reign of Oliver Cromwell) fell in curling masses across his neck. His eyes were steel-blue, keen and restless; his brow, from which the hat was pushed back, was broad at the base, narrowing and retreating at the top, his nose aquiline, with thin and expanded nostrils, his lips compressed, but well formed,—the entire countenance denoting the iron will and determination of the man who was the authorised agent of the Duke of York, with power-of-attorney to dispose of Long Island, and with the choice of retaining for his own the goodly area of 12,000 acres of such a portion of the grant as he should designate. And he had chosen Robins' Island, an emerald gem set in the heart of Great Peconic Bay, and Manhansett-aha-quash-a-warnuck [2] as his share in the land covered by the grant of the Duke of York across the blue waves; but to procure a title from the "Lords of the Soil" might prove a far more difficult task.

Twice had the granted lands been disposed of by the usurper,—first, through his own sale to a single purchaser, who, in turn, had conveyed it to four grantees. They strenuously insisted upon a confirmation of their title from the King of the Manhansetts, whose dominions had been thus summarily possessed, and who, foreseeing the threatened extermination of his race, as well as the wholesale appropriation of its lands, had set his face as adamant, and turned a deaf ear to every solicitation that might aid in the encroachment of the pale-faces.

James Farret, the silver-tongued agent, had been

---

[2] *Manhansett-aha-quash-a-warnuck.*—Island sheltered by islands. Indian name for Shelter Island.

chosen as the fittest ambassador,—the man of all others to win the confidence of Poggatticut.

Side by side they stood, one a polished courtier, a diplomat from what had been the gayest court in Europe; the other, grand, majestic, even with a century of years weighing upon his mental and physical strength, a giant in intellect, a very bulwark to his people.

That the frosts of age had chilled his blood was apparent from the fact that, although the balmy May breezes were soft and warm, beneath his furry mantle he wore a loosely-fitting jacket of buckskin. His limbs were encased in fringed leggings reaching to the thigh, daintily ornamented with coloured quills and beads, patiently wrought from the purple suck-au-hock,[3] while the girdle at his waist, from which depended his broad knife, was of the same precious shell, so highly valued by all the tribes.

A single eagle plume was interwoven with the flowing scalp-lock, the symbol of authority, the coronet of an Indian king.

Presently the white man spoke:

"I am come, Great Chief, upon a mission of importance, to ask that a council of your chief men may be called, to deliberate upon a matter of the gravest importance both to my red and white

---

[3] *Suck-au-hock.*—From the Indian "sucki," signifying black. "Black money." *Seawan* was the name of Indian money, of which there were two kinds: Wampum, signifying *white*, was manufactured from the stem of the periwinkle. Suck-au-hock was made from the inside shell of the quahaug. The Indians broke off half an inch of purple colour from the lining of the shell and converted it into beads. These were bored by sharp stones and strung on the sinews of deer, and when interwoven to a hand-breadth were called a *seawan* or *wampum* belt. A black bead, one-third of an inch long, bored longitudinally and well, was the gold of the Indians—twice the value of the white. Either kind was esteemed by the Indians of much more value than European coin. It was both money and an ornament.

brothers. My path has been long and weary, even from the fort at Saybrook. I must, perforce, crave the shelter of your wigwam and food whereby I may sustain my strength while I tarry. Will the Great Sachem of the Manhansetts give what I ask?"

The chief turned his head and fixed his flashing eyes full upon the face of the white man, as if he would read his very soul, ere he replied:

"Before the pale-face came from beyond the sunrise, the red man held power and dominion from the waters of the big sea to the land of the setting sun, and when the pale-face brother came to the wigwam of the red man he was naked, cold and hungry, and with no shelter for his head; the red man gave him of the fur of the beaver, the skin of the bear and the elk, and warmed him by his wigwam blaze, fed him with corn and the flesh of the bear and the deer, and the fish of the stream and the sea, and gave him whereon to dwell. Shall the King of the Manhansetts do less?" inquired the chief, proudly.

"He will do no less; the hospitality of the great Sachem has never been doubted," returned Farret; "and though the Sachem of the Manhansetts cannot accept the gold of the new pale-face brother in exchange for shelter and food, let us drink to our better understanding, to the continued friendship which has so long existed between the red men of sea-wan-ha-ka and Manhansett-aha-quash-a-warnuck and their white brothers at Saybrook Fort."

The Sachem drew himself to his loftiest height, fairly transfixing the eyes of his tempter by the kindling spark in his own, and with a disdainful gesture waved back the hand that held a silver flask from which the stopper had been unloosed, and a strong scent of brandy emanated.

"Listen, white brother," he replied, sternly. "How has the pale-face repaid his red brother? Like the serpent he spoke with a forked tongue; he stung the bosom that warmed him back to life—his heart was black; he gave strong water to the red man that made him weak and foolish, and when he was drunk with the fire-water the pale-face would buy the red man's country and give him nothing for something. Poggatticut spurns the strong water as he does the fang of the serpent!"

The foiled diplomat bit his lip in intense anger, and for a moment his resentment nearly overmastered his sense of prudence, but conquering his rising passion, he returned to the subject which had brought him many a league into the heart of the wilderness.

"As you will," he returned in a smooth tone; "I have offered the fire-water that makes the heart strong, according to the custom of my people, who, from the earliest times, have quaffed from the loving-cup, as the red man smokes the calumet around the council fire."

He paused, but the dignified Sachem vouchsafed no response to the apology.

"Will the great Sachem of the Manhansetts call together the wise men of his counsellors, that the pale-face brother may smoke with them the calumet, and lay before the council the weighty matter he is here to adjust?" inquired Farret, his eyes hidden beneath the drooping lids, that the Indian might not read their expression.

The Sachem still sat with his glowing eyes fixed upon the downcast face, and remained silent for a space. At length he opened his lips.

"Let my white brother speak with a straight tongue; let him tell his red brother what brought him here, and why he asks that the Sachem of the Manhansetts should bring his counsellors around the council fire—his red brother will answer. Poggatticut's ears are open."

Thus adjured, the wily agent felt compelled to speak.

"Many moons ago the Great Father across the green waters granted to his subjects a tract of land, that they might live among their red brethren in peace and harmony, that they might teach them the arts known among Europeans, and appointed me as their agent, with full power to negotiate for all sales; but the great King of the Manhansetts has never ratified the sale by giving consent; wherefore, I am come, that the title may be confirmed. Then can the pale-faces and their red brothers dwell together in peace and harmony, and to this end have I asked that the council fire may be kindled."

"You have come, as they came to our brothers on the mainland,—the Wampanoags, the Narragansetts and the Pequots,—and when the red men had given them a home the pale-face struck them like the rattlesnake; and when they would strike back the pale-face made war upon them, and they, in turn, had to show the sole of the foot in place of the white of the eye. Now, the pale-face has come with his white-winged canoes, bringing from the land of the burning sun the dark-skinned race, and, like them, he would make us his slaves. He has destroyed our forests and driven away the game, and our strong men die as with the plague. Go back over the trail you came, across the green waters to the pale-face chief whom you call the Great Father, and take to him the words of the King of the Manhansetts. Poggatticut is lord of the soil! His hand shall never affix his totem to that which will make his people slaves, his son a stranger to the burial place of his fathers!"

He turned away, and by an expressive gesture signified that the conference was at an end.

Chagrined and enraged, without a word of farewell to the haughty chief, James Farret plunged into the forest path from which he had emerged, and was quickly lost to sight.

Rising slowly to his feet, and gazing earnestly at the dying god of day, the old Nestor spoke:

"Great light of the Great Father, Poggatticut has come to say farewell. The moons of a century have waxed and waned since I first saw thy light, and in all my life you have been my unfailing friend, bringing the seasons of corn and plenty, making the earth in all its fulness glad because you smiled upon it; and when the Storm Spirit was abroad in the air, when the frost and snow came down and the waters were tied with icy hand, when the buffalo and deer had not where to feed, when the Famine Spirit whispered in the night wind, the Great Spirit would send you back to uncover the earth and make it smile and grow green again with abundant harvest, to unlock the waters and make them dance to the song of the happy birds in all the woodlands, and drive the Storm Spirit back to its home under the North Star.

"The Great Spirit has whispered to Poggatticut in the voice of the night wind, and has said, 'Come!'

"The Great Spirit is angry with His red children because we have suffered the pale-faces to take away the land which was the inheritance of our fathers, and as the pale-faces increase, the red man will be driven out and away until he is homeless, and be hunted by the pale-face as a she-wolf.

"The moons of centuries shall come and go

before the Great Spirit's anger shall pass, and He will smile again upon His red children; but when He shall frown upon the pale-face, whose black heart has made Him angry because of his treatment of his red brothers, when the pale-face young warriors are about to fall in war, like the autumn leaves, Manitou shall give a sign. He shall hide His face behind the storm-cloud and shall speak in a voice of thunder, and shall send His lightning to smite this rock,[4] that shall be my throne no longer. Poggatticut has spoken."

[4] In the summer of 1892 Sunset rock was shivered by lightning, and fell in nine portions. It was named by the Indians "Poggatticut's Throne," and there is a tradition among them that when the rock should be hurled from its foundation a portion of their ancient inheritance would be restored.

CHAPTER II

CALLED BY THE GREAT SPIRIT

"Now they are gone,—gone as the setting blaze
Goes down the west, while night is pressing on,
And with them the old tale of better days,
And trophies of remembered power are gone."

WITHIN a commodious wigwam of oblong form, fully thirty feet in length and twenty in breadth, a strange scene was transpiring.

It was the midnight hour by the solemn moon which rode high in the heavens, dimming the fainter light of the stars studding the blue firmament like myriads of diamond points.

Without the lodge was the white lustre of a May night, within the gloom of the Death Angel's wing; for, upon a couch of bear-skins, piled high, the aged chieftain of the Manhansetts lay, silent and motionless, his fast-glazing eyes fixed upon the face of a young warrior standing beside the entrance from which the matting that served as a door was drawn aside to admit the cool night breeze.

It was apparent that the impending blow had struck deep in the heart of Yo-kee; although he was exercising all the fortitude of a red man to control any exhibition of weakness.

Poggatticut lay upon his death couch, his limbs had lost the power of motion, even his lips were rigid, his jaws set.

Beside the couch, hovering over the dying, was a

strange figure, partially enveloped in a blanket wrought with strange devices, figures of serpents, beasts and fishes, with rude representations of the sun, the moon and the stars. Unlike the custom of the warriors, who wore only the scalp-lock, his hair was long and matted, falling below his shoulders. His nether limbs were encased in buckskin leggings; the hunting shirt, visible beneath the blanket, was girded at the waist by a rattlesnake skin, knotted loosely after the manner of a sash, from which depended a pouch half-filled with dried herbs.

His face was seamed and wizened, his eyes deep-set and fairly glowing from beneath the pent-house of his overhanging brows.

In a hollow, nearly in the centre of the wigwam, burned a mass of firebrands, over which a clay pot was simmering and bubbling, throwing out clouds of steam and diffusing a bitter odour that was almost stifling.

The face of the young warrior was bedewed with perspiration from the effects of the pungent steam bath, but the face of the dying chieftain was pallid and cold where the death-dews were gathering.

The dull glare from the coals fell upon the dark face of Wee-gon, the great medicine-man [1] of the Manhansetts, who, with outstretched arms, was making mysterious passes over the prostrate form upon the couch and muttering strange incantations in guttural, monotonous drone, not unlike the hum of a bumble-bee,—accented occasionally by the hiss of a

---

[1] The medicine-man was at once a prophet, physician and clergyman of his tribe. He was as unapproachable as the ruler of a civilised nation, certain forms being necessary to obtain an audience. By an unwritten law, he was not allowed to marry, but lived in solitude and in all the state of a man supposed to be gifted with occult powers. In all matters pertaining to the government of his tribe he was consulted, and considered an oracle. His person was held sacred.

serpent whose ugly head was thrust forth at intervals from the bosom of Wee-gon's hunting shirt.

"Hist, boy, hist!"

At the word of command from the strange being, the serpent withdrew his head, coiling obediently against the breast of his master, until some peculiar intonation of the voice brought the head of the reptile again into view, when the hissing was renewed.

In a dim corner of the lodge crouched an aged squaw, her face bent upon her knees, her head enveloped in the folds of a blanket, the form a blacker shadow among shadows. For hours she had sat thus, immobile as the earth upon which she rested, only the lean hands clasping her knees visible.

Ere the rising of another sun Lig-o-mee would be widowed and Yo-kee, her son, would be King of the Manhansetts.

Suddenly the dolorous invocation ceased. Wee-gon drew himself to his full height, the ugly head of the rattlesnake was hidden and an ominous silence reigned—the hush of death.

It was a weird scene, the tall form stretched upon the couch; the silent, central figure of the group,—the grim-faced Wee-gon,—the youthful warrior upon whose broad shoulders the mantle of the dead sage had fallen; the crouching squaw, motionless as a bronze statue; and, flickering fitfully over all, the light of the dying firebrands, barely making darkness visible.

With an intonation peculiar to the Lenni Lenape language, mournful as the sighing of the autumn winds among the branches of the whispering pines, the voice of Wee-gon broke the silence.

"The mighty oak has fallen, but the topmost

branch is green and full of life. The tongue of Poggatticut is silent—Yo-kee is King of the Manhansetts. Let Lig-o-mee weep with the squaws of her tribe that the mighty warrior who took her to his lodge has gone to the land of the spirits."

Without a word, the aged squaw arose and with slow step left the wigwam, not once uncovering her face or turning her eyes toward the couch whereon rested all that was mortal of the husband whom she had served for hundreds of moons; not then could she be permitted to weep over the lifeless clay. The customs of her people, dating back into the dim ages of the past, forbade any exhibition of the grief that was consuming her soul; and in silence she awaited the hour when she might relieve her overcharged heart in wailing and tears—until the period allotted to the woman when she might weep over her dead.

The face of the young chieftain was composed. Any exhibition of his grief would be unseemly; but his features were set, and the eagle eye that had lost its usual gleam was tender in its softness, but no other token was visible as the medicine-man drew his blanket over his face, and, without another word, stalked from the lodge and stood silently among the tall undergrowth hedging the path.

Presently the dull alarm of the tom-tom woke the echoes along the shore, warning the sleeping warriors that some evil event had befallen, and from the scattered lodges of the Manhansetts the chief men and counsellors came forth and listened to the story of their loss—only a brief sentence:

"Poggatticut, the Wise-man of the Manhansetts has gone. The Great Spirit has called him."

At a signal from Wee-gon a slender young Indian separated himself from his fellows and glided away, halting outside the wigwam where the dead king was lying, where he awaited the command of Yo-kee, standing as immovable as if carved in stone.

With slow, measured tread five of the wisest in council approached and entered the lodge, noiselessly as spectres, and stood with bowed heads before the young warrior who was now their chieftain.

Five minutes elapsed, while the young Indian kept his pose at the door of the wigwam, awaiting the order which he knew would come.

Presently the mat in front of the wigwam entrance was drawn aside and Yo-kee stood before him.

"Ko-zhe-osh,[2] away! Bear to the lodges of Wyandance,[3] Nowedanah and Momometou the words of Yo-kee—say that Poggatticut, the wise, the mighty warrior, has gone to the spirit land. Let the feet of Ko-zhe-osh be like the deer when he flees before the hunter, and bring word again from the brothers of my father."

The head of the Indian runner was bowed low in deference to the young chief, he laid his hand upon his heart, as he replied, the deep tones, musical, yet sad, betraying his grief:

"The feet of Ko-zhe-osh are swift as the flight of the eagle, his limbs tireless as the seabird's wing. He will bring word from the great Sachems."

He settled his knife in his belt, and grasped his tomahawk with a tighter grip.

Placing a wampum belt[4] in the hand of the messenger, Yo-kee swept his arm from right to left, indicating the order in which the intelligence was to be conveyed, and, without another word, the young

[2] *Ko-zhe-osh.*—Fleet Flyer.
[3] *Wyandance.*—Warrior King.
[4] Among the Indian tribes a message sent without the wampum belt was an empty word.

runner glided away with the easy, sinuous motion and silence of a serpent, and was quickly lost to view.

Outside the lodge a concourse of braves and warriors had gathered; the harsh, monotonous beat of the drum, the long-drawn howls of an army of dogs in unison, echoed through the leafy forest, but not the sound of a human voice was heard among the five hundred stalwart warriors whom the King of the Manhansetts could bring into battle, gathered in groups beneath the forest shade, while within the lodge the few privileged to robe the dead form, which no sacrilegious hand might profane with even a touch, were performing their office, arraying the sacred person of their king in his robes of state for the burial.[5]

In profound silence they wrought, touching the cold clay with reverent hands, as gently as if the inanimate form could feel the touch of their fingers.

It was over at last, and the body wrapped in the kingly robe fashioned from the skins of the grizzly bear, curiously painted and ornamented with the costly suck-au-hock; a belt of the same precious shell beads, a hand-breadth in width, girdled the soft buckskin shirt about the waist, the breast was adorned with numerous strings of beads and a necklace of the gleaming white teeth of the savage bear and catamount, trophies of the chieftain's skill and prowess as a renowned hunter. The pulseless wrists were clasped by oddly interwoven bracelets of purple shell; leggings and moccasins, inwrought with all the skill of Lig-o-mee, the well-beloved squaw of the dead Sachem, the mother of Yo-kee, encased his feet and lower limbs, but, as in life, the thighs were left bare to the breechcloth, revealing the contour of

---

[5] So much was Poggatticut held in reverence that but few of even his chief counsellors were allowed to touch his dead body.

CALLED BY GREAT SPIRIT

the still powerful limbs.[6] A fillet of suck-au-hock surmounted by the eagle plume [7] encircled the copper-coloured forehead, which the hand of death had paled to a softer tint.

One by one the trio whose hands had touched the body stole from the wigwam, leaving Yo-kee alone with his dead.

Anon the pearly gates of morning rolled back and the first beams of the rising sun fell in rosy and amber radiance upon the still, set features of the aged monarch, noble and dignified, even in death. Like a statue wrought in bronze he lay upon his couch, his ponderous bow by his side, a quiver filled with arrows resting against his arm, his tomahawk and knife within his girdle.

To the very last hour of his life Poggatticut had steadily opposed the sale of the lands of his tribe—often had his voice been heard in the council, not for opposing the pale-faces in warlike array, but for a steady refusal to resign any portion of his domain. How little dreamed the sorrowing warriors of that powerful tribe that the sinewy hand at the nation's helm would ere long sign away the land of his fathers which the aged king had held with so firm a grasp!

[6] To the aboriginal Indian the constraint of a covering to the kneejoint or wrists would have been considered intolerable.
[7] Eagle plume—emblem of royalty among the aborigines.

CHAPTER III

HEATHER FLOWER

"Dim was the woodland and fair was the weather,
  And blue were the skies of the beautiful May,
When laughing and singing, we wandered together,
  With hearts attuned to the happy day.
We sought the shades where the birds were singing
  And busily building the summer nest,
Where the branches, ever swaying and swinging,
  Should rock the twittering brood to rest."

IN the very heart of a dense forest, upon the highlands of Montauk,[1] known as the Heather woods, nestled a cluster of lodges, the village of the renowned Montauk Sachem, Wyandance, one of the four brothers, kings of Sea-wan-ha-ka[2] and Manhansett-aha-quash-a-warnuck, and Sachem of the totem tribe, to whom twelve minor tribes paid tribute annually in seawan.[3]

It was a lovely sylvan spot where the music of the birds and the ceaseless murmur of purling brooks and whispering zephyrs soothed the senses and delighted the ear.

The great lodge, standing apart from the cluster, was commodious enough to have sheltered two or even three families, when compared with the usual dimensions of wigwams of warriors and braves, yet here the great Montauk Sachem dwelt in state, with his son, Wyancombone, his queen, Wic-chi-tau-bit,

[1] *Montauk.*—The place of lookout.
[2] *Sea-wan-ha-ka.*—Island of shells.
[3] *Seawan.*—Indian money.

and his daughter, Ash-kick-o-tau-tup,⁴ and a woman of burden, Tom-a-la, upon whom devolved the duty of planting his corn, beans and pumpkins, harvesting his winter store, cooking his venison, and performing the many menial services which fall to the lot of the Indian squaw,⁵ from which, by the happy circumstance of birth, Ash-kick-o-tau-tup, his beloved daughter, and Wic-chi-tau-bit, his queen, who was of royal race among the Iroquois, were exempt.

The afternoon was waning; above the heavily-wooded heights floated shoals of fleecy clouds, their amber-tipped edges changing rapidly in form, pencilling a series of cloud-pictures with the rapidity of a panoramic view. Low in the western sky the sun hung like a jewel of flame; the balmy southern-breeze-ruffled waters of Gardiner Bay away to the east; to the south and west the dense forest of maple, oak, ash and walnut had but recently donned the spring attire of tender green, while the dark fir and pine tossed their plumed branches of darker, more sombre hue, in pleasing contrast.

Over the placid waters of the bay the seabird winged his way, hovering low over the curling waves; in the tree-tops the birds sang their vespers, bright-eyed squirrels leaped from bough to bough, insects chirped in the long grass, the drowsy hum of the honey-laden bee on his homeward flight, mingled in rhythm with the plash of the brooklet on the boulders that obstructed the placid flow between the green, violet-tufted banks.

Sixty feet below the crest of the bold promontory, and at its foot, stretched a long strip of sandy beach, washed by the bright waters of the bay, and

⁴ *Ash-kick-o-tau-tup.*—Heather Flower.
⁵ The entire labour of planting, harvesting, and making and rearing wigwams, and every item of labour, save hunting and fishing, is performed by the squaws.

sparsely clothed with alder and the wales of red willow, with their grey, furry buds beaded upon the slender, pliant twigs.

Upon a brow of the promontory, a point overlooking the blue waters of Fort Pond Bay and the eastern end of Long Island Sound, and commanding a view of Man-cho-nock [6] in the distance, and the lesser islands dotting the vista that stretched away to the shores of the mainland to the north, two maidens were standing, looking out seaward.

The eldest appeared scarcely twenty years of age. In stature she was tall, with a form beautifully moulded and splendidly developed, the contour revealed by the piquant Indian costume—a garment of finest doeskin, fitting the rounded bust, and confined at the waistline by a glistening belt of bright-hued beads and stained quills, fully four inches in width, and falling in strands from the hip to the edge of the skirt reaching to the knee. The leggings and moccasins, of the same material as the tunic, were also fancifully adorned with coloured quills of the porcupine and designs in beads. A fillet of bright-hued feathers. the plumage of the bluebird, the cardinal grosbeak and the snowy pigeon bound back a cascade of purplish black hair which fell in shining mass [7] below the waist.

In form and feature Heather Flower was a type of beauty such as is rarely met, even at the courts of Christian kings, among the famed beauties of Circassia, or in sunny Spain. Her face was a per-

---

[6] *Man-cho-nock.*—Named Island of Wight by its proprietor, Lyon Gardiner; now known as Gardiner Island. In the Indian tongue it signifies " Place of many dead."

[7] The shining black hair of the aborigines was glossy and abundant; but the custom of plucking the hair, leaving only the scalplock, was universal among the males, while the females retained the shining tresses which nature had bountifully bestowed.

fect oval, her complexion olive rather than copper, a rich creamy tint flushed with the warm blood that tinged her cheeks and turned the lips to coral. Her large Syrian eyes were brilliant, of intense blackness, with the latent fires of love or hatred smouldering in their depths.

It was not so much the brilliant colouring, the regularity of the features, or the statuesque form that attracted the observer, as the promise of wild daring, or unyielding will, powerful either for intense love or fierce hatred, a nature at once passionate, impulsive, fiery, daring, proud, even to haughtiness, and yet gentle and capable of the most intense devotion to a beloved object.

Her companion presented a contrast that was almost startling, exhibiting, as it did, such a different type of rare loveliness.

She was a slender little creature, childish and almost fairy-like in form, with luminous violet eyes, a complexion of pearly whiteness, a wild-rose flush just staining the rounded cheeks, and a cloud of yellow hair falling over an exquisitely moulded neck and shoulders, shining like gold in the sunshine.

The rosebud lips wreathed in smiles, disclosing the pearly teeth, her hands and feet sylph-like in their proportions, her arms of milky whiteness.

A Juno from Olympus, and an Undine fresh from a bath beneath the ocean waves, shimmering in the sunbeams, the twain appeared, outlined against the background of forest, an enchanting picture in a grand setting.

Side by side they stood, Ash-kick-o-tau-tup, the Indian princess, daughter of a lord of the soil, called Heather Flower by the English, and Damaris Gordon, descendant of a long line of haughty ancestors across the blue sea, in " Merrie England," the two whose life-paths were to intermingle and cross in a tragedy lying in the dark bosom of the future.

But no premonition of the evil so near at hand marred the happiness of the friends, no shadow of the coming doom cast blackness over the bright anticipations in which they indulged.

"They are coming, Snowbird—Poniute and the young pale-face brave. See yon dark speck dancing on the water?"

Heather Flower pointed in the direction of the dark line upon the horizon, away to the westward, the fringe of the trees marking the shore of Mancho-nock, and speaking in the Delaware tongue, the language common to most of the tribes.

"Your eyes are keener than mine," returned Damaris, in the same tongue, and arching her hand above her brows as she peered across the shimmering waves. "How know you that it is a red man and a pale-face?"

"A keen vision is the natural gift of the eagle and the red man, to whom the forest paths, the falling leaves, the trail of the beast and the serpent, the flight of the birds, the clouds, and the bent twig are as the marks the pale-face makes to tell his thoughts. The Indian reads the signs. The arm turning the paddle of yonder canoe is the arm of a red man. The other sitting in the canoe is a pale-face—a warrior," returned Heather Flower, positively.

A goodly-sized canoe was skimming swiftly over the sunlit waters, steering straight for the bold promontory of Montauk. The frail bark had left a strip of low-lying beach at the southeasterly end of Mancho-nock, and had nearly reached the middle point between the shores before either of the occupants broke the silence.

The Indian, plying the paddle with practised stroke, was tall and straight as a Norway pine, rather slender in build, a magnificent type of the red man, his forehead high, bold and commanding, his mouth well-formed, his nose aquiline, his jaw firm. The arms, bared to the shoulder, were rather slender, but strung with sinews of iron, and knotted by the swelling muscles; his hands were firm, his head well poised upon his column-like neck. Altogether, he might well have served as a model of an Ajax in bronze.

The white man seated in the stern was also tall, elegantly proportioned, with fair complexion, and a face that might have been mistaken for effeminate, did not the bold, flashing eyes, the air of proud superiority, the commanding poise of the head, and the soldierly bearing contradict the impression.

That he was an officer in the service of the English government was evidenced by his uniform, belt and sword, and the officer's hat set jauntily upon his wavy, chestnut locks.

With all his attractive exterior, there was an insincere expression in the curve of his handsome mouth, that might reveal *faithlessness* to a physiognomist; yet his smile was winning, his manners courteous, as became a carpet-knight, rather than the intrepid soldier which he had proved himself on more than one hard-fought field.

Such was the portrait of Guy Kingsland, the scion of a noble house, a royalist at heart, although a Lieutenant in Cromwell's —th Light Horse.

Some weeks previous to the date upon which our story opens he had arrived in the colonies, accompanied by Major Gordon, an old companion-in-arms of Captain Gardiner, late commander at Saybrook Fort, but retired from the service, and settled upon his recent acquisition, purchased from James Farret, who, as agent for the Earl of Stirling, conveyed the estate, the title having been confirmed by Wyandance, Sachem of the Montauks.

The Indian proprietors had named the island paradise Man-cho-nock, but Lyon Gardiner had re-christened his estate the Isle of Wight.

For a year Major Gordon's only child had been a guest at the Isle of Wight, and perhaps the errand upon which Lieutenant Kingsland had come to the colonies was a desire to meet Damaris Gordon, who had been his betrothed wife since her fifteenth year; perhaps some secret mission from Cromwell was the prime object of his voyage across the Atlantic; but if it was a matter of political intrigue, or interest, the secret was known only to those in power, Cromwell's officers in Saybrook Fort.

During her residence upon the island Damaris Gordon had formed a strong friendship for the beautiful daughter of Wyandance, and frequent visits had been interchanged, Damaris sometimes remaining at the lodge of Wyandance for two or three days.

After the arrival of her betrothed, she devoted much of her time to her lover, until matters of importance called him to Saybrook Fort. What the errand that brought him from England might be had never troubled her pretty head. He had returned to the Isle of Wight as suddenly as he had departed, and was now on his way to take the young girl back to the mansion.

"It is a long pull, Poniute," he observed, after a considerable pause in the conversation, during which time his eyes had been fixed upon the supple form of the young warrior in a sort of lazy admiration. "To-day the bay is smooth as a mirror, and handling the paddle is comparatively light, but in rough weather it must be a difficult feat to cross the bay—eh?"

"Poniute has the arms of the strong oak, his sinews are like the bowstring," returned the Indian, as he glanced over his shoulder, his black eyes scanning the shore they were fast nearing. "See! the Snowbird waits the coming of the young chief."

"Say you so?" asked Kingsland, fixing his eyes upon a point above the landing place upon the low beach. "Your eyesight must be as strong as your muscles, if you can descry an object the size of a human being clearly enough to discover whether male or female, at the distance of yon bluff—I can make out nothing save the bare face of rock, the great boulders, a line of forest trees and undergrowth beyond."

"Ugh! Poniute see Snowbird—see Ash-kick-o-tau-tup Sachem,"[8] returned the young brave, half contemptuously, as he again glanced over his shoulder. "Poniute eagle eye. Pale-face take long look—see too!"

Slightly nettled at the tone and manner of the young Indian, Guy Kingsland adjusted his field glass, and gazed steadily across the water. By the aid of the instrument he saw the two that had attracted Poniute's attention.

"Egad! You're right!" he exclaimed. "It is indeed she whom you call Snowbird. By the way, what remarkable, fantastic names you red men have—and who is the other? Ash-tree—and the rest of the name—what is it?"

[8] Among the tribes the daughter of a chief was designated by the title bestowed upon her father. Thus, "Ash-kick-o-tau-tup Sachem" signifies the daughter of a Sachem, or an Indian princess.

"Ash-kick-o-tau-tup Sachem," returned the Indian gravely; "father great Sachem—Wyandance."

"Ah! I comprehend; and Indian princess—I think I have heard her mentioned as 'Heather Flower.'"

The assertion was made in the tone of an inquiry, but the taciturn young brave vouchsafed no further information, and not another word was exchanged between the twain, not even when the light canoe grated upon the sandy beach and Poniute led the way up the steep ascent to the crown of the bluff, striking into a well-defined path towards the point where the two maidens awaited the approach of the visitors.

The eyes of the young Lieutenant wandered from point to point as he took a comprehensive view of the scene, noting every object within the line of vision, a half-smile upon his lips as if the view were a pleasant one, and he the prospective purchaser.

The speculative look was still in his eyes as he bowed low over the hand his betrothed extended, and murmured a few words in greeting.

The covetous gaze changed to one of surprise and undisguised admiration as he glanced toward the Indian king's daughter, who stood slightly apart, her attitude of unstudied grace peculiarly her own.

The introduction of the young Englishman to the forest beauty was a matter somewhat awkward of accomplishment, as her acquirement of the English language was limited to the simplest forms, a knowledge gained from her youthful friend, who, in turn, could converse in the Delaware dialect, with which she had become familiarised by her father, who had passed several years in the colonies, and, as a diplomat among the tribes, had gained a passable knowledge of the language.

But Guy Kingsland, perhaps for the first time, forgot the amenities and was almost guilty of rudeness. A passionate admirer of beauty, with an artistic appreciation of form and colouring, he stood gazing as he might have gazed on some beautiful creation of the artist's brush, or a vision from the Paradise of Mohammed, half in wonder, wholly in admiration.

What did she think of him, the lover of her young friend, Damaris Gordon? Did she know of the engagement that existed between the Lieutenant and Major Gordon's daughter?

He asked the mental question, hoping that his betrothed had kept the secret, as she probably had.

In an instant he had encountered the black eyes of the young warrior, glowering upon him with an expression that warned him of his folly; and turning to his betrothed, he began a lively badinage, to which she replied in like strain, as the four walked slowly along the broad trail in the direction of the Sachem's lodge.

Two sentinels barred the entrance. A single sentence, attuned to express the emotion of the speaker, arrested the steps of Heather Flower.

"Poggatticut, the great king of the Manhansetts, has gone to the spirit land—Wyandance, the great Sachem of the Montauks, mourns."

With a wave of her hand Heather Flower dismissed her guests, and without a word, turned away, disappearing within a small wigwam.*

"Now, by my faith, a decidedly cavalier way of dismissing one's guests!" exclaimed Kingsland, in a nettled tone, "One would imagine that the Czar

---

* According to a custom among the tribes, upon the death of a relative the Sachem of the tribe secludes himself within his wigwam, from which every member of the royal family is excluded until he signifies his wish for their return.

of all the Russians had shuffled off the mortal coil. This chieftain with the unpronounceable name must be held in high veneration."

He addressed Damaris, but it was Poniute who replied.

"Poggatticut great warrior—big hunter—Manitou give him wise head—still tongue."

"If you intend that as a rebuke for my natural curiosity, I'll refrain from further questioning," returned Kingsland. "There's nothing for it, I opine, but a pull back to the Isle of Wight. Can you take us across?" he added, turning to Poniute.

"Poniute's arms are strong. When moon walks there, pale-face chief shall be there," returned the Indian, pointing to the eastern sky, and then to the distant island.

"Lead on—we will follow," answered Kingsland, and drawing the hand of his betrothed within his arm he led her down the steep pathway to the spot where the canoe was beached.

The moon was skirting the eastern horizon when the lovers reached Gardiner Hall, but it was sinking low in the west when Lieutenant Kingsland fell asleep to dream—not of his amber-tressed, lily-fair Damaris, but of the bewitching, glowing beauty of Ash-kick-o-tau-tup, the Heather Flower of the Montauks.

CHAPTER IV

AN INDIAN SHRINE

"With reverent steps we come
To gather round his tomb,
The honoured brave!
And still from year to year,
Shall pilgrims journey here,
And many a holy tear
Shall here be shed."

FOR three days had the body of Poggatticut lain in state, for three days had the young chief Yo-kee remained secluded within the lodge, attended only by the great medicine-man, Wee-gon. For three days neither the young chieftain nor the medicine-man, whose mission it was to comfort, had spoken, save in low murmurs, and at long intervals. Not a morsel of food had passed their lips, not a drop of water had moistened their parched tongues.

On either side of the closed entrance a warrior stood guard, upright, silent, motionless as Hindoo devotees, not a contortion of their bronzed faces, not the quiver of a muscle, betraying the fatigue or gnawing hunger they were enduring so stoically.

Throughout the entire domains of Sea-wan-ha-ka and Manhansett-aha-quash-a-warnuck a solemn silence brooded, indicative of the great calamity that had befallen the nation.

In the three villages of Wyandance, King of the Montauks, Nowedanah, Grand Sachem of the Shinnecocks, and Momometou, Sagamore of the Mattitucks, the ordinary occupations were suspended, and not once had warriors, braves or squaws beheld faces or forms of their kings, who, like David of old, mourned in solitude, not only for a brother dead, but for a great statesman, a wise counsellor, a profound philosopher, a nobleman of nature's fashioning, whose voice would never again be heard in the councils of his people.

Through the dense forest shades the deer, the moose, the bear and elk might roam in safety, the partridge might lead her young. No twang of bow disturbed the stillness of the leafy coverts, no hunter's knife flashed in the green gloom, no spear of fisherman cleft the limpid waters of the bright streams.

Within their lodges the royal family abode, beneath the shelter of wigwams the squaws huddled, the warriors and braves spoke in the low, plaintive tones so suggestive, in the Delaware language, of profound grief, taking the place of tears in the eyes of the pale races, and their sentences were of the briefest.

The morning of the fourth day dawned in cloudless splendour. From his ocean bed on the eastern horizon the golden luminary rose majestically, turning the waters of the bay to a vast sheet of burnished silver, sparkling and shimmering with myraid crystal points, tinting the topmost tassels of the forest trees with vivid emerald, and piercing the green aisles with stealthy arrows tipped with crimson and gold.

From the villages runners had come in, bearing dispatches from the three kings and the tributary chieftains of the minor tribes. Already the grave had been hollowed beneath the green oak crowning the highlands of Montauk, the burial place of kings who had slumbered beneath the sod for thousands of moons. Swift runners had been sent in all directions, and by this means the arrangements for the funeral march had been completed in every detail.

The runners from Wyandance had conveyed the intelligence that he would meet the funeral cortège at the high bluff within the domain of Montauk overlooking the three or four miles of sandy beach stretching away to the westward between the place of look-out and Amagansett. And lastly, the tireless messenger was sent by Yo-kee to signify his acquiescence in the arrangement.

There was no outward sign of grief when Yo-kee joined his people; the period for mourning in state had passed, and a long line of warriors, braves and squaws passed in review beside the bier and looked for the last time upon the face of the dead, as he lay robed in all the panoply of a great warrior about to go forth upon a long journey.

Only the four principal men of the tribe were privileged to become the bearers; and reverently they raised the litter around which costly furs were bound, enveloping the dead.

With measured step they took their way on the march to the burial-place, Yo-kee following the bier with his retinue of warriors, all habited in gala attire, as befitted the occasion, and midway of the line the litter upon which the aged widow Lig-o-mee reclined, borne upon the shoulders of four athletic braves.

A long line of warriors and braves followed; the procession swelled to a great concourse at Dancing Meadow, where the deputation of Mattitucks, under their Sachem, Momometou, joined the train.

There was a formal exchange of greetings, then, observing a decorous silence, the entire party entered the capacious canoes, and obedient to the swift strokes of the paddles the little flotilla glided across the waters of Peconic Bay.

Disembarking at Hog-a-nock, they resumed their march through Accobonac [1] to Amagansett,[2] where they were joined by Nowedanah and his Shinnecock warriors. Again formal greetings were exchanged, and the journey was resumed.

Once only from Hog-a-nock to Amagansett the bearers halted during their weary march. Not once had the body been allowed to rest upon the earth, and the endurance of even the strong bearers was taxed to its utmost limit.

With willing hands, two of the young warriors scooped a little hollow in the centre of a bank of fragrant arbutus, and with awed faces, as if they bore the ark of the covenant, the bearers rested the feet of the dead king within the depression, and supported the form upright.[3]

For hours the deputation of Montauks had remained at Amagansett, awaiting the arrival of the procession, while, alone upon the high point of land overlooking the shining waters, Wyandance watched for the coming of the funeral cortège.

[1] *Accobonac*, the hunting ground of the Montauks—the level stretch of forest extending westward from Napeague, the northern shores of which are washed by the waters of Gardiner's and Little Peconic Bays, the south by the Atlantic, and bounded on the west by an imaginary line from the southeasternmost point of Hog-a-nock, southward to the sea, at a point called *Sagaponac* (Council-place).

[2] *Amagansett*.—Fishing-place.

[3] This Sachem was regarded with a species of adoration. The body was held too sacred even to touch the earth until it was placed within the grave, and when, from sheer exhaustion, the bearers were compelled to rest, a hollow was made in which to place his feet, that his body might be supported in an upright position. For more than a century after his burial the depression touched by his feet was an Indian shrine, and an Indian was never known to pass the sacred spot without kneeling and clearing whatever debris might have accumulated. The locality bears the name of Buckskill. (*Buc-usk-kil*.—Resting-place.)

AN INDIAN SHRINE

Below extended the long strip of sandy plain, and just as the sun neared the tree-tops away to the westward his eagle eye descried the head of the column as it emerged from the deep forest and entered the pathway across the lonely beach.

Not the quiver of a muscle betrayed his sorrow, although no human eye could have witnessed his emotion. True to the teachings of his race and station, he observed the decorum obligatory upon a great chief, but his heart was full as his gaze followed the movements of the four bearing upon their brawny shoulders the litter upon which rested the remains of one who had been his adviser, his well-beloved brother.

A few stunted shrubs dotted the sandy beach over which the procession was slowly moving, straight as an arrow's flight to where the trail wound upward to the forest-crowned headland where Wyandance watched and waited.

The three brothers gravely exchanged salutations, and the train moved on.

At a spot adjacent to the edge of the cliff overhanging the beach, and within the shadows of the Heather woods, the grave was made,—not the long and narrow trench to entomb a European, but a deep well, excavated beneath the shade of a flourishing oak. Far below stretched the bright waters of the bay and the Sound dotted with islands, near at hand Man-cho-nock and Gull Island, dark with woods, and far out upon the bosom of the Sound a violet line marked the shores of the mainland and Block Island.

The amber light streamed over a weird scene. Within the narrow excavation they placed the body of the aged king, the face toward the setting sun.

With slow and measured movement the warriors

gathered around the grave; outside the circle the squaws hovered, with blankets folded across their faces. A deathly stillness reigned, even the papooses slung at their mothers' shoulders, or clinging to their hands, made no outcry.

Presently Wyandance, bearing a bow and arrows, stepped beside the open grave, and with outstretched hand thus addressed the dead:

"Ka-har-wee! Ka-har-wee!⁴ why hast thou left the world? Thou, whose strong arm could once bend the bow and wield the tomahawk like this, or wield the spear like this!"

His form seemed to dilate, his eyes flashed fiercely, every muscle appeared tense as the bowstring he drew to the arrow head, and instantly the arm was raised as if in the act of hurling the tomahawk and thrusting the spear.

Instinctively every warrior drew his form to its full height, as the chieftain stood there, the very incarnation of an Ajax defying the lightning.

Suddenly the tension of the muscles relaxed, his demeanour changed, his voice rose plaintively, as he continued his adjuration.

"But now thy hand lies low and a child might conquer thee. Thou comest from the shores of light, thy face is toward the place of darkness, like the setting sun. Take this bow and quiver of arrows to be your protection on your long and dangerous journey to the land of spirits."

Bending over the grave, he placed the bow and arrows beside the dead, and took his place in the circle of warriors.

Tomahawk in hand, Nowedanah approached the grave and thus spoke:

"Ka-har-wee! Ka-har-wee! The Great Spirit

⁴ *Ka-har-wee.*—Brother.

AN INDIAN SHRINE 35

has called thee to the happy hunting grounds. Never again will you know what it is to tire in the hunt or chase, never again will you be hungry or cold, for always the eye of the Manitou will be upon thee while you hunt the buffalo, the deer, the wolf and the bear. No more war there! No more warpath in the land where you will meet with the fathers that tradition tells us have been there for ages of moons. Take this tomahawk to defend yourself against the enemies that lie in ambush in the dark forests and the dismal swamps you must cross in the land of shadows."

Placing the tomahawk beside the bow and arrows, Nowedanah retired to give place to the King of the Mattitucks.

Momometou's gift to the departed was a robe of fur, which the chief assured his dead brother would protect him from the dews of night and storms of day.

With a firm step Yo-kee took his station beside the grave.

An ornament of almost priceless value, when viewed from the Indians' standpoint, girded his waist, a belt of the precious suck-au-hock, wrought in strange devices, and of a length to sweep below the knee. In his hand he carried many fathoms of seawan strung upon the tough sinews of the deer. At his feet crouched a milk-white dog, who raised his appealing eyes to his master's face, as if he comprehended the purpose for which he had been brought.

Yo-kee's sonorous voice rang out clarion-like:

"My father: Your way leads through the pathless wilderness which the feet of the living have never trod, and dreary deserts which must be passed before you reach the happy hunting grounds where the wise Mon-go-tuck-see,[5] your father, will welcome his son.

"Can my father, the wise King who has reigned over the warlike Manhansetts, go to a strange land with an empty word? Take this belt as a record of the transactions between the sons of Mon-go-tuck-see, the four kings of the Manhansetts, the Montauks, the Shinnecocks and the Mattitucks, and the bold, bad enemies, the Narragansetts, the Pequots and the Mohawks."

Drawing his tomahawk from his belt he raised it. It fell with crushing force, and the dog at his feet lay lifeless before him.

Twining the seawan about the dead animal's neck, he again raised his voice in invocation.

"Take with you this dog as a sacrifice to Tha-lon-ghy-a-waa-gon; let him bear upon his neck the wampum with which to cheat the enemies sent by Ho-bam-o-koo to stay your flight to the happy hunting grounds.[6] Yok-ee has spoken."

Carefully depositing the slain animal within the grave, he placed the belt upon the offering of his kinsmen.

A very babel of sounds followed, and while the bearers filled in the fresh mould the tom-toms were

[5] *Mon-go-tuck-see.*—Long Knife. He once reigned lord of the Montauks and other neighbouring tribes; he had a canal constructed at Merosuck (Canoe Place) from the north to the south bay.
[6] It was the belief among the Indian tribes that during the passage of a spirit through the country they must traverse before reaching the happy hunting grounds, lay a land of darkness and shadows, infested with ravenous beasts and deadly serpents, a desert where no food can be found. A vast number of evil spirits sent by Hobamokoo (the Devil) follow swiftly to prevent the released spirit from making the journey. Therefore it was necessary to provide the traveller with a quantity of wampum, which he might scatter in the path where the pursuing fiends would tarry to gather it, and thus allow the fleeing spirit to escape.

AN INDIAN SHRINE

furiously beaten,[7] and singing the death-chant the warriors moved in a circle about the grave, accompanying their wailing notes with the pantomime of twanging the bow, throwing the tomahawk, paddling the canoe, or casting the spear.

These ceremonials completed, the throng moved away on the homeward route, to the village of Wyandance.

The time for mourning had come, and throughout the village naught save the sound of wailing was heard. Within the chief's lodge the four kings sat in council. Numerous fires blazed in the green dells of the Heather woods, where the braves had gathered in groups to rehearse the deeds of the dead warrior and smoke the calumet, the cries and moans of the squaws floating in the air about them like the wails of lost souls, as they hacked their flesh with sharpened stones, tore their hair, and besmeared their faces with ashes, crooning, swaying their bodies, and exhibiting every phase of the grief pent within their breasts until the time allotted to silence had passed.

But human nature is the same with the red man as the white, and presently the clamour ceased, while the squaws prepared the feast, to which their lords sat down with keen appetites, sharpened by the fasting and fatigue they had endured; but it was long past midnight when all sounds of mourning ceased, and wrapping their blankets around them the warriors lay down to slumber.

[7] To frighten away the evil spirits.

CHAPTER V

AN INDIAN WOOING

> "O Jealousy,
> Thou ugliest fiend of hell! thy deadly venom
> Preys on my vitals, turns the healthful hue
> Of my fresh cheeks to haggard sallowness,
> And drinks my spirit up!"

WHEN Guy Kingsland first met Heather Flower his surprised demeanour and unguarded admiration for her was not entirely lost upon the Indian maiden. Like the pale-face daughters of Eve, she was not proof against the adulation of the sterner sex, and certainly not insensible to the fascinations of the young English officer with the dashing air that so well became him and a grace of manner at once careless and high bred, and whose bold blue eyes were fairly searching her face.

She had heard of the coming of the pale-face cavalier, but Guy Kingsland was correct in his surmise that his betrothed would not confide the secret of her engagement even to her bosom friend.

The contract had been made without reference to the wishes of the maiden, who, as in duty bound, had acquiesced in the arrangement which would unite two goodly fortunes.

But not even to Heather Flower could she confess that her heart had been given to the dashing young soldier who was proud of her beauty and had played the part of the adoring lover with an energy that was part and parcel of his nature.

Heather Flower's vanity had asserted itself when, with a woman's intuition, she detected the look of undisguised admiration in Kingsland's flashing blue eyes.

To say that the Indian maiden had seen the suns of twenty summers without having a lover would be idle, but to not one among the young warriors who had sought her favour had she given more than a passing regard.

According to the customs of her people, her hand had been sought in marriage by more than one of her father's braves, but with that freedom peculiar to her station, while she had not discouraged the civilities of any, she carefully refrained from looking with more favour upon one than upon another. Every inch a princess, pure-minded, gentle, with an absence of the arrogant pride that too often possesses her sisters of more favoured races, she was lovable and much beloved by all her people.

In all matters of the heart, so far as her father was concerned, she was left to her own sweet will—not that he was unmindful of the happiness of his daughter, but because of the affairs of state that at all times weighed heavily upon him, and of his confidence in his daughter's fitness and sagacity to take care of herself, and so it happened that he had never annoyed her with even an attempt at matchmaking.

After the savage fashion, she was a progressive woman, far beyond the average of her sisters. She was jealous for the renown of her chieftain father, he being the Totem or Grand Sachem over all Seawan-ha-ka. The valour of her father's warriors and the prowess of his hunters were her pride. She was the patroness of all games or exercises tending to a high order of efficiency on the warpath and in the chase, and encouraged, by her presence, the athletic sports and pastimes so conducive to physical endurance, which, among her people, was the crowning glory of its possessor.

The regal beauty and grace of Heather Flower was known far and wide, for yearly came the ambassadors from twelve minor Sagamores, bringing wampum with which to pay tribute to her father, Wyandance, and many were the tales told of the great king's comely daughter, and many a brave had longed to take back the Heather Flower to his lodge as his wife; but the fact that he was a vassal, bearing tribute, placed the beautiful princess beyond his ambition, and so it was that her suitors must be among the warriors of her own nation.

The rivalry between two of these suitors for the hand of the king's daughter was, ere long, to end in a bloody tragedy that would cast a gloomy shadow across the sunlit path of Heather Flower. They were Mandush, a brave warrior and trusted lieutenant of Wyandance, and To-cus, some years the junior of Mandush, a typical Indian brave, bold, ambitious, impetuous and daring.

Being favourites of Wyandance, and the companions in the chase of his son, Wyancombone, both Mandush and To-cus enjoyed the hospitalities of the Sachem's lodge to a greater extent, perhaps, than their fellows, if we except Poniute, who was the chieftain's confidential messenger, and oft-times his companion and attendant in his visits to the palefaces.

Poniute's eagle eye guarded all the paths of Heather Flower, whom he loved in secret and worshipped at a distance.

As a natural sequence, these young braves, enjoying the freedom of their master's lodge and the companionship of his only son, became the slaves of the young princess.

It was upon the occasions of these visits that Mandush and To-cus, as opportunity offered, would make bold to proffer her some gallantry; that, seeing her seated upon her mat engaged in beadwork (the handicraft peculiar to the women of her race), the suitor would make bold to take his seat—not beside her, but at her back, the twain facing in opposite directions, according to the custom of Indian wooing; and if he chanced to have a branch of the sweet maple or the aromatic birch, he would pass it over his shoulder and to the lips of the maiden; if she chose to nibble at the offering he understood at once that he was an accepted suitor. Or, perchance, it might be a nosegay of fragrant flowers, or a spray of wintergreen with its spicy berries, which he brought as a medium to declare his love.

More than once had the rivals proffered these tokens, which proved to be at least premature,'if not presumptuous; for their attentions were received with an indifferent air, and neither of her suitors could boast that he was her recognised lover.

Neither had dared to make a positive test by complying with certain conditions of etiquette customary with all the Indian tribes. In making love to a maiden, the lover must choose a favourable moment to lay his offering of fruit, flowers, or fragrant bark at the entrance to her wigwam, and must pass on, looking neither to the right nor left. If he is accepted, his offering, whatever it may be, will be appropriated by the maiden; but if he is rejected, his gift will remain where he left it until he returns and takes it away, and it is only after a lover is thus accepted and looked upon with favour by the parents that he is admitted to the lodge as a suitor.

During the wooing, which continues for a longer or shorter time, as circumstances may dictate, the maid is chaperoned by her mother, or some elderly duenna, and the lovers are never allowed to remain alone together until after formal betrothal. At that time all parental restraint is abandoned and the affianced pair are allowed to roam at will, to come and go as they please. No conventionalities [1] of savage wooing had been observed by the ardent admirers of Heather Flower; but each in turn had sought to win the maiden's favour by a less circuitous route, and each had been eager to make the most of his opportunity. The ambition of each was known to the other, and jealousy, the dragon that curses its victim of any race or clime, seized upon these dusky sons of the forest, and a fierce hatred sprang up between the rivals.

Ah! what a complex thing is the human heart, when it is at the same time under the influence of both love and hate. At one moment the fierce fires of love and devotion consume the soul; and at the sight of a hated rival a very hell of mingled hatred, contempt and revenge burns deep in the heart.

A beautiful glen in the heather woods, a very boudoir of nature, was the playground of the Montauks—the arena of all the sports and athletic games.

In the afternoon of a perfect day in spring, when the older squaws of the tribe were away from their wigwams, engaged in planting corn in the Indian field, the braves and warriors had repaired to the glen for an afternoon of competitive drill in the arts

---

[1] It is a singular fact that before the advent of Europeans and the demoralising effect of their fire-water, the primitive Indian was chaste to a degree. Any lapse from the strictest code of morality was punishable with death or banishment. Among the tribes the "baton" was unknown.

"With the quickness of thought, Mandush adjusted an arrow to the bowstring——"

of savage warfare and athletic sports, where they were followed by the younger members of the tribe.

It was at these gatherings that Heather Flower, with her retinue of attendant maidens, always occupied a place of vantage, and encouraged by her presence and approval the prowess and cleverness of her kinsmen. It was also at these tournaments that the rival warriors were brought together in fiercest competition, and as all were adepts with every weapon in use among the tribes, each vied with the other in all contests of strength and skill.

A word or look of approbation from Heather Flower to either of the rivals intensified the bitterness of the other.

On this balmy spring day the games had been contested with more than usual interest, and the braves were indulging in competitive archery.

Mandush, an expert archer, had half emptied his quiver, and he glanced towards Heather Flower for a smile of approval.

"Hist!"

The sharp call cut the air like a knife, and was followed by a babel of sounds.

Following the direction, up the wooded slope, pointed out by the index fingers, he beheld a strange spectacle. A large golden owl, belated in its migration, and seeking repose for a day in the dark wood of the high promontory, had been discovered by a flock of crows, which had set upon him, and with all the boisterous demonstration peculiar to them were attacking him on all sides, until the hapless intruder was compelled to seek safety in headlong flight, beset on every hand by his black tormentors.

Just as the pursued and pursuers were overhead, with the quickness of thought Mandush adjusted an arrow to the bow-string and with unerring aim sent the shaft on its message of death.

Cleaving the air like a lightning bolt, it struck the golden beauty beneath its wing, piercing the heart. With a shrill cry of pain the luckless bird plunged headlong to the earth, dead.

The cloud of crows sought safety in flight, filling the air with their discordant caws.

A murmur of admiration and surprise went up from the concourse of braves and squaws at the masterstroke of Mandush's marksmanship, and with a proud step he approached the prostrate bird, and after assuring himself that life was extinct, he lifted it by the arrow that had transfixed it, and, bearing it in triumph to Heather Flower, presented her with the beautiful trophy, its golden plumage, tinted with blue and crimson, unruffled and unmarred.

Accepting the gift with maidenly grace, Heather Flower complimented him upon his superior ability in the arts so much admired in an Indian warrior.

With a glance of triumph that was not lost upon To-cus, who was a witness of all that had transpired, Mandush returned to his station to exhaust his quiver of arrows. This being done, he turned leisurely to retrace his steps in the direction of Heather Flower, darting from the depths of his fiery, serpent-like eyes a look of mingled triumph and contempt toward his hated rival.

The chagrin of To-cus at the apparent advantage Mandush had gained maddened him, but his innate cunning prevented him from any exhibition of rashness, and stifling the rage that strove for the mastery over prudence, he abruptly left the field, and strode with haughty and impatient step up the path leading to a rocky bluff northward. The pent-up rage seething in his heart nearly consumed him, and yet, what could he do? To approach the medicine-man and offer a bribe for an amulet with which to charm Heather Flower would bring only exposure and disgrace; to importune the chieftain, without first obtaining the maiden's consent, was certain to bring only humiliation, and his proud spirit fairly writhed in the contemplation of the rebuff he was certain to meet—that he was only a squaw, and if he could not win the consent of the daughter he was not worthy of her affection.

Arriving at the brow of the rocky bluff, he surprised a flock of crows who had alighted upon a narrow sand-pit below and were dissecting the carcass of a fish that had been cast up by the waves. Taking aim at one of the fleeing scavengers, he let fly an arrow and the next instant the stricken bird was fluttering upon the bosom of the waves where it had fallen. Descending the cliff, the marksman waited for the bird to drift ashore, and, concealing it about his person, he made his way to his wigwam, where he arrived just as the shadows of evening were falling.

The moon, only a silver crescent, was sinking below the western horizon when the young warrior stole with a soundless tread from his lodge, and crept, cat-like among the shadows cast by the clustered wigwams, halting at last at the entrance of his rival's lodge. Only a brief period, and when he stole silently away a dead crow, pierced through with an arrow, was swaying beside the entrance.

When Mandush at early dawn emerged from his lodge he found the object which served as a gauntlet fastened to his lodge-pole, a challenge to deadly combat. An examination of the arrow proved its ownership. Not for an instant did he hesitate—he must accept the challenge, or ever after wear the white feather, and be accounted only worthy to be a squaw. Ere the sun had skirted the horizon the bird was hanging to the lodge-pole of his rival's lodge, pierced with a second arrow from the opposite side, a shaft from Mandush's quiver. The gauntlet had been thrown and taken.

According to code the challenged had the choice of weapons, and before the sun was an hour in the heavens the rumour spread through the village that Mandush and To-cus were to settle their feud by a duel with knives.

The remonstrances of their friends and kinsmen were unavailing. Their meeting in deadly strife could signify naught but the death of one or both, for nothing but the life of the rival would appease the fierce hatred of the other.

CHAPTER VI

INCONSTANCY

"Holy St. Francis! what a change is here!
Is Rosalind whom thou did'st love so dear
So soon forsaken? Young men's love, then, lies
Not truly in their hearts, but in their eyes."

A GRAND mansion for the period, and the colonies, was Gardiner Hall, the only residence on the Isle of Wight, as its proprietor had named his estate.

Lyon Gardiner, late commandant of Saybrook Fort, had an innate dislike for modern dwellings and modern furnishing, and his mansion had been built after an antique style, a copy of the manor in Scotland where many generations of his ancestors had been born, lived and died, and if the old hall, standing grim and grey upon the Scottish coast, had been, like Aladdin's palace, transported across seas and planted upon the green island, the ancient could not have been told from the new.

In 1635, late in November, a barque of twenty-five tons, sent by Lords Say and Brook, with Lyon Gardiner on board, with provisions of all sorts to begin a fort, arrived at the mouth of the Connecticut River. Gardiner, an expert engineer, or work-base, who had been employed to superintend the construction of the fort, was a man of worth and great ability, and had served with distinction as a lieutenant in the British army in the Low Countries. He was a staunch Republican, with Hamden, Oliver Cromwell, and others of the same spirit.

In 1639 he took possession of and removed to the island he had purchased.

The woodland had been cleared of undergrowth for a distance from the hall at a comparatively slight expense, and the forest trees were as grand as those that dotted the Scottish park, and here the deer roamed in all their wild freedom.

The building was an irregular, cumbrous structure of grey stone, the main edifice flanked by two wings enclosing a wide court-yard on three sides. There was a keeper's lodge beside the great gate, opening beneath the stone arch, upon which the family coat-of-arms was emblazoned, a mailed hand grasping a battle-axe, with the motto, "*Veni, vidi, vici.*"

A strong palisade bristling with sharp, iron spikes enclosed the extensive grounds surrounding the mansion, a long avenue of horse-chestnuts led from the gateway to the ponderous entrance of the central building, a door of oak set deep in the wall, studded with spikes, and hooded by a massive porch supported by thick oak columns.

Palisaded and strongly built, it was a veritable stronghold that might serve as a fortress in case of an invasion of hostile Indians of the warlike tribes upon the mainland.

And here, in almost regal state, dwelt Lyon Gardiner with his lady and their three children, a son, David, a stripling of athletic mould, and two lovely daughters, Elizabeth and Mary, aged respectively twelve and nine years.

The son and eldest daughter had been born at Saybrook Fort, but pretty Mary's birthplace was the beautiful Island of Wight.

Four stout yeomen and two bondsmen, all of English birth, and two Mohicans from the region about the mouth of the Connecticut River, made up the force of plantation hands, and a like number of female servitors were employed about the mansion. Of the latter, three were staunch family servants who emigrated with the family in the barque that brought Lyon Gardiner from England to Saybrook Fort, four were deft-handed, strong-armed dames from the Connecticut colony, and one, named by her master, " Xantippe," an African slave who had been brought from the Virginia plantation in a trading vessel.

A stern-faced overseer, one Cyrus Howell, superintended the plantation hands, while Patience, his wife, filled the position of housekeeper at the hall. The couple occupied a one-story frame building adjoining the manor house.

Twenty-three souls, men, women, and children, made up the household at the date of which we write, but Gardiner Hall was the very abode of colonial hospitality, and guests were the rule rather than the exception.

Damaris Gordon's stay upon the island promised to be an indefinite visit, and Major Gordon, with Guy Kingsland, his prospective son-in-law, made the mansion a kind of headquarters while they made frequent journeys, visiting the villages of the friendly tribes upon the islands and the mainland.

Many times Guy Kingsland had crossed to Montauk, sometimes for a day's hunting, but oftener his visit was confined to the lodge of Wyandance, with whom he was on a more familiar footing than the haughty chieftain usually accorded to any of the English race, with the exception of Lyon Gardiner, who had won the entire confidence of the Sachem.

On several occasions Kingsland had met Heather Flower, but only in the presence of her father, Wicchi-tau-bit, her mother, or of Damaris Gordon, who usually accompanied the young Lieutenant to the island.

The friendship existing between the two maidens suffered no abatement as the days went by, but several circumstances that Damaris had noticed puzzled her not a little.

Frequently she had observed Poniute near at hand, upon occasions when walking in the paths near the village accompanied by the Indian girl, and might have regarded his distant attendance as a safeguard against the attacks from beasts or reptiles but from the fact that it was only when Lieutenant Kingsland accompanied the twain upon a stroll through the leafy glades or to the brow of the bluff (where an Indian picket constantly kept watch and ward) that the young brave hovered near, never joining the trio, but flitting from shadow to shadow, or wandering along the pathway skirting the cliff, as if he would guard the young princess from some lurking danger.

Guy Kingsland had not once noticed him, and if Heather Flower had knowledge of his presence she made no sign.

For some reason the dashing young Lieutenant felt extremely dissatisfied; his vanity was wounded by the apparent indifference of the chief's daughter. He was annoyed that the fascinations that had won the smiles of high bred beauties in London's fashionable circles—the Lady Dorothys, Marys, and Calistas—should be lost upon this untutored child of the wilderness, whose inborn pride exceeded even the studied haughtiness of the fair English dames of rank.

Did he love her? He could not have told; he was fascinated, bewildered, enthralled; and yet, had circumstances favoured, he would not have made her his wife. Upon that point he was assured, but his thoughts were a medley of conflicting elements.

Curiously enough, his mind reverted to the marriage of John Rolfe with the Indian princess, Pocahontas; but then Rolfe, so far as known, had not been hampered with a previous engagement—"hampered" was the mental designation of his betrothal. Perhaps the young scion of nobility was dimly conscious of his own fickleness and shrank from what he feared would be an exacting affection, even if he could win the heart of the young forest queen. It would be a hazardous pastime, but he reflected that he should return to England at no distant period, and be safe from the pursuit of lurking savage or jealous maiden.

Of the feuds and heartburnings of Mandush and To-cus he knew nothing, for the affairs relating to domestic life among the tribes were strictly guarded from strangers, and thus, while one tragedy was nearly at its culmination, the germ of a second was springing into life.

By adroit questioning he assured himself that not in words, at least, had Damaris revealed her engagement, and he resolved that, if it were possible, he would seek an interview with the Indian girl and risk the result, a determination that was fostered by his pique at her apparent indifference; and in this frame of mind he rowed over to the island and betook himself to the woods for a day's hunt, hoping that he might be fortunate enough to meet with the goddess of his day-dreams.

"No, the idea of marriage with an Indian squaw would be preposterous, notwithstanding she is the daughter of a sovereign who is as potent in his realm as Cromwell the Protector, who rules the three kingdoms with a rod of iron," mused Guy. "Unfortunately, or contrariwise, I am bound to the fair Damaris by ties that I could not sever if I would—um-m-m!—would not if I could; she will be a wife of whom even a Kingsland may be proud. Egad! I wonder what my lily-fair lady-love would think could she take a peep behind the scenes—read my thoughts? Methinks my chances in that quarter would be reduced to naught. Zounds! the fire-eating old Major would call me out!—On the other hand, should I succeed with my olive-skinned divinity, what then? The haughty old chief, her daddy, would demand my intentions with as much hauteur as the noblest lord in England might—that to a dead certainty. Um-m-m-m! I might contract one of those left-handed Indian marriages so convenient as a salve to the tender conscience of my princess, that would be in no wise binding across the big pond; but the objection to such an arrangement is that it could not be kept from the Major or Captain Gardiner, for the old Sachem would never consent to turn off his beautiful daughter without a great wedding feast. What a pity that she isn't one of the squaws whose existence isn't worth a rush. Ye gods! should old Wyandance get wind of my intentions, my scalp would be dangling at his belt in less time than I would take to shoot a quail. If the Major and his daughter had never come to the colonies I could see my way clear; I would wed my uplifted red Cleopatra after the most approved Indian mode, take her to my wigwam, and when I tired of her love the first ship sailing to England would waft me away to home and the high-born maiden who is destined to be my wife, leaving the proud King of the Montauks to chew the cud of sweet and bitter fancies. Heigh-ho! I wonder how it will end!"

INCONSTANCY

He was roused from his musing in a startling manner. He was slowly making his way across an opening in the Heather woods, his eyes bent upon the ground. A lithe figure sprang from the copse of alders surrounding the glade, a lonely spot lying in a basin between high hills, a tomahawk whirled through the air barely missing the target at which it was aimed, Lieutenant Kingsland's handsome head. An involuntary start of surprise had saved his life.

The young Englishman was without weapon, save his firelock, which had been discharged, and he realised the imminence of his danger at a glance.

Alone in this wilderness, he was at the mercy of this powerful young brave, whom he recognised as Poniute, whose visage was almost demoniacal in its expression.

Guy Kingsland was no coward, and his usually cheerful face grew set and stern, his nerves like steel, as he confronted the young warrior; and with a leap widened the distance between himself and the Indian, who was rushing upon him with uplifted knife.

"Pale-face dog not take away Heather Flower! Black-heart die here—now—bear and wolf eat bones!" snarled the young brave, viciously.

The keen knife would have been buried in Kingsland's heart but with a bound he met his assailant, swinging his clubbed musket; the Indian, eluding the stroke, closed in. Guy grasped his wrist and strove with the strength of despair to wrest the knife from the sinewy fingers. A terrific struggle ensued.

The combatants were equally matched in point of stature and weight, but the trained muscles in the Indian's arms were the more powerful of the twain. He tugged and strained every nerve to free his right hand, and at length, with a mighty wrench, succeeded, and raised his arm for the fatal stroke.

Kingsland closed his eyes, and a half-groan escaped his lips.

A strange sound broke the silence; there was a low cry in a tone of command; from the adjoining thicket a huge form rose in a half-circle, and the young Indian felt the fangs of an animal buried deep in his shoulder; his hand relaxed its hold, the knife fell to the rocky shingle with a clang, and he was drawn backward and hurled to the earth.

Kingsland opened his eyes when the clutch upon his throat relaxed, heard a fierce growl, a word in the Delaware tongue, felt a plash of hot blood in his face, and involuntarily turning his head he beheld the supple figure of the Indian princess,

CHAPTER VII

FOR GOOD OR EVIL?

"Pansy, born in the royal purple,
  Say have I read your story aright,
What do you read in me that you tremble,
  Hiding way in sudden affright?

"Saw you, under my calm-eyed gazing,
  Something I've hidden from all beside?
Keep my secret, O thoughtful flower,
  Tell not the daisy close by your side.

"Tell not the rose that is bending to listen,
  Tell not the passion-flower over your head,
That my heart is trembling to love's sweet music,
  Oh, pansy, tell not a word that I've said."

GUY KINGSLAND stood staring mechanically at the apparition before him, for Heather Flower's steps had been noiseless, and the bound of the savage wolf-dog was the first intimation that any living creature was within the distance of five miles.

Upon the ground at her feet lay Poniute, struggling fiercely with the great brute, who, with his blood-shot eyes turned toward his mistress, as if awaiting her command, held his prisoner securely, but carefully avoiding further mangling of the young warrior, who was showering heavy blows upon his thick shoulders.

" Would Poniute kill the friend of Wyandance? "

Heather Flower asked the question in the Delaware tongue, and although Kingsland was nearly ignorant of the language, he divined the purport from the name of the Sagamore, coupled with that of the assailant, and the contempt in the tone of the questioner.

Poniute made no reply, but ceased his struggles, and at a word from the Indian girl the animal released his hold, and Poniute bounded to his feet.

Heather Flower addressed him in a few short sentences, and pointing an imperious finger in the direction of the village, turned her back upon the warrior, who scowled fiercely in the face of the Lieutenant and stalked into the forest.

"Is the pale-face warrior hurt?" asked Heather Flower, as Guy pushed back the clustering locks from his forehead and glanced at his hand, which was stained with blood.

"No—I don't know," he replied, again passing his fingers across his brow. "I can feel no pain, and yet—let the Heather Flower find whether or not there is a wound."

Pressing his hand upon his eyes as if a sudden faintness had seized him, he sank back upon a rock and bowed his head upon his palm.

Words and action were but an artifice; he had noted the swift pallor of the olive cheek, the tender light leaping to the dark eyes, the quick compression of the mobile lips, but not yet did he dare approach her with words of love. She might spurn him, but in her pity, so near akin to love, she must unbend from her reserved demeanour. He had read a woman's heart aright—his ruse was successful.

Bending over him as he half-reclined upon the rock, she placed her slender hand upon his forehead and tenderly threaded the chestnut locks dabbled in the blood of his assailant. He remembered now, perfectly, of feeling the great drops from Poniute's naked shoulder sprinkle his face when the long

FOR GOOD OR EVIL? 57

sharp fangs of the dog fastened themselves in the flesh.

That magnetic touch from the soft fingers thrilled his whole being and sent the life-current rushing in a lava torrent through his veins. He made no sign, but sitting with drooping head, smiled inwardly at the fortunate chance which had removed the barrier of reserve he had thus far found it impossible to cross.

"What has the pale-face chief done? Why did Poniute try to kill him?" she questioned, anxiously.

"Will Heather Flower bring water from the spring that I may drink?" he said, evasively, for like an inspiration of evil an idea had flashed through his subtle brain, "I—hear the—murmur of —water—I——"

He sank back, resting his head upon the mossy stone, and closed his eyes as if about to swoon.

In an instant she darted away, making straight for a tiny spring bubbling from beneath a shelving rock at a short distance from the spot where he was reclining.

Scarcely had she disappeared when he took from his waistcoat pocket a keen-edged pocket-knife, and opening the blade he drew the sharp point across his crown in such a manner as to allow the blood to flow, yet making but a superficial wound.

She must not know that he was uninjured; that would spoil the effect of his acting, he argued, and thrusting the knife back in his pocket he awaited her return.

Her absence was of brief duration, and bearing a cup hastily improvised from the bark of the silver birch, which she had fashioned and lined with cool, green leaves, she offered him a draught of pure, cold water, which he drank eagerly.

Carefully cleansing the stains from his forehead, she quickly discovered the scalp-wound, and again hastening into the copse she gathered a dry mushroom, filled with a fine, brown powder, the fungus known among Europeans as a puff-ball, with which she was enabled to staunch the flow of blood.

"Will the pale-face warrior tell why the Montauk brave would kill him—will the white brother tell Heather Flower with a straight tongue?"

His eyes took on an evil glitter which was veiled by the half-closed lids, as he replied:

"Shall the white warrior speak truly, and will the Heather Flower be angry if he tells her why the Montauk warrior sought his life?"

"Let the young white brave speak with a straight tongue, Heather Flower will not be angry."

"The Sachem's daughter has bidden me speak. Poniute has looked in the heart of the white chief and has seen the love that has been hidden from all the world. He has the keen eye of jealousy; he knows that the white warrior loves the princess of the Montauks."

The warm fingers fell away from the curling locks of the tempter, and she turned away her head in maidenly confusion, the swift blushes staining her cheek to a peachy hue.

"Is my forest queen angry? Does the love of a true heart offend her because the lover is of the pale-faces?"

A deeper bloom suffused her cheek, but her lips were silent.

"If the Heather Flower is angry, the white chief will go away; the first white-winged canoe that sails shall bear him across the blue waters, and Heather Flower shall be troubled with his presence no longer —she shall see his face no more."

"Heather Flower is not angry that the pale-face chief speaks with a straight tongue. But she must stay in the lodges of her people. Let the young chief take counsel with the King of the Montauks. If her father will give her in marriage, she will go to the wigwam of the young white chief who loves her."

"The pale-face lover will speak to the great Sachem of the Montauks, but not now. For a time, the secret of our love must be locked within our hearts," he whispered, his lips close to her ear, his tone a caress. "Will my forest flower consent to remain silent until I give her leave to speak—until I have completed my arrangements? Listen, love of my soul, the Great Chief across the blue water has sent me here upon matters of much importance, and should it become known to my people that I had taken a wife from among the red men I might be carried to England loaded with chains, nay, I might be convicted of treason to my sovereign lord, and suffer an ignominious death; would my forest flower know what I must endure should some enemy represent my motives falsely? I might be hanged upon a gibbet to suffer the pangs of strangulation, but only for a moment, then my heart would be torn from my breast, my limbs would be severed, and my head placed upon the highest spike on Temple Bar, a spectacle for the gaping crowd! Can my forest queen ask the sacrifice, when, by her silence, she might save me?"

She but partially comprehended the language, but the tone, the pantomime accompanying the statement, conveyed the meaning only too surely.

"But the daughter of a king is a fitting mate for the greatest chief among the pale-faces!" returned Heather Flower, proudly, withdrawing herself from her lover's encircling arm, a red flush mounting to her brow.

With caressing words he soothed her wounded pride, picturing in vivid colouring the happiness that would crown their lives when, as his idolised wife, he would take her to England and present her at the English Court, just as John Rolfe had presented his beautiful bride, Pocahontas, the daughter of King Powhattan.

From her own people Heather Flower had heard the story of the Indian princess and the renowned Captain Smith, of her marriage to the young Englishman who had taken her to his native land; but the truth did not wholly satisfy her own conviction of right.

"The great warrior whose life Pocahontas saved was the warrior she loved, so it is told beside the lodge fires of my people; why, then, did they take her to the lodge of another white chief?" she asked. "From a warrior of the Manhansetts, who was carried away in the white-winged canoe to be the white man's slave, and come back after many moons to the lodges of his people, his red brothers know that, when in the great lodge of the pale-face father she looked upon the war-chief whose life she had saved, she covered her face with her blanket and wept, that, for love of the brave war-captain she died; did the red warrior of the Manhansetts speak with a straight tongue?"

"It is not certainly known, but it is believed that Pocahontas gave her love to the gallant Rolfe; at all events, she became his wife of her own free will," returned Kingsland, "a marriage of convenience, of diplomacy upon her father's part, it may have been; such are not uncommon."

It required all the arts of which he was past-master to combat the objection of the forest girl to the course marked out by her treacherous lover, that she would meet him at intervals, and in secret, that both should use the strictest rule of etiquette usual among her people when in the presence of others, and that their betrothal should not be made known until his secret mission was concluded and he was free to claim her as his wife.

With all the sophistry at his command, he explained that by the laws of his people one engaged in a secret mission must, upon no account, become entangled in a matrimonial alliance; that such an entanglement subjected him to arrest, imprisonment, perhaps death, should an enemy arise to bear false witness; and she, ignorant of the white man's laws, believed, implicitly, his honeyed speech.

In haste to divert her attention, he cunningly turned the conversation into another and less dangerous channel.

"I shall be on my guard at all times, and it is unlikely that Poniute will be able to take me at a disadvantage; but remember he is stealthy of foot, familiar with every path in his native forest, while I, a stranger in woodcraft, might easily fall a prey, pierced to the heart by an arrow sent from ambush. His eyes must be blinded to the truth, or my heart's idol may chance to see my scalp in the belt of the red warrior."

"Should my white chief be sent to the spirit land Heather Flower would go to him; she would live no longer; but should he turn from her, should his words be false, should he take a pale-faced maiden to his lodge, then would Heather Flower take his scalp in her hand and laugh at his groans!"

Despite his hardihood, Guy Kingsland was startled out of his self-possession. He had not looked for such an early exhibition of the fierce nature lying dormant beneath the usually calm demeanour, and for the moment he heartily wished he had not committed himself. This magnificent woman who was a very dove in her constancy and depth of affection could prove a tigress were her jealousy once aroused.

Her eyes were blazing, her cheeks had lost their colour, her face was illuminated with a baleful flame at the bare contemplation of treachery. Should she fathom the depths of his meditated perfidy, what would be the consequence? He shuddered involuntarily, dimly realising the horrible vengeance she was capable of meting out should he continue in the course he had mapped.

But the novelty of possession, the triumph of knowing that this untamed, beautiful maiden loved him, blinded him to the peril. His love was too passionate, too selfish, to endure, he knew that; but he promised himself that ere the truth could come to the Indian girl he would be safely on board ship and on his way to " Merrie England."

With tender caresses he quelled the momentary ebullition of anger, and almost as suddenly as her jealousy had arisen her mood changed to the softness of the cooing dove.

" If I ever forget my vow may Heaven forget me in my hour of sorest need," he whispered, feeling a wild sense of exultation that he held a loyal heart in the hollow of his hand, that this regal beauty loved him with a wild worship that she had given no other earthly being, and quite forgetting that thus had he raved of the charms of the lily-fair English maid who was his betrothed, and whom he meant to make his wife.

The afternoon had waned, the sun was casting long shadows across highland and glen, when the lovers parted, he with the memory of the promise she had made that until his mission was accomplished and he was at liberty to demand her of her father, to all the world they should be as the merest acquaintances; she, only conscious that she had never been so happy, never had the song of the birds charmed her so entirely, never had the sun shone so brightly, and only longing for the hour when she might again meet her false love, the man she deemed so perfect.

Ah, happier would it have been for both had they never met. But for that meeting many a dark tragedy enacted within the gloomy recesses of the pine and fir forest would have been lost to the traditions of the Lords of the Soil.

CHAPTER VIII

AN INVOCATION TO HO-BAM-O-KOO

*"May the grass wither from thy feet; the woods
Deny thee shelter! earth a home! the dust
A grave! the sun his light! and heaven her God!"*

THE red glory of a setting summer sun was blazing aslant beneath the tangled branches of the willow, maple and oak grove clothing the islet Manchoage,[1] set like an aquamarine gem in the centre of the lake that lay hidden in the heart of the Heather woods, and turning the waters into patches of gold, crystal and crimson where the rays fell, deepening the lengthened shadows cast by the dark boles of the trees fringing the shore.

Over the smooth surface a canoe was gliding, propelled by the strong arms of an Indian paddler.

Around a weird silence reigned, no barking of dog or croak of frog smote the drowsy air, the only sign of human presence the thin line of smoke curling from the apex of a solitary lodge in a dense grove, through which, however, a well-worn path led straight from the shore of the tiny island.

Beaching his canoe, the young warrior strode up the steep bank in the direction of the lodge, but halting at a few yards distance from the solitary wigwam he gave a peculiar, long-drawn call, like the cry of a night-bird, but no living thing appeared. Twice again, with a moment's interval of silence,

[1] *Manchoage.*—Now known as the Great Pond Island.

AN INVOCATION

Poniute repeated the call, and ere the echoes died away the mat covering the entrance was lifted, and Wee-gon, the great medicine-man of the Montauks, stood in the opening, and with a beckoning finger invited the young warrior to enter.

Filled with the awe which the presence of the wizard of the tribe always inspires in the minds of his people, Poniute followed the medicine-man into the lodge.

Even to a white man, the appearance of the strange being must have been nerve-chilling, as were the surroundings within the mystic abode.

His blanket was laid aside, and his face, exposed to the view of the visitor, was not of the prevailing coppery hue of the red man's skin, but rather of an ashen shade resembling the pallor of death. His thin lips were slightly parted, revealing a line of pointed, sharp teeth; his eyes, set deeply in their cavernous sockets, were intensely black and piercing, lighting up the ghastly features with an uncanny glow. His garments and surroundings were quite in keeping with his personality. A loose robe of deerskin, bedizened with curious and hideous devices—coiling serpents, lizards, fishes, tortoises and scorpions, insects and skeleton bones, mingled in fantastic groups and standing out fearfully life-like covered the gaunt form. His waist was girdled by the stuffed skin of a rattlesnake, the head and notched tail of the reptile falling from hip to knee, seeming to assume life with every motion of the wearer.

Skeletons of birds, snakes and beasts were heaped in a mass upon the earth at the right of the entrance, within the wigwam; a grinning skull suspended from a wooden hook, the conformation denoting it to be a remnant of the skeleton of a gigantic negro; in the centre of the lodge, directly above the smoke of the lodge fire, a hoop was suspended, fringed around its entire circumference with scalps, all of the shining lengths of the Indian scalp-locks, trophies of combats with the enemies of the Montauks dwelling upon the mainland.

Altogether the interior of the wizard's lair resembled a heathen temple rather than the abode of man, and the presiding genius looked not unlike a sacrificial priest of a Druid altar.

Placing his hand upon his heart, Poniute bent his head low in obeisance, and stood with lowered crest, awaiting the speech of the medicine-man, who presently motioned his visitor to a seat upon the broad mat spread in the faint light from a handful of coals glowing in the centre of the lodge, although the summer heat was oppressive.

Seating himself upon a second mat, near the elbow of his visitor, Wee-gon slowly lighted a pipe, drew a score of whiffs and passed the calumet to the young warrior, who silently puffed the smoke, then gravely returned it to the weird man.

"Why are the toes of the young brave's moccasins turned toward the lodge of the medicine-man of the Montauks?" asked Wee-gon, after a pause, during which his fierce eyes had been fixed upon the countenance of the young warrior. "Shall Wee-gon speak? Shall he say that it is not for counsel for a brave upon the war-path; not for a charm to bring down the game in the hunt, but to avenge for the wound in his shoulder where the teeth of the great wolf-dog sunk deep in the flesh; because the very dogs are turned against their masters, and lick the hands of their enemies; because the heart of the young warrior is hot with anger against the pale-face who would tear the Heather Flower from her

AN INVOCATION

native soil to bloom in his lodge until he tired of the wild flower of the forest, only to cast her forth, faded, withered, dying, while he sails away in his white-winged canoe."

The speech was delivered with an intensity that betrayed the pent-up fury raging within the breast of the wizard.

"The great medicine-man of the Montauks is wise; he reads the heart of Poniute as a broad trail in the noonday light. How can the wise man know what brought Poniute to his lodge?" asked the young Indian, as he met the fiery glance of his questioner.

"The leaves of the forest have whispered the story; the birds of the air have sung it; the wise serpent has come from his den in the cleft of the rocks to whisper it in the ear of Wee-gon. Has the young warrior seen the great serpent? Did he meet him on his way hither?"

"Poniute saw nothing of the great serpent," returned the young brave. "He comes forth in the sunlight to warm himself in the heat, and hides when the moon and stars light the earth."

Rising from his seat, Wee-gon stalked into the moonlight, beckoning his visitor to follow.

The rays of the rising orb of night fell in level sheen across the waters of the lake. The necromancer spread his hands and brought the palms together with a soft, soundless touch, repeating the motion a score of times.

"Can Poniute see aught of a serpent?" he asked, without moving a muscle of his face.

"Poniute sees nothing."

The wizard repeated the movement of the hands, and an invocation issued from his lips in a droning tone.

"Great serpent from the cave beneath the water, Wee-gon says come!"

There was the soft rustle of the tall grass, and above the green plumes of a mass of flags upon the border of the lake an ugly head upreared. The white moonlight fell upon the distended jaws and glittering eyes shining like sparks of fire as the reptile swayed its head from side to side.

Again the wizard waved his hand with a beckoning movement, and, obedient to the unspoken command, the snake glided from his covert and approached the lodge with slow, lazy motion; but when within five yards, it coiled with a lightning motion, its head, raised three feet and swinging from side to side with the even strokes of a pendulum, oscillated in unison with the magician's index finger, a low hum issuing from its open jaws.

Involuntarily Poniute stepped backward, for the attitude of the reptile was that of preparation for the fatal spring. It was of a species not common in the forest, fully eight feet in length, its body thick in proportion, but faded by age from a glistening black to a dingy brown, a broad white ring encircling the neck, of the genus, that, like the anaconda of the tropics, crushes its prey in its hideous folds, attacking man or brute without the slightest provocation, giving no warning of its presence until the deadly coils are fastened about the victim.

"Is the young warrior afraid?" asked Wee-gon, in a contemptuous tone. "See!" he continued, awaiting no reply, "Ponny[2] would aid the young brave. He has sent his serpent to whisper in the ear of Wee-gon. Here, boy, here! Give to the

[2] *Ponny.*—One of the names by which the Evil Spirit was known among the island tribes.

AN INVOCATION

great medicine-man of the Montauks the charm [3] that will bring Heather Flower to the lodge of the young warrior of the Montauks; let the swift runner Ponny has sent warm himself in the bosom of Wee-gon. Here, boy, here!"

Slowly uncoiling, the reptile crawled toward the wizard, and, as if ascending a tree trunk, crept upward, its folds lightly encircling the waist and chest of the conjurer, the wicked head rising above his shoulder, close to his ear, while a low hiss broke startlingly upon the night air.[4]

Notwithstanding the stoicism by which the Indian is enabled to conceal his emotions, either of joy, fear, anger or grief, Poniute was unable to repress a shudder.

The enchanter was standing motionless and rigid, his eyes dilated in a mystic stare, his jaws set, and even under the moonlight Poniute could discern the exceeding pallor that had stolen over his features from brow to chin, but leaving the lips blue.

Presently a voice so chill, so hollow, as seemingly to proceed from the chest of a corpse, broke the silence.

"Wee-gon looks into the bosom of the future and sees there what will come to the enemy of the red man, the white warrior who would steal like a thief and take away the young Queen of the Montauks.

"I see the moon hidden behind the black clouds, the stars are put out by the Storm Spirit; the white

---

[3] Charms against evil spirits, to propitiate demons, and to guard the wearer from harm, were given by the medicine-men. Love potions were concocted, also spells to remove a rival. The wizard was also supposed by practise of the black art to torture an enemy, or cause a lingering death.

[4] The singular power to charm venomous serpents possessed by the medicine-men of the various tribes has been demonstrated since the earliest settlement of Europeans in the New World, a power akin to that of East Indian snake-charmers.

light Manitou sends with the snow that makes the dark forest light like the day; the pines bend low with the mighty wind. By the snowflakes the Great Spirit sends to light the earth, the medicine-man sees a pale-face stretched upon the ground, lying in his own blood; it is the young chief of the pale-faces, and over him Poniute stands, holding in his hand the scalp he has taken. His arrow is sticking in the flesh of the enemy at his feet.

"But first our enemies must come upon the warpath across the shining water."

He waved his hand in the direction of the mainland.

"When next the great light of day looks down on the topmost branches of the trees [5] let the young brave go to the wigwam of Cut-was the arrow-maker,[6] and bring back to the lodge of Wee-gon an arrow fashioned long and narrow. Bring bow and quiver, that Wee-gon may make the arrow sure to carry swift death to the heart of his enemy."

"Poniute hears the words of the great medicine-man of the Montauks; when the sun touches the hilltops to the west Poniute will come again, bringing the arrow that will drink the life blood of the paleface warrior," returned the young brave, eagerly, "before three times the sun rises Poniute will take his enemy's scalp."

"No! Let Poniute wait; let him close his lips, let his tongue be silent, let him lie in ambush. Wee-gon has seen the great bow in the sky—it is red with blood; the enemies of the Montauks must come across the water in their war canoes; the soil will drink blood, the forest will ring with the war-whoop of our enemies, for the Evil Spirit will blind the eyes

[5] Noon.
[6] Arrow making was a distinct trade among the Indian tribes.

AN INVOCATION 71

of the watchman on the great rocks. A moon must pass before the enemies of the Montauks drink blood. Moons must come and go before the white chief lies at the feet of Poniute in the Mah-chon-it-chuge. Wee-gon has spoken."

Turning abruptly, the medicine-man vanished within the lodge, and the young warrior was standing alone in the moonlight. The strange conference was ended.

CHAPTER IX

A RED ESAU

"He was the mildest mannered man
That ever scuttled ship, or cut a throat!
With such true breeding of a gentleman,
You never could divine his real thought."

THE village adjacent to the clear lake upon the shore of Manhansett-aha-quash-a-warnuck, the summer abode of the Manhansetts, was in a state of unusual, though suppressed excitement.

Within the great council lodge two-score of chieftains and principal men of the tribes were assembled in council with three white men, while outside groups of younger braves and youths were gathered, debating in low murmurs the subject which was under discussion within the council-lodge, the confirmation of the titles to the lands which had been granted by the Earl of Stirling to James Farret, a measure against which the wise old King Poggatticut had set his face as a flint.[1]

[1] In the power-of-attorney executed by William Alexander, Earl of Stirling, to James Farret, authorising him to dispose of Long Island, he was at liberty to select for his own use 12,000 acres, in consequence of which he made a choice of Shelter Island and Robins Island in Peconic Bay, both of which, on the 18th of May, 1641, he sold to Stephen Goodyear, who afterward conveyed the same to Thomas Middleton, Thomas Rouse, Constant Sylvester and Nathaniel Sylvester, for 1600 wt. good merchantable (Muscovado) sugar.

The grantees procured an immediate confirmation of the title from Yokee, the Manhansett Sachem, and his chief men, who covenanted and agreed at the same time to put away all their dogs, and in case any damage was done to the purchasers by them, to make a proper satisfaction for the same forthwith.

Now the sage was dead; Yo-kee, his son, reigned in his stead, and Wyandance, Sachem of the Montauks, was the staunch friend of the pale-faces.

Would Yo-kee, like a second Esau, sell his birthright for a mess of pottage? That was the question that occupied the thoughts of James Farret, Major Gordon and Lieutenant Kingsland, as they sat in the circle around the fire kindled within the council-lodge, each observing the silence and decorum considered essential at all assemblies of the red men.

The circle of Sachems and chief men was complete, and presently Wyandance lighted the calumet, an elaborate specimen of Indian workmanship, and drawing several whiffs, gravely presented it to Farret, who smoked with the deliberation usual upon such occasions, and placed the pipe in Major Gordon's hand.

Guy Kingsland's fastidious taste could ill brook this indiscriminate use of the pipe, but conquering his squeamishness by an effort, he gripped the stem between his teeth, sending forth three successive curls of blue smoke.

In like manner the calumet passed from lip to lip until it had thrice circulated and was returned to Wyandance.

During the ceremony not a sound was heard, not a syllable spoken, but at its conclusion Wyandance, as king of the Totem[2] tribe, arose, and in the terse, but comprehensive speech of his people, explained the purpose for which the council had been convened.

" Listen, my brothers: The Great Spirit has been good to His children and desires that they should live in peace and harmony together. To that end,

---

[2] *Totem.*—A sort of coat-of-arms among the tribes, without which no signature was held valid by them.

we have smoked the pipe of peace that the friendship of the red man for his pale-faced brother may last as long as grass grows green and water runs downward.

"Listen! I am always glad the Great Spirit gave me hereon to dwell, where the hills are first kissed by the morning sun as he leaves his bed in the land of sunrise beyond the great waters, to bring light and warm His red children, and where I may watch for the coming of the white-winged canoes, and be the first to see and welcome the coming of the white man.

"Listen! Since the coming of the pale-face brother there have been disputes and misunderstandings about the land. When the Dutch came among us they did not want to buy our land, but bought our furs and wampum, and we knew them as our friends. We are sorry they are gone. But when the English came they told us they wanted whereon to build their wigwams, and to plant corn, and to worship the Great Spirit in their own way.

"Listen! When we had sold them land for this purpose they went away with a smile, for their red brothers had made them glad.

"When they come to us again they bring us strange nothings, parchments that speak with tongues we do not understand, that tell us we have sold all our land to the pale-face, and we are asked to put our mark on them.

"Listen! The pale brother tells us that his Great Father across the big water has given him all the land that we see. How can these things be? How could he give away a land that he has not seen, and that was not his to give, and leave the red man without a home in the land which the Great Spirit had given to his fathers? If it was his to give, why did the white man buy any from his red brother, and why are we now asked to put our hand to his lying papers before the land can be his?

"Listen! Now that the council fire is kindled and we have smoked the council pipe, I hope that all will speak freely, and with straight tongues, that all our differences may be settled, that we may not dig up the hatchet, because we love peace better than war, and because we desire to remain the friends of the white man. Wyandance has spoken."

Amid the profound silence that reigned after the Sachem took his seat, James Farret arose, his features composed to the gravity befitting the occasion.

"Let my red brother listen while his pale-face brother speaks with a straight tongue to his red brothers.

"Many moons ago the white man came across the great waters, because in his own land he might not worship the Great Spirit in his own way, and because his Great Father, who was like a mighty Sachem among the red men, was angry with his children.

"We came to the land of the red man, where we were welcomed, and where we taught the red brother to do many things he did not know; the Great Spirit sent us to teach these things, for the pale-face does not live by hunting and fishing as his red brother does, but by tilling the soil and causing the plants to grow, the trees to bear the fruit that there may be enough for all, and to spare. The Great Spirit taught these things to the pale-face and sent him across the great waters where there is room enough for the pale-face and the red man.

"In the land across the water everyone has his land apportioned, that one may not encroach upon another, and that all may do as they choose, and thus avoid misunderstandings and disputes; and to secure to each brother in what is his own, the pale-face has papers which speak to all, and tell what he has given for the land whereon he builds his wigwam; parchments that speak always the same words to keep in remembrance what has been done, to speak to his children after he has gone to the spirit world.

"The pale-face would not steal from his red brother, but he brings, from his own land across the waters, implements with which to till the soil; he brings strange animals of which his red brother has never heard: the cow to yield her milk which is good for food, as the mother's milk is food for the papoose; the horse to carry his rider swiftly across the country, like the swiftest Indian runner, and as sure-footed and tireless; the ox to plough his fields; the sheep to give his red brother the wherewithal to make his blankets; and he will teach his red brother how to card and spin and weave the wool into soft, warm clothing. He brings the seed of strange plants that are good for food, that the squaws may plant and reap. In return what does the pale-face ask? Nothing save that his red brother will give him the land whereon to raise his grain and his fruit, a pasture whereon to feed his cattle and to rear his lodge, while his red brother has room in these vast forests wherein to hunt his game, and the streams from which to take fish. The white man desires to live in peace with his red brothers, to buy furs and wampum, and in exchange to give him of the comforts such as he has known in his own land.

"Let my red brothers ponder my words in their hearts."

With a wave of the hand in token that his address was ended, Farret took his seat, and Yo-kee rose to his feet.

"My Brothers: I am come from the home of the Manhansetts. My heart is yet heavy for the death of my father, Poggatticut, the wisest counsellor Sea-wan-ha-ka has ever known. In his lifetime we were glad to sit around the council fire and listen to his words of wisdom, and were always safe and happy under his guidance.

"Since the Great Spirit whispered and called him to live with his fathers, strange things have come to pass, and I have had none to counsel me, so I have asked that the council fire be kindled that I may understand the things of which I shall now speak.

"When the Great Spirit called away my father in the voice of the night wind, he had seen the moons come and go until the saplings had grown into gnarled and withered oaks, and the moss of a century clung to their rugged trunks, and yet, in all his time, and from the time when the stars were young, and before the small hills had grown to tall mountains, our traditions tell us the Great Spirit planted us here and gave us the land, and none came to claim it until the pale brother came and told us his Great Father across the big water had given him all the red men's land.

"Then he tells us the land has been bought and sold by men we have never seen. He speaks with a double tongue, and his heart is black, for now he comes and asks us to put our hands to this paper that speaks with words we cannot hear and do not understand.

"They tell us we must do this before the land is theirs, that is already theirs by gift and purchase.

"I am like a squaw who is old and blind—I cannot see. I am like a young papoose—I cannot understand.

"I am told that if my father had lived he would

have put his hand to this paper—that he had promised to do so. I do not know this. My father never spoke with a forked tongue. Who is there to say that the tongue of Poggatticut was not straight? He spurned the pale-faces for bringing the dark children of the night and making of them slaves, whom he scourges at will. Their spirits are broken with the lash, and with drooping head and downcast eyes they are bought and sold as we sell the bear and deer skin, or the fur of the otter and beaver.

"Poggatticut's heart was never open to the pale-faces, because they bring strong water that is very bad medicine for us.

"First the white men told us that we must kill all our dogs,[3] and we did this to satisfy them and to save their sheep.

"Now they tell us the land is theirs, and we must go away from the home of our fathers that was left us, to a place we know not where.

"My people are restless and uneasy because of these things, and I am anxious that the wisdom of the council will settle the matter, so that the red children of the Great Father may sit down in their wigwams again, and be always contented and happy. Yo-kee has spoken."

The young chieftain gravely took his seat. His allusions to the wholesale appropriation of land, and to the evil effects of the introduction of slaves, had made a strong impression upon the assembled sachems and counsellors. Major Gordon saw that he must counteract the effect, and waited for a moment to collect his mental forces ere he ventured upon a reply.

[3] When the English commenced the first settlement of Long Island, the Indians annoyed them much by the multitude of dogs they kept, which originally were young wolves brought up tame, and continuing of a very ravenous nature.

It would require the utmost finesse upon his part, else the Manhansett Sachem would not only refuse to sign the transfer, but the entire council would oppose further negotiations.

In a slightly hesitating voice he began:

"My Red Brothers: I have asked that the council fire be kindled that the misunderstandings between the pale-face and his red brother may be explained; that both the white man and the red man may sit peaceably beside their lodge-fires and be happy.

"The coming of the pale-face to the country of the red men may result most favourably for both.

"Before the white man built his forts, the tribes of Sea-wan-ha-ka were forced to pay tribute to their neighbours upon the mainland. Now all may be changed.

"Have we not protected you from the war-clubs and tomahawks of the wicked Narragansetts, who have taken many scalps from the Montauks, the Manhansetts, and other tribes upon these islands?

"The Great Spirit has sent to your relief great warriors from across the blue water, with war canoes, with guns that speak in thunder and flash the lightning. We will teach our red friends their use, and when Ninigret would destroy you, we will protect you until you are strong enough to protect yourselves, until the Narragansetts shall become few, and weak like squaws, and the red men of Sea-wan-ha-ka shall become more in number than the leaves upon the forest trees. In return what do we ask? That we may have land that the red man does not plant; and, by the white man's law, that it may be freely used to the advantage of all, and that the industrious may not be obliged to support the idle, we wish to divide it in tracts, to have the bounds set whereon the white brother may dwell, while he leaves to the red brother the vast forests in which to hunt, and the streams from which to take the fish as he has always done. We would not send the red man away from the lands he has had from his fathers. Here let him remain, here let his children be born, here let him die and be buried with his people, while his tribe multiplies and grows strong under the protection of the white brother, who only wishes to live in peace and comfort in the land that is broad enough for all.

"Let the wise men speak and say if I do not tell them with a straight tongue. Let them consider and be wise."

The stern-browed warriors still frowned, but preserved a decorous silence, while Momometou, chief of the Corchaigs, arose to reply to the conciliatory address of the Major.

The old Sachem's voice rose in sad, but distinct utterance:

"Listen, my brothers: The words of Yo-kee have awakened memories of our traditions that have long slept in the caves of the past.

"In my youth, when the oaks that cast their shadows around us to-day were hiding in the acorn shell, I have listened to our old men while they spoke of what their fathers had told them of the time in the long-ago—so far in the past that they long since had forgotten to count the moons, that our ancestors had come from a warm and sunny land that lies in the far southwest, and that we were the first that the Great Spirit taught to fashion the wampum from the shells of the quahaug and sucki which He gave us for food, and which He had made to grow in plenty in all the waters that at every sun come in and go out[4] again to the great sea. Since then we

[4] Ebb and flow of the tide.

have never been an idle people, as our ancestors were in the hot and sultry clime from whence they came.

"This pleased the Great Spirit, and our wampum was the standard of value and the medium of exchange among all his red children until the coming of the pale-faced brother.

"When he came to us he spoke with the voice of a squaw, his eyes were as the sky in summer. He told us he was fleeing from his Great Father, who was angry with him, and he asked to be allowed to stay and build his wigwam and plant corn and worship the Great Spirit in his own way, and be at peace.

"He brought with him the 'black-coat,'[5] with a book filled with the words of the Great Spirit to His children, that told us that the Great Spirit, when He was angry with His children, spoke, with His thunder from a mountain of fire and smoke, these words: 'Thou shalt not lie'; 'Thou shalt not kill'; 'Thou shalt not take thy brother's wife nor anything that is his.'

"But the pale-face spoke with the forked tongue of a serpent. We have no need of these teachings, for we knew and practised them always.

"When we gave the pale-face whereon to live, we fixed the bounds and marked them with stones set in the earth. Then we gave him of turf and twig as a sign that the gift was perpetual.

"For this the white man said 'Tat-a-my! Tat-a-my!'[6] but in the night, when we slept in our wigwams, he carried the stones away as if they had never been, so that the bounds were lost. Then he came with parchments, with strange characters that we had not seen, and told us that the Great Father had given him all the land that belonged to the Corchaigs, and now he tells us to put our hands to his

[5] *Black-coat.*—Minister. [6] *Tat-a-my.*—Thank you, thank you.

parchments. His voice is no longer soft and sweet, but he grins and snarls as the bear, and his eye is wicked and cold as the eye of the sea-wolf.[7]

"If, as you say, the Great Father was so angry with you, because you had displeased him, that you fled from your homes to save your lives, why has he given you all the land of the Indian? Was it to reward your disobedience? Why have you forgot the words of the Great Spirit that are in the Book from which you would teach your red brothers? Our ears are open to hear the truth, and our hearts will be glad when we see the white man's heart is white, and that he speaks with a straight tongue, and remembers the words of the Great Spirit, 'Thou shalt not lie!' I have spoken."

James Farret had promised to act as interpreter for Guy Kingsland, who understood the Delaware tongue but imperfectly, and the Lieutenant declined to reply until each of the sachems had made complaint and entered his protest.

Of the three white men at the council, where so much was at stake, the young man was the most wily, the most persuasive of speech, the most winning in person and address. He wished to get the consensus of opinion before he made the final stroke. Confident of his own power, he bided his time for the final oration, when his silver tongue might scatter the objections to the winds.

"I am but a sapling among mighty oaks, and would hearken to the counsel of warriors whose years and experience so far exceed my own," he explained, through the interpretation of Farret.

His seeming respect and humility drew a nod of approval from the dignified sachems, and Nowedanah, Sachem of the Shinnecocks, stood up.

[7] *Sea-wolf.*—Shark.

"Listen, my brothers! I will speak to you with a straight tongue, for I am not a serpent and I will show you that my heart is not black.

"When the pale-faces first came to our lodges they gave us the green bough and held up their palms to tell us that they were the children of peace. They brought us strong water, and knives, and looking-glasses, and in return we gave them some of our land upon which to build their lodges and sit down. We taught them that the seed-time had come when the sun unbound the waters that had been locked by the icy hand of the Storm King, when the serpent crawled forth from his long sleep in his den, and the turtle from his hiding-place, when the fish-hawk came again to build her nest and rear her brood among the trees around our wigwams; and how to plant corn when the leaves of the white oaks were no bigger than the squirrel's ear.

"When the harvest came we told him, and when the Indian summer came and the Frost Spirit, with gentle breath, breathed his war-paint on all the leaves, that made them to wither and fall, and the flowers to droop and die, we told him this was to tell us of the return of the Snow Spirit with his icy breath. For a time we lived in peace, but soon the pale-faces were joined by their brothers from over the big water. They wanted more land, and we were told to move on.

"Now all is changed. The white man is no longer the friend of his red brother.

"Only the last winter one of my old men, with his squaw, was returning from Meanticut, where they had been to visit relatives, to his wigwam at the Canoe-place, when the night came on and they were met by a storm. The breath of the Ice King chilled their blood, for they were old; the blinding snow came down and threatened to bury them—the wolf howled upon their trail. Afraid to cross the hills with his squaw on such a night, he turned aside at Agawan, and sought the lodge of the black-coat for food and shelter for the night.

"'No room for Indian dog,' the black-coat said, and sent them away. The squaw would fain lie down in the snow to perish, but the old warrior would not allow it, so they returned to the black-coat's lodge to ask where to find the lodge of a *Christian,* and the black-coat dropped his head, but his white squaw said, 'Come in,' and she let them lay on the floor and sleep; but before the wolf had sought his covert, or the sun looked from under the black blanket of night, they were awakened, and, without food, were told to move on.

"The pale-face is no longer the friend of his red brother; he comes to our wigwams to trade for our furs, and bring strong water that makes us walk like a crazy squaw, and then we sleep like dead men; our bow-strings are cut, and our arrows are broken.

"Twelve moons ago, when one of the great canoes of the pale-faces was broken by the big water at Agawan,[8] one of the pale-faces was killed by the Pequots, who had come to talk and ask us to join them and make war on all the whites, and who were hiding in the woods, and would not remain in our wigwams because we were the friends of the pale-faces. When the Pequots had gone, the white men came to our village and demanded two of our young men, whom they charged with the murder of their brother, and when we refused to give them up they threatened to bring the red-coats,[9] and kill us all.

[8] A vessel was wrecked, but the crew got ashore. One of the white men was murdered by the Pequots. The murder was charged to the Shinnecocks, and two braves of that tribe were executed.

[9] *Red-coats.*—Soldiers.

Then they took our young men and hung them for a murder committed by our enemy, the Pequots.

"You tell us that the Great Father across the big water loves his red children, and wants them to live in peace with his white children and not make war upon them; but he sends his great war canoes here, that throw out thunder and fire and smoke. They are filled with red-coats, who carry muskets and long knives; they build strong lodges,[10] and make war on their red brothers.

"You tell us the Great Father has given you all the land of his red children. If he loves us why has he robbed us? When they were in dispute over the land we sold them, why were we, with our brother, Poggatticut, called to meet them at Wegmaganuck, to fix and define the bounds, that they might live in peace?

"You tell us so rich and powerful is your Great Father that the sun never sets on his domain. If this be true, is it because the Great Spirit is afraid to trust his white children in the dark?

"Our traditions tell us that in the long-ago the pale-faced strangers came from the North and lived in the country of the Passamaquoddies, the Penobscots and the Wampanoags, and later they lived in the country of the Narragansetts, without molestation, until they returned to their own country afar off, leaving behind them a stone lodge,[11] which the red man has been careful to preserve as a sign of the friendship that existed between them and the white man.

"The sun warms us, the earth feeds us, we rest in her bosom where our fathers have slept since the sun first kissed and smiled upon her before her red children had learned to count the moons. Who,

---

[10] *Strong Lodges.*—Forts.   [11] Stone tower at Newport.

then, will say the land is not ours? Where would they have us go? We send our respects to the Great Father, and shake hands with him, and say 'How-dy.' We desire to live in peace with his white children, and trust they will deal justly with us and make all things plain to us before we put our hands to this parchment. I have spoken."

The aged Sachem took his seat. The frowns had become absolute scowls, and the elder white men could scarcely hide their chagrin at what they feared to be the failure of their schemes; but with a serene brow and smiling eyes Guy Kingsland stood up to deliver the final oration on the part of the white men.

Awed by the wisdom of the great Sachems who had spoken, the counsellors declined to add anything to their counsel, judging that a repetition of their sentiments would add nothing, but rather weaken the effect of their remonstrances.

Kingsland's intonation was singularly sweet, his gestures perfect, his personality magnetic.

"Red Brothers: You have long been the friends of the white man. Although I cannot speak to you in your own tongue, I have listened to its music, and my brother has interpreted its sense.

"All my red brothers have said is true, in a sense, for, as among the Indian tribes, there are good men and true and there are bad men among us. Shall we judge the lords of Sea-wan-ha-ka by the wickedness of the Narragansetts, who have so cruelly exacted tribute from their brothers on these islands? No, we cannot! From the land beyond where the sun rises good men came that they might be free to worship the Great Spirit in their own way. The red men fed and clothed them, and they, in their turn, were the friends of the red brother.

"By and by came others, men outlawed by the Great Father over the sea, for their crimes, and the same evil acts that drove them from their native land were renewed in this land. They brought, in their great white canoes, men from the land of the burning sun, and sold them for slaves. It was but a merciful act to purchase these men and women who had been confined in loathsome prisons, in the depths of their great canoes, and far down beneath the waters, where the sunlight never shines; it was merciful for white men to make these poor black children of the Great Spirit their own, that they might clothe and feed the poor, helpless creatures who had been torn from their homes by cruel white men who dare not uncover their faces in their own land lest they should be placed in prison, or hanged for their crimes.

"Mark you, red brothers, how sleek and fat and happy your best friend, Lyon Gardiner, has made the dark-skinned squaw whom he has called Xantippe.

"These men also brought the fire-water, which is a medicine that makes the heart glad, while it is taken only in moderation; but they told not to the red brother that if taken too freely it would cause him to stagger like a wounded deer.

"It is only the wicked men, outlaws from their own race, that would take away the land, and would drive the red brother from his inheritance. These are the bad men whom we would scourge from our midst. The good white men would dwell beside their red brothers in peace. We bring seeds for the planting, we bring cattle and horses, we bring implements to make the cloth with which to clothe ourselves and our red brothers, we take in exchange their furs and wampum, as one Indian would trade with another.

"More than all, with our muskets and our swords we will protect our friends; the red-coats are here but for the protection of good white men and good Indians alike, and that the Montauk warriors may no more be murdered, no more shall the scalp of a Montauk, a Manhansett, a Mattituck or a Shinnecock dangle at the belt of an enemy, or dry in the smoke of his lodge fire.

"No more shall the lords of Sea-wan-ha-ka pay tribute to their enemies, but to their friends, the English, who will protect them while their people multiply and live in peace beside their protectors, while they hunt in the forest, take fish from the streams, the sucki from their beds, and enjoy to the full the lands their fathers have given them.

"True, our Great Father across the blue water has given us parchments which say that the land is ours by his gift. How can he give it when it is not his? He cannot, and we come, with open palms and straight tongues, and ask our red brothers to sell us their land, to set the bounds. We do this that there may be no misunderstanding. We do not wish to have the Indians go away.

"Brothers, would you have revenge upon your enemies, would you have the red-coats to send the thunder of their guns into the forests where your enemies dwell, would you grow great and powerful, that every tribe upon the mainland might fear your warriors? If so, sign the parchment in acknowledgment that we are your friends, that we are welcome among you, that we, too, may sit down peaceably in our homes, knowing that the Indians of Sea-wan-ha-ka are our friends, that we are their brothers. Sign this parchment in token of the friendship that shall be closer as the moons come and go. Thus can the tribes of Sea-wan-ha-ka free themselves from the hated tribute,[12] and be revenged upon their enemies."

Guy Kingsland had touched the master-chord that never ceases to vibrate in an Indian's breast—revenge, which they consider a cardinal virtue.

What the threats and arguments of those more powerful had failed to accomplish, the sophistry, and more than all, the magnetic influence of this wily young lieutenant had surmounted.

In five minutes Yo-kee, the red Esau, had relinquished his hold upon the land of his fathers, had bartered his birthright for a mess of pottage.

Momometou of the Mattitucks, Nowedanah, Sachem of the Shinnecocks, and, lastly, Wyandance, King of the Montauks, the Totem tribe, had affixed their signatures, and the renunciation was complete.

[12] "The Montauks were doubtless superior in numbers and warlike skill to any other of the Long Island tribes, and this superiority was acknowledged by the payment of tribute. The Pequots had once subdued the Montauks, and the whole of the Long Island Indians were obliged to pay to their conquerors an annual tribute.

"After 1637 they seem to have considered themselves in subjection to the English, and paid them for their protection the same amount they had previously paid to the Pequots.

"In 1650, in consequence of their failure to pay, the New England commissioners sent Captain Mason to Long Island to require payment of the tribute due from the Indians, and to make arrangements for their more punctual discharge in the future. In 1656 the Montauk chief visited the commissioners at Boston, and acquainted them with the fact that he had paid the tribute due from him at Hartford for the space of ten years, but that it was in arrears for the last four years, in consequence of the war in which they had been engaged with the Narragansetts, on which account the commissioners consented to release the payment of it. It is not easy at this date to perceive the justice of the imposition of this tribute by the white people.

"The Pequots, who had also been tributary to the English in 1650, remonstrated against the injustice of exacting tribute from them, in answer to which the commissioners said it was imposed in 1635 for the murders they had committed. It was exacted from the Long Island Indians under the pretence that the whites afforded them protection against their red brethren, to whom they would otherwise have been forced to pay tribute."

CHAPTER X

À LA MORT

"To hell allegiance! vows to the blackest devil!
Conscience, and grace, to the profoundest pit!
I dare damnation: To this point I stand,—
That both the worlds I give to negligence,
Let come what comes; only I'll be revenged."

IN all ages of the world duelling always has and always will appeal to the brutal side of humanity. Where or with whom it originated is conjecture.
If we delve amid the ruins of ancient Egypt we find the duellist perpetuated in hieroglyphics upon the sculptured marble of a forgotten past.

We find Moses, the Law-giver of ancient Israel, fleeing into the land of Midian, after indulging in a duel with an Egyptian, in which the latter was slain. Again, we find the youthful David, the most valiant of King Saul's army, going out to meet Goliath, the Philistine giant, in the valley of Elah, in a duel, in which the proud and boastful warrior succumbed to the stripling.

So it has been that the duellist has always had a place, whether on the plains of mediæval Troy or within the confines of classic Greece or in the Roman amphitheatre.

In the feudal age of knight-errantry, or in the days of modern civilisation, the role of the duellist has been, and is, peculiar. He has determined the destiny of nations as well as of individuals, and disturbs and distorts, alike, the history of every race.

What wonder, then, that he should have his place among the North American Indians? His progenitors may have brought the practice with them on the voyage of the *Atlantis*, or, perchance, it has come by the many other avenues if, as fancy has imagined, the new world was peopled from the old. In what manner the Indian became imbued with a love for the duel we leave everyone to reach by his own conclusions. Certain it is that he was ever a lover of hand-to-hand, single combat, and certain too it is that the brute side of human nature has always been a willing witness to a duel. Thus, we find the love for the sin not confined to class or caste, and also that in so-called " defence of honour " of a duelling nature, that is regulated or prohibited by law, we discover in the throngs who witness these exhibitions, an equal percentage of indifferent law-makers and law-breakers.

It is said of the lion and tiger, that after once tasting human blood their thirst for the same is never satiated. So it is with their biped brother who has once vanquished an adversary on the field of honour, or dishonour; he is ever athirst for blood.

The decline and overthrow of the power of the Narragansetts was determined and hastened by Uncas, the cunning and wily Mohican chieftain, who, when he learned that Miantonomoh, his enemy, with a large force of warriors, was about to invade his country, gathered his forces and went forth to battle, and when the opposing armies met Uncas challenged the Narragansett Sachem to single combat.

By a preconcerted plot, as soon as Miantonomoh was apart from his warriors, the Mohicans sent a shower of arrows upon the passive and unsuspecting Narragansetts, then seized and pinioned Miantonomoh, and carried him in triumph before the paleface commissioners at Hartford, a captive.

Those Christian monstrosities, while feigning unbounded friendship for both, with matchless treachery committed a noble captive to the care of his merciless captor, to be conducted safely back to his own domain, well knowing he would be foully murdered *en route*.

There is no ambition, real or imaginary, no virtue or vice within the realm of human thought, for which a duel has not been fought, and in every instance the victor and vanquished have, in turn, been lionised or lamented.

In Indian warfare a challenge is often implied by the war-whoop, and accepted by an answering whoop, from an enemy. Oft, in the heat of battle, a challenge is conveyed by the brandishing of a spear or war-club in a threatening manner, or tapping, significantly, the hilt of a hunting knife or the handle of a tomahawk.

Such a challenge is accepted when the same gestures are returned by an adversary.

It is an unwritten law of savage warfare that the combats are always held under a truce. Often the fortunes of war were decided by them, or at their close the battle was abandoned or renewed according to the terms of the truce.

When a duel is fought between members of the same tribe the conditions are that the survivor contributes to the support of the victim's widow.

From the day that To-cus challenged Mandush to mortal combat, and the day for the fray had been fixed upon, the village of the Montauks had been alive with excitement concerning the result of the fight.

At last the day on which the fate of one or both

was to be decided, dawned, and the hour for a battle to the death was upon them.

The arena was a wooded dell, a deep and wide ravine, peculiar to the wild region that, at some remote period of the past ages, had been a watercourse connecting the waters of the sea at the south with those of the bay on the north, with wooded slopes stretching upward and away on either hand; while the valley on the bed of the ancient stream, from which the waters had long since subsided, was carpeted in a luxuriant coat of verdure, flanked on either side by abundant and variegated flora that filled the air with sweet incense.

The giant oaks and maples that had kept the vigils of centuries, overgrown with the moss that clung to their trunks and drooped from their branches, fitting reminders of the patriarchs of old, stood here, mute and rugged sentinels that had witnessed the shrouding of the dead, weird, mysterious, echoless past.

It was at the early hour of morning, before the sunbeams had drunk the dew from flower and leaf and grass. The day was faultless but for that oppressive stillness with which nature is sometimes hushed, not unlike the calm that precedes the hurricane.

The very woods seemed deserted by the feathered songsters that inhabited them, so deathlike was the silence, save for the moaning surge of the ever-restless sea to the southward, that in shimmering undulations greeted the eye. The leaves hung motionless.

Suddenly the oppressive silence was broken. Across the silvery waters of the bay came the shrill, peculiar call of the great sprat, or sea-loon, filling the air with mournful cadence, echoing through the green forest, while far up the heights, defined against the azure sky, an eagle floated on fearless pinion, soaring in circles, as if surveying the scene below.

When the principals, coming from opposite directions, and bared to the waist, made their appearance upon the scene, they found that the entire population of the village had preceded them, and was awaiting their arrival in grim silence.

Let us pen-sketch the untutored warriors, Mandush and To-cus, who have met to engage in deadly strife, each for the other's undoing.

Mandush, the incarnation of majestic bearing, a warrior cast in heroic mould, giant in strength, heavily set, deep-chested, with fearless courage and determination outlined in the contour of his face and flashing from the depths of his fiery, deep-set eyes.

To-cus, his rival, was fashioned in a different pattern. He was some years the junior of his antagonist, a perfect type of physical manhood, more agile and panther-like than his foeman. With muscles of steel and nerves of iron, a steady eye, and of unquestioned courage and reckless daring, he was well worth the steel of his enemy.

The weapons to be used were knives, heavy, cruel-looking blades.

An aged warrior, tomahawk in hand, strode into the arena, as master-of-ceremonies, and at his signal four warriors came forward, the two first proceeding to securely pinion the left hand of one of the combatants upon his back, while the second two performed the same office for the other.

When this was done, the master-of-ceremonies addressed the duellists, stating the terms to be observed.

The battle was to the death; no quarter was to be shown, and the victor must bind himself, during his lifetime, to contribute to the support of those who were dependent upon the vanquished.

The words were enunciated distinctly, then, with lightning-like rapidity, he encircled his head, once, twice, thrice, with his tomahawk and hurled it at a tree trunk, into which it sank, and the fight was on.

Simultaneously with the thud of the tomahawk, with knives drawn, with quickened breath and set lips, with nostrils distended and eyes scintillating, the mortal foes, quivering in every limb with convulsions of hate that were consuming both, with the impetus of a whirlwind rushed upon each other.

As the waves are thrown back from the ocean-bound rock, each in turn was hurled away from the other, neither uttering a sound, but each fighting with desperate valour and ferocity, now striking, thrusting, lunging, fencing, sparring and parrying, they fought with the fury of demons, each in turn driving and being driven.

So terrible was the battle that it seemed as if, in one dread moment, the peaceful vale had been transformed into a heathen temple of sacrifice.

It was soon apparent, from the sanguinary pace set, that the battle would be short. Blood was flowing freely from both contestants, but neither had reached a vital spot. Ere long it was seen that Mandush began to flag, and was more on the defensive, being older, heavier, and less agile than the sinewy and more cat-like To-cus, who, ever alert, avoided his adversary's dangerous onsets with adroit cleverness.

Meanwhile Mandush received a slash across the forehead from which the blood flowed freely, crimsoning his visage and obstructing his vision. In this unfortunate condition he was at the mercy of his merciless foe, who, seizing the advantage, reached the throat of his adversary, severing the neck to the bone, and then, with a fierce yell of exultation, he plunged the knife to the hilt, and wrenching it from right to left, nearly disembowelled his victim.

The hapless Mandush sank down, and ere the thirsty earth had drunk his life-blood the death-song had died upon his lips, the warlike soul had embarked in the mystic, white canoe to cross the fathomless, trackless sea for the shore of the spirit land.

CHAPTER XI

A BOW WITH TWO STRINGS

"The air is full of hints of grief,
Strange voices, filled with pain—
The pathos of the falling leaf,
And rustling of the rain."

THE late June roses were rocking in the balmy evening breeze, the full moon was rising from beneath the silvery waters, lighting up the Isle of Wight with its calm, white sheen, the insect voices and the lonely call of the whip-poor-will mingled with the wash of the waves upon the shore, and tempted by the exceeding beauty of the night Damaris Gordon strolled down the path leading to the grove of elm and maple skirting the bluff above the beach.

Swiftly time had glided by, and twice each week Guy Kingsland had rowed over to Montauk, upon each occasion meeting with the beautiful Indian girl whose heart he had won—for what?

In his inmost soul he knew that the passion she had inspired was of the earth earthy, and as evanescent as the scores of flirtations in which he had engaged during his youth and young manhood, and already he was tiring of the pursuit; the object he had sought with such ardour he desired no longer, for, with the true purity that had been taught her by precept and example, he found, to his chagrin, that her honour was greater than even her love, and that a marriage-ceremony by the rites of her people was the only means through which he might claim her.

Had she been the daughter of an obscure member of the tribe small ceremony would have been required, and the farce of a marriage might have attracted little attention and might have been accomplished without the knowledge of the white residents upon the island; but for an Indian princess there must be a grand feast and all the ceremony befitting her rank.

Guy Kingsland was in a dilemma from which it might be difficult to extricate himself, and, cursing his folly, he drifted on. Fearing to arouse the suspicion of Heather Flower, he continued his visits, to be received, upon each occasion, with such rapturous greeting that even his fickle heart was stirred, half with a consciousness of his own villainy, but more by a dread of the consequences should she discover his falsity, and dimly realising the fierceness of her passions when unchained.

Heather Flower, however, in her absorbing and implicit trust and love suspected nothing. His fervid, impassioned glances, his magnetic presence, his caressing tones, had awakened into active life all the passionate tenderness that was so blended in her dual nature with the fierceness of the savage.

Meantime, by well-timed but casual remarks he had intimated to Major Gordon that the frequent visits Damaris paid her Indian friend were in scarcely good form, and that the growing intimacy between the two maidens should be curtailed as far as possible.

Acting under the suggestion, the Major had prohibited his daughter's visits to the Sachem's lodge, except escorted by her father or lover, and hinting vaguely at some threatened rising of the tribes upon the mainland or a descent of the Mohawks, a war between the tribes that might break out at any moment; and that, should a white girl be found with the Montauks, by either Narragansetts or Mohawks, she would be made captive or slaughtered. At the same time he cautioned her against mentioning the matter to Heather Flower, declaring that it might give her needless anxiety, as the outbreak might, after all, not occur.

As for Damaris, she regarded her false lover as the embodiment of all that was chivalrous, brave and true, believing that he worshipped her with the ardour of a first and abiding passion, and trusting him with a blindness which naught save the unmasking of his treachery could unseal, and so matters drifted on to a crisis which could not long be delayed.

"Great Heavens! what a dolt, what an idiot, I have made of myself!" thought Kinsgland. "What evil genius prompted me to imperil my peace, my ambition, even my personal safety? I was mad to mistake the fleeting fancy for that fierce tigress of an American forest for love—a fatal error for which I may pay dearly. Fortunately, her severe code of virtue has baffled my advances and completely balked me, else I might be in deeper seas. As it is, I am between the devil and the deep sea, for I cannot shake off the superstitious foreboding of evil until the waves of the Atlantic roll between me and this vindictive daughter of a savage, fiery race. Double-dyed fool that I was to risk the loss of the innocent child who loves me, by an entanglement with one for whom I really care nothing; yet the play must be played out, the farce carried on to the end; Ye gods! it looks as if it might end in a tragedy, and when my mission is concluded, I shall lose not a moment in leaving the colonies; I'll drive this land-grabbing game with all speed, and then good-bye to these black forests where a savage or a wild beast lurks in every covert. Um-m-m! I'll take a constitutional on the bluff and drive away the blue devils before it is time to turn in."

Crushing his hat over his eyes, he went out into the night.

The warm June evening down in the shadow of the greenwood was inexpressibly soothing, the crystal dew-drops glittered on grass blade and leaf, as he strode on beneath the overarching arms of giant oaks and maples; the air was redolent of the perfume of wild roses, honeysuckles, swamp-pinks and fern.

"I'll cheat destiny itself, but I must be cunning as the fox, subtle as the serpent," he muttered. "If I were a fatalist, I should believe that some demon was on my track, some unseen spirit of evil at my heels —but pshaw! who believes in destiny nowadays?"

How little he dreamed that even at that moment he was entering the fatal circle of destiny and doom.

Down upon the slope of an overhanging bluff, beneath the branches of a graceful elm, Damaris had a favourite resort, and almost unconsciously Guy bent his steps in that direction.

She was sitting there, as he half fancied she would be, the moonlight sifting through the branches falling upon the slender, girlish figure and the stately little head crowned with an aureole of golden ringlets.

With all the artist's love of the beautiful, Guy Kingsland noted the perfect pose, the delicate profile, and his heart quickened its pulsations when he reflected that this was his promised bride, and the haunting presence of the Indian maid, that had but the previous moment seemed a reality, faded from his mental vision.

Damaris welcomed him with a smile, but he noticed a shadow of abstraction, all unusual, upon her fair face as he took a seat beside her upon the rustic bench he had fashioned for her, and unconsciously a sigh escaped her lips.

"You are distrait, my darling—why that sigh? One might imagine my presence an intrusion," he said, half-reproachfully, half-jestingly. "Are you unhappy, love?"

"Not unhappy, Guy, only nervous—it is but my foolish fancies," she replied.

"Fancies, dearest; surely you should have only bright waking dreams. Tell me, fairest Damaris, what troubles you? surely I have a right to know, I, your promised husband," he answered, a secret misgiving at his heart that she might harbour a suspicion of the cause of his frequent visits to Montauk.

"I am quite sure you would laugh at what you would consider nonsense," she returned.

"I will promise not even to smile, if I can help it," he answered, gaily. "I have the greatest curiosity to learn what untoward fancy can bring a cloud to your fair brow."

"I cannot tell why, but since I have been sitting here I have felt as if some evil presence overshadowed me, a creeping chill, such as one feels when one says, 'Someone is walking over my grave,' a presentiment of some calamity, an apprehension I cannot shake off, reason as I may. Guy, do you believe in warnings?"

"No-o-o," he replied, tardily, his own sense of a haunting presence returning more strongly as he listened, "I am not superstitious; ghosts, wraiths and presentiments are only auld-wives' tales for the amusement of the goodies and gaffers around the winter fireside. Belike the fancy is engendered by the rather heavy dinner we indulged in; a good digestion is the most effectual cure for the blue-devils. Shake off morbid fancies and be again my own bright, light-hearted Damaris."

"I beg you will not be angry with me, Guy," she answered, deprecatingly, as she noted the pronounced frown between his eyes. "I suppose I was silly to give expression to my thoughts."

"Angry! not in the least," he replied, "only surprised and sorry that you should be disturbed by chimeras; and now let us change the subject for some topic more in consonance with this sylvan scene and this delicious moonlight. Suppose we stroll down the Sachem's walk and see what exercise can effect in the way of laying the phantom of your imagination."

She rose at once, his arm about her slender waist.

"I have often wondered what gives the name to this beautiful path," Guy said, inquiringly, as they sauntered down the leafy arcade between two lines of magnificent trees as accurately planted by the hand of nature as if designed for an avenue, and from which Gardiner's woodmen had carefully cleared the undergrowth; "I suppose some doughty, red Sachem had here a wigwam, or something equally interesting. I never remembered to ask Gardiner."

"The Captain has told me nothing, but I have heard a queer old legend told by the Indians over at Montauk—you know their traditions are handed down from generation to generation, just as we preserve a written history of olden days in England;

Heather Flower has told me the story. Why, you are cold!" broke off Damaris, as she felt the slight shudder in the arm about her waist, evidence of the shock the mention of that name had given.

"Cold? Oh, no! what put such an idea in your pretty head?"

"You were shivering, I am quite sure," she returned, peering in his face, "and you look quite pale."

"Another of your odd conceits; it is only the moonlight that plays strange tricks," he smiled, "but you have not told me the tradition."

"We are upon the very spot with which the legend is connected, and it was here that Heather Flower told me the story—— Why, you are certainly chilly, and your heart bounded suddenly, I am sure. What is the matter?"

"Nonsense!" he exclaimed, almost angrily; "probably a little palpitation to which I—all lovers are subject when blessed with the companionship of a sweetheart." He abruptly changed the tone and manner as he saw her look of surprise: "I am sure I shall never get at the story with so many interruptions."

He was angry with himself, angry with his companion that she should so persist in mentioning the name that chilled him in spite of reason and brought that unseen, uncanny presence so near.

"Many moons ago, as the Indians tell, the trail leading through the forest at this point was soft and grass-grown its entire length; these paving-stones, laid with such care, were brought here from the ledge upon the other side of the brook. Here dwelt one of the minor tribes tributary to the King of the Montauks, who were at war with the Narragansetts, and here a sanguinary battle was fought. In fact, there have been many battles upon this island, and warriors' graves are scattered the length and breadth, from which circumstance the Indians gave it the name of Man-cho-nock, the place of many dead; but I am wandering from the story. Confronted by a force of Narragansetts triple their own in number, the Montauks fell, one by one, slaughtered miserably by their foes, asking no quarter, until but the chieftain and one of his principal warriors were left, and these were spared only for torture.

"It was then that these paving stones were brought, laid, and heated by fires built upon them the entire length and breadth, and the unfortunate Sachem and his chief counsellor were compelled to walk barefoot over the glowing rocks until they fell and expired.

"The enmity of the Narragansetts was aroused solely because the Montauks had refused to aid them in destroying the whites, but on the contrary, they had divulged the plot to massacre the English, thus frustrating the design."

"And, thus, the Montauk chief had to pay the penalty of his devotion with his life?" asked Guy, a twinge of conscience reminding him that he, at least, was guilty of treachery in the sight of Heaven for the deed he meditated against one who was regarded by her people with the deepest affection and a kind of reverence, and, unconsciously the words of Holy Writ escaped his lips:

"Vengeance is mine, I will repay," his guilty soul trembling as if involuntarily he had pronounced upon himself the sentence of doom.

"But these children of the forest, reared in a heathen faith, know nothing of the Christian religion," returned Damaris, gravely. "To them warfare is a glory, to slay from ambush a military necessity, death upon the battle-field a passport to the happy hunting grounds. In their ignorance, I believe the Good Shepherd will excuse them, but surely the vengeance of a just God must fall upon a Christian who would wilfully injure or defraud these untutored people who have conveyed their lands to strangers, all unknowing of the value of these princely estates they have bartered for a song. According to statements, the price paid to the Indians for this beautiful island of thousands of acres was only one black dog, one gun and ammunition, some rum, and a few Dutch blankets; besides, I understand that the sum of five pounds sterling is to be paid annually, not to the Indians, mark you, but to the Earl of Stirling, or his heirs, if demanded; but I cannot understand this barter, or what right King Charles, Cromwell, or any other English ruler can possibly have to a country already populated by those who have been lords of the soil for centuries, may be——"

"Prithee, don't meddle with politics, lassie; it is according to the law of survival of the fittest, and I make no doubt that ere a century has waned the race inhabiting these islands, and the mainland as well, will have become extinct, or practically so, and these manors apportioned by the English grants will be of immense value, the proprietors among the great of the earth," said Guy, loftily. "I have already secured a big tract, and there is Farret, who has possession of a dukedom; it was rather up-hill work we had to get Yo-kee's signature, and had the old Sachem, his father, lived, we should have obtained possession only at the point of the bayonet. As it is, many valuable lives are saved, for the war must have been long and bloody, but now the Lord has given the land to his followers, the saints possess a goodly dwelling place," concluded the hypocrite, adopting the popular style of expression.

"I am but a girl, but I can reason; and truly, Guy, I can see nothing saintly, or even just, in this land-grabbing; I think it is a cruel thing to take advantage of the ignorance and hospitality of these poor people—confess that you believe that," returned Damaris, firmly.

"I choose to look rather on the reverse side of the question—self-interest must ever outweigh sentiment; I must confess I have little sentiment, neither do I deal in heroics; I could not change matters if I would, would not if I could. If the red Sachem who perished here could but take a glimpse of mundane affairs, he would be slightly astonished, no doubt."

"Perchance he does return; how can we tell what is permitted to departed spirits? Tradition has it that when the moon is at the full, the period when the Sachem suffered a horrible death, his ghastly form rushes with headlong bounds over the rocky way, and at the dead midnight hour the war-whoop of the Montauks, uttered by no mortal lips, peals through these leafy aisles, the defiant death-shriek of the doomed Sachem," concluded Damaris, in an awed half-whisper.

Silence fell between the pair when the narration was concluded, and they sauntered on, reaching an open glade commanding a view of the bay ere they turned to retrace their steps. An angle in the path brought them to the lower extremity of the vista across the stretch of paving, the scene of the tragedy now wrapped in deep shade. The dark, woodland aisle, the masses of fern on either hand casting a denser shadow, looked mysteriously beautiful in the patches of moonlight breaking at intervals between the umbrageous foliage overhead.

Suddenly a wailing note smote the air, a prolonged, unearthly peal that echoed through the forest, cutting the air like a knife.

"The terrible war-whoop of the Montauks!" shuddered Damaris, as she clung closely within the encircling arm of her lover.

"Are you sure?" answered Guy. "Might it not be the call of a loon, or some strange night bird—a screech owl or something of the kind?"

"Oh, no! I am quite positive that it was the war-whoop of the Montauks. I heard it but once from Wyancombone's lips, just to gratify my curiosity, but I can never forget it, or mistake it."

CHAPTER XII

THE WAR-WHOOP OF THE MONTAUKS

> "A scream! 'tis but the panther's—naught
> Breaks the calm sunshine there;
> A thicket stirs, a deer has sought
> From sight a closer lair."

HASTENING along the avenue in the direction from which the uncanny cry had proceeded, the lovers gained a point upon a knoll commanding a view of the hall and grounds and adown the vistas cut by three paths leading shorewards, but not a living thing was in sight.

"It must have been Macrobow or Tehemon, one of the Captain's henchmen, who thinks to amuse himself at our expense," suggested Guy. "Either could have reached his wigwam before we could make the distance by the circuitous path."

"It is neither of the Mohicans," declared Damaris; "I cannot be mistaken. I shall never forget that piercing, mournful note. It was the war-cry of the Montauks, whether a human sound, or uttered by spirit lips."

"You surprise me; I imagined that a war-whoop was just a war-whoop; I had no idea that there was a variation of the blood-curdling call I have heard so much of, but never listened to. Unless you are correct, and that was a veritable whoop, which I do not care to hear again, I must confess," declared the Lieutenant, "of all the unearthly shrieks I ever dreamed, that is the climax."

"Each tribe has its own peculiar war-cry, so Wyancombone says; besides, he imitated the battle call of the Narragansetts and the Mohicans, the Mohawks and the Pequots, all of which differ as much as the language of the English from the French and Dutch. That was the cry of a Montauk," asserted Damaris, almost petulantly.

"Well, my love, it was not a particularly inspiring sound in the ears of an Englishman, and let us forget it; it is quite probable that as Wyancombone can imitate the whoop of a Mohican, a member of that tribe can duplicate a Montauk, and it must have been one of our own Indians, for certain it is that there's not a Montauk nearer the Isle of Wight than Montauk cliffs."

"I suppose you must be in the right; it may have been one of the Mohicans, probably from a sudden whim, and without an idea that he may have been frightening anyone,—neither are malicious," assented Damaris, rather reluctantly, and the subject was dropped.

As they walked toward the hall the little episode which had so alarmed them for the moment was forgotten, while he murmured those fond words so sweet to a lover's ears, so foolish to a listener, so heart-sickening to a jealous rival such as hovered near, yet unseen by the lovers, who, absorbed in each other, looked neither to the right nor left.

With his arm around the maiden's waist, his handsome head bowed until his lips nearly touched her shining hair, Kingsland walked beside his betrothed, all unconscious of the presence of the two dogging his footsteps, gliding from bush to bush like sleuth hounds, and silent as shadows.

From the moment Guy joined his sweetheart the watchers had remained near enough to the pair to mark every caress, and though his words were mostly inaudible, the tender inflection, the kisses and embraces were unmistakable language.

The cry that had disturbed the pair was indeed uttered by Wyancombone, who had rowed his sister over to the island. Heather Flower would fain gratify her desire to look upon the face of the man she loved, for although she might not speak freely to him in the presence of others, she longed for a glance of the expressive blue eyes, a tender pressure of the hand, or even a sight of his manly form.

Wearied with the object he had sought with such ardour, the game he had pursued, Guy Kingsland dared not avow his true sentiments, but was ready with plausible excuses for his failures to meet Heather Flower, which were now so frequent, and this was evening, after a day she had waited long at the trysting, a secluded spot not far from the village.

But it was Wyancombone, a handsome stripling in his teens, but strangely delicate and sensitive, the brother of Heather Flower, who had proposed the excursion to Man-cho-nock, which he had visited only the previous evening, returning to the lodge with a dark cloud upon his boyish face, that was noted with anxiety by his fond mother, Wic-chi-tau-bit, although, with all the outward stoicism of her race, she asked no questions.

With a purpose of his own he had timed his arrival at a moment just before the full moon rose from her bath beneath the waves while yet the boat and its occupants were but indistinct objects upon the waters; but scarcely had the pair stepped ashore when the white lustre of the silver disc flooded sea and shore.

Somewhat to the surprise of his sister, Wyancombone paddled his light craft to a narrow belt of sandy, beach overshadowed by shelving banks, at quite a distance from the usual landing, and mooring the canoe, he led the way up a precipitous path, overhung by a thick curtain of red willow, and seldom trodden by the white people upon the island.

Presently he turned sharply to the right, in the direction of the lodge nestled in the dark shade of two oaks, where abode the Mohicans employed by Lyon Gardiner upon his plantation.

If Heather Flower marvelled, she made no sign, and soon the brother and sister reached a thick copse of willow in the midst of a growth of alders so entangled with creeping vines as to form a miniature jungle scarcely fifty feet from the rustic bench that Heather Flower knew was a favourite resting place for her friend.

Still she made no inquiry, not even when Wyancombone motioned her to a seat upon a spur of rock within the network of shrubs and vines. She knew, from his demeanour at the start, that there was something of moment, some discovery he had made; but of its real nature she had not the slightest suspicion, as he stood by her side his attention fixed upon the path leading down from the palisade gates.

Five minutes passed, when the crackling of twigs beneath a light footstep warned the watchers of the approach of a third party—Damaris Gordon.

Grasping his sister's arm to enforce continued silence, Wyancombone still watched, his gaze fixed, not upon the slight figure upon the rustic seat near at hand, but the avenue, his face strangely set under the pencil of moonlight falling whitely through a broad interstice overhead, a dogged expression in his eyes quite at variance with his youthful features.

Again his patience was rewarded. Down the avenue came the Lieutenant, who emerged full into view of both watchers, his debonair face handsomer than its wont under the softening crystal moonlight, as he took his seat beside the graceful figure, wound his arm about her as one who had the right, and, bending down, pressed a kiss upon the coral lips.

The young Indian lad clenched his hands, his black eyes glaring like those of a panther.

And Heather Flower—for her the traitor's mask had been torn from her false lover; instinctively she pressed one brown hand upon her heart as if recoiling from a mortal stab. There was a tightening of the lips, a maniacal glitter in the magnificent black eyes, but not even a sigh escaped her lips to tell of the agony, the fierce whirlwind of passion, that swept her heart-strings.

On the instant she comprehended the truth—her brother had discovered her secret; he had learned the perfidy of the man she loved, and had taken this means of warning and guarding his sister.

The sound of their voices came faintly; she saw the kisses pressed upon the lip and brow of the innocent girl she had called her white sister, evidences that changed the loving, trusting Indian maiden into a fury, and a low hiss broke from Wyancombone's lips as he noiselessly fitted an arrow and drew it to the head.

A hand grasped his arm like a fetter of steel, a grip that made him wince and drew him back, while his sister's lips, pressed to his ear, whispered a few sentences in the Delaware tongue. The tough bow slipped to the ground and he fairly held his breath in his intense excitement. She had touched the right chord—a future revenge more torturing than a sudden death by the swift arrow.

Motioning Heather Flower to remain in her concealment, the youth glided away, not a rustle of a

"The traitor's mask had been torn from her false lover"

leaf betraying his passage, while, almost breathless, Heather Flower sat, her eyes fairly devouring the lovers, all the devotion, the self-sacrificing idolatry she had given the traitor changed in an instant to bitter, relentless hate. Verily she required no further proof of Kingsland's villainy. The man she would have trusted with her soul's salvation, for whom she would have gloried to have suffered death by slow torture, was false—a knowledge more terrible to the untutored daughter of a savage king than had he been guilty of a hundred cold-blooded murders. She had loved him madly, trusted him with all the blindness inspired by such devotion, and the awakening was fearful.

Had it been the case with Damaris Gordon she would have wept in secret, suffered in silence, and in time pride would have conquered her love; but no thought of vengeance would have reared a hydra head; her grief might have been deep, but naught compared to the terrible despair, the fierce, burning thirst for revenge seething beneath an icy exterior, a calm more to be dreaded in an Indian girl than the wildest exhibition of rage.

Well might the fair English maid sitting beside her betrothed husband shudder under the vindictive glare of those fierce orbs, unseen, yet felt.

Yet, amid all the heart-agony, with all the burning desire for vengeance upon the man who had wrecked her life, Heather Flower was magnanimous; no thought of evil against the white lily she had cherished as tenderly as she might a sister found lodgment in her breast; her nobility of nature asserted itself as she whispered:

"The Snowbird did not take the Black-heart from her red sister—he was the white-lily's own before he came to the Heather Flower with a lie in his mouth;

a lie to the Indian girl is as nothing in his eyes—he has taken the Indians' land, he has made the breast of the Sachem's child a burning fire of hate! He must pay, but Heather Flower will not harm the pale-face sister who has rested her head upon this heart while she slept, the white lily who did not know that the young white warrior, whom she thought her own, spoke with a forked tongue. Wolf of a pale-face, you have killed the heart of Heather Flower! Better for you that you had placed your hand upon the crest of a rattle-snake. Pale-face dog, you have taken the Indians' land—you shall keep it! you shall sleep beneath the dark earth where the foot of a white man has never trod, while your spirit roams through the black forests and over icy plains where the breath of summer never comes, or over the burning sands where the feet blister with the heat; you shall suffer cold, heat, hunger and thirst, always pursued by evil spirits, while ages and ages of moons come and go. The Princess of the Montauks curses you!"

The pair sitting upon the rustic seat rose and passed slowly down the Sachem's walk, and were lost to her sight. A solemn silence reigned, while the Indian maid waited for the return of Wyancombone.

Suddenly the wild war-whoop of her tribe pealed out, fairly rousing her from the dark reverie into which she had fallen.

At once she divined the cause. Unable to restrain himself, her brother had given vent to his rage in the defiant war-cry, the fearful challenge coming from a point distant from her place of concealment. Presently she saw the lovers emerge from the avenue and slowly cross the open glade, heard the muttered words of dismay as Guy searched for an intruder, and his angry ejaculation when his face came in contact with the thicket of briars hedging her in and proving a barrier to his further investigation in that direction; but even her acute ear failed to catch the faintest warning of her brother's stealthy movements as he stole to her side.

Alarmed, as well they might be, by the uncanny yell, the pair of lovers tarried no longer, while the wily children of the forest glided along in their wake as they returned to the hall.

Among Mrs. Gardiner's pet aversions was remaining up late at night, and when Guy and his companion entered the house the drawing-room was deserted, but a cluster of wax candles was burning brightly, trailing a long line of ruddy light far out upon the lawn, while fainter gleams came from the single candles burning in the bed-chambers, for every member of the family had retired to their respective apartments, except Lyon Gardiner and his guest, Major Gordon.

Entering the great central hall, the lovers exchanged a parting kiss while standing under the full glare of the candelabra, and Damaris, with cheeks blushing like wild roses, ran lightly up the shallow stairs, leaving the Lieutenant to make his way to the library where her father and Captain Gardiner usually passed their time in studying maps and drawing plans of the various grants apportioned to the colonists who had come from Lynn and the adjacent townships of the Massachusetts colony. There were thirty families who were the first settlers of Maidstone.[1]

---

[1] The present town of Easthampton, L. I., was, at its first settlement, named Maidstone, from the fact that Lyon Gardiner, with several others, came from Maidstone, in the County of Kent, England. After a time the name was changed to Easthampton. It is situated on the southern branch of Long Island, and includes the peninsula of Montauk and Gardiner's Island.

Upon this particular evening they were discussing the boundary of the township.[2]

Guy saw nothing of the two figures hovering in the borders of the hedge within the park. They witnessed the tender parting with his lady-love, and the good-night kiss he pressed upon her lips; then the intruders flitted away like phantoms, past the great gates of the encircling palisade, and just in time to make their egress before the plantation overseer, Cyrus Howell, made his last rounds to see that the entrance was properly secured with lock and bar, for, from ten o'clock of the evening until sunrise, Gardiner Hall became a fortress capable of resisting the attacks of a savage horde.

"Ha' ye seen e'er an Indian from the outside, MacPherson?" he inquired of Sandy, the lodge-keeper, who was in the act of turning the ponderous key; "I fancied I got sight o' some'un as I turned into the path."

"De'il tak' me if I ha'," responded Sandy, as he thrust the thick bolts in the sockets. "I dinna ken if a body ha' coom in sen' Maister Guy an' the young leddy wi' him."

"Hech, sir!" interrupted Janet MacPherson, from the doorway of the lodge, "don't 'ee stan' theer talkin' luk a twa-handed crack, Sandy, mon!

[2] Easthampton, formerly called Maidstone, was bounded on the east by the confluence of the Ocean with the Sound, on the south by the Atlantic Ocean, on the west by Southampton, and on the north by Gardiner's Bay and the Sound. The south shore is in some places a low, sandy beach, in others formed into hills of every variety of shape; but upon Montauk there are high and rugged cliffs against whose base the waves dash with almost continued violence, anything like a perfect calm here being a rare occurrence. Previous to the settlement of Maidstone arangements were made with the governors of New Haven and Connecticut to obtain a title to the lands from the Indian proprietors. The undertaking was soon accomplished, and the conveyance procured from the native chiefs.

Wheen ye war smokin' ye pipe twa bodies slipped through yon gate luk twa speerits, an' war gane i' the clappin' o' an ee' luk warlocks i' the moonlight."

"Aye, woman," answered Howell, "belike it was some stray redskin from Montauk who has been to the kitchen for some'at to eat an' some'at to drink—theer outside, whomsoever they might o' been." And satisfied that all was safe within his jurisdiction, Cyrus betook himself to his comfortable tenement in the rear of the hall, where his good dame, Patience Howell, housekeeper at the hall, awaited his coming with a tankard of 'ome-brewed beer as a nightcap.

Out upon the placid, moonlit waters a canoe was dancing, propelled by the arms of the Indian stripling, Wyancombone, and in the frail, birchen craft his sister sat, gazing with stony eyes across to the cliffs bounding her father's domain, motionless with the chill calmness of despair and a dread resolve— the quiet that precedes the tornado that may burst at any moment to deal death and desolation.

CHAPTER XIII

THE LAW OF THE WHITE MAN

"I will go to my tent and lie down in despair;
I will paint me with black and sever my hair;
I will sit on the shore when the hurricane blows,
And reveal to the God of the tempest my woes;
I will weep for a season, on bitterness fed,
For my kindred are gone to the hills of the dead,
But they died not of hunger, or lingering decay—
The hand of the white man hath swept them away."

"OH, Lawrence, lad! when did you arrive? I'd as soon have expected to see Cromwell himself, as to find you here!" greeted Lieutenant Kingsland, as he held out a welcoming hand to the grave-looking man who had risen from his seat and taken a step forward to meet his old companion-in-arms.

"I came less than an hour since. Crossed from Connecticut Colony in Captain How's vessel, on its voyage to Southampton plantation," returned Colonel Lawrence. "Learning that the Major had taken up his quarters here, I determined to make a stop—I had no idea that you had crossed the big puddle until the Captain told me. Glad to see you! But, man alive, what ails you? You are looking like your own wraith!" broke off Henry Lawrence.

"A slight headache, nothing more serious, I assure you, Colonel," returned Kingsland, striving to speak lightly; but the memory of that threatening war-whoop still troubled him, and, notwithstanding he had made light of the matter to Damaris, he could not shake off the impression that there was something sinister and boding to himself in that singular demonstration.

"Where have you been, lad? Zounds! that headache must be something tremendous to knock you out after such a fashion!" chimed in Captain Gardiner, who, with Major Gordon, was seated at the table, which was strewn with papers and documents bearing heavy seals, and written in the blackest of ink with the coarsest of quills. "Here, take a sup of brandy, it will set you up—you and my lass been out mooning, eh?"

The Lieutenant drained the glass the Captain offered, handed it back to his host, and dropped into a chair beside Lawrence.

He was an eminently handsome, distinguished-looking man, this Lawrence, a soldier who had served under Cromwell, and for gallantry on hard-fought fields had risen to the rank of Colonel in the Soldier-Dictator's army.

He was perhaps thirty years of age, of magnificent physique, with a face tanned of the bronze peculiar to one who has seen long service under tropic suns. The dark, keen, proud eyes were shadowed by lashes that softened their brilliancy, lending a half-dreamy expression. A clear-cut profile, a handsome, resolute mouth, a square chin, and a noble head crowned by dark, glossy hair made up the portrait of an ex-colonel of the British army, and lord over one of the finest manors in Lancashire.

Upon the death of his father, and his consequent accession, he had sold out his commission and retired from the service.

Those who knew him best asserted that his principles inclined him to the rule of old "Ironsides," under whom he had served, rather than to a maudlin sympathy with Charles, afterward called the "Merrie Monarch," and whom the Royalist party would fain seat upon the throne that was in reality occupied by Oliver Cromwell.

But Cromwell was alive, and the time had not come when the weaker son, Richard, would allow the reins of government to slip from his hands, and Charles Stuart to be proclaimed England's king.

"Have I interrupted a business meeting?" asked Guy, as he glanced over the array of documents upon the table.

"Not interrupted," returned Major Gordon, as he picked up a paper; "I was about to examine these title deeds, just to refresh my memory and enlighten the Colonel."

"Tut, tut!" demurred Lawrence, "small need for military titles after a man is fairly out of the service—plain Lawrence will satisfy me."

"Ha, lad! has that weapon a double edge?" laughed the Major, good-naturedly. "My military title appears to cling, even in the American wilderness among savages and rude colonists, for there is much of the ruder material mixed with the sprinkling of gentlemen who have migrated to the colonies. But we have use for them should there be an uprising of the Indians. Every arm will count. In a few years, however, we shall have removed the last inducement our red brothers have to remain here, and they will migrate westward of their own free will."

"How so?" asked the Colonel. "These rightful owners of the soil have retained their right to hunt and fish, which, according to their mode of life, is nearly all that is required, besides the small amount of cultivation. Under such circumstances are they likely to abandon their homes?"

"Marry-come-up, good sir; have you lost sight, as they appear to have, of the fact that we have the right to fell these forests, which at present shelter the game they value so highly, especially the bears and wolves. Besides, we have already two gristmills in operation over in Southampton, and shall soon have many others reared along the streams. That will banish the fish from the vicinity. Take away the forests, scatter the fish, and there will soon be an exodus westward," returned Gordon jubilantly.

"According to my judgment, Englishmen will be compelled to fight for the land they have obtained by—diplomacy," said the Colonel, substituting the more pacific word for the term *fraud*, that had trembled upon his tongue.

"Not so," chimed in Kingsland, "they are certain to become involved in wars between themselves. Now there is Uncas, the Mohican chief, one of the most wily and ambitious savages in America, who is the enemy of the Narragansetts, who, in their turn, have a most violent hatred of the Montauks."

"What is the cause of their enmity?" queried Lawrence.

"The Captain can explain better than I. He is thoroughly informed on all affairs that pertain to Indians on the islands," answered Kingsland, lighting his pipe.

"I can enlighten you, Colonel," agreed Gardiner, "It is the simplest thing in creation. It appears that Ninigret, Sachem of the Narragansetts, some time since made overtures to the Montauk Sachem to join him in a plot to destroy all the white settlers— that is, the English; but instead of uniting with the Narragansetts, Wyandance revealed the plot to us, thus frustrating the design of the Narragansetts, and saving the settlers from extermination; Wyandance, the Long Island Sachem, told me that, as all the plots of the Narragansetts had been discovered, they had now concluded to let the English alone until they had destroyed Uncas, the Mohican chief, and himself; then, with the assistance of the Mohawks and Indians beyond the Dutch, they could easily destroy us, *every man and mother's son*," concluded Captain Gardiner.

"This Wyandance appears to be a staunch friend of yours," remarked Lawrence, turning to Captain Gardiner; "at least I judge as much by reason of his imparting to you the knowledge of the contemplated massacre."

"Yes, true as steel to his white neighbours, and I flatter myself that I have more influence with him than any other white man alive," assented Gardiner, with a smile. "He has dealt munificently with me, and not once have I been disturbed in the quiet possession of my plantation."

"Which is extensive—a goodly inheritance for your children, judging from the observation I made from the deck of the *Blessing*," said the Colonel. "What is the extent?"

"It contains three thousand, three hundred acres, all told—that is including the beaches and ponds; the soil is fine. As yet, it is a separate plantation."

"Zounds, man!" exclaimed the astonished Colonel, "but you are in luck! and this Indian potentate gave you a clear title?"

"Most assuredly," smiled Gardiner.

"Your ruling planet must have been propitious; it seems that luck has attended you since coming to the colonies. I wouldn't object to getting a goodly slice of these fertile vales and heavily timbered lands; still I must insist that I could not have the conscience to take land at such unheard-of terms. I am inclined to see this generous savage and make an honourable purchase of a few hundred acres, in exchange for good old English pounds and shillings."

"Tut! tut! not the slightest use. Wyandance refuses to sell another foot of his broad acres; there's a tract I have my mind set upon, but the Sachem is hard as iron, even to me; I think he begins to dread the encroachment of the white man," put in Kingsland.

"And I have a tract in my mind's eye which I intend to force him to disgorge," remarked Major Gordon, with a greedy glitter in his deep-set eyes.

"And you will fail," returned Gardiner. "Had Poggatticut lived, we should not have been able to get his signature, but although Yo-kee put up a good fight, he was less stubborn. Should Wyandance die, then, indeed, young Wyancombone will be more easily handled."

"I don't propose to wait for the old Sachem to go to the land of spirits. He comes of a tough race; his brother, Poggatticut, lived over a century, if tradition speaks truly; nevertheless, I have a plan in my brain by which that hard-bitted old heathen will become as wax in my hands. No use asking questions, as I perceive you have a mind to do, gentlemen; wait and see," concluded the Major in an oracular tone.

CHAPTER XIV

WIC-CHI-TAU-BIT

"My resolution's placed, and I have nothing
Of woman in me: Now from head to foot
I am marble-constant."

THERE was something terrible in the fixed look of despair, the hushed storm brooding upon the features of Heather Flower as she stepped from the canoe, which Wyancombone moored without a word, and strode away, taking the path to the cliff above, where, day and night, a stout warrior kept constant watch.

With a delicacy scarcely to be expected, the young savage had left his sister to the silence and solitude she craved.

The scene upon Man-cho-nock had been a fatal revelation, tearing her heart strings in twain. The blood coursed madly through her veins and throbbed in her temples, her limbs seemed benumbed, for she felt naught of the sharp thorns piercing her hands and arms as she tore through the rough brambles in a direct line for her father's lodge, avoiding the cleared way lest she might meet some stroller from the village.

In all the wide world there was but one human being who could comfort her, Wic-chi-tau-bit, her tender, loving mother.

Unheeding when she emerged from the thorny tangle, she came upon the beaten path. On either hand the plumed ferns, clusters of sweet briar, clumps of honeysuckle and tall mountain laurel lined the way, waving softly above the green carpeting of moss and diffusing a subtle perfume.

With an inarticulate cry, such as an animal might give when suffering intense agony, she cast herself upon a bed of moss, her frame quivering, her hands clenched, her teeth set tightly to suppress the storm of sobs that threatened to rend their way from heart to lip. Face downward, she gave vent to her anguish in low moans and gasps.

The fearful gust of sorrow and anger was over at last, but the moon rode high in the heavens when she rose from her recumbent attitude. How long she had lain there she never knew.

A deep silence brooded, and when the first fierce throes of passion had subsided her thoughts ran in a quieter, but deadlier channel, and she began to consider the future. Her mind had been almost a blank, but now a subtle chain of thought was weaving out a plot through which she might wreak a fearful vengeance upon the man who had wrought her woe.

Tossing back her dishevelled tresses, and smoothing her garments, she approached the lodge with swift, noiseless steps, and peered through the entrance from which the bear-skin robe had been partially drawn aside, and hung banner-like, flapping heavily in the breeze that blew up damply from the ocean.

She drew a long breath of relief. The stern Sachem was absent, but Wic-chi-tau-bit was sitting upon a couch of furs, her elbows resting on her knees, after the patient attitude of an Indian woman. Alone, she was waiting the coming of her children.

With the soft step of a leopardess, the girl crept to her mother's side and sat down, twining her arms with unwonted tenderness about the crouching figure.

Wic-chi-tau-bit raised her head, and without a

word drew her daughter to her breast, noting that the girl's cheek was burning, that the fingers resting against her neck were icy cold, and that the supple form was shivering in every nerve. Still she asked no question, but waited with all the endurance characteristic of her race for her child to speak.

"Mother! oh, my mother! comfort your child, for her heart is breaking!"

The passionate appeal broke from the girl's lips in a wailing cry.

"How can Wic-chi-tau-bit comfort her child when she knows not the sorrow that is in her heart?" asked the mother, softly, wonderingly. "Tell me, my child, that I may know how to bring joy to the life of my heart," returned Wic-chi-tau-bit, in the cooing tones more suggestive of the deep affection of the Indian mother than the mere words.

Heather Flower clung closer to the bosom upon which her head rested, and for several minutes the mournful whispers of the maiden alone broke the stillness.

The gasping breath, the quivering form, attested the fearful tension that upheld the girl as she repeated the story of her ill-starred love and the white man's perfidy. Shame, scorn, anger, hate, love and revenge were expressed by turns in the low, intense tones of the narrator, and when the story was ended she drew a long, tremulous breath, a sigh forced from the depths of a wounded spirit, while Wic-chi-tau-bit drew her in a closer embrace, placing her hand caressingly upon the throbbing heart, as if thus she would heal the wound an envenomed arrow had inflicted, and where it still rankled.

There was silence for a moment, broken at length by the Indian mother, in an impressive tone, singularly sweet with the emotion it expressed.

"My child, since the hour when I first felt your head nestling against my heart, I have loved you with all the strong love an Indian woman gives her offspring; as the mother bird shelters her young, so have I sheltered you. Wic-chi-tau-bit has learned to read her child's face as the white man reads the words traced on the parchment, as the warrior reads the signs in the sky, the cry of the birds, the call of the insects, the growl of beasts, the blue water, and to follow the trail. She has seen her child's face brighten when the sound of the young white chief's moccasins made music to her ear, has seen her eyelids droop and her cheek wear the colour of the ripened peach did he but speak; the sound of his voice was soft as the breath of the south wind when he spoke to Heather Flower. Wic-chi-tau-bit spoke no word, for she knew her child was beautiful—more beautiful than the pale daughter of the English chief. She saw the eye of the young white brave light and his bosom heave, and she believed that in time he might be the son of the great Sachem of the Montauks. Such things have been, the traditions of our fathers tell us, and Wic-chi-tau-bit has watched and waited; she believed his heart was white, that he spoke with a straight tongue; Heather Flower is the daughter of a great king, like Powhattan. Her mother is a princess of the Mohawks. Their daughter is a fitting mate for the white eagle."

"He is a traitor!" exclaimed Heather Flower, "but he shall pay for his treachery with his life; the daughter of Wyandance will not crouch at his feet and weep like a puling white papoose, for she has trampled her heart under her feet, she has no more tears, they are dried; to such insult she has but one answer to give; she can avenge her wrongs. Let the pale-face dog beware! he shall wash away the stain in his heart-blood, the bitter wrong offered a princess of the Montauks!"

Her face was blanched, her eyes glittered with a smouldering fire, flecks of foam beaded her white lips, and her limbs quivered as if in the death agony. Ah! more than revenge spoke in the hollow accents, a heart-desolation that would have moved the most savage among her father's trusty warriors to pity, to vengeance that would be terrible.

"Mother, when I saw him fold the Snowbird in his arms, saw his lips pressed to her cheek, the warm, living heart in my bosom died, frozen to stone it lay, and in that moment Wyandance's daughter swore a terrible oath of vengeance! She will keep it though a thousand red-coat warriors guard him day and night. The arrow or knife shall drink his blood, his scalp shall hang in the smoke of Heather Flower's wigwam!"

"Listen, my daughter!" commanded Wic-chi-tau-bit, in a calm, soothing tone, "the traitor must die, but not by the hand of my child; he must fall where none but the slayer and the eye of the Great Spirit can look upon the deed, his burial place must be where the white man cannot search the spot. The Narragansetts are our enemies. Should Englishmen suspect that a princess of the Montauks or a Montauk warrior had slain the young white chief, their vengeance would fall upon the people of Wyandance. None of our tribe, even, must know how or where he died."

Heather Flower drew a sharp, quick breath.

"Listen, my daughter! To-cus is a great brave; it was for your hand he fought Mandush to the death; his wounds are healing fast, and he will ask you of the Sachem, your father—our people believe that you are to go to his wigwam. Let it be so—you will do as our people expect, according to our customs. There will be a great feast, as befits the marriage of a princess of the Montauks. Then the pale-face dog will forget and he will think that Heather Flower has forgotten her wrongs, or is afraid, and like the fox he will fall into the snare. To-cus shall lure him to the swamp of Mah-chon-it-chuge. He will go, but he will never come back to the lodges of the pale-faces, for the poisoned quagmire shall drink his blood, the fishes of the black lake shall feed upon his body, and the white man shall never dream that the hand of an Indian brave sent their brother to the spirit land. Would you save your people from a deadly revenge, from being swept from the earth like the falling leaves in autumn when the Frost Spirit is abroad, while you have your revenge, heed the counsel of Wic-chi-tau-bit and be wise."

Heather Flower listened silently, and as her mother ended she stood up, her head raised proudly, her eyes kindling, her form seeming to take a loftier height, all the rich beauty of her face re-touched as by a wizard's wand.

"My mother speaks the words of wisdom, the blood of Wyandance flows again hot through his daughter's veins; she will go to the lodge of To-cus as his wife, there shall be feasting and games, a great merry-making such as has not been since Wic-chi-tau-bit, a Mohawk princess, came to the wigwam of the King of the Montauks. The warriors, squaws and maidens of the tribe shall rejoice; they shall share the joy of Heather Flower!" she said, with mocking emphasis. "But the daughter of a king is proud. She must not speak the words to To-cus that tell him the price of the hand of an Indian princess, and why he must kill the white wolf."

"Heather Flower is the daughter of a great Sachem; she shall hide herself while Wic-chi-tau-bit seeks the lodge of To-cus, to say the words his ears are open to hear," was the mother's reply.

"And Wyancombone, he knows," whispered Heather Flower.

"He will keep his own counsel; few moons have shone upon his life, but he has the wisdom of a warrior whose hair is silvered with the frosts of many winters. Will the future king of the Montauks speak idle words that would trample his sister in the dust? Heather Flower speaks like a silly child," returned Wic-chi-tau-bit. "When the deed is done and the serpent comes to the lodges of the pale-faces no more, Wyancombone will dream whither he has gone, but his lips will be silent. Now, let the Heather Flower go to her rest."

It was past the hour of midnight when Heather Flower fell into the deep sleep of utter exhaustion, and the patient mother watching by her side rose silently, wrapped her mantle about her shoulders and stole out into the moonlight.

Fortunately for her purpose, Wyandance was absent on a visit to Yo-kee, his nephew, and she was free to work out the scheme in hand without question from the stern-browed chieftain.

Her Mohawk blood was on fire at the insult and injury to her child, and To-cus was the instrument she had chosen to secure her revenge.

Like a grey ghost she flitted down the winding pathway and was presently lost in the gloom of a thick grove of firs that she must cross to reach the lodge of To-cus, the warrior whose prowess in slaying Mandush was the topic of every tongue.

Under different circumstances, Wic-chi-tau-bit would have summoned Ko-zhe-osh to do her bidding in rousing To-cus, but not to a living soul would she entrust the secret meeting with the man she sought, whose wigwam loomed up blackly against the trunks of the towering trees overshadowing it, as she halted a few yards distant, debating how best to rouse the occupant.

The question was speedily solved, the matting at the entrance was lifted and To-cus stood before her.

Even the Indian stoicism was not sufficient to prevent a slight start of surprise at the presence of the Indian queen in that place at that hour, but the young warrior merely bowed his head in silent respect for the wife of his Sachem, while he waited for her to address him.

His figure was erect, and over his shoulders hung an Indian blanket, worn with all the regal grace of a Roman toga, and from beneath his heavy brows his eyes blazed with their wonted fierce light that had been unquenched by the lingering fever and suffering he had endured after the terrible contest in which he had slain his rival.

The half-cicatrised wounds, one crossing the bridge of the nose, another traversing the cheek from temple to chin, a third that had severed upper and under lip in twain, rendered his otherwise comely countenance almost repulsive, and deepened the sinister expression which nature had painted in unmistakable characters, and quite in keeping with the fiery eyes from which the bravest might have shrunk.

A fourth wound, in the breast, was still covered with a mass of pulp of healing leaves, bound thickly across his chest, and his left wrist was bandaged.

All this Wic-chi-tau-bit noted as the young warrior stood where the light from a burning pine knot in the centre of the wigwam fell full upon his face and form in a background of dull red.

"The Queen of the Montauks would whisper in the ear of To-cus."

Wic-chi-tau-bit uttered the sentence in a low tone, and silently the young brave stepped aside that she might enter his lodge.

"Will the squaw of the great Sachem rest in the wigwam of To-cus?" he asked, waving his hand towards the pile of matting which was covered with a bear-skin, a trophy of his skill in the chase, and bowing her assent, Wic-chi-tau-bit took the proffered seat.

The Indian queen was a woman of majestic presence. As the daughter of an Iroquois chief she had never been a woman of burden, and her highest ambition had been gratified in her union with the powerful Montauk Sachem. So far as the customs of her people would allow, hers had been a love match, and she exercised a powerful influence over her stern, dark-browed lord.

Her features were singularly pleasing; in her youth her lips had been accustomed only to smiles, and as a matron she had known far less of sorrow than usually falls to the lot of the Indian squaw, comparatively none, save the anxiety she felt when her lord was absent upon the war-path.

Her long, abundant hair, yet untouched by a silver thread, hung in thick masses over her gorgeous robe of crimson cloth, edged with costly fur and confined at the waist by a belt of suck-au-hock, for the grey mantle had fallen back revealing her costume. Her head was crowned by a coronet of soft, blood-red feathers, the plumage of the cardinal grosbeak, plaited in a band of the costly wampum, that glittered in the glow of the pine knot like diamonds. Bracelets of purple wampum and beads of the same encircled arms and throat. Her moccasins were daintily broidered with coloured quills, beads and shells, and laced with scarlet cord terminating in tassels of beads.

To-cus did not presume to sit in her presence, but stood in the centre of the lodge, gravely awaiting the communication of his visitor, who cast a searching glance around the wigwam, and then turned her eyes with keen scrutiny upon the scarred warrior.

"The young brave would wed the daughter of the great Sachem of the Montauks," she said, abruptly.

"To-cus would take the young princess to his lodge," he returned, his eyes flashing. His voice had a ring of triumph which did not escape the keen perception of his visitor.

"It was that he might take Heather Flower to his lodge that he sought Mandush in mortal combat; it was that hope that made his arm powerful to kill his rival?" queried Wic-chi-tau-bit, in a tone of assertion.

His eyes blazed with the mingled fire of gratified vanity and ferocity as he answered:

"The Queen of the Montauks speaks with a straight tongue—she is wise—she sees the truth deep down in the heart of To-cus."

"Heather Flower will go to the lodge of the young brave who slew Mandush in honourable, hand-to-hand combat, but—on condition," returned Wic-chi-tau-bit.

"Let the Queen of the Montauks speak—the ears of To-cus are open," replied the warrior.

"Listen, while Wic-chi-tau-bit whispers that which the winds must not breathe, of which no other, save the Great Spirit, can hear the sound, and then let To-cus say if he will, of his own choice, do the bidding of Heather Flower."

"The ears of To-cus are open," repeated the young Indian.

"First, swear by the Great Spirit that never shall the tongue of the young warrior repeat the words that Heather Flower will speak through her mother's lips, not even to save his life," returned the Indian queen.

"Not even to save his body from fire at the stake will To-cus open his lips," he replied grimly.

"Listen: a pale-face came to the nest of the great Eagle of the Montauks, a hawk clothed in the plumage of a dove. His voice was like the murmur of the brook, pleasant to the ear as the silvery tinkle of the cascade in the heart of the forest. With a lying tongue and honeyed lips he stole the heart of the forest flower, only to trample it in the dust. When the moon was yet rising from the blue waters in the east, Heather Flower listened to his words of love to another, a pale-faced maiden, one of his own race, who promised many moons ago to go to his lodge across the great waters. What shall be the vengeance inflicted upon the pale-face vulture who has offered such an insult to the daughter of the Warrior King?"

"Death by slow torture!" uttered the grim savage, in a tone of such deadly menace that Wic-chi-tau-bit knew she had found the instrument of revenge she sought. "And when he is dead?"

The last sentence was a question.

"His slayer shall take Heather Flower to his lodge before he takes revenge—his promise will not be broken. First, the feast must be spread, the warriors shall make merry at the marriage festivities. Afterwards Heather Flower's lord shall seek out the white serpent; he shall lay in ambush until he finds opportunity to satisfy his revenge. But he must follow the trail secretly, for the English must never know that their brother died by the hand of a Montauk; therefore, let the wedding feast be set, the young princess be taken to the lodge of To-cus; then, when the white wolf believes that Heather Flower is crouching in fear, let To-cus bring his scalp to hang in the smoke of her wigwam fire. Is it well?"

"It is well. To-cus hears, and will obey; Heather Flower shall dry the scalp of the white chief the palefaces call Guy Kingsland."

"How can the young warrior know the name of the viper his heel must crush?" asked Wic-chi-tau-bit.

"Has To-cus no eyes to see, no ears to hear?" asked the warrior. "Had the white wolf stolen the forest flower from the lodges of her people, unless the wedding feast had first been eaten among her kin, the knife of To-cus would have found his black heart; five hundred knives would have been sharpened, five hundred tomahawks ready to drink his blood, but it should have been the knife of To-cus that would take his scalp."

"It is well," returned the red queen, with a satisfied air. "Before the coming of the young moon To-cus shall take the princess of the Montauks to his wigwam."

Without another word, or even a glance toward the young savage, she was gone, and To-cus stood alone beside his lodge fire, his eyes alight with the fierce fires of gratified pride and ambition.

CHAPTER XV

BIRDS OF PREY

"The devil can cite Scripture for his purpose;
An evil soul producing holy witness
Is like a villain with a smiling cheek;
A goodly apple rotten at the heart;
O, what a goodly outside falsehood hath."

"A fellow by the hand of nature mark'd,
Quoted and sign'd to do a deed of shame."

THE fort at Saybrook was but a blockhouse, a cumbrous affair of logs within a stout stockade and abatis, with rather commodious quarters for the officers and their families, and ample storage for arms and ammunition, a sort of depot from whence supplies were drawn by the settlements on Long Island and the interior plantations of Connecticut colony.

Hither prisoners were brought, whites and Indians, for safe keeping, and the small vessels plying between the fort and the ports on the mainland and islands were usually well passengered.

The fort was surrounded by dense forests, the clearing being fairly hewed from the heart of the wilderness that was still the abode of savages, seamed with their war-paths, and still the haunt of wild beasts.

It was in the early twilight of a sultry day when the gruff challenge of the guard came clearly to the ears of the Commandant, who was just seated at table, and presently a guest was announced.

"Eh! Kingsland! what brings you here? glad to see you, of course!" greeted Captain Mason, cordially.

"But surprised that I am back so soon, eh?" returned the Lieutenant, with a short, half uneasy laugh. "In this beastly country, even the sudden visit of a friend becomes a trifle startling; a matter of moment demanding immediate attention brought me here—this letter from Major Gordon will explain all."

"Here, Quash, you rascal, lay a cover and be quick about it!" called the Captain, turning to a negro with charcoal-black skin; "bring another decanter of old rum, a plate of venison and a dish of succotash!"

Quash grinned until two rows of ivory lighted up the lower portion of his visage like a streak of pale moonlight, and as he disappeared the outer door opened and Colonel Lawrence entered.

The two officers exchanged greetings.

"Like our host, you hardly thought to see me here so soon after you left the island," smiled Kingsland.

"Hardly," assented the Colonel; "it must be an errand of importance that can tear you from the presence of your 'ladye faire.'"

"Of some import," admitted Kingsland, rather guardedly. "I am the bearer of a letter from the Major."

"Sit down, sit down, gentlemen, we will have some'at to eat and some'at to drink before we discuss business," said the Captain, hospitably, turning to his guests, who had placed their hats upon the broad antlers of a deer that served for a rack.

The three seated themselves at table, the host at the head.

"Been beastly warm all day, wind freshening, going to be a blow," said Kingsland. "If the *Nancy* goes out to-night it will be in a howling gale, not safe for so small a craft, I should say."

"A mere tub," declared Captain Mason. "I'm of the opinion it will blow great guns before midnight. Fall to—fall to, gentlemen, don't allow me to disturb your appetite. Permit me to glance over the Major's letter."

Quash had placed a haunch of venison, a platter of succotash, and a decanter upon the board and waited to serve the viands.

"Be off with you, varlet!" growled the Commandant. "See that you remain within ear-shot of the bell, if it chances that you are wanted," whereupon Quash ducked his head and vanished.

"Gad-Zuchus! here's a deuced piece o' handiwork cut out for us, it strikes me!" exclaimed the Captain, as he laid down the open sheet and smoothed the folds, his eyes raised with a puzzled stare. "A devilish risky job from first to last. Whose brain hatched such a brood? It is raising a nest of hornets with a vengeance, if I clearly understand the instructions. The wording is curious—hear what he says: 'We must handle this plank with care or somebody will get slivers in their fingers.'"

"On a par with the Delphic oracle," laughed Kingsland.

"What is the consideration?" asked the Captain.

"As much territory as can be wrung from this red potentate, who has the bad taste of absolutely refusing to dispose of another foot of land for love or money; he is getting obstinate, and what cannot be obtained by force or persuasion must be gained by stratagem. All is fair in love and war, and old

Wyandance will never begrudge a few square miles of land in return for the rescue of his daughter," replied the Lieutenant.

A frown settled between the Colonel's eyes that were slowly gathering flame beneath the drooping lids, and his lips compressed as he began to comprehend the drift of the conversation.

The Lieutenant caught the expression, but mistook the signification.

"See here, Colonel, rather rude—at least not in good form to discuss an obscure subject in presence of a third party not in the secret, eh? No cause to look glum or like a mute at a funeral, you are heartily welcome to the knowledge. A British officer can be trusted with even so delicate matter as we have in hand. The whole affair lies in a nutshell; Gordon has a plan on foot to connive at the abduction of the young squaw, Wyandance's daughter; the plan is cut and dried. Ninigret, Sachem of the Narragansetts, has agreed to carry the girl off, then she shall be rescued by the good offices of her father's white friends. Ha! ha! And in his gratitude the old Sachem will shell out a dukedom; he will do anything to recover his daughter."

"And the Major desires my co-operation," observed the Captain. "I' faith! I don't clearly perceive the honourable side of the question, and don't relish getting into the war-kettle, or I may chance to get my hands full of splinters, and my soldiers spitted with arrows as well."

"Tush, man!" returned the Lieutenant, petulantly, "you are over-squeamish. Who the devil said the Major had anything to do with the abduction? Allow me to explain. You are aware that the Narragansetts and Montauks are mortal foes, and that Ninigret has sworn a deadly revenge upon his enemy for some innovation—a revenge that he proposes to accomplish by carrying off the red beauty for ransom, and also strike a fearful blow by obliging his ancient foe to pay an annual tribute."

"If I understood you correctly, you have but now admitted that the Major has a plan on foot to 'connive'—I think that was the word—at the abduction of the Indian girl. That was the substance of the remark, was it not?" asked Lawrence.

"A mere slip of the tongue," replied Kingsland, "it is only this, that Gordon became acquainted with the particulars of the plot through a drunken Narragansett. By some means, the Major has come to an understanding with Ninigret, by which he is to pay to that chief a sum in goods of English manufacture, and gew-gaws, such as beads, blankets, knives and looking-glasses, a mere bagatelle in a white man's estimation, but a dazzling bait to a redskin.

"In return the Narragansett will release the captive to him, after a sham battle, or something of the sort, and the Major will make his own terms with Wyandance—perfectly laudable exchange, you perceive."

"Hardly! looks like land-grabbing with a vengeance. But how came Gordon to be so deep in the confidence of this blood-thirsty Narragansett—or is it a custom of these savages to impart information of their contemplated attacks to their white neighbours?" asked Lawrence.

"How should I know? It is one of the Major's secrets. He is a dark one, Gordon, you know. Certain it is that he has great influence with Ninigret—some debt of gratitude, I fancy, or so he gives one to understand. These savages never forget a favour I'm told, nor forgive an injury."

"A favourable contrast to the boasted civilisation

of Europeans," commented Lawrence, with a shrug of his broad shoulders.

"As I observed," began Captain Mason, "my instructions are decidedly vague; the Major tells me you will explain the part I am expected to take—all I clearly understand is that the girl is to be abducted, and held until ransomed. How does the Narragansett chief propose to get possession of his prize? Plain speech is what is needed."

"Here's the plan in detail. I imagined Gordon had the sense to explain," returned Kingsland, his face flushing slightly. "We do not propose to have anything to do with carrying off the red beauty. It seems she is to be married within the week, and already her white friends at the Isle of Wight have been bidden to the marriage feast. Needless to say the invitations will be promptly accepted, but the Major will find some means of detaining the family upon the island. While the festivities are at their height a swarm of Narragansetts will land from their war canoes, burst upon the unsuspicious Montauks, take what scalps they can, and in the heat of the conflict a detailed squad will seize the bride, convey her to a canoe and paddle away for Block Island."

"And then?" queried the Commandant.

"The Major will hold a conference with old Wyandance, and offer his services in restoring Heather Flower to her people."

"Still, I can see no way in which my assistance can be necessary," said Captain Mason.

"Merely to order a detachment from the garrison aboard ship, the soldiers to be under the command of Major Gordon, to make the run to Block Island where Ninigret will be encamped—mere figureheads to give colouring to a rescue—a blind to the hawk-eyed Indian. Not a shot will be fired. The

Major will go ashore, meet the chief, arrange for the ransom, which will be delivered from the ship, and take away the prisoner; plenty of glory with not the slightest danger to life or limb—neat piece of strategy, eh?"

Captain Mason's lip curled slightly, for the barefaced fraud was abhorrent to his nature. He was a rough soldier, with the true courage befitting the position he occupied.

A hot flush shot up to the Colonel's forehead as he replied to the question addressed to the Captain, who remained silent.

"I deem it a dastardly act considered from any standpoint. I had supposed Major Gordon imbued with the chivalry that should be the birthright of every true Briton, certainly of every officer in the service—I fear I have placed a too high estimate."

"That is as it may be—depends upon circumstances. Hark'ee, Colonel, the Narragansetts will carry off the girl in spite of every effort to restrain them—that point is clear. Now is it not the part of a gentleman, an officer in the British service, a man who chances to possess the means, to restore her without bloodshed, in other words, to use his power for doing good? or would you consider it more honourable, the more humane plan, to leave her in the clutches of her father's deadliest foes, who might murder her with as little compunction as they would spear a fish?"

"If you put it in the light of an act of generosity and humanity, that alters the case; but the ransom her father must pay the Major puts another phase on the affair—miles of fertile land in exchange for such disinterested friendship!" exclaimed Lawrence.

"Vastly fine in theory, such opinions may be, my

fastidious Hotspur," laughed Kingsland, " but decidedly unwise in practice; in this case the Major will reap the benefit, it is true, but if the girl is left for ransom this Ninigret will exact an annual tribute, which will place the proud Montauk Sachem under his heel; on the other hand, should the girl be murdered, a long and bloody war will follow, that must involve the colonists."

"If Gordon intended to be a true friend to the Montauk chief, why does he not warn him of the intended attack, that he may be prepared and prevent the abduction?" asked Lawrence.

"Aye, lad, and bring the powerful Narragansetts swarming upon the Isle of Wight! Ninigret is cunning as the fox, bloodthirsty as the tiger! I tell you there must be no interference with his plans, else there will be five hundred howling savages about Gardiner Hall, and another Indian massacre. At present Captain Gardiner is on the friendliest terms with the Indians upon the mainland and upon the islands; a poor return for his hospitality should the Major, by word or deed, involve him in a difficulty with the savages. As a friend, I would advise you not to meddle in the affair, as I thought at first of doing. Upon mature reflection I came to the conclusion that any interference could be productive only of mischief," said Kingsland, with an assumption of candour.

"I have no power to interfere, but my high opinion of Gordon is—modified," returned Lawrence.

"Aye, well, gentlemen, we can only allow the matter to rest. It appears the preliminaries are too well adjusted to admit of a remedy; the girl must not be left in the hands of her enemies, who, it is quite certain, would have no scruples in slaughtering her. When Gordon is prepared to take command, a detachment will be detailed from the garrison, and, after all, I suppose it is as well that he should receive the reward, as that Wyandance be forced to annual tribute, and certainly cheaper, in the end, for the proud old Sachem," reasoned Captain Mason, with a meditative air. "When is the attack to be made?"

"As I have said, on the occasion of the wedding feast—that takes place within a week. It is really a mercy to the girl, for the bridegroom-elect is as ugly as Vulcan; not but that nature has been kind to him in the matter of good looks—that is, of a savage style; but his face is disfigured by great gashes, his nose half severed, his lips split in twain, and the wounds are scarcely healed; he is a sight for gods and men— absolutely disgusting in the eyes of the white woman, however much he may be prized by a red damsel. He would make but a sorry mate for Heather Flower," explained Kingsland, with a half sigh.

"And she—I have heard that she is well looking," remarked Captain Mason.

"Handsome as a Cleopatra, proud as a Boadicea, keen as a hawk, lithe as a tigress, a regular Venus in bronze; a white man would not make a bad speculation in marrying her outright and getting possession of some of the broad lands over which her dusky father is lord, were it not for the disagreeable fact that she has the temper of the very devil; with her it is either the coo of the ring-dove or the talon of the falcon."

A flush mounted to his forehead, for Lawrence's keen eyes were searching his face curiously.

"Our Lieutenant appears to be well versed in the moods of this forest beauty," smiled the Colonel, in a tone that brought a still deeper glow to Kingsland's cheek. "How does it happen that she is mating with this scarred warrior?"

"Oh, I believe he received the wounds in fair combat—a duel with a rival for her hand, and according to the customs of her people she is bound in honour to marry the survivor; fortunately for her, from a white man's standpoint, To-cus is marked for a victim to the hatchets of the Narragansetts, and she will escape a union that must be repulsive to her whole nature, for she surely has no more affection for the bridegroom selected for her than for one of the wolf dogs that infest the Indian village."

"Tolerably conversant with her affairs of the heart. Ha! ha!" laughed the Captain.

"I' faith!" exclaimed Kingsland, in a nettled tone, "you are pleased to be facetious; man alive, if you are at all acquainted with savage customs, you must understand that she is, in a way, compelled to accept the victor. These unwritten laws of the aborigines are rigidly adhered to, and she is almost as much bound to accept this surly, scarred warrior as a woman of burden might be. Thus, you perceive, the Major has provided for her absolute safety by his interference, and saved her from the talons of her ugly lover; besides, he has the word of Ninigret, that she shall be held in all honour; an Indian chief holds his oath sacred."

"Pity our white race could not follow the same line," remarked Lawrence. "This is an ugly affair to be mixed in. I still marvel that Gordon should become a party."

"For further information concerning his motives I must refer you to the Major," returned Kingsland, a trifle stiffly. "I imagine, however, that in order to make the attack a success it was necessary to secure the co-operation of someone upon Man-cho-nock."

"How so?" asked Captain Mason.

"Look'ee, it is only an opinion," returned the

Lieutenant, cautiously, " as there are lookouts constantly stationed on Montauk cliff, the war canoes must cross from the mainland during the night, and must make an attack during the day; to obviate the danger of being seen, should they make the voyage in daylight, they might cross during the darkness, provided they might lie in ambush until the night. On the shores of Man-cho-nock there are coves where a regiment might hide in safety, with no danger of being discovered by the inhabitants; the Narragansetts might conceal their canoes in the thick undergrowth overhanging a creek, ensconce themselves in the swamp, and wait until nightfall, when they might easily paddle across and fall upon their unsuspecting foes—a complete surprise."

"Could not this be done without informing anyone upon the island?" asked the Captain.

"It might; but remember that the proprietor of Man-cho-nock and his family and guests are invited to the feast, and should they accept, as they assuredly will, everyone, male and female, would most likely be massacred. The Major has contrived some means by which they will remain at home upon the occasion."

"By what means?" asked the Colonel.

"I am not a principal in this business, and as I have said, a knowledge of motives and means must be obtained from the Major himself. I cannot say that this savage mode of warfare is to my taste, but if our English settlers try to arrange matters and settle the ancient feuds existing between the different tribes of aborigines, they will but embroil themselves and provoke a general uprising," answered the Lieutenant. "Rest assured that the Major will prevent the attendance of Gardiner's family, even if he is obliged to reveal the circumstances to the Captain himself."

"It strikes me that this wholesale appropriation of land is a greater provocation than any petty dispute might be, or the friendliness of the Narragansetts and Montauks, to provoke hostilities, and I can scarcely find it in my heart to censure these sons of the forest if they were to inaugurate a war of extermination against the usurping whites," rejoined Lawrence.

"A truce to further discussion," called Captain Mason, good-humouredly. "Let's fill our glasses and drink to the good health of this Indian princess."

CHAPTER XVI

THE SIGNAL FIRE

> "Mammon led them on:
> Mammon, the least erected spirit that fell
> From heaven; for e'en in heaven his looks and thoughts
> Were always downward bent."
>
> . . .
>
> "The lust of gold succeeds the rags of conquest:
> The lust of gold unfeeling and remorseless!
> The last corruption of degenerate man."

SEVERAL weeks had passed since the duel between To-cus and Mandush, and while the former lay suffering tortures ere his wounds were healed, important events had followed each other in quick succession.

Friction between the whites and Indians in all the New England colonies was growing rapidly; duplicity and treachery were the rule rather than the exception in the policy of the colonists towards the Indians, and the latter, when duped and fleeced, feeling and knowing the injustice, were fast awakening from their delusion, and their hatred and resentment were daily becoming more menacing.

Many of the more powerful and warlike tribes were already on the war-path to wreak a merited vengeance upon the conscienceless hypocrites, and tribes that in time past had made war upon each other were becoming allies of their ancient enemies and uniting for the purpose of driving out the common enemy.

The upright among the colonists saw the danger,

THE SIGNAL FIRE 149

but were powerless to stay the workings of a policy which had for its object the acquisition of the whole country.

Emissaries from the hostiles were being sent in all directions to form an alliance of the tribes that were neutral or friendly to the pale-faces.

A knowledge of this on the part of the more avaricious and unprincipled of the whites afforded them an opportunity for the exhibition of that nameless deviltry miscalled *diplomacy*, the equal of which the world has never seen, and for which they must forever stand pre-eminently as past-masters in perfidy. While flattering and professing unbounded friendship for their red brothers, the most cold-blooded and inhuman atrocities were perpetrated from time to time, as the advantage favoured, that were ever inflicted by a civilised upon a savage race, since God spoke light out of darkness, order out of chaos, and all in the name of a living and ascended Christ. They were systematically creating strife between rival chieftains, provoking each to war upon the other and then when the tribes were weakened by the ravage of fierce strife, becoming the allies of the one to annihilate the other, and, serpent-like, re-coiling and striking the bosoms that had been bared in their defence, often employing modes of torture, and practicing upon the unfortunate victims a refinement of cruelty to which even the inventive genius of the red Indian was a stranger.

Instances were not wanting where white men, by premeditated action, had surprised and butchered whole villages of peaceable Indians, not to mete out vengeance, for surely the women and children were innocent, but to indulge the love for the shedding of blood, or to check the growth in population among the tribes.

Since his contact with civilisation,—that child of the serpent, that charity that vaunteth itself and is puffed up,—the Indian has been, and is, what his environment, together with the curse of strong water and the injustice practiced upon him in unnameable ways at the hands of the white race, have made him.

Secret emissaries had visited the various tribes of Sea-wan-ha-ka to induce them to raise the tomahawk against the pale-faces; but notwithstanding the fact that they were smarting under the injustice shared by their brothers in the colonies, they were restrained through the unbounded influence of Lyon Gardiner over Wyandance.

The ships of the English navy that were engaged in protecting the colonists along the seaboard, and in watching the Dutch at New Amsterdam, were wont to rendezvous in Gardiner Bay, that afforded ample protection to the whites in the country adjacent, who, with impunity, subjected the Indians to every indignity, while the presence of the ships served to restrain and intimidate the latter.

So much, then, for the vaunted friendship of Wyandance for the pale-faces.

True it is that he saw much of them, and to a degree was, in turn, flattered and coerced by them, now promised protection and rich reward to do this or that, or threatened with abandonment and disaster if he demurred.

In company with and under the protection of the whites, he visited some of the forts and seats of government of the colonies. He saw and knew their growing power, and keenly felt the helplessness of his people to rebel, so isolated were they in their island home, so completely were they encircled by the coils of the serpent.

Deeply conscious of this, and trembling for the

THE SIGNAL FIRE

fate of his race, what wonder that, from time to time, we find him relinquishing, with unwilling hand, the heritage of the Lords of the Soil.

Advancing in years, his power broken, and feeling sadly the loss of his elder brother, he was weary of life.

But recently he had been bullied into releasing Manhansett-aha-quash-a-warnuck to the white man, for his signature as Grand Sachem of the United Tribes was necessary to secure the island over which his nephew, Yo-kee, reigned.

He had dreamed that ere long he would be called to the spirit land, and in this frame of mind we find him giving willing consent to the marriage of his daughter with To-cus, that she might have a protector when the spirit of her father had gone to join its kindred in the home of the Manitou.

The perfidy of Guy Kingsland and his hypocritical attempt to win the love of Heather Flower had at last been laid bare before the proud Sachem, and had incensed him not a little.

Enraged and mortified at his discomfiture to compass the ruin of the daughter of the Montauks, and profoundly mystified at the sudden failure of the princess to meet him at the trysting, Kingsland had, for wholesome reasons, discontinued his visits to Montauk, and in his inmost heart he had sworn vengeance, and vowed to humiliate the proud and fiery princess, whose visits to her friend had abruptly ceased, much to the wonder and grief of Damaris.

Major Gordon had concluded to entrust his future son-in-law with the details of his plot, which, it is needless to say, met with the most hearty approval from the Lieutenant, although the Major had not the slightest suspicion of Kingsland's defection towards his promised bride.

The ignorance of the details of the plot, even to minute particulars, had been feigned when the Lieutenant acted as an envoy to Captain Mason.

The intimate political relations existing between the proprietor of the Isle of Wight and the Commandant of the English fort at Saybrook, their frequent exchange of visits to each other, and on board the English ships that frequented the adjacent waters, and the vigilance and caution observed by them at all times, rendered it improbable that any considerable number of Indians in canoes could cross, unseen, the waters that separated Montauk from the mainland on the north.

About this period the friendliness of the Narragansetts towards the whites was strengthened by divers means, and by conferences between the Commandant at Saybrook and Ninigret, that, in the light of events closely following, is open to speculation. Certain it is that Ninigret became fully and accurately informed of the time and place of the contemplated wedding of Heather Flower, the daughter of his old enemy, Wyandance.

The reward he received for the significant part he played in the stirring events we are about to chronicle is not certainly known, but an extensive tract of land, several square miles in extent, and lying in the westward end of Sea-wan-ha-ka, was coveted by Major Gordon, who had been an adventurous and speculative land-grabber, and who, thus far, had failed to bring any influence to bear upon Wyandance to induce that Sachem to sell the land, which, ere long, he was to give as a ransom.

Meanwhile, the preparations for the wedding of Heather Flower had been ripening and were fully completed when the appointed time came.

On the night preceding the nuptial eve a strange,

THE SIGNAL FIRE

phantom-like scene was being enacted on the waters and upon the neighbouring island in close proximity to the home of the Montauks.

At the hour of midnight a signal fire was lighted on a bluff at the northern end of Man-cho-nock, and immediately a canoe was launched and put off seaward, with its two silent occupants.

When a few cable-lengths from shore their ears were greeted with the soft plash of muffled paddles to the east, but these sounds appeared to be expected by the two persons in the canoe.

"Egad! the red devils are on time!"

The exclamation fell in a hoarse whisper from the man at the helm.

"Um-m-m! I wonder how many of the greasy cutthroats there are," was the rejoinder, in the same stage whisper.

Further conversation was cut short as a huge war canoe hove in sight, filled with dusky Narragansett warriors in full war paint, mute and grim as statues.

Fourteen other canoes, of equal size, filled with warriors, following closely in the wake of the first, slackened the strokes of their paddles, when, by the reflection of the signal fire upon the water, they espied the canoe from shore, and as others ranged up the leader was brought to a standstill alongside the boat from shore, and a short colloquy ensued.

"Well, Chief?"

"Ugh!"

"How many canoes have you?"

"Fifteen."

"How many warriors in each?"

"Ten."

"Good! Follow me."

With measured strokes the whole flotilla resumed its course toward the bluff where the signal fire was smouldering, and very soon a landing was made. The prows of the birchen vessels grated lightly on the sandy beach, and Ninigret, with a hundred and fifty warriors, stood upon the shores of Nan-cho-nock.

No sound save the shuffling of moccasined feet disturbed the still night.

The landing was made at a point where a small stream that took its rise in a nearby swamp emptied its waters into the bay.

In an incredibly short time the little birchen fleet had been waded up the stream and safely moored from sight under the dense overhanging branches of tangled underbrush and forest trees in the swamp, and the entire band of red warriors had secreted themselves in the thicket, an almost impenetrable forest that crowned the highland upon that portion of the island, where they remained in hiding during the entire day following.

When morning dawned not a sign was visible of what had transpired during the night. Every trace had been effectually effaced by the action of the tides.

CHAPTER XVII

"NOCHE TRISTE"

> "Then more fierce
> The conflict grew, the din of arms, the yell
> Of savage rage, the shriek of agony,
> The groan of death, commingled in one sound
> Of undistinguished horrors."
>
> . . . .
>
> "The deathshot hissing from afar—
> The shock—the shout—the groan of war—
> Reverberates along that vale
> More suited to the shepherd's tale;
> Though few the numbers—theirs the strife
> That neither spares, nor speaks for life."

THERE were signs of life at an unusually early hour in the village of the Montauks, nestling along the northern slopes of the high promontory. The whole population was astir, all was bustle and excitement.

While the day was yet young, troops of Indian girls were flitting through the woodland trails in all directions, gathering wild flowers with which to adorn themselves and garland the litter upon which the bride, escorted by her retinue of maidens, was to be carried to the wildwood arena which was chosen for the wedding ceremonies.

The women were busy in preparing the feast of dainty viands that had been gathered from forest and field, from sea and lake.

Fires were built in rude ovens of cobble-stones, made in the earth, from which, ere long, was emitted the savoury odour of venison, bear and wild fowl, while an immense mound, oval in shape, and well rounded, with a base of stones heated to whiteness sent out occasional whiffs of steam from bushels of quahaugs, oysters and mussels that were roasting as only Indian squaws could prepare them.

The men were engaged in various occupations, each having for his aim the completion in detail of the arrangements to commemorate the wedding by indulging in a great feast.

The sun was sinking in billows of crimson and gold, bathing the landscape in its warm rays, and with a good-night kiss flooding the blue waves with its departing glory.

The feast was prepared, and as the shadows fell and thickened and twilight stole over sea and shore, fires were lighted in the green amphitheatre where the festivities were to be held, and the populace, in gala attire, began to assemble before the hour appointed for the arrival of the pale-face guests who were expected from Man-cho-nock.

The minutes lengthened into an hour, and the time for the ceremony came, the revels had already begun. Everyone was freely mingling in the dance that was the order of the hour preceding the coming of the bride. Still the pale-faces had not arrived, no boat was in sight, and the warriors were impatient at the delay.

As the last gleam of twilight was hidden within the mystic folds of the curtain of night another act in the drama was in progress at the northern end of Man-cho-nock.

Dusky forms were flitting like unquiet spirits in and out of the dense undergrowth of the " thicket," and presently there emerged from the gloomy recesses of the wood the stalwart forms of Ninigret's warriors, bearing their canoes upon their brawny shoulders, across the low beach, and launching them once more upon the bosom of the dark waters.

Noiselessly as spirits of evil they took their places in the light crafts, and the voyage was resumed towards the south.

Stealing in and out among the wave-washed rocks flanking the shore, they glided onward, until, in rounding a projecting highland, the fierce warriors descried the bright fires at the village of the Montauks, streaming up in bold relief against the dark background of night, bonfires of death that served as beacon lights to guide, with unerring precision, these savage despoilers upon their unarmed and unsuspecting foes.

At a signal from the occupants of the leading canoe the others sprang forward like things of life, propelled by numerous paddles wielded by the powerful arms of grim athletes.

Presently their ears were saluted with the tumult of revelry echoing over the waters from the illumined camp of the Montauks.

Effecting, unseen, a landing above and below the village, the Narragansetts, from opposite directions, began their stealthy approach.

The amphitheatre, girdled by a dark forest, was a scene that might appeal to the lover of the picturesque, a memory to be retained during a lifetime; the pennons of flame fluttering from the bonfires, streamed upward, casting lambent arrows of lurid light between the brown boles and emerald boughs of the belt of forest trees enclosing the glade, and falling redly upon the lines of warriors circling the encampment like a cordon of cardinal birds in full feather.

The thirteen minor tribes tributary to the Grand

Sachem were represented by their bravest chiefs, wisest counsellors, and most renowned braves.

With noiseless footsteps To-cus entered the circle and took his position near the mass of rich furs piled high beneath a rustic arch garlanded with bright flowers.

Among that assemblage of stalwart sons of the forest he was a fine figure, despite the scars that seamed his features. His broad breast, bared, save for the necklace of bears' claws, trophies of his prowess in the chase, bore livid marks of freshly healed wounds, honourable scars which he cared not to conceal, medals which bore the impress of their intrinsic value which all might read.

From his shoulders depended a blanket of scarlet cloth, inwrought with devices in quills and beads, over which his long scalp-lock trailed like a black cloud, and from beneath his heavy brows his eyes blazed with a triumphant light, veiling the deadly fire of anger from which the bravest warrior might well have shrunk, were he a foeman.

There was a strain, soft and sweet as of falling waters, the voices of the maidens chosen by the young princess as her attendants, and the swarthy face of the bridegroom lighted as if by magic.

Just as the flower-bedecked litter upon which Heather Flower was seated, surrounded by her dancing, singing maidens, was borne within the circle of light, there rose an awful cry from the heart of the forest. To the east, to the west, to the north and to the south, the sudden blood-curdling slogan of the Narragansetts pealed out fiercely, and a hundred and fifty plumed warriors, hideous in war-paint, broke from the cover of the night, leaped forward like ravenous beasts, and with irresistible onset began the fearful butchery of the terror-stricken Montauks,

"She was seized and borne shoreward by two powerful warriors"

many of whom made desperate but fruitless efforts to escape.

In vain Wyandance rushed like an incarnate spirit of war among his braves, and amidst a storm of arrows besought them to rally, his fierce war-cry ringing out like a clarion. All in vain.

Arrows cut the air like hissing serpents, tomahawks rained, knives flashed. Numbers were transfixed with flint-headed lances, many fell with heads battered by war-clubs or cloven by tomahawks, others, gashed and maimed by knives, lay upon the earth, the green turf and moss streaming with the life-blood flowing from gaping wounds.

The comparatively few in numbers of the Montauks had instantly recognised the war shout of the Narragansetts, but, taken so completely at a disadvantage by their surprise, they could scarcely offer a semblance of resistance.

Like a flash of lightning it had dawned upon all that the abduction of their princess was the prime object of the attack, for almost at the first onset she was seized and borne shoreward by two powerful warriors, who showed not the slightest disposition to do her bodily injury, but on the contrary appeared only anxious to escape with their captive unharmed.

Their retreat was covered by a score of warriors, whose only desire seemed to be to expedite the escape of the abductors, and, perceiving this, the Montauks, led by their Sachem, rushed as one man to rescue their beloved princess, but were overcome by numbers and slaughtered.

Battling with the desperation of despair to reach the captors and wrest his bride from their grasp, To-cus was literally cut in pieces with tomahawks and repeatedly pierced with spears, but to the last he struck out blindly, until crushed to earth by a blow from a war-club wielded by the arm of a gigantic foeman.

Wyandance fought with the ferocity of a tiger to reach his daughter's side, but was foiled at every point; and yet, as if by design, he received no harm, not even a scratch. He was finally overpowered by numbers, borne down, and securely pinioned to the trunk of a giant oak, but suffered no further indignity except the taunts of his arch enemy, Ninigret:

"The great Sachem of the Montauks is a squaw! Let him plant the corn, dress the skins, cook the venison and build the wigwams!"

A defiant yell was the only response from the chief.

The horrible deed was done. Heather Flower was a captive to her father's deadliest foe, To-cus was dead, many of her people slain, and their scalps hung at the belts of their murderers; the fate of her father was unknown to her, and she was upon the dark waters, captive of the fierce and revengeful Ninigret.

The first shock of battle was over, but the carnage that followed was not less terrible, as amid the green aisles and in the dark thickets red-handed Murder stalked.

From the outset, the murderers were indiscriminate as to age or sex. At least a score of squaws and children were among the victims. Their piteous appeals and shrieks were alike disregarded, and one by one, in quick succession, they were impaled upon spears, or their foreheads cleft by the tomahawk, and scarcely were their voices stilled in death ere their scalps hung from the girdles of the red demons. It was truly a saturnalia of blood.

A number, seeing the hopelessness of defence, fled to the dense thickets to hide from the demons who were ravenous for blood. The shrieks of the victims

"NOCHE TRISTE"

were stilled by the blows that brought death; the fiendish yells of the slayers grew less and less frequent, and finally ceased, to be succeeded by the swift, stealthy pressure of moccasined feet, as straggling, one by one the satiated victors left the ensanguined spot and hastened to their canoes.

A score of Montauk braves lay just as they had fallen, in strangely distorted postures, within the area encircling the arch their living hands had reared, dead ere the leaves and blossoms had withered, their dark faces upturned to the silvery moon, now at the full and just rising to light the retreating conquerors on their path across the heaving waters.

But the invaders had not escaped scathless. The knives of the Montauks, their only weapons, had laid low half a score of their enemies, and these lay among the dead Montauks, mute, ghastly evidences of the devotion and prowess of the warriors who had given their lives in the vain effort to save the daughter of their chief.

Where scores of living had stood, but one whose pulse beat with life remained—the wretched, almost heart-broken Wyandance, his arms pinioned, his body securely bound to the trunk of a mighty oak.

He stood there with drooping head, mute, motionless, with scarce a sign of life upon his features save the burning flash in his eagle eyes. Wic-chi-tau-bit was safe, probably within her wigwam; by a rare fortune she had not arrived at the festive scene. Did she know of the awful massacre?

Patter-patter-patter—a foot-fall so light as to scarcely be heard above the chirp of insects and the monotonous cry of the night-hawk with his doleful plaint, "beem! be-em, beem!" that for a time had been stilled; and yet to the agonised, sharpened senses of the Sachem the cautious fall of the moccasined foot was recognised.

His face lighted with a gleam of hope as the swaying vines were cautiously parted, a face appeared, and Wyancombone glided from the shadows. In an instant his keen blade, yet wet with blood, severed the bonds that confined his father, and the proud chieftain stood free, looking mournfully upon the desolation around him.

One by one those who had succeeded in screening themselves stole back to the battlefield where the fires still smouldered.

Three prisoners besides Heather Flower had been carried away by the marauders, an aged warrior, Ascassasatic, his daughter Wy-tit-tee, whose husband, Nabamacow, lay among the slain, and her child, a tiny girl of three years.

Ascassasatic had long been one of the chief counsellors of Wyandance, a warrior of courage and renown, whose voice had ever been raised against the encroachments of the whites, and the unrelenting foe of the Narragansetts.

A sorrowing cry went up, swelling upon the air like a moan from the sounding sea, the lamentation for the slain from the lips of mothers and widows bereft, rising and falling like the sighing of a strong wind through the branches of the forest trees, an invocation of the wrath of the Deity upon the guilty. It had been indeed a " Night of Sorrow."

CHAPTER XVIII

"EVEN TO THE HALF OF MY KINGDOM"

> "So the struck eagle stretched upon the plain,
> No more through rolling clouds to soar again,
> Viewed his own feather on the fatal dart,
> And wing'd the shaft that quivered in his heart;
> Keen were his pains, but keener far to feel
> He nursed the pinion which impelled the steel."

A ROUND yellow moon was sailing up the midnight heavens in its path of opal and azure, hemmed in by floating fleeces of misty cloud, a thousand stars glimmered golden, their light paling in the beams of the night queen, and in the weird, softening sheen the fleet of canoes sped onward, cleaving the waters like arrows sent from a strong bow; and as they glided among the rocks skirting Man-cho-nock, two figures emerged from the shadows of a fringe of firs and peered eagerly out over the waters.

On came the fleet of canoes, winding in and out among the treacherous rocks, breasting the waves like giant water-fowls.

"Curse the luck! I wonder now if they have failed in securing the squaw! If so, we are none the richer. What the devil do we care to have Ninigret slaughter a dozen or so greasy bucks for his own glory, or to take a few squaws' scalps? By Jupiter! if he has been successful the red rascal fails to give the signal!" growled Major Gordon, stepping a pace nearer the edge of the bluff in his anxiety to behold what he wished.

"Have a care, Major! if the girl is there she may discover you and our game is up. She has the vision of a hawk, and is keen as a briar. The Narragansett chief has an eye on the prize money, and I'll wager a crown she is there safe enough," whispered Guy Kingsland. "I wouldn't have her suspect our agency for a king's ransom."

"Ha! she's there! there goes the signal!" interrupted Gordon in an exultant whisper.

Like a bird checked in flight the foremost canoe paused, rocked upon the tide, and a sudden, dull red glow of flame shot over the faces and forms of the occupants, the muscular figure of Ninigret, and half-a-dozen warriors, grim and hideous beneath the mask of war-paint and blood. Their companions who had made up the complement of the canoe-load were lying upon the awful shore they had quitted. The red gleam was from a freshly lighted torch that reddened the waves with its sinister glow, and fell upon another figure seated in the stern—the captive maiden.

"It is she, they have her safe enough," whispered Gordon, exultingly. "The Narragansett has done his work well—and now, let us away."

"I'll not say ye nay," answered Kingsland. "I' faith, I have no desire to be seen and recognised by the forest beauty, whose bridegroom is sleeping yon, the earth his bridal couch!"

"An' ye will, we'll to our beds. Egad! this has been a profitable speculation for us, and we can afford to sleep," returned Gordon.

"'To sleep, perchance to dream—aye, there's the rub,'" quoted Kingsland. "Heigh-ho! I am completely knocked out with this beastly uncertainty."

The ruddy torchlight flared for a moment, turning the waves to blood, then whirled far out across the water, hurled by the chief's brawny hand, and floated away, still burning like a meteor, while the flotilla swept on, swiftly receding from the view of the watchers on the bluff and swallowed up in the impalpable sea mist.

Major Gordon and his no less guilty coadjutor turned and retraced their steps to the hall, there to await the further development of their scheme.

Both retired to rest, creeping as stealthily through the postern door and up the narrow staircase to their chambers as if shod with the shoes of silence; but sleep was a stranger to their eyelids. The stirring events of the night, of which they had been the instigators, their fears lest their plot might yet miscarry, kept them awake; besides, they were in expectation that a call for assistance would be sent from the Indian village.

As they had anticipated, a messenger came. While yet the rosy tints of coming morn were dispersing the violet of dawn, a canoe grated upon the beach, and Wyancombone stood at the gate of the stockade demanding admittance.

Not a word of explanation did he vouchsafe to the wondering Sandy, except the peremptory exclamation:

"Cap'n Gardiner—Wyancombone see 'em!"

"Hech! but I dinna ken ef the maister's oot o' bed th' marn!" expostulated Sandy, ogling the young Indian with inquisitive eyes.

"Wyancombone find 'em, now!" insisted the youth with an imperious wave of the hand.

"Theer coom the Major noo!" exclaimed Sandy. "Ye maun gain speech wi' him. Unco strange what brings him oot this airly i' the marn!"

But the canny Scot addressed the latter portion of his remarks and speculations to empty air, for the young Indian had bounded away and was already speaking to the Major.

The appearance of Gordon upon the scene is easily accounted for. From his window he had witnessed the coming of the messenger for whom he was watching since the dark hour preceding the dawn, and when the canoe approached swiftly he had hastily dressed and hurried out into the park to be the first to meet the visitor.

In his terse mode, Wyancombone related the events of the night, while the crafty white man listened with a well-assumed degree of horror and surprise.

"Ninigret has attacked your people? Heather Flower carried away?" he exclaimed in a tone of incredulity. "How dared he? the wretch! the villain! By heaven, he shall suffer for such a horrible slaughter of women and children! There's no time to lose! I will acquaint the Captain at once! Ho, there, Sandy!" beckoning to the lodge-keeper, "that unequalled devil, Ninigret, has made an attack upon our friends over at Montauk. There has been a frightful massacre—two-score warriors and a dozen or more of the women and children are lying dead, and the chief's daughter, with old Ascassasatic, Wy-tit-tee, and her child, little Mary, have been carried away prisoners; I'm going over with the young chief here. Tell Gardiner to follow with half a dozen of his henchmen; they need help yon, and that without delay,—and hark'ee, don't frighten the ladies, for the Narragansetts are far on their way to Block Island."

"Art sure?" demanded Sandy. "How can 'ee tell but wha' they maun't be in hidin' wi' us?"

"Not likely, they are sure to have made good their retreat under cover of night. Don't stand there wasting precious minutes. Bring my weapons and I'll be off!"

Sandy hastened to obey, and Gordon, his sword clanking by his side, pistols in his belt, and powder horn and bullet-pouch filled, hastened away, and was presently seated in the canoe, with the prow pointed in the direction of Montauk cliffs.

The interview he desired with Wyandance was of a nature that might render witnesses unpleasant; besides, it was his policy to be the first to reach the scene of slaughter and tender his services to the bereaved father.

Rapidly the light bark crossed the intervening space, and mooring the canoe, Wyancombone led the way by a straight line to the battle-ground.

For a moment even the cold-blooded Gordon recoiled, familiar as he had been with scenes of bloodshed, in his military career.

All around lay the dead, young and innocent maidens, tiny children, mothers with infants beside them or clasped in their stiffened arms; sinewy warriors, each scalped and mutilated almost beyond recognition. Even the Narragansetts had not been spared—their scalps hung at the belts of the Sagamore and his son.

With an impressive gesture the youth hurried the white man forward to the great lodge now made desolate.

As the twain approached, the matting was thrown aside and Wyandance emerged into the open air, the sternness of the warrior merged in the grief of the father, and the anguish in those keen, deep-set eyes smote heavily upon the conscience of the man whose diabolical arts had compassed the crime; for an instant he half repented of what he had done, but avarice triumphed, and an exultant throb of his heart succeeded what he termed his momentary weakness. In this mood the chief would be as wax in his hands—the land so long coveted would be his.

"Why were not my pale-face brothers here when the feast was spread? They were bidden; did they know that the Narragansetts would steal upon us like the serpent, like the hunter upon the game, and did they fear his fangs would be buried in their flesh?" asked Wyandance after the first formal nod, for the Sachem had not offered his palm to the white man, who shrank from the stern and searching gaze as if he feared it might read his soul.

"No, chief," returned Gordon, with an assumed air of injured innocence, "when we would have launched our boats, we could not find them; some mischievous person had taken them away, and although we made diligent search we found not a trace of them until we were fain to give up the search, long after the moon had risen, when we discovered them within a deep cove beneath a black growth of hemlock that had been broken and placed within them in a manner to appear like saplings growing from the rocks. Then it was too late to visit the island; a white man's eyes would not have noticed the deception—it was the Mohicans who found out the hidden boats," explained the Major, with an air of such sincerity that the chief doubted not but that he spoke the truth.

"Indian find 'em?" asked Wyandance.

"Yes, the Mohicans—they have a keen eye."

"Ugh! Mohican know where find—wolf find cubs in den where hide 'em—snake find small ones in throat, where eat 'em," answered the chief.

"I know not," returned the Major, with an air of candour, as if revolving a problem in his own mind. "The Captain has always trusted them, besides the Mohicans are the enemies of the Narragansetts—we did not suspect them, but it is possible we are mistaken," answered Gordon.

The boats had been hidden, but it was by Guy Kingsland, who had adopted the Indian mode of concealing an object, with a view to implicating the Mohicans should a suspicion be aroused.

The two conspirators had done their work well, not an item that would betray their complicity with the Narragansett chief, or their treachery, had been left unprovided for.

"Here is my hand, Sachem, take it in token of the friendship I have always felt for my red brothers. I came hither to devise some means by which the princess of the Montauks may either be ransomed or taken by force from your enemy. Once, many moons ago, I had the opportunity of doing this same Ninigret a service; the Narragansetts are not at war with the pale-faces. I will seek the chief and use my best efforts to effect a release, either by an appeal to his gratitude, as I will claim his promise, or I will offer ransom. If both means fail then English arms must be tried."

He tapped his sword sheath suggestively.

"Will my white brother do this?" asked the chief. "Does he speak with a straight tongue?"

"Could I do otherwise?" asked the Major, in a tone of reproach, "when I feel assured that I can treat with this red-handed chief with greater advantage than even the great Sachem of the Montauks, from whom Ninigret would assuredly demand a tribute that shall be forever. Allow me to deal with him and all will be well; Heather Flower shall be restored to her father, and no more shall the Montauk pay tribute to the Narragansett."

"It is good," assented the chief, "my white brother speaks well. He shall go to the country of the Narragansett and take away the daughter of Wyandance, then shall Wyandance give to the white warrior of the lands he will not give the pale-faces for wampum, for knives or blankets. The Sachem of the Montauks has spoken. He never speaks with a crooked tongue. Give him his child and take the broad lands that Wyandance will give for his daughter."

CHAPTER XIX

"UNKNELLED, UNCOFFINED, AND UNKNOWN"

"The sea is still and deep,
All things within its bosom sleep!
A single step, and all is o'er;
A plunge, a bubble, and no more."

GORDON'S heart beat high with triumph. He had not asked for a recompense—he would have done that later, but this great-hearted Lord of the Soil had pledged him a dukedom.

"Great Cæsar!" he whispered, inwardly, "the chief has promised of his own will, and he will not break his word. Deucedly fortunate I am not dealing with a white man, else I'd not be certain before a contract was drawn in black and white with quill and parchment; but in dealing with this red Indian the land is as surely my own as if the bond had been signed, sealed and delivered."

Unconsciously he had admitted a truth that has held good since the hour a European foot pressed the soil in the primeval forests of America.

"The white brother shall dwell in peace with the red men over whom Wyandance is king, for when Heather Flower comes again to her father's lodge, then shall the land be the white chief's for his own; Wyandance will place the totem of the Grand Sachem to the parchment that the white brother shall make according to the custom of his people," spoke the chief, as if in reply to the secret musings of the treacherous visitor.

"Look ye, lad—your eyes are keener than mine— see you aught of a boat? Is not the Captain yon in the distance?" the Major inquired, turning to Wyancombone, who was standing at a little distance, a silent witness to the transaction between his sire and the Major.

"The eyes of Wyancombone are like the eagle's. He has seen the white man's canoe, it brings the white chief and so many of his people," returned the youth, raising his right hand and the index finger of his left.

"The Captain with a half-dozen of his henchmen; they are on their way to help the Montauks bury their dead," explained Gordon.

Numbers of warriors were gathered upon the beach and grouped beneath the shelter of the trees, conversing at intervals, and as the boat came near they began a dismal death-song, echoed by the mournful wail of the squaws, the sound fairly chilling the blood of the guilty listener.

The boat touched the landing, the white men stepped ashore. Captain Gardiner and Guy Kingsland met the sorrowing chief with extended hand; he took the Captain's hand in his own, but paid no attention to the Lieutenant, other than a muttered word.

He had not forgotten the part the young man played in winning the heart of the young princess, although his pride would not allow him to proclaim the fact; besides, he cared not to put the hypocrite on his guard.

It was a gruesome task, composing those stark forms for burial. The Montauks, where they had fallen in defense of their princess, were wrapped in their blankets, laid in a line, and then the search for the dead, scattered in the recesses of the forest, began.

One by one they were brought forth, and beneath the shade of a group of oaks the graves were hollowed, Captain Gardiner, Major Gordon, the serving men, and even Guy Kingsland using the spades the party had brought from the Isle of Wight; and in the trenches thus prepared the Montauks laid their dead brothers and the innocent maidens, women, and little children who had fallen in the dreadful massacre.

With their weapons in their hands, the warriors were seated to rest in their graves, the maidens, in their gala attire, were lowered tenderly, the garlands they had woven and the withered flowers they had plucked laid upon their pulseless bosoms.

There was deathly silence broken only by the soft fall of the earth upon the uncoffined forms as the white men performed their office.

When all was over, Wyandance moved to the head of the long line of graves, and in obedience to a wave of his hand the warriors fell back. The stricken chief stood alone, and with his right arm stretched over the grave thus vented his grief and voiced the sorrow of his people:

"Listen, my brothers: Our hearts are very sore, and the eyes of our women and children are heavy with weeping for our dead warriors slain by our enemies—not in battle, but when we had laid away our weapons to make our hearts glad; when the Heather Flower would go to the lodge of To-cus to carry the sunshine that would live there always to gladden his heart.

"Listen! Who is the enemy of the Montauks who told the Narragansetts when to strike them, when we had buried the tomahawk and forgotten war in the hope to live in peace?"

The chieftain paused, while his eagle eye was riveted on the faces of the white men, as if he would read there any sign of a criminal knowledge; instinctively the Major and Kingsland bit their lips and reddened faintly, each comprehending that the stern-browed chief more than half-suspected their complicity in the crime. After a slight pause the sorrowing Sachem continued:

"Listen! Our traditions tell us that long ago when we were not a numerous people, the Narragansetts demanded tribute of us and we refused to pay it. They invaded our country, burned our wigwams, slew our braves in battle, and drove us from our hunting grounds. But when we had joined forces with our three brother tribes, the Narragansetts, in turn, had to show the sole of the foot in the place of the white of the eye, and we were left to live in peace in all our borders. Then, later, the Pequots came and made war upon us, and we were made to pay tribute to them.

"At length a daughter of the Iroquois came to the wigwam of a Montauk and we were about to form an alliance with the Mohawks, the ancient enemies of the Pequots, when the pale-faces came with soft and cooing words, and we were their friends. When the Mohawks saw this they left us alone to be despoiled by our friends and murdered by our enemies.

"Listen, my children: The Great Spirit is angry with the Montauks because we have been the white man's friend and have remained in peace at home when the Pequots and Narragansetts would induce us to go upon the war-path that our tomahawks might drink the white man's blood. For this the Great Spirit caused the eyes of the Montauks to be heavy and dim on Shag-a-nock hill,[1] that they did not see Nin-e-croft,[2] in his war canoes, coming to carry the daughter of Wyandance, we know not where."

For the moment the Sachem's composure nearly forsook him, but with kingly grace and bearing he controlled and stilled the storm that raged within his heaving bosom, and snatching, with impatient hand, the toga from his head, he stood erect, his matchless form dilating with righteous anger, his fierce eyes kindling and flashing as the lightning plays upon the storm-cloud's crest, as he continued:

"Listen, my brothers: Swear by the Great Spirit, swear by the earth, sea, sun and sky, by the bones of your fathers, that they who betrayed us to the Narragansetts, that they who struck the blow that has sent so many Montauks to the happy hunting grounds, our brothers whose bodies are here hidden in the earth to-day, that we may not look upon them again, that they who have robbed our wigwams of the bravest warriors, shall die! Swear by the bodies of our dead maidens, women and children, that they who took Heather Flower from us, from her home and all she loved, shall be food for the sea-wolves, the wolf and panther, and that the deed can only be washed out by the blood of our enemies!"

A deep, guttural murmur of approval came from the assembled Montauks.

At the head of his warriors the stern chief retraced his steps, his eyes kindled with ferocity, his brow darkening as he stood beside the remains of the Narragansetts who had fallen in the strife.

His fingers worked nervously about the haft of his knife, telling more plainly than words could have done of the vengeful feelings in his breast.

---

[1] *Shag-a-nock.*—End of the land.   [2] *Nin-e-croft.*—Ninigret.

The wailing cry for the dead was stilled upon the lips of the squaws, and in sullen gloom the warriors awaited the command of their Sachem.

After holding a short conference with Captain Gardiner and the Major, he addressed a few words to his followers, when half a score separated themselves from their companions and strode shoreward.

At a gesture from the chief his warriors clutched their dead enemies by the feet and dragged them away, followed by a procession of braves, squaws and papooses, the latter bringing up the rear as they moved forward to the beach, where several canoes were awaiting the gruesome freight; and like slaughtered wolves the lifeless Narragansetts were piled in ghastly heaps within the birchen vessels, which were tethered together with strong lines, fashioned from the sinews of the deer.

The flotilla was firmly secured to three canoes, in which a complement of Montauks were seated, the rowers bent to their task, and the gruesome cortège swept onward.

Upon the highest point of the bold headland Wyandance stood upright, his gaze fixed steadfastly upon the receding canoes until they came to a sudden standstill, in plain sight of his elevated point of observation.

Dragging the canoes containing the scalpless warriors alongside the leading boats, the Montauks raised the dead from the bottom of the canoe, and one by one they were plunged into the depths by the grim undertakers.

Through a field glass Major Gordon and Kingsland watched each act of the drama, plainly saw the fin of a shark rise to the surface, the glistening white belly of the man-eater exposed to view for an instant ere the monster seized upon his prey, that disappeared from sight as if engulfed within the circles of a maelstrom.

Another and yet another sea-wolf flashed to the surface, to disappear as suddenly as the first, while a fierce yell of gratified revenge floated across the waters, answered by the Montauk war-whoop from the braves gathered upon the promontory, and supplemented by the weird wailing of the squaws mourning for their own dead.

"The graves of our enemies are in the jaws of the sea-wolves—their spirits must roam forever amid the swamps and deserts, pursued by Ho-bam-o-koo, chilled by frosts, burned by hot sands, but never can they reach the happy hunting grounds where the Montauk warriors they have slain will hunt the deer, the moose and the bear—it is well!" exclaimed Wyandance, in a deep solemn voice. "And for the traitor who betrayed the Montauks to their enemies, may he, like the Narragansetts, our foes, find his grave in the stomach of the wild beast of the forest!"

With a shudder, Major Gordon walked away, his face whitening, his limbs trembling. Would the curse follow him and the no less guilty Kingsland?

The sorrowing Sachem sought the solitude of his desolate wigwam to receive the faithful ministrations of his devoted Wic-chi-tau-bit.

CHAPTER XX

AN INTRICATE WEB

> "O, serpent heart, hid with a flow'ring face!
> Did ever dragon keep so fair a cave?
> Beautiful tryant! fiend angelical!
> Dove-feathered raven! wolfish-ravening lamb!
> Despised substance of divinest show!
> Just oposite to what thou justly seem'st,
> A damned saint, an honourable villain!"

FROM the chaos of mind Heather Flower awakened slowly as from a fearful dream. Nearly an hour had elapsed since she was ruthlessly torn from her friends, in the very midst of the wedding festivities which had been suddenly turned to a scene of woe. The shock had been so terrible as to stupefy her faculties and benumb her limbs.

She remembered the gay pageant upon which her eyes had rested; the cooing tones of her maidens sounded in her ears, voices so swiftly stilled in death; again the red torchlights flashed before her eyes, again she saw the green arch, the garlands, the moving figures of the dancers in the centre of the amphitheatre, the revelry to be succeeded by the awful war-whoop of the Narragansetts hemming in the revellers as they rushed upon their prey; again she heard the whizzing of arrows, saw the whirling tomahawks raining blows upon the defenceless heads of her defenders, and then in fancy she beheld the torchlights shedding a lurid glow upon the forms lying around her, the dead bodies of her people. She remembered that neither age nor sex had been spared by the ruthless assassins, and again she turned deathly sick and faint.

A heavy fur robe had been suddenly thrown over her head and secured about her neck so closely as to stifle her breath and muffle the horrid din, and she had felt herself raised and borne swiftly along through the thick forest, for the green-leaved twigs of the undergrowth had struck sharply against her limbs and the thorns had clung to her garments as her captors made their passage, while the fearful sound of conflict, the cries of the wounded, the groans of the dying grew fainter, and she knew that she was a captive of the brawny Narragansetts whose arms encircled her form, and was being carried away from all she held dear on earth, and into a bondage that might prove worse than death.

All passed before her like a phantasmagoria of a frightful dream, and yet she realised that it was a dread reality.

She felt herself lowered and placed in a sitting posture, and knew by the rocking motion that she was in a canoe, and that only two persons stepped in after her; then the birchen vessel was pushed off, and that the paddles were wielded with powerful strokes she felt by the motion of the light craft and the swiftness with which it shot over the waters. All this she perceived only by circumstances, for her eyes were blinded, and not a word had been spoken by her captors.

On, on, sped the war-canoe, like a bird upon the wing, riding lightly upon the smooth waters, and at length rocking idly, for the stout oarsmen rested from their labours; and although the frightful spectacle she had witnessed was appalling, the helpless captive knew that it was but a prelude to the awful tragedy that was being enacted on the shore she had left.

Of the flight of time she could take no note, her breath came in gasps, and then the hardy child of the forest fainted.

When she awoke from the dead stupor that had steeped her senses in a merciful oblivion, the heavy robe was removed from her face and wrapped about her shoulders, the moonlight was falling whitely upon her bared head, which was pillowed against the naked breast of a swarthy Narragansett; a hot breath scorched her cheek, and she raised her heavy eyes to encounter the basilisk gaze of her father's arch enemy, Ninigret.

With a sudden movement she wrenched herself free from his enfolding arm and sprang to her feet. The canoe rocked dangerously with the impetus of her motion, and the chief grasped her arm with a grip of steel, forcing her back to the bottom of the canoe.

"Let the daughter of Wyandance be still or Ninigret's knife shall drink her blood!" exclaimed the chief, in menacing tones, while his hand sought his knife haft.

"Let the murderer of women and children strike! He can fight only the Montauks who have no bows in their hands, no tomahawks at their belts!" exclaimed the girl, with dauntless mien, her eyes blazing, her nostrils dilating scornfully. "Ninigret is a squaw who dares not look in the face of a Montauk who carries a spear in his hand!"

In an instant the keen knife was in the air, poised above her heart; but with a mighty effort the wily Narragansett quelled the fierce gust of passion her taunts had raised, and his hand dropped to his side, though still clutching the weapon.

The canoe in which he was seated was in the lead, and there were but half a dozen warriors in the boat besides the chief. Their companions were lying stark and cold on the blood-stained shore they had quitted.

Following closely was a flotilla of war-canoes, heavily laden with warriors, hideous as satyrs, and in the nearest canoe three captives were huddled, whom the Indian girl recognised as her father's chief counsellor, Ascassasatic, his daughter and his little grandchild. Heather Flower knew that the unfortunate Wy-tit-tee was a widow, her infant daughter fatherless, for she had seen the young warrior stricken down by an arrow.

The scene was familiar, for the Indian rowers were steering among the outlying rocks close upon the shore of Man-cho-nock, and as the captive turned her eyes toward the headland she descried a figure flitting across a white patch of moonlit sward, to be lost in the blackness of the timber belt upon the verge of the bluff.

Only the hawk-like vision of an Indian, or the keen eyes of love or hate, could have recognised a friend or foe, but the three qualities were combined in that glimpse.

"The Black-heart!" she whispered through her clenched teeth. "What does he here when the moon is in the midnight sky?"

A torch was burning at the prow of the canoe, and the action of Ninigret confirmed her suspicions.

Grasping the blazing pine knot, the chief whirled it thrice about his head, poised it so that the light fell full upon his captive's face and form, ere he hurled it far out over the dark waters, where it whirled and danced like the fiery eye of a Cyclops.

"A signal light! *He* is the traitor! *he* said the

words that told the Narragansetts when to strike to the hearts of the Montauks!"

The conviction settled upon heart and brain like a red-hot iron, as the paddles again dipped and the flotilla dashed onward, leaving ghostly manes of snow-white, like the bleached locks of drowned mariners tossing upon the waves.

Had Guy Kingsland guessed that he had been seen and recognised by the Indian girl whom he had made his deadly foe, the pillow which his head pressed so heavily would have been indeed a bed of thorns.

Three days later an encampment of Narragansetts was located upon a spot near the beach on Block Island. The point was not one frequently used as a camping ground, and the party was small, numbering not more than a score, too few for a war party, too numerous for a fishing party; besides their movements were singular.

Only one lodge had been erected, large and commodious as befitted the lodging place of a chief of the Narragansetts, for the leader was Ninigret.

Upon the cliff above the beach a vidette was posted at a station commanding an extended view of the Sound in the direction of the Connecticut shore.

Both by looks and gestures it was apparent the watch was expecting the approach of either friend or foe by water.

The sun was sinking low in the western horizon when the lookout descried a sail, a mere speck at first, but gradually growing on the sight, and patiently the warrior watched it until he was assured he had not been mistaken in the character of the craft, and as he gazed the sun dipped lower, finally sinking beneath the wave upon which its last beams lingered, a sheet of flame reflected from the hidden fires in the horizon.

AN INTRICATE WEB 183

There was no mistake. More rapidly as the boat neared, the white sails enlarged, the rigging of a ship loomed up, and presently the dark hull was plainly visible.

Not until then did the sentinel leave his post and hasten to the wigwam, and as he neared the entrance the chief stepped forth to meet him.

Bending his head in presence of the Sachem, the young brave awaited his speech.

"The white man's canoe comes?" asked Ninigret.

"War-canoe there!" replied the brave, pointing seaward.

Summoning his warriors by a sweep of his hand, Ninigret made his way to the crest of the bluff to await the coming of the ship that was now in plain view, and that presently cast anchor.

Upon the deck stood a detachment of soldiers in the uniform of the English army, the last red glow of the dying day deepening their scarlet coats to blood-red, and burnishing the hilts of their weapons in Roman gold. A boat was quickly lowered and manned, and a man of soldierly bearing stepped in and was rowed ashore.

With a few peremptory commands to his boatmen, he stepped upon the beach and climbed up the rough pathway, meeting the chief upon the escarpment.

CHAPTER XXI

TRUE TO BIRTH AND BREEDING

"I do oppose
My patience to his fury; and am arm'd
To suffer with a quietness of spirit,
The very tyranny and rage of his."

"THE white chief is welcome in the lodge of his red brother," greeted the Sachem, as he took Major Gordon's extended hand in a strong grip. "Is my white brother afraid that he brings so many red-coats from the strong lodge where the waters meet?"

"Not for protection, chief," returned the Major, "but as a precaution to blind the eyes of the Montauk Sachem; Wyandance is cunning as the fox, and had I not taken with me a detachment of English soldiers his daughter would surely have suspected that the affair had been cut and dried, and such a suspicion would bring the Montauk warriors about our ears like a nest of hornets."

"Wagh! Narragansett braves take sting from Montauk wasp! make 'em 'fraid strike white brothers! Ugh!" exclaimed Ninigret, contemptuously.

"You took some scalps, eh?" questioned Gordon.

"Much scalp—see!" assented Ninigret, brushing the long tufts of purple-black hair trailing to his knee. "Montauks squaws—not fight warriors."

"Well, Sachem, we bring the ransom agreed upon

for the caged red bird: ten blankets, twenty-four hatchets, ten spades, forty knives, many fathoms of beads, with the rings, and a cask of New England rum—that was what was agreed upon, and I think it is ample ransom for a warrior, and this is only a squaw; I have dealt handsomely by you, Sachem."

"Not like other squaw, not woman of burden—mother princess of Iroquois, father Sachem; blood in heart of Wyandance, life of his veins, Montauk chief love daughter deep here!" he added, pressing his hand upon his breast.

"Aye, and shall pay roundly in broad lands," Gordon said in his heart, with a sinister smile upon his thin lips, then aloud, "Zooks! I have done you a good turn, Sachem, scalps and glory and a round ransom for the Narragansetts, land for me."

"Land!" sneered Ninigret, almost fiercely, "always land—more land! pale-face take all land bime-by, drive red man away towards setting sun where his fathers once dwelt before they drove away their enemies, hundreds of moon ago and made a path to where the sun rises from the Great Waters.[1] White man take no more land from the Narragansetts."

The usually astute white man had stumbled upon dangerous ground, and aroused the jealousy concerning the land transactions, a common cause that might, ere long, cement the various tribes in a confederation that would prove highly dangerous and disastrous to the settlers.

Ninigret's gloomy brow grew dark and his deep-set eyes kindled.

"Well, Sachem, let that pass," the Major re-

[1] The Long Island and mainland tribes had a tradition that their forefathers came from a land far to the westward, fought and conquered the ancient tribes inhabiting the islands and seaboard and took possession of the country which their descendants have since occupied.

turned smoothly. " I have performed my part of the contract, or am prepared; the merchandise is in yon ship awaiting your pleasure—shall I have it brought ashore at once? "

" Ninigret much sorry—like keep squaw—take her to lodge—Ninigret's wife—then Montauk fight with Narragansett brothers, drive away pale-faces," replied the Sachem, moodily.

" But the great chief of the Narragansetts has promised, surely he will not break his word! " exclaimed Gordon, his lips twitching nervously.

" Ninigret is a great chief—white man make promise—forget—wind blow away his word, like this! Pouf! " he puffed spitefully. " Narragansett not forget—but sorry—much sorry—never lie; let my white brother bring the ransom and take away the squaw."

The Major was angry, nettled, chagrined, but disguising his ill-humour, he asked:

" She is here? "

" Squaw in lodge," answered the chief, pointing towards the wigwam.

" And has received neither insult nor injury except such inconvenience as was unavoidable under the circumstances? " questioned Gordon.

" Ninigret is not a pale-face, he is not a serpent to speak with a forked tongue! He is a great Sachem. He made a promise—he has kept it—Ninigret owe no more debt to white brother! "

The proud chieftain spoke sternly, drawing up his figure to its stateliest height.

Without further comment Gordon signalled the ship, and presently a second boat was lowered, a quantity of freight stowed, and heavily-laden it was propelled to shore.

The crew lifted the burden from the boat and bore it up across the rugged rocks, depositing it in the

TRUE TO BIRTH 187

centre of the encampment, a labour which Ninigret's warriors disdained.

Within the circle of savages at whose girdles hung the freshly taken scalps of the Montauks, some of which Gordon recognised as those of white-haired warriors whom he had known, half a dozen white men were engaged in unbinding the articles they had brought, while the Narragansetts crouched upon the ground, their eyes eagerly bent upon the cask they knew contained the fire-water so much coveted.

"Will my white brother sleep in the lodge of the Narragansetts?" asked the Sachem, with native hospitality.

But neither the Major or his boat's crew cared to remain ashore, a witness to the orgies that would follow after the fiery liquor had transformed the red men into maniacs; and, truth to tell, the Major feared to trust himself under the protection of even so powerful a personage as the Sachem.

"No, we must be away as soon as possible—it would not be consistent with our professions to remain; therefore let my red brother deliver the squaw into our possession, and we will go on board ship at once—when the sun rises the young squaw must be in her father's lodge," replied Gordon.

Heather Flower was seated upon a pile of mats where the shadows fell thickest within the lodge, her face buried in her hands, her long hair unbound and veiling neck and bust. She was bearing her suffering with the dumb endurance so characteristic of her Indian blood, true to her birth and breeding.

A light touch aroused her and she sprang to her feet, looking in the face of her captor with fierce, feverish eyes.

"Come! Why does the daughter of a chief bow herself and cry like a pale-face papoose?" asked Ninigret, in a harsh tone. "Is it because her father is a squaw, his warriors dogs that crouch and whine when the arrows of their enemies fly through the air?"

"The Narragansett is a thief! Heather Flower is the daughter of a great chief, she is not afraid! she disdains to ask mercy of the snake who crawls upon an unarmed enemy and makes war upon squaws and papooses! A Montauk would scorn to wear the scalp of a squaw or a papoose at his belt!" exclaimed the proud Indian maiden, pointing significantly at the scalps he displayed at his girdle, and speaking in accents of such withering contempt that even the fierce Narragansett could not repress a thrill of shame.

"Does Wyandance ever forget to take vengeance for a wrong? His only answer to insult is death! His warriors will lie in ambush, and when Ninigret is their captive, they will give him to be the sport of their women of burden! The aged squaws shall take his scalp as he has taken these!"

She pointed to the long, raven tresses, the scalps of her murdered maidens, and the soft fringes torn from papooses slung at their mothers' backs.

"Dog of a Narragansett, why does he not slay Heather Flower, that he may hang another scalp of a squaw at his belt? Is it because the blood of the great Warrior King flows hot through his daughter's veins that Ninigret fears to take her life? Strike, crawling serpent with the poisoned teeth that fears to meet the Montauks when the sun shines!" she exclaimed, drawing herself to her fullest stature. "Heather Flower has not even a bending reed with which to defend herself!"

She had feared that the hated Sachem would make her his wife by force, and death was far preferable, therefore she had striven to taunt him into giving her a death blow. All the fire in her haughty soul kindled in her flashing eyes and burned in fever spots upon her cheeks, transforming the face that had been so wan and despairing into the lineaments befitting a Boadicea.

She had too nearly succeeded, for, driven to a perfect frenzy of fury by her taunts, the chief snatched his knife from his belt, and in an instant the sharp blade would have pierced the heart of the captive.

"Shame! will the great Sachem of the Narragansetts let the words of a squaw make him forget that he is a warrior?"

The deep, stern voice of Major Gordon broke the spell. The chief thrust the knife in his belt and turned a scowling visage toward the intruder.

"Take her away!" he hissed, "her tongue has the poison of the rattlesnake, her words are like the hot breath of the fire at the stake! Go! lest the great chief of the Narragansetts forgets that his white brother has paid the ransom, and leaves him nothing but the dead to carry to the enemy of Ninigret!"

Turning upon his heel, without a backward glance or word of parting, the surly chief disappeared in the blackness of a tangled thicket.

If Heather Flower felt surprise that a white man should appear upon the scene at such an opportune moment, she evinced none as she followed her rescuer to the waiting boat, asking no question, but taking her place within the boat that was rowed swiftly to the ship.

It would be hours before the moon, now in its last quarter, would light the scene, but myriads of stars hung their silver lamps in the cloudless blue above and were faintly mirrored in the waters as the craft swiftly ploughed its way, sailing under a fresh breeze toward its point of destination, the grey cliffs of Montauk.

CHAPTER XXII

"BLUE LAWS"

"I think that friars and their hoods,
 Their doctrines and their maggots,
Have lighted up too many feuds,
 And far too many faggots;
I think, while zealots fast and frown,
 And fight for two or seven,
That there are fifty roads to town,
 And rather more to heaven."

"ARE you for a row over to Maidstone[1] this morning?"

Guy Kingsland asked the question as he entered the breakfast room at Gardiner Hall, where he found Colonel Lawrence, who had accepted the pressing invitation of Lyon Gardiner that he would make the hall his home a portion of the time while he remained in the colonies.

"Really, I have thought nothing about the matter," returned Lawrence, looking up from the pages of a letter he had been reading, with rather a puzzled expression in his fine eyes. "You refer to the case of the Indian squaw, I suppose?"

"Nothing of the sort. Zounds, man! it is a full-fledged warrior who is to be tried in the Court of Sessions for witchcraft. Odd affair, altogether. Gordon is going over with the Captain, I believe, and most of the Captain's henchmen—the rabble always attend anything of the kind here, as in England the middle and lower classes are always to be found at an execution."

[1] *Maidstone.*—Easthampton.

"The brute portion of the human family. I had no idea that the colonists, staid Puritans and Republicans as most profess to be, should carry their superstitions so far as to solemnly convene a court on such a flimsy accusation. What is the specific charge against the Indian, and to what tribe does he belong?"

"He is called Poniute, and is a fierce, vindictive warrior of note in the Montauk tribe; the indictment sets forth that said Poniute was and is a sorcerer, and has, on a recent occasion, bewitched and caused the death of a lad named Garlick. The Indian is confined within the stockade at Maidstone, under close guard."

"What a senseless charge—a mere farce!" exclaimed Henry Lawrence. "Was he arrested in the usual fashion?"

"I don't pretend to say as to that—I presume so, providing he allowed himself to be taken without showing fight; it appears that Wee-gon, the medicine-man of the Montauks, has been holding what the Indians call a pow-pow, a sort of worship of the devil—one of their religious observances—a short time ago, and directly afterward this lad accompanied the Indian, Poniute, upon a botanical hunt for healing herbs, or something of the sort, after which the lad was seized of a strange disorder that baffled the skill of the leech. His death was attributed to the malignant arts of this red heathen," explained Guy.

"Ridiculous! You speak of the worship of the devil—a heathen idea with a vengeance! Is it original with these Montauks, or are other tribes of the same belief?"

"The religious notions of the Montauks and other island tribes are peculiar, and are shared by the tribes upon the mainland, I think. As I understand it, they believe in a plurality of gods, and in one great and good being who controls all the others, whom they call Manitou, or the Great Spirit. They likewise believe in a devil, or evil spirit, whom they call Ho-bam-o-koo, or Ponny, and they have their conjurers or medicine men, who hold these pow-pows, a kind of worship of the devil."

"A sop to Cerberus?" smiled the Colonel.

"Something of the sort. Gardiner explains that this ceremony is so revolting in character, in the opinion of Europeans, that laws are about to be enacted for the suppression of the rites."

"You have a form of government, of course; are there provisions for occasions like the present, concerning this Poniute?" asked Lawrence.

"I must confess to ignorance on the subject of colonial laws. Again I refer you to the Captain, who is authority. But if we go over to-day we shall get a fair idea of the style in which justice is administered in this beastly wilderness. 'Fore God, I wish I were safely out of it; what with the savage beasts, and still more savage natives, a man has but a sorry shave to keep his head upon his shoulders or his scalp from drying in a smoky Indian lodge," returned Guy, with a short, uneasy laugh. "If it were not for the circumstance that my future wife and her respected parent are in a way compelled to tarry awhile, I would sail in the next good ship crossing the high seas."

"I have not found it so bad," replied Colonel Lawrence.

"Wait until you have unwittingly incurred the enmity of some redskin. It isn't the pleasantest prospect in the world to be obliged to regard every copper-hide as a possible foe who might lie in ambush to plunge a knife in your back or plant an arrow between your ribs, with all the complacency in life; it is a constant nightmare on one's mind. I shall feel like a new man once I set sail for my native shore."

"Tush, man! you are getting the vapours. As I understand, these Long Island Indians are your good friends, the Narragansetts are allies of the English, although at war with the Montauks, and the Mohawks and other Iroquois tribes are kept at bay by dread of a combination of the redcoats and Narragansett warriors. Is it that you fear an unpleasant complication arising from the late transactions, or that the attack of the Narragansetts and the capture of the Indian girl may be laid at your door?"

The instant reddening of the Lieutenant's cheek, succeeded by the sudden pallor, might have confirmed the Colonel's chance shot.

"Bah! your morning dram must have mounted to your brain, my Colonel," returned Guy. "I was but speaking in general terms. These Montauks are on the friendliest footing with all upon the island, myself included, but they are heathen, nevertheless, and a breath, the turning of a straw, may at any moment transform them into assassins—not an agreeable fact to contemplate."

The entrance of the Captain and his lady put an end to the colloquy, much to Guy's relief, and before the morning salutations were fairly exchanged Major Gordon sauntered in. Presently Damaris appeared, laughing and chatting with Mollie and Bessie, the Captain's two young daughters, whom the breakfast bell had summoned from their romp in the garden.

"Mistress, where is David?" questioned Gardiner of his wife, and casting a severe glance toward his son's empty chair at the board, for Lyon Gardiner was the soul of punctuality, and his experience as commandant at Saybrook Fort had intensified his natural disposition in that regard, so that at all times he required its strictest observance by his family.

"Here, sir!" called David, a handsome youth of sixteen summers, tall and stalwart beyond his years, as he took his seat decorously.

"We have been discussing the nature of the laws in these colonies, Captain," remarked Guy, turning to the Captain, "a subject with which you are familiar, and I have taken the liberty of giving the Colonel an invitation to accompany us to Maidstone to attend the trial of the Montauk."

"No liberty, whatever, Lieutenant, I was about to tender him an invitation. Of course he will be one of the party; I shall not take a denial," said the Captain, heartily.

"That is what brought up the question as to what article under colonial laws this case comes; you are better able to expound the statutes more fully than I can possibly do, and I referred him to you."

"Um-m-m-m!" hemmed Gardiner; "the Indian was arrested and confined under a suspicion of practising sorcery upon a lad, from which acts the youth died. By the code, persons punishable with death are:

"'Those who shall in any wise deny the true God, or His attributes; those who commit a wilful or premeditated murder; he who slays another with a sword or dagger, that hath not any weapon to defend himself; those who lie in wait; poisoning, or any such wicked conspiracy; taking away life by false and malicious testimony; man stealing; resisting the government by arms; conspiracy against the public; children above the age of sixteen, and of sufficient understanding, smiting their natural father and mother, unless in self-defence from maiming or death,'" explained Captain Gardiner.

"I' faith! I can discover nothing under the provisions applicable in this Indian's case, if I understand Kingsland correctly," returned Colonel Lawrence.

"Perhaps not, unless it is proven a case of poisoning; but there is another clause that may be brought to bear: 'That no person employed about the bed of any man, woman or child, as surgeon, midwife, physician, or other person, presume to exercise or put in practice and act contrary to the approved rules of the art in each mystery or occupation.'"

"This latter provision will probably apply. The lad, while strolling in the forest with the Indian, who was initiating him in the mysteries of botany as known among the tribes, and quite out of the known, approved rules of the art, suddenly became ill—seized with violent cramps; and he acknowledged having eaten a goodly quantity of some strange berries which the Indian declared to be a virulent poison, who immediately searched for a certain root which he professed, as it probably was, to be an antidote to the poison which the lad had taken; which, after the lad had chewed, he professed himself in less pain, and he continued chewing until he reached his father's cabin; but his parents, being alarmed, commanded him to desist, and cast the remaining portion of the roots into the fire. In a short time the pain returned, and Goodman Garlick summoned the leech, but when the physician arrived the lad was past all earthly aid, and expired in fearful convulsions.

"His relatives, who are deeply imbued with the common belief in the arts of the sorcerer, stoutly maintained that the youth came to his death through foul means, to wit, the conjurer's practice—arts exercised by Poniute, who, as they asserted, had obtained some diabolical agency from old Wee-gon. They entered a formal complaint, and in consequence of this proceeding the Indian was promptly apprehended and held for trial."

"The upshot of the matter is that this Indian is arrested and held under suspicion of witchcraft?" said Lawrence, inquiringly.

"That is the charge," assented Captain Gardiner; "and for my part I hold it a senseless accusation; it was either a case of accidental poisoning through the lad's carelessness, or an attack of cramp which probably would have yielded to the efficacy of the root prescribed and furnished by the Indian had the lad been allowed to continue its use, for these Indians are wonderfully well informed concerning the medicinal properties of plants."

"And the punishment for practising the art is—what is it?" asked the Colonel.

"If proven, the fellow will be hanged or drowned —probably the former; if doubtful, a punishment will be inflicted according to the discretion of the Court. If you do us the honour of making one of the party you will hear the proceedings, and doubtless be greatly edified thereby; at all events you will be better able to judge of the merits of the case. I must acknowledge that our laws when applied to these Indians are apt to be severe," returned Captain Gardiner, candidly.

"For my part I hope they will hang the redskin

as high as Haman!" put in Major Gordon, vindictively.

"I agree with you, Major," declared Lieutenant Kingsland. "I have often seen this Poniute, who is said to be a pestilent fellow, and morose and revengeful, if his face does not belie him; if he is permitted to escape there will be no end of trouble. Make an example of him and it will serve to intimidate his tribe. It is believed that they are on the eve of an outbreak, and it is certain that they are getting bold and restless."

"Hang him, guilty or not guilty, eh?" questioned Lawrence. "It strikes me that it is an extremely odd, not to say cruel policy that obtains, of which I have observed the workings on one or more occasions since I came to the colonies. Now who, in all conscience, can blame these untutored savages should they unite to drive out the invaders from the land over which their ancestors reigned Lords of the Soil ere the white man came to the shores of the New World? In a civilised nation, such action would be considered righteous, a duty, even a necessity, for the preservation of life, liberty and country, yet with these untamed savages self-defence is punished as a crime, their protestations are accounted unworthy of regard, while a demand is constantly made for mile after mile of their territory, and the land taken either by cajolery or masked force; I acknowledge I have little patience with such proceedings."

"Tut! tut!" remonstrated Captain Gardiner. "Look 'ee, lad, 'When you are in Rome do as Romans do.' I have argued as you do, but of what avail? I can only drift with the tide. Harkee, no individual, or even a score of men, can right the wrongs of a community, and mere protestations are but idle breath that involve one in a sea of trouble."

Glancing at the tall clock upon the stair landing, through the open door, he arose from the table.

"Excuse me, gentlemen, sorry to interrupt, but if we would be in time to secure comfortable seats at the trial, we must e'en hasten. Here comes my boatmen, and we will be off at once."

CHAPTER XXIII

ON CHARGE OF WITCHCRAFT

> "Chained in the market-place he stood,
>   A man of giant frame,
> Amid the gathering multitude,
>   That shrunk to hear his name;
> All stern of look and strong of limb,
>   His dark eye on the ground,
> And silently they gazed on him,
>   As on a lion bound."

ALL Maidstone was astir. At the moment the doors of the stone church, used also as a court house, were opened, a motley crowd rushed in; every inch of space except a small semi-circle reserved for the officers of the law, and the rough bench allotted as a prisoners' dock, was occupied, but the throng parted right and left when Lyon Gardiner entered, followed by Major Gordon, Colonel Lawrence, and Lieutenant Kingsland, for the Captain was a man of note and renown among the colonists, and he had no difficulty in securing seats for himself and his party where they could hear and observe the proceedings.

The crowd was getting restless, the mutterings finally gathering volume until the impatient growls rose to vociferous calls, but as the clamour waxed stronger the prisoner was brought in by the sheriff, assisted by four stout guards, who placed the warrior within the dock.

Everyone was in a fever of excitement and on tiptoe with curiosity to get a view of the savage, for the infamy of his supposed crime, and the circumstances attending his arrest had been blazoned through every settlement on the island.

He was well worth the scrutiny he was obliged to face from that assembly, a savage proud of his renown as a warrior, and a statesman in the councils of his people, a red Hercules towering half a head above the stalwart yeomen who hemmed him in. His arms were pinioned, chains clanked at his ankles.

Colonel Lawrence noted the blaze of anger that swept over that bronzed face, and the fierce fire gathering in his sloe-black eyes, saw the heaving of the brawny chest and the compression of the thin lips the only outward signs of the volcano of passion raging within.

As he took his stand, for by a haughty gesture he refused to be seated, a pin might have been heard to drop, so profound was the hush, but when he turned his fierce, unflinching gaze upon the sea of faces a low growl of anger rose on all sides.

The sharp clang of the tithing-man's wand compelled instant silence, and the indictment was read, a composition quite in keeping with the times and the superstitions.

"The constable and overseers of the town of Maidstone in the east riding of Yorkshire, upon Long Island, do present for our sovereign lord, Protector of England, that Poniute, an Indian of the Montauk tribe, upon the twentieth day of August, and several other days and times previous, by some wicked and detestable arts, commonly called witchcraft and sorcery, did (as is suspected) maliciously and feloniously practice and exercise the same, at the said east riding of Yorkshire, on Long Island aforesaid.

"Moreover, the constable and overseers of the said towne of Maidstone, in the east riding of Yorkshire, upon Long Island aforesaid, do further present for our sovereign lord, that the said Indian named Poniute, did (as is suspected) divers times, by the like wicked and detestable arts, commonly called witchcraft and sorcery, maliciously and feloniously practise and exercise at the said towne of Maidstone, in the east riding of Yorkshire upon Long Island aforesaid, on the person of a lad called Charles Garlick, by which wicked and detestable arts the said lad (as is suspected) most dangerously and mortally sickened and languished, and not long after by the same wicked and detestable arts (as is likewise suspected,) died; and so the said constable and overseers do present that said Charles Garlick, by the ways and means aforesaid, most wickedly and maliciously, and feloniously was (as is suspected) murdered by the said Indian, Poniute, at the time and place aforesaid, against the peace and against the laws of this government in such cases provided."

The first witness called was the father of the lad who had died so suddenly, who deposed on oath, that early in the morning, on the day of his death, the youth left his home and accompanied the Indian in search of herbs. He was then in his usual health. That, on his return late in the afternoon, he complained that he had been suffering from violent cramps, but that an herb which the Indian had given him had relieved the pain in a goodly degree, but fearing that his son had been foully dealt with, the father of the lad burned the remains of the herb which had been left to complete the cure according to the Indian's direction. Scarcely had he arrived at his home when the cramps returned, and rapidly increased in violence, whereupon the leech was summoned, but, dwelling at a distance, he came too late to be of assistance. The boy was breathing his last.

Goodwife Garlick,[1] the mother of the youth, but confirmed her husband's testimony, and was dismissed, when the physician took the stand, but could add little to the testimony; the lad had died in spasms, and was past all earthly aid before the doctor's arrival.

Thereafter several depositions were read from persons accusing the prisoner of having been seen crossing the lake and entering the wigwam of the medicine-man, presumably to obtain some philter or poison concocted by the medicine-man while practising the unholy rite called the pow-wow.

When the depositions had been read and the testimony concluded, the clerk, calling the name of the prisoner in a loud voice, ordered him to raise his hand, which the prisoner refused to do, remaining immovable and glowering in the faces of the constable and magistrate without making answer.

Aware of the stubborn nature with which he had to deal, the magistrate signed the clerk to proceed with his duty, whereupon the clerk read as follows:

" Poniute, thou standest here indicted for that, having not the fear of God before thine eyes, thou didst, upon the twentieth day of August, and at several other occasions before (as is suspected), by some wicked and detestable arts, commonly called witchcraft and sorcery, maliciously and feloniously practise and exercise upon the body of Charles Garlick, by which said arts the said Charles Garlick, (as is suspected) most dangerously and mortally fell sick, and languished unto death. Poniute, what dost

[1] Goodwife Garlick, at a later date, was herself arraigned for being suspected of practising witchcraft, and sent to Hartford for trial.

thou say for thyself? Art thou guilty or not guilty?"

"The white man lies!"

Specks of foam had settled upon the prisoner's writhing lips, his eyes were lurid with smouldering fire, his voice broke forth deep as the rumble of distant thunder.

The violent thumping of the tithing man's wand came as an echo to the defiant answer; the Court gazed across the sea of faces upturned to catch every expression of the prisoner's features.

Through the open door the magistrate perceived a score of scowling visages—copper-hued braves were hovering near, and his heart gave a bound of terror.

"Thy lack of knowledge of the laws of the country and ignorance of civilised courts must excuse thy insolence, prisoner at the bar," he declared; "I therefore refer thy case to the jury."

The Indian's eyes gleamed with contempt as he turned his head and looked significantly in the direction where the tufted heads of the warriors broke the monotony of the rough hats of the settlers in the background.

"In conclusion I would recommend the prisoner to the mercy of the twelve jurors, good men and true, and I charge you to weigh well the evidence, that no injustice be done our red brother," concluded the magistrate in a sonorous tone that was easily heard beyond the open door.

The jury, twelve hard-headed planters, with stern faces and grave demeanour, retired apart to consult, and scarcely ten minutes were consumed in summing up the evidence and bringing a verdict:

"We, having the fear of God before our eyes, and having severally considered the case committed to our charge against the prisoner at the bar, and having well weighed the evidence, we find there are some suspicions by the evidence, of what the man is charged with, but nothing considerable of value to take away his life. However, we find that he is guilty of consulting with conjurers who perform the worship of the devil. We would recommend him to the mercy of the Court."

Whereupon the Court arose and pronounced sentence:

"By the laws it is enacted that 'no Indian shall be suffered to pow-wow, or perform worship to the devil, in any town within this government,' and in accordance with the law, and whereas the prisoner has been found guilty of consulting and consorting with a sorcerer, it is the decree of this Court that said prisoner be taken hence to the public whipping-post, there to receive two dozen stripes, after which punishment he shall be released and hath liberty to remain in the towne where he now resides, or anywhere else within the government during his pleasure."

CHAPTER XXIV

THE MAJESTY OF THE LAW

> "Is not the winding up of witnesses,
> And nicking, more than half the business?
> For witnesses, like watches, go
> Just as they're set, too fast, or slow;
> And where in conscience they're straight-lac'd,
> 'Tis ten to one that side is cast."

PONIUTE, manacled as he was, was taken away, his chains clanking dismally as he followed the constable, a stout guard walking on his right and left, while gruff laughter and gibing scoffs were indulged in by the more reckless among the crowd, as the rabble rushed to the square where the whipping-post stood, in proximity with two other instruments of torture that were considered, by the most humane, part and parcel of a settlement in the early colonial days, the pillory [1] and the stocks.[2]

---

[1] The pillory was an instrument of punishment in early colonial days. A heavy plank was tilted to an angle and raised or lowered by means of thick pins fitted in two supporting posts. In apertures fitted to the size of his neck and wrists the culprit was fastened in a manner that allowed his chin and hands to rest upon the upper side of the plank, which was graded to a height allowing his toes only to rest upon the ground. Did his muscles relax for an instant from the fearful strain, he was suspended and compelled by strangulation to sustain his weight upon his toes.

[2] *Stocks.*—A kind of frame or fence constructed of planks, two in number, nailed to posts. Through apertures in the lower plank his ankles were secured, and the wrists similarly secured in an upper plank. The culprit being seated upon the ground, with feet and arms raised at an angle of forty-five degrees, was forced to maintain a most painful attitude for hours.

One stall in each was occupied, the pillory by a white man of brutal visage, whose inflamed eyes and puffy cheeks marked him as an inordinate tippler, and who was suffering the punishment under an action for defamation, the verdict of the jury having been rendered thus:

"Wee finde for ye Plaintive, first our charges, and the said James Gill to be placed five hours in ye pillory, and then to be banished out of this jurisdiction; with this proviso, y^t his creditors will bee bound to keep him in good behaviour, or else to sell him out of our jurisdiction for two years' service, and the towne be noe more troubled with him."

Judgment was granted accordingly by the Court, and the offender was undergoing the preliminary punishment.

Near at hand a powerful Indian was confined in the stocks. His offence had been a trivial one, but it was a breach of the law, that "Noe Indian shall Digg for ground-nuts in the plain, or digg in any ground, upon penalty of sitting in the stocks for ye first fault, and for the second to be whipped. And if any of ye English see any Indian howing [3] or digging as aforesaid, they may peaceably bring them to the magistrates, if they can; if not to take the hoes or digging instruments away from them; and this to take effect as soon as the Sachem or Indians have warning thereof."

Confined by wrists and ankles, seated upon the ground, his body leaning forward, the Indian was enduring the punishment and worse than all, the galling taunts of the bystanders who pointed the finger of scorn.

His eyes glittered with a deadlier light as Poniute was led past the spot and conducted to the whip-

[3] *Howing.*—Hoeing.

"Slowly, with an interval between each stroke, the cat-o-nine tails fell —"

ping-post, which was thickly crusted with spots that had been crimson ere the sun and storm had darkened them to brown.

The haughty savage neared the spot, looking in every direction save the shameful goal, and shout after shout of derision greeted his ears as he halted.

For a moment he struggled fiercely with the manacles that clasped his limbs—all in vain; the rough irons but wounded the flesh, the strong clasps held him as in a vice, and his struggles ceased.

It was the work of a moment to secure his wrists to the thick ring driven in the post, his back was bared, and the punishment began. Slowly, with an interval between each stroke, the cat-o'-nine-tails [4] fell, while the copper-hued back began to trickle with redder drops, as with straining eyeballs and clenched hands the proud warrior underwent the degrading torture, only the quickened heaving of his broad chest telling of the pain he was enduring. Not even a sigh escaped his lips.

Again and again with cruel precision the blows fell, the lashes hissing spitefully, the man who wielded it, with long sinewy arms, applying himself to his task as if it were a pleasure rather than a duty, while the crowd watched the proceedings, some with mere curiosity, others with callousness that told the hatred that human beings often feel for those whom they have already wronged.

Henry Lawrence stood at a little distance, his teeth set hard, his face whitening with suppressed anger.

"This is infamous, under the circumstances!" he exclaimed, heedless that his remonstrance might be construed into a breach of law. "Had this poor

---

[4] *Cat-o'-nine-tails.*—A whip having nine lashes, used for flogging in the navy and army.

fellow been proved guilty of a crime there would be an excuse for such barbarity, but on a trumped-up charge—faugh! it makes the punishment an outrage on humanity!"

The Indian's quick ear caught the words, which he evidently understood, for he turned his bloodshot eyes on the speaker, a glance of gratitude breaking through the expression of agony and revenge.

"Have a care, lad!" admonished Lyon Gardiner, to whom the remarks had been addressed. "The punishment is certainly severe, and in my opinion unjust, but an open expression of such sentiments will but add fuel to the fire, and can be productive of no good. While I freely admit to you that I do not approve of such high-handed measures, I am powerless to stop, or even mitigate, the punishment. Thank God, it will soon be over!"

"I have had enough of it! let us go," returned Lawrence. "I have seen flogging in the army, but never without cause, or what was made apparent by reliable testimony; if I read that warrior's expression aright there will be retribution for this day's work."

"What's the haste? What's to do?" called Guy Kingsland. "This is the first punishment I have seen dealt out to a redskin, and I've a mind to see if he will stand it without flinching to the end. Alack-a-day! thus far he bears it like a Spartan; might be a block of stone for all the sign he has given—game to the core, eh?"

Major Gordon stood beside the Lieutenant, solacing himself with frequent pinches of Scotch snuff from a gold-inlaid teak-wood box of ample dimensions, watching the proceedings grimly, but making no remark.

With an exclamation of anger and pity, Lawrence turned away, elbowing the crowd until he stood outside the cordon of human beings. intent on witnessing the punishment.

Captain Gardiner followed at his heels, but the scene must have possessed a peculiar fascination for both the Major and Lieutenant, for they remained near the post until the full measure of the sentence had been inflicted, and the executioner dropped the blood-stained lash upon the green sward, where it trailed like a glistening crimson snake-knot, while the man leaned against the post, panting heavily from the violence of his late exercise.

A rough plantation hand stepped forward and released the prisoner, who, in spite of his nerve and iron will, staggered helplessly forward, his arms hanging limply by his side. One moment he reeled dizzily, and then, by an almost superhuman effort, the degraded warrior raised himself to his full height and looked about him, the maniacal glare of the gladiator, pitted against wild beasts, in his eyes. All the ferocity of his nature was aroused, and barely held in abeyance, while his fingers clenched and unclenched, and his white teeth ground together with a click that caused Kingsland to shiver as he heard the sound and met the stare in that basilisk eye.

Again, in spite of all his firmness, the proud warrior faltered as he reached the spot where Captain Gardiner and Colonel Lawrence awaited the coming of their companions.

Nature, even Indian nature, could endure no more; notwithstanding his utmost efforts to conquer his weakness, Poniute reeled blindly against the trunk of a knotted oak, and sank to the ground like some savage animal wounded to the death, his sightless eyes open wide.

In a moment Henry Lawrence was kneeling by his side.

"Hark'ee, Captain, there's nothing in your beastly laws that will forbid an act of mercy to this poor devil, and if there is, why, demme, I'll e'en take the consequences! Here, poor fellow, take a pull at my brandy flask, it will set you up, lad!"

He held the flask to the swooning man's lips, and the Indian swallowed a hearty draught.

"Look alive, Colonel!" exclaimed Lieutenant Kingsland, who had hastened to join his friends. "If I am informed correctly you are breaking the law at this blessed minute; you have no authority to give an Indian brandy—there's a statute against it!"

"What's all that clatter?" asked the Colonel.

"Is it not so, Captain?" asked Guy, turning to Gardiner.

"Verily," returned the Captain, "the statute says no person shall 'sell, truck, barter, give or deliver any strong liquor to an Indian under penalty of forty shillings for one pint, and in proportion for any greater or lesser quantity, except in case of sudden extremity, and then not exceeding two drams.' So the law reads, but marry, my lad, it strikes me this is a case of sudden extremity."

"I'll give him a full pint if he needs it, and pay my fine without a grimace. Gramercy! it strikes me that the statutes to protect white men are multiplied, but where is the law for the Indian? Courage, man!" addressing the warrior, who had partly raised himself from the ground, but fell back exhausted and setting his teeth hard from the pain he was enduring, "let me lift this rough blanket which is no fit covering for such bruises. God A'mighty! Look here Captain, this is horrible!"

The Colonel ground out the words between his

teeth as he lifted the heavy blanket and exposed the lacerated shoulders that were seamed as if from the strokes of a knife blade.

"Zounds! what do you think of that, Major?" cried Captain Gardiner, in angry tones.

But the Major made no reply, and neither he nor the Lieutenant offered the slightest assistance while Gardiner brought water in his hat from a stream near at hand and held it, and the Colonel bathed the wounds by dipping his handkerchief in the cool water and laving the surface as tenderly as if his were a woman's hands.

"Demme, Captain, that fellow yon must have the strength of a giant to inflict such punishment. One would imagine he was chosen for the strength of muscle," grumbled the Colonel.

"The yokel was obliged to do his duty, else he might have chanced to get a taste of the cat upon his own shoulders," said the Major, philosophically.

"It is unsafe to carry such a free tongue while on trial, and it is not altogether safe for even officers of the English army to cavil at the punishment awarded to law-breakers," put in the Lieutenant.

Kingsland believed the sufferer to be too insensible to make out the drift of the conversation, but that Poniute both heard and understood Captain Gardiner knew by the sudden fierce gleam shot from between his half closed lids.

The wounds were cleansed at last, and while the Captain cast the water from his dripping hat, which he shook sharply ere he replaced it upon his head, the Colonel took from his own neck a silken scarf, and spreading it smoothly across the lacerated shoulders, he drew the blanket over it.

"Take another pull at the brandy, my friend,

God knows you need it!" spoke Lawrence, again holding the flask to the Indian's lips.

"White brother pay fine," answered the warrior. "Poniute go now."

"Take it, it will make my red brother strong. You know there is a law against an Indian being found loitering in the town; the sooner you get back to the village the safer you will be," advised Captain Gardiner. "Take it," insisted the Captain; "never mind the fine, you must not risk another dozen, my lad."

"Demme, Captain, let's take him to his lodge; he is not strong enough to go by himself," protested the Colonel. "There shall be no more such infernal work and I stand by!"

Ere the Captain could reply Poniute raised his hands to his lips and gave a long, peculiar cry, a shrill, wailing sound that reverberated through the forest like the call of some hoarse night bird.

In response a score of warriors emerged from the shelter of a wall of boulders skirting the path, each armed with tomahawk and knife, which he drew from beneath the folds of his blanket, and at the sudden apparition Kingsland and the Major started violently, while a smile of derision hovered upon the lips of the wounded man.

"Pale-face brothers go now—Poniute's red brothers take him to his wigwam—Indian not forget good white brothers—remember bad white men too."

Evidently the Indians were prepared for the emergency, and dragging a litter from its concealment in the thick undergrowth of brush and vines they spread blankets thereon, lifted their companion, and in another moment the soft tread of their moccasins died away on the path carpeted with a thick layer of pine needles.

CHAPTER XXV

NINIGRET'S CAPTIVES

"The sun sets at night and the stars shun the day,
But glory remains when the light fades away;
Begin, ye tormenters, your threats are in vain,
For the son of Alnoomock will never complain.

"Remember the arrows he shot from his bow,
Remember your chiefs by his hatchet laid low;
O why do ye wait till I shrink from my pain?
For the son of Alnoomock will never complain.

"Remember the spot where in ambush he lay,
The scalps that he bore from your nation away,
The flame rises fast, you exult in my pain,
But the son of Alnoomock will never complain.

"I will go to the land where my father has gone,
And he shall exult in the fame of his son;
Death comes, like a friend, to release me from pain,
And the son of Alnoomock will never complain."

A LINE of unbroken forest fringing the shore of Block Island, save for a green glade opening, fan-like, from the water's edge, and sloping gradually upward to the point where the forest trees met at the apex of the angle, the earth softly carpeted with moss and starry with autumn flowers, a sylvan nook fashioned by nature's hand, upon which the moon, now but a narrow sickle in the western sky, shed a faint, ghostly light, but myriads of solemn stars floated in the dome above, their light paling in the red glare of torches throwing out sheets of flame and dancing in fantastic swirls upon the figures moving backward and forward in the lurid light, like gnomes and satyrs.

Such was the picture presented to the crew, the knot of soldiers, and the two passengers grouped upon the deck of an armed brig floating the cross of St. George, one of many that were constantly cruising among the islands and along the shores of the mainland as a protection to the English settlements.

From the shore fierce cries and infernal whoops rent the air, rolling out over the waters where the stars kissed the waves rippling softly against the keel of the *Gerfalcon* in strange contrast to that red, angry beacon of death upon shore.

Suddenly the mad dance ceased, a yell rose as a pennon of flame shot upward from a dark mass of brushwood, narrow at first like the cleft tongue of a serpent reaching for its prey, but widening to a broad banner of lurid red.

Again and again that ferocious howl went up, gathering in volume as savage after savage took up the yell.

Congregated within that circle of light were fully a hundred screeching fiends, brandishing their tomahawks, war-clubs, spears and scalping-knives, each leaping, dancing and gesticulating in the horrid illumination reaching far out over the waters in a red glare, and lighting the background of forest trees with a brazen pencil from Tophet.

The two passengers were Colonel Lawrence and Captain Gardiner, who were aboard the *Gerfalcon* for the benefit of a cruise along shore; both were standing upon deck.

"For God's sake, Captain, look yon!" exclaimed the Colonel; "there are three victims bound to that infernal stake, a man, a little child, and—my God! I believe it is a woman!"

"Your glass, Colonel," cried the Captain, excitedly. "I think I recognise the victims—I must make sure."

"Ah-h!" groaned he, after looking intently through the glass, "it is as I thought,—old Ascassasatic, his daughter, Wy-tit-tee, and her little daughter Mary—named for my dame. I knew they were prisoners, but had no idea the Narragansetts, bold as they are, would carry their vengeance to such a pitch—that the three would be held for ransom I made sure."

Even as he spoke fresh heaps of pine boughs were piled in the circle, and as the flames shot higher, lancing the black smoke-clouds eddying in circles, tiny spires of flame licked the boughs and ignited the foliage of the trees, against which the three nearly nude figures stood out with startling distinctness.

The child, a mere infant of four years, stretched her wee arms toward her mother, who bent forward as far as possible, that her long abundant hair, falling in a black cloud to her waist, might veil her babe from the rain of burning pine needles falling like a shower of blazing stars, while she tugged madly at the bonds that held her waist and wrists.

To the trunk of a second tree but a few feet distant the tall, majestic figure of an aged warrior was bound, his hair bleached by the snows of nearly four score winters.

"The cursed Narragansetts are putting them to the torture, ne'er a doubt," exclaimed Captain How. "On my soul, it must be the three you speak of. If I am well informed, this Ascassasatic is the chief counsellor of Wyandance, and as such an object of dread to his enemies."

"No matter who they are!" broke in Lawrence,

eagerly, "there is no time to lose—we must rescue them at once, or we shall be too late!"

"Prithee, Colonel, I've no authority to risk my men in such a case as this," spoke Captain How, uneasily; "if they were white prisoners the case would be different. We have to consider that the devils outnumber us four to one. See how they swarm! more than a hundred, if there's one!"

Every eye was scanning the terrible tableau.

A low murmur deepened to a groan.

"See, Captain, the men are chafing like tigers—let them loose, for the love of God, and allow me to call for volunteers. There's not one among the ship's crew or soldiers but would eagerly respond, I'll lay fifty pounds," urged Lawrence. "See the flames are creeping closer! even now the helpless woman and child must begin to feel the scorching heat; let me have a handful of your men, only such as are willing to follow me!" pleaded Lawrence.

"It is sheer madness, but have your will, Colonel," returned Captain How. "Make your call, and all who volunteer are at liberty to go, provided there are men enough left to work the ship."

"Ho, men, soldiers and crew of the *Gerfalcon!* who among you will follow me on shore to save that woman, that babe, that infirm old man from being roasted alive?" called the Colonel, in stentorian tones.

"I!" responded Captain Gardiner.

"I!" "I!" "I!" and the hearty response came from every man on that deck, soldiers, sailors, and even the cabin boy.

"Lower the boats!" shouted Captain How. "Let enough remain aboard to fire a broadside, if necessary; we may be obliged to throw a few balls among that cursed herd!"

The order was obeyed with alacrity, only a sufficient number remained aboard, and reluctantly enough, to stand ready for an emergency. Like swallows the boats skimmed across the water, and speedily the party landed, with the exception of the oarsmen, who remained to care for the boats.

From the deck of the *Gerfalcon* the picture had been frightful, but near at hand the horrors were intensified.

The loud shrieks of the child, who already began to feel the blistering heat, rose sharply, and the poor young mother strove frantically to sever the cruel bonds and gather her infant to her bosom, all the agony she was enduring pictured in her face, while groans and entreaties broke from her lips—not that her enemies would spare her life, but that they would save her child.

Lyon Gardiner heard and understood her frenzied appeal, and the tears coursed down his cheeks as he rushed silently forward, by the Colonel's side, clearing the ground with great bounds, followed closely by the detachment, all, as yet unseen by the savages, their approach being covered by the dense darkness beneath the thick pines.

The aged Indian, true to his race and breeding, was singing or rather chaunting his death-song, his taunting notes rising above the horrid discord of voices, the crackling of the flames and the frightful din of beating tom-toms, as the nearly nude demons danced, whirled and leaped in the red glare of the death-fire, horrible in war-paint, bedizened in feathers, their tossing scalplocks writhing like serpents endowed with life.

Derisively Ascassasatic flaunted his deeds of daring when on the war-path against the Narragansetts, boasting of the scalps he had taken from their nation, of his prowess in single combat, until the passions of his tormentors were raised to a pitch of insane fury, and one brave, a young man, suddenly halted and flung his tomahawk full at the head of the gibing prisoner.

A hand gripped the youthful brave, as Ninigret hurled him backward with a force that felled him to the earth, while the tomahawk, barely missing the head of the old warrior, quivered in the trunk of the tree to which he was bound, scarcely a hair's-breadth from his ear.

Fortunately the fagots had been piled at a distance from the stakes, that the victims might suffer a greater, more lingering torture; but as Lawrence and his men leaped ashore fresh bundles of pine were cast upon the still green branches, and for a moment a thick volume of smoke rolled up, hiding the victims from view. Then the flames burst forth afresh, dancing and curling in the light breeze that sprang up to fan them, and roaring like insatiate dragons. And again the smoke lifted, disclosing the three forms of the sufferers, and a fiercer, deadlier yell arose—howls that were suddenly silenced by a roar of musketry from the thicket on their right, their left, and in the rear, and a storm of bullets that rattled like hailstones, or struck with a dull thud, was poured in by the assailants who had separated, one division, under Colonel Lawrence filing to the right, the second, led by Captain Gardiner, marching to the left after gaining the rear of the encampment, thus forming a semicircle, hemming in the Narragansetts on every side except where the sea hindered their flight.

The suddenness and fierceness of the onset threw them in dire confusion. Not a foeman was in view.

So completely had they been absorbed in their cruel pastime that they had not turned their eyes seaward, and had failed to notice the brig looming up like a dim ghost under the faint light of the stars and the young moon floating upon the very edge of the western horizon like a fairy boat.

A second volley was poured in on flank and rear, and with howls of rage the brawny warriors leaped back from the circle of light into the gloom.

With a ringing shout Colonel Lawrence led in the fray upon the right, Captain Gardiner on the left, as the assailants burst from their covert and rushed, with drawn cutlasses, upon the panic-stricken horde.

CHAPTER XXVI

A PARTHIAN SHOT

"He is a soldier, fit to stand by Cæsar
And give direction."

IT was a terrific battle that raged for the space of five minutes around that circle of fire-brands that had been scattered in the brushwood, where the flames caught in the resinous pine needles and ran riot among the dry leaves and creeping vines carpeting the earth, shrivelling the green foliage and darting dragon-tongued, hither and thither as the spears of tall grass or brown twigs fed and determined their course.

Animated by the ringing shouts of their leaders, the white men fought with a fury that was irresistible, and one after another the red men went down beneath the murderous sweep of the broadsword and cutlass, wielded by stout arms, their tufted heads cloven by the weapons against which their knives were but a sorry defence.

The whiz of arrows, the crash of descending tomahawks and murderous war-clubs, the spiteful bark of the English bulldogs,[1] the hiss of the circling broadswords, mingled with the groans of the wounded and dying.

In five minutes, upon the spot where the death-fire had been kindled, there remained only a few smouldering embers and half-consumed boughs,

---
[1] *English bulldogs.*—Pistols of heavy calibre.

blackened, and emitting little puffs of pungent smoke. The trees to which the prisoners had been bound stood with scorched branches, the green withes with which they had been secured lay coiled about the roots. The prisoners had vanished, for, at the first onset the broadsword in the hands of a marine had severed the bonds, and the scorched prisoners had fled like hares in the direction of the boats to which the soldier pointed, and were safe in the light ship's boat floating upon the water, waiting for the human freight.

Through all the carnage the tall, lordly Lawrence passed unscathed, his sword flashing in circles or descending like a lightning bolt, beneath which many a plumed warrior sank.

Panic-stricken, the surviving Narragansetts fled into the denser depths of the fastnesses, scattering like a pack of wolves driven frightened from their prey, their inhuman yells stilled, their hideous orgies ended.

The field was won, but as Henry Lawrence turned to gather his followers an arrow sped, almost as noiselessly as a dead leaf falls, from an unseen marksman concealed in a tangle of dwarf alders. A keen pain darted through his frame as the blunt arrowhead was buried in his shoulder.

It was a Parthian shot from Ninigret's bow, and with a loud yell of defiance the chief bounded away after his flying savages, the swift crashing of brush and brake telling of the speed of his flight.

It would have been madness to follow, and the little detachment of white men made their way to the waiting boats, two bearing a dead comrade, others assisting the Colonel and the three sailors who had been wounded, leaving the dead and wounded Narragansetts prone upon the battlefield, beneath the stars now paling in a murky cloud settling low above the tree tops, and darkening the azure heavens as if a storm lay embosomed in a circumscribed space above the shore line.

A lively pull brought the boats alongside the *Gerfalcon*, and obedient to the surgeon's orders the wounded were conveyed below, and the dead sailor was taken to a sheltered portion of the deck and wrapped in a roll of sail-cloth.

"Poor Crowell, he'll never reef sail again," sighed Captain How. "He was as fine a hand and as brave a lad as ever sailed the seas!"

"Dead as Pharaoh," answered the mate. "His head was crushed in by a blow from a war-club at the very last moment before the devils broke and run."

"Ye gods and little fishes! There's an encampment on that slope beyond the pine belt, and the wigwams are ablaze! What the devil, man! did you set their lodges afire?" exclaimed Captain How.

"Faith! not we!" returned Captain Gardiner, indignantly. "There was too much of that kind of work when the Pequot fort was burned, and women and children perished miserably in the flames. Good God, see! Look at the squaws and papooses yon, running like partridges!" he continued as a volume of flame shot above the tree tops, dancing and swirling in red sheets that lit up the scene with frightful distinctness.

It was owing to their preoccupation on board the *Gerfalcon* that none had noticed the smoke on shore, and guessed nothing of the truth.

"Thank God we had nothing to do with that work!" called the Colonel. "They set their own fire when they lighted the funeral pyre yon, and it must be that when we scattered the burning brands the fire caught the pine needles; the woods are dry as tinder at this season, and the blaze they set with their own hands is burning them out."

A breeze that suddenly sprang up was driving the flame shoreward, the conflagration lighting up the green, foam-fringed waves as it swept rapidly toward the water's edge.

"An' ye had naught to do with the setting o' the fire, we have naught to do with the quenching," declared Captain How.

The errand upon which they had landed was accomplished, and as soon as all the ship's crew were aboard and accounted for, it was decided to return to Gardiner Hall on account of the wound sustained by Colonel Lawrence.

"Get the brig under weigh, Mr. Morle!" called Captain How, to the mate.

"Aye, aye, sir!" responded the mate.

A moment later all hands were piped to quarters by the boatswain's whistle, then came the order, bawled from the quarterdeck.

"Be lively, there, my hearties! man the braces, stand by your halyards! Hoist away on your jib and flying jib! Pay her off to port, and then haul close to the wind!"

"Aye, aye, sir!" was the hearty response, and in an incredibly short time the *Gerfalcon*, that had been under spanker and forestay sail while Lawrence and his men had gone to the rescue of the Montauks, was bowling along, close-hauled, with her starboard tacks aboard, careening to the strong breeze that had sprung up from the southwest at the early morn, with the high headland of Montauk bearing ahead.

Meanwhile the arrow-head wound in Henry Lawrence's shoulder was giving him no little pain, and was a source of the greatest apprehension, as the pain was becoming more unbearable with each succeeding moment.

Upon examination it was found that the arrow had pierced the shoulder below the armpit, and had struck the point of the blade. That the arrow had been poisoned the swelling and telltale purplish hue of the skin attested, Captains How and Gardiner both averred, and finally old Ascassasatic, who had just been saved from a horrible death at the stake, was summoned to the cabin to look at the wound and prescribe.

"Arrow poison—no coup,"[2] was all he said. Then pressing the swollen incision between the thumb and index finger of each hand, and pressing it gently, but firmly, he began sucking the wound with a power that made the patient groan with pain.

"Keep your nerve, lad!" exclaimed Gardiner. "I know the old buck has the right of it! Ne'er a fear that the operation is an experiment with him."

Meanwhile the Indian had succeeded in extracting a quantity of heavy black blood from the now gaping, bleeding wound, and after a time he desisted and desired some tobacco, with which he made a poultice and applied it to the wounded part, which soon had a soothing effect.

This done, the old Indian explained that the wound would not be dangerous, as the bone had stopped the arrow, and the surrounding tissues did not readily absorb the poison.

In due time the *Gerfalcon*, which was accounted a good sailor, having held her wind and aided by a strong flood tide, had reached her destined haven, standing in well, for the water there was very bold. The brig was brought to the wind two cables' length

[2] *Coup.*—Kill.

from the shore, and the village of the Montauks was abeam.

Tacks and sheets were lighted, braces were slackened, topsails were clewed up, and the *Gerfalcon* lay off-and-on while a boat was lowered and manned to land the three Montauks who had been rescued from the Narragansetts.

When this was accomplished the vessel was again hauled on the wind with her port tacks aboard, to run over to Man-cho-nock, where in due time she was rounded-to and cast anchor in the offing adjacent to Gardiner Hall, and the Captain, with his chivalrous guest, returned to shore to recount to their friends the stirring events of the voyage.

CHAPTER XXVII

"'TWIXT LOVE AND DUTY"

"Why did she love him? Curious fool! be still;
Is human love the growth of human will?"

"Then there were sighs, the deeper for suppression,
And stolen glances, sweeter for the theft,
And burning blushes, tho' for no transgression,
Tremblings when met, and restlessness when left."

THE weeks glided past, summer had merged into autumn, and the brief Indian summer came, glorious October days when nature, attired in her gorgeous robes of crimson, orange, russet, and the few remaining touches of the summer's tender green, appears in her most lovely and enticing aspect.

It was not until Colonel Lawrence had been a guest at Gardiner Hall for days that Damaris Gordon discovered the poetic, tender nature hidden beneath his usually cold, but courteous manner, and insensibly she began to yield admiration to the subtle charm of his personality.

A spirit worship for all that was grand and ennobling had ever been a trait in the character of the young girl, a sort of hero worship which the worldly, ambitious nature of Guy Kingsland had failed to satisfy.

Betrothed in childhood, no thought of escaping the bonds forged for her had ever crossed in her mind. And Kingsland, aware of her loyalty of heart and her strict, almost morbid sense of duty, and with naught but a thoroughly selfish love actuating his conduct, never dreamed of danger from the companionship of his fiancée with this sedate, self-contained man, so many years her senior, and with a degree of reserve, even stiffness of manner, that was by no means calculated to attract a young and sensitive girl whom the gay Lieutenant treated with such flattery as he would have bestowed upon a spoiled child, whispering soft words and highly seasoned compliments in the pretty pink ear, which, truth to tell, palled upon her appetite, but were received as a matter of course, as they had been from her childhood.

And so it came to pass that Guy, at length believing Heather Flower heedless of the past, forgot his fears and rowed almost daily to Montauk, where he followed the chase or whiled away his hours in the sport of fishing, in reality feeling vastly relieved of what he had come to consider the rather irksome duty of entertaining his betrothed; while she, all unconscious of danger, beguiled the tedious hours of the Colonel's convalescence from the illness induced by his wound, by reading or conversation.

In truth she had been his nurse and companion, for the Major, indolent by nature, and with a brain filled with schemes for his own benefit, had evaded the monotony of a life within doors, while Captain Gardiner, the most active of individuals, had a perfect horror of a sick room, contenting himself with morning and evening calls, and a tender of all the hall afforded; and Mrs. Gardiner, busied with the superintendence of her household and the welfare of her children, had scant time for the care of the invalid, gladly delegating to Damaris what she considered a trifling duty.

And Damaris, ere she was aware, began to remember the hours spent in the sick room as something to to be looked forward to, a pleasure rather than a duty.

There was a depth of intellect, a brilliancy, a vivid imagination, a poetic soul hidden beneath Colonel Lawrence's reserve that stirred her young heart like a strain of martial music and awakened the melody dormant in her own soul like the hand of a master spirit. By degrees the beauties of his grand character were revealed, the strength of principle, the wealth of intellect, the tenderness underlying the outward hauteur came to the surface.

She had thought him cold and impassive; he had regarded her as a child, petted and spoiled, a mere butterfly basking in the sunlight of affection, beautiful—he acknowledged that, but frivolous and thoughtless, with no depth of character, and fitted only to grace a drawing-room, as became the wife of precisely such a man as he knew Guy Kingsland to be.

And in this mistaken estimate of each other their great danger lay, and had not fate sufficed to draw them in daily companionship they might never have understood each other.

But the hours passed in the seclusion of the low-ceiled, commodious drawing-room at the hall, or in rambling in the leafy avenues intersecting the forest, after the Colonel was sufficiently convalescent to admit of out-of-door exercise, revealed the knowledge that was like a thunderbolt.

The maiden he had deemed so frivolous he found to be loving, spirited, tender and truthful. His eyes were opened and he knew why that dwelling in the wilderness had been suddenly transformed to a paradise, that forest-shadowed, sea-girt spot to an Eden.

Then it was that his nobility of soul asserted itself;

his fine sense of honour forbade the slightest expression of love to the betrothed of another, and marked out his course. Even before his health was perfectly restored he absented himself from the society of the maiden as frequently as possible without provoking comment, sometimes joining Guy in his hunting trips, or wandering away upon long excursions to some remote portion of the island, thus avoiding the companionship that had become so perilously sweet, while she, piqued by his sudden coolness, remained in her own chamber for hours, and when, by chance, she met Colonel Lawrence her replies to his courteous but formal greetings were as distant as the strictest etiquette would permit.

But in spite of his iron will, his stern resolve, he loved Damaris Gordon with all the strength of his noble soul; the love that had conquered him could not be exorcised by even his brave, loyal spirit.

With his sudden reticence came the awakening to the gentle maiden that, all unsought, she had given the love that had never been Guy's into the keeping of this king among men; the heart that had been sleeping had been touched with a burning coal from love's altar, and the knowledge brought a keen pang such as she had never experienced. She had been a dreaming child—now she was a loving woman and must pay the penalty of her heart-worship; but with all the subtle instinct born of that love she knew his heart was all her own, and that her lover was striving with the strength of an upright nature to silence the voice of affection deep in his heart, to maintain the honour that bade him conquer, for the sake of the being he loved.

Not a thought of breaking her troth-plight occurred to Damaris Gordon, while the love the gallant Colonel bore that pure young maiden was too deep and fervent to admit of a step that might bring her the deepest sorrow, for he divined that Major Gordon would never consent to a severance of the chain that bound his fair young daughter to the man of his choice.

And thus both struggled against the love that had stolen upon them unawares, and which Henry Lawrence vainly strove to mould into the semblance of friendship. Delusive effort, for with the opportunity came the day when the mutual confession flashed from eye to eye, and in the electric thrill when their hands met by chance, until, at last, their lips confessed in spite of the strict guard both had kept over every action.

It was by chance, or rather fate, that the twain met upon the very spot where, weeks before, Guy Kingsland had been detected by Heather Flower in his interview with his betrothed which had resulted in such fearful changes in the lives of more than the twain.

In the gloaming Damaris had wandered to the secluded nook and seated herself upon the rustic bench which Guy's hands had fashioned. Twilight deepened into night, the moon sailed up from the broad expanse of waters to the eastward, that already mirrored countless stars set in the arch of blue.

Her heart was heavy, her eyes dimmed with unshed tears. Lawrence was going away, in spite of the efforts of Captain Gardiner and his lady to dissuade him, and too well Damaris divined the cause.

He had made the announcement, in the most matter-of-fact tone, at the breakfast table, and no eye, save his own, had noted the sudden pallor that mounted to her brow, or the drooping eyelids and quivering lips, and now she was quite unconscious that the slow tears had again gathered in her violet eyes and were falling, one by one, upon the slender hands lying idly in her lap.

The rustle of autumn leaves carpeting the path, the sound of a footfall, roused her from her painful reverie, a step she had learned to listen for and to recognise with quickening heartbeats.

Henry Lawrence—she knew that before the steps suddenly ceased and he stood before her in the moonlight.

She felt the blood surging to her forehead and receding, a deadly faintness overcoming her will,—her lips moved as if she would have spoken and bade him welcome, but no sound came.

For a moment he stood silently regarding her; then he quietly took a seat by her side.

He must have divined the cause of her agitation, for his own face paled, and his hand trembled as he stretched out his arm as if to enfold her, then instantly drew back, his lips closing firmly over his white teeth.

He felt the necessity of speech, but there was a choking huskiness in the voice he strove to render steady, and the words he uttered were the very opposite of what he had intended—the cry of a strong man from the depths of a wounded heart.

"How perfect is the evening—the last we shall ever spend together, for—to-morrow I must be far away. The delusive dreams I have cherished will mock me many a weary hour, and yet—yet the remembrance will be sweet, an oasis in my past—the dearest memory in life."

He spoke drearily, haltingly, rather as if communing with his own heart than addressing the gentle girl by his side.

The very thought of his leaving her was torture. She strove to raise her head, to frame a reply, but the beating of her heart was suffocating her, and only a half sob broke from her tremulous lips.

Strong man that he was, strong in his honour and integrity, he was powerless now to stem the torrent of love that swept away the barrier between two loving hearts. In that mad moment both forgot the tie that bound her to another, forgot all save that both loved, both suffered.

"My God!" he exclaimed, hoarsely, "has it indeed come to this? that I—I who would give life itself to save you from a single pang, should be the cause of your sorrow! Why did I not leave you while your heart was untouched by this fatal love? And yet, the angels in heaven might bear me witness that I never intended to win your heart—I had no intention of wronging the man whose plighted wife you are—the man whom you might have still continued to love had I not come between you, and unwittingly tempted you from your allegiance. May God forgive me and pity you!"

His strong arms encircled her, her cold, tear-wet cheek rested upon his breast.

"May God pardon me—I have never loved him!" whispered Damaris brokenly. "This love that binds me now was never his, not for one brief moment, but oh! I did not know that it was only such affection as a sister might give a brother that I gave him. How should I? I never dreamed of wronging him, and yet, how wicked I have been!"

"Don't! Don't!" he pleaded, softly. "Poor little lass, the sin, the wrong is mine—all my own. You are as innocent as an angel!"

His clasp tightened about the slender form he held in his embrace.

"Would to God mine alone could be the suffering," he groaned; "but that cannot be. We must part—better now than to put off the evil day. Hour after hour I have felt in my heart the danger of remaining, the while I have been too weak to sever the ties that bound me. God knows I love you too dearly to willingly inflict this pain. My darling, best beloved of my soul, can you forgive me?"

He gazed down into the white, frightened face resting so closely against his heart that she could count its muffled throbs, his eyes aglitter with pain, as he pleaded.

"I have nothing to forgive—nothing," she moaned. "The past has been but a dream, too bright to last, but it is useless to strive to deceive ourselves longer—yes—you must—must go away, and—in time we may—forget."

"I will go—will try to dissemble, but never, while life and memory remains, can I forget you, the one love of my life, my peerless, innocent Damaris—let me call you mine but this one, short moment," he answered, drearily, as he drew her in a closer embrace. "My own love, this must be our real parting, for to-morrow we must take leave only—only as friends."

A quick, springing step startled the lovers, Guy Kingsland, both knew, as he came swiftly down the path, trolling gaily the bars of a favourite army song:

> "In London lived a noble ladye,
> She was beautiful and gay,
> But this fair ladye had declared,
> No man alive her groom should be;
> Except it be some man of honour,
> Or some young man that she had seen,
> At length two suitors came a-courting,
> This fair ladye for to win."

"It is he, Kingsland, your betrothed husband. Damaris, for your own sake, be strong—for his, for mine," whispered Lawrence, as he rose from his seat, and forcing an outward calmness, nerved himself to meet the man who, in his inmost soul he distrusted, but scorned to wrong.

> "The one he was a brisk lieutenant,
> With sword and pistols by his side,
> The other, he was a brave young captain—"

"Halloa, Colonel!" broke off Guy, abruptly, as he came out into the moonlight. "I took you for nothing but a spook looming up in the ghostly moonlight. What the devil took you here? A thousand pardons for using naughty words in your presence, lassie," he continued, as he caught sight of Damaris, still seated upon the rustic bench. "'Pon honour, I did not see you."

Henry Lawrence had purposely interposed his tall figure between the agitated girl and her betrothed, to allow her a moment in which to compose her features and collect her thoughts.

Had Guy Kingsland loved deeply he might have taken alarm at her unwonted silence, but he was quite incapable of any depth of affection, and noticed nothing in the manner of either the girl or Colonel Lawrence to arouse a suspicion of the truth.

How thoroughly Damaris despised herself as Guy wound his arm about her waist with the freedom of an accepted lover, soon to be her husband, and led her away, her lips quivering in a grieved way as she saw the Colonel stretch out his hand involuntarily as if he would snatch her from the embrace of the man to whom she was bound.

Only for an instant. Then the brave soldier was himself again, and with a stern, set face he turned away in the direction of the beach, saying that he would linger yet a little under the bewitching moonlight.

And this was the real parting between the pair whom an ill-starred love had made miserable.

It was in the early morning that the few, brief words of a formal farewell were spoken, all that was granted those two who were parted by an inexorable fate, and then the wretched girl fled away to her own chamber, there to shed the bitterest tears that had ever fallen from her eyes during her short, bright life.

CHAPTER XXVIII

AN ANCIENT FAMILY

"Of noble race was Shenkin."

"He, above the rest
In shape and gesture proudly eminent
Stood like a tower."

UPON a peninsula stretching out between Flushing Bay and Whitestone, its shores washed by the green waters of Long Island Sound, a tract containing nine hundred acres of fertile land, and at the time of which we write called "Lawrence Neck," a dwelling had been reared that, even at the present time, would be considered a substantial mansion, and at the date of which we write was occupied by its proprietor, Captain William Lawrence, who had selected this woodland paradise as a fit setting for his home in America.

It was built of stone, and after the castellated style so frequently found in Old England, the long façade fronting on the Sound, the main building flanked by massive towers, the thick stone walls pierced for musketry, just below the parapet, the narrow slits serving also as outlooks in case of an attack from hostile savage or invading Dutch.

There was no stockade, such as was frequent in early colonial days, the dwelling itself being a stronghold capable of withstanding a storm of cannon-balls, and within the embrasure upon the heavy battlement crowning the eastern tower a swivel gun had been mounted, capable of a range that might sweep the dense, primeval forest framing in the mansion on three sides, crescent-formed, and which, as yet, the destroying axe had scarcely touched; the great gun also commanded the waters of the Sound dashing against the rock-ribbed shore at the foot of the long slope which the mansion crowned.

During the summer months Lawrence Hall was usually filled with guests, and hunting parties roamed through the woods or fished in the streams; but in late autumn and winter, and far into the spring, all was silent and dreary, the deep snows rendering the trails impassable, while the traffic between the hall and the outer world was carried on mainly through the medium of sloops and trading vessels touching at the little landing below the mansion.

Among the planters whose residences were scattered at long intervals along the shore, the Lawrence brothers, three in number, were famed alike for their high courage, their probity and their pride, as men quick and fierce to resent an insult or avenge an injury, but humane, upright in their dealings, and generous to a fault, withal bitter as foemen, or staunch as friends.

From time immemorial the Lawrences had been soldiers, serving in army or navy, and, as the annals of the family ran, the first known ancestor was a certain Sir Robert Laurens of Lancashire, who was knighted by Richard of the Lion Heart, under whom he served in the Crusades, his knighthood dating from 1191; coming down the line from this warlike progenitor the family traced their descent from Sir John Lawrence, who flourished in 1491, the ninth in descent from Sir Robert.

Inheriting all the valour and fiery temper of the old Crusader, Sir John had the misfortune to kill a gentleman usher of King Henry VII, for which act he was outlawed, and he died in exile, in France.

At that time Ashton Hall, his family seat in Lancashire, and the remainder of his estates passed by decree to his relatives, Lords Monteagle and Girard.

From generation to generation the fiery blood of Sir Robert, one of the boldest knights that drew sword against the Saracens in the Holy Land, had passed without adulteration to his descendants, and coursed as hotly in the veins of Henry Lawrence and his cousins, William Lawrence of Lawrence Hall, and Thomas and John, large landholders on the western portion of Long Island, as it had in the heart of their warlike progenitors.

The last red ray of the setting sun had faded slowly to amber and deepened to violet in the west, in the east a round, yellow moon sailed up in an opal sky, and one by one the stars flashed out.

Under the silvery light the forest trees, clothed in their gay autumnal attire, and the massive building looming up on the crest of the bold shore looked very fair and peaceful, and so thought Henry Lawrence as he leaned over the taffrail of the little schooner *Nightingale,* that was gallantly ploughing the green waves, leaving a long line of foam-wreath in its wake.

From the green gloom of the pines and firs lining the beach came the dismal hoot of the owl echoing over the waters and through the groves, like a warwhoop from savage throats.

"Well, Colonel, you're nigh the end of your journey. Yon is Lawrence's Neck, and we shall be at the landing presently," called Captain Dixon; "we've made a quick run, sir."

"Egad! I'm not sorry," returned Lawrence. "Listen to the hoarse croak of that bird of ill-omen.

Enough to give one the creeps, pealing out in the silence like the warning cry of the Banshee they prate of back there in Ireland. Prithee, but it is altogether a strange country, and a lonely, this. Ha! rather an imposing structure, judging from this distance, and by moonlight, my cousin's house, eh?"

"Aye, that is Lawrence Hall," replied Captain Dixon, "one of the finest dwellings in these parts, or in all the colonies, I should say, and I've sailed to all parts from the Penobscot to the James; but I fear me much as ye'll soon tire o' the loneliness o' the place."

"Not I, faith! I'm becoming accustomed to the isolation of your American forests, and the spice of danger from the wild beasts and wilder natives is rather attractive than otherwise—keeps one's blood from stagnating," smiled the Colonel.

"There spoke the true Lawrence. I'd 'a' known ye for one o' the old stock!" exclaimed Captain Dixon, with real admiration in his tone. "A dauntless race be these Lawrences, and a bold, so 'tis said in these parts; there be few, sir, who would wantonly raise their ire—but I forget I'm speaking of your kin. No offence, I hope," apologised Captain Dixon.

"None in the least. We're a hot-blooded race, and truth needs no apology," replied the Colonel, with one of the rare smiles that lit up his usually grave face like a ray of sunshine.

"Methinks if you tarry long at the Hall your courage may stand you in good stead," returned the Captain. "There are rumours of an uprising among the Indians. The Nis-se-quags and other tribes upon the island are reported to be getting uneasy, and it would not greatly surprise me if, on some dark night, they should make an attack upon the plantations, Captain Lawrence's among the first."

"Marry, Captain, and if that be truth I shall not curtail my stay at my kinsman's house from dread of a descent by the Indians," answered the Colonel; "I should have made the hall my abiding place, while I tarry in the colonies, but for the fact that business called me to the other extremity of the island; besides, although John, William and Thomas are my cousins, I have never met either, while Captain Gardiner is an acquaintance of my early years."

"Lyon Gardiner is safe enough, e'en granting there should be a general uprising—you know, Colonel, he is under the especial protection of old Wyandance, Chief Sachem of all these petty tribes, and the Isle of Wight is as safe as if his dwelling was in the very heart o' Lunnon," responded Captain Dixon.

"For which thank God!" ejaculated Lawrence, with such fervour that Captain Dixon looked keenly in his face as if striving to comprehend his meaning.

"I doubt if Captain Gardiner has anything like fear in his make-up. He's a brave officer, as everyone in these parts can testify, and up to all the Indian devilment, for he led many a band into the wilderness in pursuit of the hostiles, while at the Fort. I' faith, it is better to have a friend in old Wyandance than an enemy, that goes without saying, Colonel."

But Colonel Lawrence was not thinking of the safety of Captain Gardiner, but of the beautiful girl he loved to madness, from whom he had voluntarily exiled himself that he might preserve the honour that was dearer to him than life, and a long-drawn sigh escaped his lips, as memory but too faithfully mirrored that fair face he could not forget, strive as he might to banish the image.

Captain Dixon walked away to give the necessary

AN ANCIENT FAMILY

orders for landing his passenger, and presently the schooner came to anchor and a boat put off to the landing, bearing Captain Dixon's passenger, who waved an adieu to the officers aboard, and then turned his attention to the shore he was nearing.

At the landing he dismissed his boatmen and hurried up the long avenue leading to the hall and winding beneath a canopy of boughs, an arch frescoed in crimson, yellow, amber and russet hung with green banners where the giant tamaracks raised their scaly trunks and spread out their broad arms.

Inexpressibly lonely looked the depths of the woodland, the black patches of fern which the Frost King had nipped and left standing, and the broad sweeps of dank sward from which the undergrowth had been cleared.

Portmanteau in hand he strode forward, but the mansion, which from the deck of the schooner had seemed so near at hand, was, by the windings of the avenue, quite a distance from the shore, making the ascent gradual to the crown of the headland.

Suddenly he stopped—stood stock still in the gloom, a low whistle of intense astonishment escaping his lips.

From a path crossing the main avenue at right angles a strange apparition came suddenly into view, the tall figure of a man astride the back of an enormous bull, that went crashing through the scattered pine cones and blackened brakes at a tremendous pace, a thick-necked, ebon-hued brute, with lowered head armed with a pair of thick, pointed horns to which broad leathern straps were secured, serving the rider in place of reins, and which he grasped as easily as if guiding an Arabian steed.

"Angels and ministers of grace defend us! What is that, I wonder, the Devil turned Centaur?

Methinks nothing short of his Satanic Majesty could bestride that fierce brute. Mayhap it is a second edition of Androcles and his lion!" exclaimed Lawrence, in his unbounded amazement.

Man and beast had rushed upon the scene at but a few yards' distance, and before the Colonel had recovered from his astonishment the bull and his rider had disappeared around a curve in the avenue in advance of the watcher, and were lost to sight, heading in the direction of the mansion.

The Colonel could not repress a second prolonged whistle.

"Whew-w-w-w! that equestrian would take first prize in a genuine bull fight, such as we witnessed back there in Spain, I ween. Mayhap I have the key to the mystery of the supernatural monster which these red men prate of—the gigantic apparition astride a strange monster breathing flame from its red nostrils, a precursor of ill to the unfortunate beholder; I have witnessed some odd things since setting foot in the colonies, but of all uncanny modes of locomotion this is the climax!"

Thus musing, Colonel Lawrence pursued his walk, presently emerging from the shaded avenue into the broad park, that had been literally hewn from the dense forest.

As the visitor hastened up the path leading straight across the slope to the vine-wreathed porch overhanging the main entrance, a pleasing scene opened to his sight.

The spike-studded door lay open wide, through which a full view of the interior was permitted, the great entrance hall with its gulf of a chimney and elaborately carved mantel, the oaken staircase sweeping up to the second story, with thick twisted rail and immense baluster posts set in the flooring of red and white stone flags, the wainscotted walls bristling with huge antlers of the red deer, from which depended articles of value and curios; a rusty suit of armour, worn lang-syne by the Crusader, Robert Laurens, at the battles of Acre and Antioch, and near at hand a broad, curved scimitar taken by the warrior from a turbaned Moslem.

Upon other and smaller antlers were disposed pistols and cumbersome muskets, cutlasses, rapiers, broadswords, and stilettos, all of ancient pattern.

Set in the oaken panels were family portraits, Lords Monteagle and Girard, but so dimmed by time that the features appeared half hidden by the veil which the years had woven, and there were portraits of stately ladies in ruff and stomacher, equally obscured by the flight of time.

A group of paintings were fresh—portraits of the master of Lawrence Hall, and of his two brothers, John and Thomas, all broad-shouldered, handsome and eagle-eyed, as it was in the nature of the bold Lawrences to be.

On the right of the three last named two portraits stood out strongly in the light of the great log fire blazing upon the hearth, a lady, beautiful, youthful and blonde, and a gentleman in the court costume of the days of Henry VII.

The features, in the red light, looked singularly life-like, the dark, flashing eyes of the courtier seeming to bid an unspoken welcome to the man standing upon the threshold, the living, breathing counterpart of that face in the oaken frame.

This portrait had been renovated at great expense, and the colouring was perfect.

Henry Lawrence started as if he had unexpectedly looked in a mirror, for, if he had been habited in the antique costume of his dead and gone ancestor, the Colonel might well have been mistaken for the original of the portrait of John, the knight who had died in exile two hundred years agone.

He had taken this hasty survey of the hall and its furnishing while yet the echoes of the brass knocker resounded through the mansion, and ere he had recovered from his momentary astonishment at the reflection of his own image, the old butler stalked down the hall with measured, solid tread—Aleck McGregor, a solemn-faced Scot who had served the family years before they set foot upon American soil.

"Is your master at home?" asked the Colonel.

"Laird be gude till us!" ejaculated the old servitor, involuntarily glancing toward the portrait, and then staring hard at the visitor; "I maun beg yer lairdship's pardon, but ye gie a mon an unco turn. Aweel, the maister's hame, an' wull ye cam in frae the nicht?" concluded McGregor, with a prolonged stare at the figure looming up stately and handsome in the shadow of the entrance porch.

Three oaken doors opened on right and left, and the old butler led the way to the third upon the right, which was partially open, disclosing a scene of comfort, even luxury, hardly to be expected in the colonies. A glowing fire in the wide fireplace shone on polished brass andirons, cushioned chairs with elaborately carved backs, a massive table with great bear's claws terminating each twisted leg, an inlaid sideboard, heavy damask curtains, a square of rug in the centre of the polished oak floor, and the spinnet, where a tall, graceful figure presided, a woman in the very heyday of her beauty, her blonde hair arranged high upon her head, after the fashion of the period, and confined by an immense comb of tortoise shell and gold.

Two gentlemen were seated, occupying the

chimney corners opposite each other, one of whom was easily recognised by the visitor, as his relative, by the eagle eyes, the lofty poise of head and the stalwart figure characterising the Lawrence race. In the opposite corner sat the muscular rider of the bovine monster Henry Lawrence had encountered in the park.

CHAPTER XXIX

"BULL SMITH"

"Men are the sport of circumstances, when
The circumstances seem the sport of men."

"I have a room whereinto no one enters
Save I myself alone;
There sits a blessed memory on a throne,
There my life centres."

"LAIRD JAHRN, maister!"

Old McGregor made the announcement as he flung wide the partially open door, and noiselessly retreated, leaving the guest to introduce himself more definitely to the relatives whom he had never seen, while Aleck hurried away, muttering as he went:

"Hoot, Aleck mon! ye maun be feckless an' daft, but the lad be braw an' brent, as like t' Laird Jahrn as his ain wraith, his lith an' limb."

William Lawrence rose to receive his visitor, stopped short in the centre of the room, and staring almost as fixedly as had the old servitor.

"Beg pardon, but I did not understand the name, sir," he apologised, offering his hand.

"Henry Lawrence, of Lancashire, England,—your kinsman," returned the Colonel, as he took the offered palm in a cordial grasp.

"And right glad are we to welcome ye to our hearthstone, cousin!" exclaimed the host, heartily. "Elizabeth, allow me to present our kinsman,

Cousin Henry Lawrence—you have often heard me make mention of him, although we have never met," continued William, turning to his wife, who had risen from the spinnet and now came forward to greet the guest.

It was Colonel Lawrence's turn to be astonished when Elizabeth introduced the rider of the elephantine Taurus as " My father, Richard Smith," and he felt the grip of a strong muscular hand and marked the half smile in the keen grey eyes looking into his own.

" I am assured we have met before, sir," remarked Richard Smith, in a deep, hearty voice, " as I came hither I noticed a tall gentleman, who halted as I passed. I might have addressed him, but, truth to tell, Whisper was in an ugly mood, and a stranger might not have relished a nearer approach. Ha! ha! ha! "

The speaker, herculean in stature, but so perfectly proportioned and of so fine a physique as to neutralise any appearance of ungainliness, was a man whose age it was difficult to determine accurately; his erect figure, fresh complexion, clear eyes and perfect teeth bespoke the man of not more than forty-five, but the deep furrows between the heavy, grey eyebrows and the grizzled hair would mark his winters at not less than sixty.

His garments were a compound of the dress worn by the English planter of the period and the gala attire of an Indian chief.

" Right glad to make your acquaintance, my lad; son William has often talked of you; welcome to America. Aye, lad, it makes the heart glad to take the hand of one from Old England, the home we have not forgotten. Ye'll bide wi' us many a day, I hope."

"For a time," replied the Colonel.

"What good wind brought you to the colonies, cousin?" asked Captain Lawrence, after the group were seated around the hearth.

"Business in the first place, an innate love of adventure, in the second," returned Henry Lawrence. "I have been in the colonies several weeks, and should have paid my respects to you earlier, had it not been that the business upon which I came kept me at the Isle of Wight and vicinity for a time; besides, I learned that you were absent from the island, together with John and Thomas, and that fact delayed me for the last few days."

"True; we have been as far as Nova Scotia, with two others, on a commission to settle some land disputes; it is scarcely a week since our return," returned Captain Lawrence. "Bess, wife, have you observed what a capital likeness our kinsman bears to the portrait of Sir John?"

He turned to his wife, as he abruptly changed the subject.

"A most striking resemblance. I noticed it at a glance," returned Elizabeth. "One might fancy you sat for the picture, cousin."

"I think old McGregor must have been struck with the counterpart," remarked Richard Smith. "Did you note, lass, how he stumbled and mumbled something about 'Laird Jarhn'?"

"I heard, but imagined he must have been informed that our cousin was named John," answered Mrs. Lawrence.

"How do you like the country?" inquired Captain Lawrence, "decidedly rough, after a residence in one of our English cities, eh?"

"I am rather pleased than otherwise," returned Henry, "although I must confess I should scarcely care to take up my abode permanently in the wilderness."

"I wot not, cousin," responded William, "but it is a country in which to replenish one's coffers."

"Presumably," returned the Colonel. "How have you contrived to amass all these home luxuries, William?"

"The articles came over in several shipments from Old England," returned Captain Lawrence, complacently. "It is pleasant to see one's surroundings such as he has been accustomed to in the land of his birth."

"And the mansion itself—you have succeeded admirably in rendering it uncommonly like the homes of England, as well as in giving it an ancient tone. One would imagine the structure half a century old, at the least."

"There is a surplus of stone on the island, and the most expensive woods are to be had for the labour of cutting; besides, we have arrived at the dignity of having sawmills, while skilled carpenters and artisans of all trades are at hand; thus, you perceive the rearing of a considerable mansion is not as serious an undertaking as might appear," returned William.

"We have effaced the newness that is so conducive to homesickness in the colonies, stains and varnishes having accomplished miracles in the way of converting newly erected and furnished dwellings into specimens of older homes we loved in England. The family portraits, plate, bric-à-brac, clocks and furniture came from England, of course; we are free from being obliged to make the numerous repairs so often required in the baronial mansions of the mother country, which those born and reared in England so often complain of—there are no smoking chimneys, no draughts to chill one to the marrow," said Elizabeth.

"Bess takes a practical and most sensible view," laughed William.

"And a correct one," agreed Henry.

"Dinner is served!" announced Aleck McGregor, from the threshold, his eyes turned in the direction where Colonel Lawrence sat, for the striking likeness the Colonel bore to the portrait gracing the wall of the entrance hall was yet a source of superstitious wonder to the old Scot, who half persuaded himself at heart that the spirit of the fiery Sir John had returned to inhabit an earthly tenement.

"Prithee, cousin, you are a-hungered enough to accept of a fricassee of chicken and game," chimed in Richard Smith. "You perceive I make myself quite at home in the Captain's house."

"As you should, father," rejoined the Captain, pleasantly.

Colonel Lawrence offered his arm to Elizabeth and the four entered the dining hall, which was illuminated by lighted wax candles and a cheerful blaze upon the hearth that flickered redly upon the table, spread with the whitest of damask, and bright with silver and rare old china. The drapery at the windows was drawn close, for the evening air was chill.

It was a pleasant family party gathered at the hospitable board; Colonel Lawrence was seated at the right of the host, with Elizabeth and her father as their vis-à-vis, the mistress of the mansion very fair and graceful in her robe of dark blue, the flowing sleeves falling back from her rounded arms. Often she raised her clear, earnest eyes to the Colonel's face as he talked of the friends across seas, and of those at the Isle of Wight, with whom she was on terms of intimacy.

"Colonel Lawrence offered his arm to Elizabeth —"

"And Major Gordon; he has often promised to visit us and bring his pretty daughter—affianced to Kingsland, you know. Pity, say I—such a mere child; should be in pinafores, so Bess says," Captain Lawrence remarked, and the lady caught sight of the flush that mounted to the Colonel's forehead, succeeded by a swift pallor and a compression of the lips, and with the keen intuition of a sensitive woman she half divined his secret.

"For myself, I'm not particularly put about that he has deferred his visit," put in Smith, bluntly. "I should not mind, truth to tell, if he should forget us altogether—I don't fancy him—never did! Oddsbobs! I don't know the reason, but mayhap it is because he is too sweet to be wholesome."

"'I do not like you, Doctor Fell,
The reason why I cannot tell,'"

quoted Elizabeth. "But you must acknowledge, father, that Damaris is a dear little thing, a child in years, but with plenty of character, when it is developed, I assure you."

"The lass is pretty and good," assented Smith, heartily, "too good and innocent to have sprung from such stock. But alack! she will suffer from his tyranny, as did her mother before her! She favours the distaff side of the house—is the moral of her mother; I was acquainted with poor Lucy Graham before she was wed to the Major—he was a Lieutenant then. If all tales are true he led her the devil of a life. How does the Major strike you, Colonel?"

There was a dead silence for a moment following this abrupt question, and Elizabeth observed that the Colonel had paled again, from chin to brow, and that he made no reply.

"No, I don't like him!" reiterated Smith, positively. "There's a sharp claw beneath that velvet paw, I'll dare warrant; I'd sooner trust the friendship of my bull, Whisper, who is the nobler animal of the twain."

"An original Rosinante, sir. May I inquire how you chanced to select such a steed?" asked the Colonel, anxious to change the subject which was so painful and embarrassing to him, for Richard Smith had voiced his own secret dislike for the Major.

"Nothing singular, when you reflect that there's scarcely a charger to be had for love or money here in the colonies; and I having been accustomed to the saddle from the day I was but a lad, it occurred to me that the powerful brute might serve as an excellent make-shift. He was but a calf when I made the first experiment, and he demurred for a time, you may make sure, but after a plenty of discipline he became manageable and I had a saddle fitted to his sharp back. His stride is rather ungainly, and he jolts his rider somewhat, but not nearly as much as a camel, and he takes me over these rough trails safely and at a speed scarcely inferior to that of a saddle horse; besides, he is a sure-footed beast."

"The name you have chosen is quite as original as your choice of an animal," laughed the Colonel. "Isn't it rather a misnomer?"

"Rather; a bit o' sarcasm on the strength of his lungs," returned Smith, with an answering laugh. "His bellow is like the rumble of a volcano, but, in addition to his other useful qualities, he is a protection against wild animals, a strolling wolf or bear, for instance; his horns are sharp and strong as iron prongs, and he is nearly as powerful as a rhinoceros. I'm known the length and breadth of the island as 'Bull Smith,' and the name pleases me right well."

Enlivened with laugh and jest the dinner hour

passed, and after a bottle of grape wine had been discussed the party returned to the drawing-room.

"Bess, lass, sing us the song I've not heard for a twelve-month, my favourite—you know what that is," coaxed Richard Smith, as he took his seat in the chimney corner, and at the request his daughter sat down to the spinnet.

"You have several favourites, father, what particular song do you wish?"

"You should know well enough, lass; there's not a better than the good old Scotch song—'Mary's Dream.'"

"Which is also a favourite of my own," chimed in the Colonel.

Elizabeth was an accomplished performer, and her fingers swept the keys in a weird prelude, and glided into the ancient ballad, of the ghostly, sombre stamp so popular at that date.

"The moon had climbed the highest hill
   That rises o'er the source of Dee,
And from her eastern summit shed
   Her silvery light on tower and tree.
Then Mary laid her down to rest,
   Her thoughts on Sandy, far at sea,
When, soft and low, a voice she heard,
   Saying, 'Mary, weep no more for me.'

"She gently from her pillow raised,
   To see and ask who there might be,
And she saw young Sandy shivering stand,
   With pallid cheek and hollow eye.
'O Mary dear, cold is my clay,
   It lies beneath the stormy sea,
Far, far away I sleep in death,
   So, 'Mary, weep no more for me.'

"Three stormy nights and stormy days,
   We tossed upon the raging main,
And hard we strove our bark to save,
   But all our striving was in vain;

> And then, when horror filled my breast,
>   My heart was filled with love for thee,
> The storm is past, and I'm at rest,
>   So, 'Mary, weep no more for me.'
>
> "Loud sang the lark, the shadow fled,
>   No more of Sandy could she see,
> At length the passing spirit said,
>   'Sweet Mary, weep no more for me.'"

The song was a favourite with the Colonel, as he had said, and he strove to appear interested, listening politely, but ere the song was half finished his thoughts had strayed far away. Again in fancy he beheld the delicate, high-bred features of his beloved, the soulful, violet eyes, the sweet, proud lips of the child-woman who could never be his; and yet, in spite of his self-command, Samson-like, he was mad, blind with the consuming fever men call love, a passion that enchained his soul, absorbed his whole being, dominated his thoughts like a waking dream.

It was late when he bade his cousins and their guest good-night and followed McGregor to the chamber assigned him, a commodious apartment, handsomely furnished.

Dismissing McGregor, he sank into the depths of an easy chair in front of the comfortable fire blazing in the wide-throated chimney, his face turning hard and drawn, his dark eyes smouldering with a rebellious light.

"Great God!" he thought, "must the memory of the few happy days I have spent upon the bright island haunt me to my dying day? I came hither, hoping, believing that absence might cure my passion, make me forget my madness, my folly—nay, more—my wickedness; and yet, the sternest censor that ever sat in judgment over an erring weak mortal could hardly blame me for the affection that grew insensibly, stole my senses like a draught of sweet wine, enthralled me like a wild, sweet dream, and which I sought vainly to curb! Why did not I fly from her enchanting presence before she was so perilously dear—ah, why?"

He rose from his chair and began pacing up and down the room with the swift stride born of the tumult of his brain, his hands locked hard, his lips closed as if to shut in the words he would have uttered, his face strangely haggard and set, under the red firelight.

"And she!" he mused, bitterly. "I have been cowardly enough to avow my love, to win her heart! Did I intend it? No, by Heaven! I never meant to tempt her from her allegiance to the man she is fated to wed! My God! had it been one with a tithe of true manhood the fatal declaration should never have passed my lips. But Guy Kingsland, I cannot trust him, and as the bluff, open-hearted Richard Smith says of her father, so say I of Guy—I do not like him. It is not jealousy, but a keen conviction that if she marries him he will break her heart. Alack! there is nothing left me but to return to England, join a marching regiment and conquer this ill-starred love if I can—aye, if I can; and if not Heaven grant that in some desperate strife it may be my fate to fall. Ah! and for her, my peerless love, my earnest prayer, even at the dying hour, shall be that she may forget, or at least, remember the past only as a dream, over and gone."

He removed only his coat, threw himself upon the couch, and lay silent, with closed eyes, but it was in the small hours when sleep came, to give him again in his dreams the blissful hours forever vanished.

CHAPTER XXX

LADY DEBORAH MOODY

> "Man, though limited
> By fate, may vainly think his actions free,
> While all he does, was at his hour of birth,
> Or by his gods, or potent stars ordained."

AND so you have fully decided to go to Gravesend, Major? Who is this Lady Moody, and what upon earth is taking you thither?"

It was Guy Kingsland who asked the question, as he leaned indolently upon the softest of cushions in the great armchair beside the open window in Major Gordon's room at Gardiner Hall.

Although the crisp October weather rendered the fire upon the hearth a luxury, the fumes of the big pipe of Indian manufacture which the Major held in his teeth were filling the room, and Guy had thrown up the sash to admit fresh air.

"I can imagine naught short of absolute fate that can send you away from your comfortable quarters here, at this season, and especially as there is a rumour of an Indian outbreak to the westward," pursued Guy, as he lighted his own pipe from the Major's glowing pipebowl.

"Aye, lad, fate in the shape of business of a pressing nature, mayhap," returned the Major, between the deep whiffs he was indulging in. "Nothing worse I ween. Who is Lady Moody? A lady well known in the colonies—odd you have not heard her discussed. Thereby hangs a tale. She is a very wealthy landholder, both in this section and in Salem, back there in Massachusetts Bay colony. Enormous estates and gold in plenty has the Lady Deborah, who is an exceedingly eccentric personage, whose peculiar tenets and talents have kicked up no end of a row among the Puritans, and also in England, where, as it appears, she was brought before the Court of the Star Chamber——"

"The Star Chamber?" echoed Guy, in astonishment. "What's to do with that court?"

"Naught to conflict with her morals, or what may be termed a crime—she is the most proper of matrons. Nothing more flagrant than a protracted residence in London, which being brought to notice, she was summoned, and the court ordered that Dame Deborah Moody and others should return to their hereditaments in forty days, in the good example necessary for the poorer classes."

"Egad! but a trifling offence," answered Guy.

"Aye, lad, but she acted in direct opposition to the statute providing that no person shall reside beyond a limited time from their own homes. As it appears, she went down to London from her home in one of the remote counties—I forget which. It is to be presumed that she had other troubles in England, from the fact that, five years later, she came to the colonies. Her summons before the court was in 1635, and in 1640 she sailed for America. Shortly after her arrival she was taken into church fellowship at Salem, where, as appears, she prospered in temporal affairs, for early in the spring of the same year the court granted her four hundred acres of land, and the following year she purchased Swamscut, the property of Deputy Governor Humfrey, for which she paid eleven hundred pounds."

"Fortunate dame," commented Guy.

"Not so fortunate in other respects. It was not long before she got into trouble, notwithstanding her wealth."

"How so? a lady of high degree should be held in reverence here—she must be worth cultivating. I'm certain I should not object to numbering her among my acquaintance. Prithee, how did it happen?"

"It was in this wise," returned the Major, taking a long puff; "she has some of the most unorthodox tenets, among others that the baptism of infants is not only unnecessary, but in truth a sinful ordinance."

"Whew-w-w-w-w!" whistled Guy, "she must be a dame of uncommonly strong individuality, to assert herself after so pronounced a manner—a shrew, I warrant!"

"There you are at sea—she is Quakeress, and in deportment the meekest woman in the three kingdoms, so 'tis said."

"And with such a heathenish idea concerning baptism—that's odd."

"Fact, nevertheless—I have it from my old acquaintance, Winthrop himself, who admitted that she was formerly a wise and anciently religious woman before she fell into the error of denying baptism to infants, for which she was dealt with by the elders, and at first only admonished, but persisting in her opinion, she was excommunicated. This brought on a climax, and she came to Sea-wan-ha-ka at the time when Kieft, then Dutch Governor of New Amsterdam, granted a patent written in both English and Dutch. The first named patentee was Lady Deborah Moody."

"Harkee, Major, an' it is brave days when an auldwife is put before her goodman; at this gait we'll have the petticoats assuming the rule of the household, and mayhap holding themselves equal with their husbands," grumbled Guy, as he refilled his pipe.

"Lady Deborah is a widow, and is certainly the first named patentee; the next written is Sir Henry Moody, Baronet, her son; then follows Ensign George Baxter, Sergeant James Hubbard, and others. I have a copy of the patent."

"I'd like a peep at the document, if you have it handy," returned Guy. "Such an extraordinary piece of penmanship should be worth the reading."

Gordon crossed over to his desk and took a paper therefrom.

"Queer kind of hieroglyphics—odd fist that!" drawled Guy. "Have the goodness to read it, an' you will; it might be Mohawk or Narragansett, for all I should be able to make of it."

"I can decipher the document, as I have waded through it several times. Ahem-m-m!" said the Major, taking the document and looking at the cramped lines.

"A certain quantity of land lying or being upon or about the westernmost part of Long Island, beginning at the north of a creek adjacent to Conyne-Island,[1] and bounded on the west part thereof with the lands belonging to Anthony Johnson and Robert Penoyre; and to run as far as the westermost part of a certain pond in an old Indian field on the north side of the plantation of the said Robert Penoyre; and from thence to run directly east as far as a valley being at the head of a fly or marsh sometime belonging to the land of Hugh Garretson; and being bounded on the south side with the main ocean, with liberty to put what cattle they shall see fitting to feed or grass upon the aforesaid Conyne-Island, and with a liberty to build a town, with such necessary fortifications as to them shall seem expedient; and to have and enjoy the free liberty of conscience according to the customs and manners of Holland, without molestation, and to establish courts, and elect magistrates, to try all causes not exceeding fifty Holland guilders."

[1] *Conyne-Island.*—Coney Island. Called by the Dutch "Conynen-Eylandt," probably from the name of a former owner of the island, or part of it.

"A curious document, deucedly odd—a patent granted to a woman, and more, her name first on the list. That is something new under the sun, King Solomon to the contrary notwithstanding!" exclaimed Guy, in a thoroughly disgusted tone. "Zounds! she must be a most remarkable filly, and —wonder of wonders, a Quakeress!"

"She is all of that—a disciple of George Fox," replied Gordon, evidently enjoying the surprise of the Lieutenant. "She has, so rumour says, an unbounded influence over Governor Stuyvesant, as she had over his predecessor, Governor Kieft."

"But, sir, I understood that the Dutch Reformed Church was the only sect tolerated by these old Dutch Patroons, and that there has been a persecution of the Quakers by these same Dutchmen. How is it?"

"Peter Stuyvesant is a brave soldier who lost his leg in the service, but he is a zealot, and a most intolerant churchman, and—whisper it softly, my lad, Lady Moody is wealthy. Besides her immense estate here, honestly paid for in good English pounds, she has, as I have said, large possessions in Salem, with money in the funds, and it is shrewdly suspected that she holds the purse-string of the thrifty Dutch Governor for a goodly amount. However that may be or may not be, she has unbounded influence with him, and it is through her intercession—or command—devil knows which, that several of the prominent Quakers who have been apprehended, and would have suffered a rigorous sort of imprisonment, besides being dragged at the tail of a cart[2] and flogged, have been released. There were a number

---

[2] *Dragging at the cart-tail.*—A punishment common in colonial days. The offender was bound with a slack halter which was secured to the rear of a cart to which horses or oxen were harnessed, and the victim was obliged to follow and keep his feet, or be dragged upon the ground.

of Quakers that came with her from Saugus,[3] others from Salem and vicinity, but oddly enough, although a Quaker persecution is raging, she still retains her influence with the Governor, which fact can only be accounted for by the supposition that her prestige comes from a moneyed power, for gold is all potent here in the colonies of America, as it is in the three kingdoms, my lad," concluded the Major, sagely.

"And is it a matter of friendship, or a more sordid sentiment that takes you to her house—personal regard or gold?" asked Guy, with a slight smile.

"Neither, in a strict sense; it is a landed interest I wish to secure from Stuyvesant, and to do this I must engage the kind offices of Lady Moody in my behalf. Backed by her influence, I must succeed."

"How about the Indian titles? They are constantly cropping up in the most annoying fashion," grumbled Guy.

"A murrain on their claims; they can settle that with old Peter, or go to the devil for all I know or care!" growled the Major.

"Ah, I perceive the same policy runs like a thread through every dealing with these aborigines. I must confess it would be devilish mean, providing they were white men, but what signifies it with these heathen? The sooner they are annihilated, root and branch, the better for the European settlers, who must eventually possess the land. So success to your mission, say I. But, seriously speaking, why should you not purchase of these Indians, and cheaper? A few gew-gaws, half a dozen blankets, a brace of dogs, a looking-glass or two, or, best of all, a few gallons of Jamaica rum, would do the business. They sell their lands for a song," advised the Lieutenant.

"To be sure, but they do not thoroughly under-

---

[3] *Saugus.*—Indian name of Lynn.

stand these transactions. To their minds they are only allowing the pale-faces to erect dwellings, to till the earth, while they reserve the right to spear fish in the rivers, hunt in the forests and roam at will over the country as of yore they and their fathers have done. It is true that the more sagacious of the Sachems are waking to the fact that their ancient domain is slipping from their grasp, that the white men are surely driving them from their possessions, and that in a few years they will be hunted from the soil like beasts of the forest—a consummation devoutly to be wished," declared the Major, with conviction.

"What tribe claims jurisdiction under Stuyvesant in the western part of the island?" asked Guy.

"The Canarsees. The Dutch have their own mode of dealing with the redskins. The governor makes the purchase of the Indians and distributes the patents in a manner that seems to him good. You can thus understand how important it is that I should obtain a patent for land already grabbed by him from these Indians, and the surest means of effecting this is through the mediation of Lady Moody."

"Land! land! land! Still more land. Between the English and Dutch there will not a rod remain to these Indians after the next half century, eh?" laughed Guy.

"Doubtless, and allow me to state that these lands will be of great value in the future. We have a footing that will continue to enlarge, while disease, drunkenness, wars between the tribes, ingeniously contrived and fostered, will diminish their population, by destroying numbers and enfeebling the remainder—a policy that will finally cause their extinction, or oblige the remnant that may be left to migrate to far distant regions to the westward. The man who is fortunate enough to get land here, at the present time, will speedily become a potentate with as great power as the feudal barons possessed in the Middle Ages, and in the future their descendants will revel in the wealth acquired by their far-seeing ancestors, who are the colonists of the present. Do you know I have a presentiment that the journey I am about to take will be the turning point in my career."

"You take ship on the good barque *Blessing*, the day after to-morrow, I believe?" said Guy, interrogatively.

"Such is my intention, and, my lad, this will be my last venture, for if I succeed I am off for Old England. To speak truth, since the moment I gave Ninigret the means of carrying off the Sachem's daughter, I have had a premonition—a dread, rather—that by some means Wyandance may become acquainted with the facts, and if he should suspect the truth a thousand fierce savages, Montauks, Manhansetts and Shinnecocks, with the warriors of other minor tribes under the control of the Grand Sachem, would be ready, at his nod, and be upon my track like blood-hounds until my scalp would hang in his wigwam. I'll secure my reward from Wyandance for my little piece of diplomacy as soon as I return from Gravesend, where I hope to make a deal with Peter Stuyvesant for another goodly bowerie,[4] and then I can afford to retire."

"Oho! sets the wind in that quarter? Excellent! If you succeed you will be one of the richest landholders in the colonies and can afford to leave the field to other prospectors," returned Guy, with a yawn.

"Precisely! I shall be one of the heaviest, except Farret—a far-seeing man is Farret; in twenty years

[4] *Bowerie.*—A farm.

—nay, in half that time, these same boweries will be increased in market value a hundred fold, and, mark me, Guy, in the next decade Europeans will be the virtual possessors of not only these islands, but a broad margin all along shore from the Penobscot to beyond Virginia. These half-nude savages will stand but a poor chance against our trained soldiers. The statute against selling guns, ammunition, or any vessel, save a canoe, to any Indian is a wise and precautionary measure, and looking directly to the end in view. An ounce of prevention is worth a pound of cure, my lad."

"Bow and arrow, tomahawk, spear and scalping-knife are but sorry weapons of warfare against firelocks, pistols, cannon and broadswords," returned Guy, serenely.

"The net is closing around them slowly but surely," answered the Major.

"Yet I fancy there will be some severe fighting before the savages yield their dominion, but without a question the race is doomed," replied Guy. "I would have dipped deeper in this land speculation but for the fact that you will secure sufficient, and I'm not greedy enough to exert myself to such an extent as I might otherwise have done. A fair bargain. I bring your daughter a title, you provide the means of sustaining it, eh?"

"You speak but truth, lad," laughed the Major. "You are constitutionally lazy. You are right, you will have a goodly settlement in your bride's dower, and there's a coronet in your family which will not be withheld for long—only one feeble life between you and an earldom. Lord Charles Erlington is in the eighties, and in a few years Damaris will be 'My Lady.'"

"Lord Charles is eighty-five come Christmas,"

answered Guy, reflectively; "a very old man. His title is deucedly near all he has to leave his heir, for we Kingslands have ever been an improvident race; but what with the dangers lurking in every shadow of this wild, lawless land, it would scarcely be surprising if, as was predicted by a soothsayer, he should be the last male of his line. He may outlive you and me."

"Tush! You have an attack of the blue devils —have 'em myself upon occasions,—and oddly enough they thrive in this confoundedly dull atmosphere. We will leave the colonies as soon as this business is off my hands—a matter of a few months. We will sail in the first ship that clears port in the spring. There shall be a grand wedding, and you will settle down with your bride to enjoy the wealth that I have amassed. As for me, I'll have my suit of apartments, my grog and my pipe as I go down into the lean and slippered stage of existence. How do you like the picture?"

"Excellently well," assented Guy. "I'm confoundedly at odds with this beastly forest and all its concomitants in the shape of red heathen, wolves, bears and reptiles, and I'm sure I shall bid these shores a long adieu without a regret."

"In a week, probably, if the winds and waves are not too boisterous, and nothing occurs to delay her passage, the staunch ship *Blessing* will drop anchor here, on her voyage to New Amsterdam. By All-Hallow Eve my fate will be decided, whether I am to be the fortunate possessor of a township or otherwise," declared the Major, as he complacently knocked the ashes from his pipe and poured a couple of glasses of brandy. "Let's drink to the success of my mission." The glasses clinked, and bidding the Major good-night Guy went to his couch to dream of—Heather Flower.

CHAPTER XXXI

HEART STRUGGLES

> "A spirit pure as hers,
> Is always pure, even while it errs;
> As sunshine, broken in the rill
> Though turned astray, is sunshine still."

"WHERE, in all this vast wilderness, is he to-night? Does he gaze on yonder moon shining so coldly, and think of one who loves him in spite of stern duty? Shall we ever meet again? Oh, that I had been free—free to love as my heart dictates, then all would have been well, but now—ah, me!"

Damaris Gordon, sitting in the firelight glow in her own chamber, was very lovely, even with the shadow of the sorrow that had come so lately clouding her face.

From her father she had inherited little besides her pride; from her gentle mother, who had died while yet her child was an infant, she derived the exquisite tenderness of her nature, the lovely face and the soul-lit, violet eyes, the wealth of amber tresses, and, more than all, the constant, true heart.

Her own nature had been a sealed book hitherto, even to herself, and she accepted the man destined by her father as her future husband without demur, never dreaming that her heart was capable of a more passionate, abiding love than the sisterly affection she had given, an affection undisturbed by even a ripple of jealousy.

Now the hidden scroll was unrolled, and her very soul trembled in the reading.

"Oh, how this love would have ennobled my whole being!" she murmured, brokenly. "It was cruel, a terrible wrong to me—to Guy, this betrothal, while neither could possibly know the evil that might result! It is horrible to feel the fetters corroding the heart, bonds that may not be broken! Guy, poor Guy! He loves me, and unwittingly I have wronged him. Thank God that this love for another was not weak. God knows how I have struggled against it, and if I cannot conquer, mine shall be the suffering, mine the martyrdom; never shall Guy be tortured with the knowledge, and may the All-Father help me to be a true and tender wife. But oh, he is so different!" and in that piteous cry the inward sense, an intuition of the shallowness of the gay young Lieutenant was uttered, and one by one the slow tears fell, for in spite of her will a leaden sense of Guy's lack of heart oppressed her.

The firelight settled in a dull, red glow within a circumscribed circle, but the white October moon streamed through the diamond-shaped panes of the window and lay in a fleecy whiteness over the forest and sea, piercing the curtain of leaves, now purple, yellow and crimson, shivering in the frosty air and fluttering down like a shower of rubies, amethysts and topaz, one by one, fast weaving a gay, parti-hued carpet upon the brown, frost-nipped sward.

The brazen-tongued clock upon the stair landing tolled out the hour—eleven solemn, measured strokes, and the sound aroused her from her painful reverie.

A long line of light was trailing like a red banner tingeing the pearly moonlight with faint pink where the rival rays met, the glow of firelight and waxlight streaming through the open window of her father's chamber, but as she looked the red-gleam was extingished, leaving naught save the misty, pearly rays, and the slipping of a sash told her that the open casement had been closed.

She was about to draw down the curtains when a moving shadow upon the edge of the grove a short distance from the mansion attracted her attention. It was at a spot where, at that hour, she would have looked for no one; yet she could not be mistaken for the figure halted just upon the edge of the fringe of shadow, and she made out the form of an Indian, slender, tall, straight-limbed.

Half frightened, wholly mystified, she watched the intruder, who finally stepped full into the moonlight, his face turned toward the dwelling, his head erect; he stood quite still, but the distance was too great to allow her to recognise the features, but she was certain that it was neither Tohemon or Macrobow—the figure was too slender.

Only a moment he remained, then he turned and was lost in the darkness shrouding the avenue.

The gait, the form, were strangely like Wyancombone, and puzzling over the question of what the presence of the young Indian might signify at that hour and in that place, she at last came to the conclusion that she had been deceived by the uncertain moonlight and that it must have been one of the Mohicans, and thus cogitating she undressed and sought her couch.

It was, in truth, Wyancombone whom she had seen as he stole down the avenue, and the errand that had brought him to Gardiner Hall had been accomplished; another link in the chain that would bring retributive justice to the guilty had been forged.

Keen of intellect, quick of perception, even beyond

the ordinary acuteness of the Indian, and far beyond his years, he had pondered upon the startling circumstances attending the attack by the Narragansetts, and every hour the conviction became deeper that Ninigret could not have accomplished his object without the assistance of a confederate who must be thoroughly acquainted with the situation, and who was fully informed regarding the exact date of the festivities. The singular occurrence concerning the concealment of the boats at Man-cho-nock, that had been so cunningly hidden that the family at the hall had been prevented from attending the wedding, and thus had been safe from the massacre, coupled with the items which the youth had gathered by dint of craftily put inquiries, that it was upon that portion of the island which Major Gordon had searched where the boats were finally discovered, was suspicious. Clearly, had it been the work of a person desirous of injuring Captain Gardiner it would have been easier to have cut them loose from their moorings and allowed them to be carried away.

That there was method in the proceeding, and that it was actuated by some deep motive, Wyancombone felt assured, but with what intent any person upon the island could have betrayed the Montauks to their deadly foes he could not divine, and brooding over the mystery he determined to solve it.

Several times he had rowed over to the island, mooring his canoe at various points distant from the usual landing, concealing himself until nightfall and contriving to approach the wigwam occupied by the Mohicans, in expectation that their unguarded conversation might give him a clew; but after a time he knew by their allusions to the subject that they were without the slightest knowledge concerning the matter.

If they were innocent, then a white man must have been the guilty party, and with all the patience of an Indian Wyancombone set himself the task of making the discovery.

It thus became necessary that he should contrive a means of scaling the palisade, a feat not easy of accomplishment. The massive gates were bolted and locked at the hour of ten each night. Heavy posts bristling with spikes had been driven deep in the ground, and so closely set that not a chink appeared in the long stretches arranged after the pattern of a regular fortress, under the direction of Captain Gardiner, who was, as we have said, an expert work-base, or engineer, who had been sent from England for the express purpose of superintending the erection of the Saybrook Fort. And in fact, the defences of his own mansion were, in form and construction, almost a counterpart of the fort, with bastions pierced for musketry, a sally-port in the rear, the immense gates barring the broad avenue leading to the shore, straight across the park which extended beyond the stockade.

At intervals apertures had been left, within three feet of the top of the palisade, to allow a convenient means of watching an enemy upon the outside, but these were but narrow slits. At a short distance from, and connected to, the cellar of the hall by a tunnelled passage, was an underground apartment serving as a storehouse for arms and ammunition, and here also was a deep well, for, although the gallant Captain lived upon terms of the utmost amity with the Indians upon Sea-wan-ha-ka, and also with the Narragansetts, yet, like a prudent general, he neglected no precaution that might serve well in event of treachery, well knowing that the breaking out of hostilities between rival tribes might involve him, and with a correct estimate that the means he had adopted for defence would be likely to deter the savages from an attack.

Even the trees near the palisade, both within and without, had been felled, with the exception of a giant pine which stood just within the wall, and had been preserved upon account of its great size and perfect symmetry; but even this had been carefully trimmed to a height of twenty feet from the ground, leaving the scaly trunk bare.

But the ingenuity of the young Indian compassed the obstacle, and he speedily devised a scheme by which he might not only scale the palisade, but also provide a way of hasty retreat.

Attaching a pebble to a slender strand of buckskin, he sent the missile whirling above the lowest branch of the pine, but retaining the slack end of the cord in his hand. In a trice he had secured a stout rawhide, capable of sustaining his weight, and when this had been done. he drew the rawhide over the limb and knotted the ends together, forming a double length. Agile as a squirrel, he raised himself, hand over hand, pressing his feet against the wall as a lever, and in a moment he had a seat upon the high perch, and sliding along the limb until he was near the tree trunk, and within the bristling line of spikes projecting from the upper edge of the palisade, he lowered the rawhide and slipped to the ground, leaving the noose dangling close against the rough trunk, as a means of instant egress should he be discovered.

Gliding with silent steps along the avenue, and by the edge of the grove within the wall, he presently stood upon the border of a rose thicket, and in the shadow cast by the building itself, directly beneath an open window from which the sound of voices came distinctly.

The evil genius of Major Gordon must have prompted him, for he was discussing the very subject with the Lieutenant that Wyancombone most desired to hear, and almost holding his breath he listened, his eyes glowing, his fingers clenched, his face black with suppressed anger. His knowledge of the English language, though limited, enabled him to form a tolerable estimate of the truth, and of the further treachery meditated by the white men.

Aware of the real character of Kingsland, and hating him with all the strength of a savage nature, Wyancombone had marked the young man as the guilty party who had deliberately delivered Heather Flower into the hands of her enemies; but of the Major he had no suspicion.

"And, my lad, this will be my last venture, for if I succeed I'm away for Old England. To speak truly, since I gave Ninigret the means of carrying off the chief's daughter I have had a premonition that by some means Wyandance might become acquainted with the facts, and a thousand redskins would be on my track like bloodhounds, until my scalp would hang in a Montauk wigwam. Neat job that, hiding the boats. I was mortally afraid lest the Captain might discover them and insist on going over to the merry-making; but the job was done before the Mohicans discovered them. I'll secure my reward from the old Sachem for my little piece of diplomacy, make a deal with Peter Stuyvesant for another goodly plantation, and then—then I'll retire on my laurels. Heigh-ho!" he yawned, sleepily.

The unseen listener remained until the parting glass was drained, the good-night exchanged, the window closed and the light extinguished, then he stole away, creeping silently on hands and knees, gained the edge of the grove and rising he turned for a parting look at the row of windows in the second story. Against the dim red background from the glowing embers upon the hearth his keen vision made out the figure of the girl seated by the window. It was to gain a glimpse of the object of his secret adoration that the stripling had paused, and it was at that instant that Damaris had seen and recognised him.

Aware of the danger of discovery, he flitted down the avenue, struck into a narrow, intersecting path and gained the shelter of the tall pine. Nimbly mounting his improvised ladder, he crept out beyond the palisade and slid to the ground, and, unloosing the thong, he coiled it about his waist and plunged into the coppice.

Making his way with swift strides he gained the water's edge, unmoored his canoe and the light bark swept out upon the bosom of the bay.

"Wyancombone has dug the fox from his hole! Is the son of Wyandance a bat that he has not seen while the white serpent burrowed like the mole? The King of the Montauks would not sell the inheritance of his fathers, the bones of his people, but the paleface, like the sea-wolf, would eat up all! It was his hand that hid away the canoes that the pale-faces might not be found upon the path of the Narragansetts when they came, like prowling wolves to kill the Montauk warriors, the squaws and papooses, to take many scalps and carry away prisoners for the torture. Great Spirit! While his hands were red with the blood of the Montauks, the squaws and papooses whom Ninigret had killed, the white snake crawled to the great chief whose heart was heavy with the loss of his daughter, and with lying eyes and false face, asked for the lands of the Montauk, not with his tongue, but with the look that speaks; then the mighty Sachem would give his land because his heart was soft with sorrow and had grown big with love for the fox who promised to bring back the daughter of the Montauks—the cruel, lying pale-face that would take all from the red man, even at the price of blood, and groans and tears! But," and his mood changed, " shall the son of Wyandance cry like a papoose when it is starving, and bury the tomahawk, because the Snowbird has made his heart weak? The Great Spirit gives him eyes that he may see the bright star that looks down into the great waters, but it will always be pale and cold for Wyancombone. He can never pluck it from the clouds, and can his hand go down into the green waves and take it? The Snowbird can never come to the lodge of Wyancombone! The false pale-face from across the shining water will go away again and take the bright star from the blue sky that will then be black to the eyes of the son of Wyandance. Let Wyancombone tear the heart from his bosom, the heart that must give, drop by drop, the life-blood that feeds it, until the Great Spirit calls him away!"

His incoherent murmurs broke into a plaintive wail, and for a moment the paddle swayed in his listless clasp as he sat, allowing the canoe to rock idly on the waves while he gazed down into the depths where the bright stars were reflected like pitying angels eyes, with an air of utter heart-weariness and desolation.

Presently his mood changed, and an angry light leaped to his eyes, like the gleam of the sunlight upon a sharpened blade, as he dashed the paddle in swift whirling motion that caused the light canoe to skim over the waters like a frightened bird.

"Let the son of Wyandance remember only that the white squaw is the daughter of the wolf whose claws and fangs have torn his people, whose breath has scorched the hearts of the Montauks and dried the blood in their veins! He must die! The dead, whose spirits wander in the forests they loved, are calling, their voices sound in the ear of Wyancombone, cold and hollow as the moaning of the deep water when the storm is upon it, bidding the Montauks to take vengeance upon the cold, proud paleface who would have robbed Wyandance of his land. They point with skeleton fingers, and whisper: 'The sea-wolf shall have land, but only to cover his bones!' Wyancombone hears and will obey. The white wolf must die, but not by the hand of a Montauk, lest it bring Englishmen like sea-wolves to destroy the tribes of Sea-wan-ha-ka. Let Wyancombone be silent, that not a warrior of his tribe may know what is in his heart. Great Spirit!" he cried aloud, his voice ringing over the waters like the vibrations of a deep-toned bell, "spirits of dead warriors that cannot rest, listen to the voice of Wyancombone while he breathes the words he has spoken in his heart. Wyancombone swears by the bones of his fathers, never to rest until the Englishman finds a grave in the earth he would have stolen!"

More than revenge breathed in that cry—there was a dull, dreary note of desolation, for that vow was a renunciation of the hopeless love he bore the daughter of the man he had sworn to destroy.

CHAPTER XXXII

VENGEANCE CONQUERS LOVE

> "If we do but watch the hour
> There never yet was human power
> Which could evade, if unforgiven,
> The patient search and vigil long,
> Of him who treasures up a wrong."

"UGH!"

The guttural utterance came from the throat of an Indian who was lying, securely bound, upon the earth, within a low-browed lodge in the centre of the Indian village, a Mohawk runner, the ambassador from his tribe bearing overtures to the Montauk king, that the tribes of Sea-wan-ha-ka would dig up the hatchet and unite with the fierce tribes of the Five Nations in a contemplated massacre of the English upon the islands and the mainland.

Not for a moment did the noble old Sachem waver in his loyalty to those he yet deemed his friends, but instantly disarmed the messenger and confined him within a lodge.

The savage captive had been sleeping soundly when a light hand upon his shoulder elicited the exclamation.

"Sh-h-h-h!"

The warning came in a sibilant whisper, and by the pencil of moonlight sifting through a crack in the entrance the captive beheld the youthful Wyancombone, whose slender hand had pressed his

VENGEANCE CONQUERS LOVE

shoulder, causing the sleeper to raise himself to a sitting position, while he peered in the face of the youth half in surprise, half in anger.

"Would Wa-ne-no return to his people?" asked the young Indian in a cautious tone.

Deeming the question but an insult, the Mohawk vouchsafed no reply; but the visitor was not to be baffled, and again he asked the question, with the explanation of his singular query.

"Wa-ne-no came to the great Sachem of the Montauks with the wampum belt as a token that Wyandance should dig up the hatchet and join with the Mohawks to destroy the pale-faces who are the friends of the Montauks. The great Sachem will not make war upon his friends, but he has bound the Mohawk brave with thongs."

A grunt of defiance was the only reply.

"Listen! In the council of wise men the fire has been lighted, and when the sun burns in the east Wa-ne-no will be sent away to the great council fire of the pale-faces, who, maybe, will kill him; maybe keep him a prisoner for many moons; maybe hang him up like a snared fox. Does the Mohawk brave know this?"

"Wa-ne-no is a great brave of the Mohawks—not a papoose," muttered the warrior, with a shrug of his shoulders, and an intonation that pointed his meaning to the stripling. "Let the papoose listen. Wa-ne-no is not afraid. The Sachem of the Montauks is blind like an old squaw. The pale-faces spit on him—take away his land—take dogs—by-and-bye take all—take the burial place of his fathers!

"Listen! Let the ears of the papoose hear the words of Wa-ne-no, let his tongue speak them to the blind squaw who is his father. When his red brother comes with the token, asking him to go upon the war-path and drive away the white wolf who is making the red man without a country, without a home, he makes him a prisoner and carries him to the white man's council fire to make sport for the white warriors! Does the chief of the Montauks forget the lashes his white brothers gave to Poniute? A little bird sung it in the ears of the Montauks, but the Sachem of the Montauks forgets!

"Listen, papoose! When the pale-face came across the great water he was but as a feeble sprout; the red man was a strong oak, and the little, withering plant would fain be sheltered under its branches. But the plant was poison and sapped the strength of the great oak until it began to wither and its trunk to decay; the feeble plant was a thrifty, poisonous sapling sucking up the moisture that was the blood of the green oak for hundreds of moons. By-and-bye the oak will be leafless, its trunk dry for the burning, the poison sapling will be a green tree with spreading branches that will take all the moisture of the earth, and the roots of the oak will be dead. But the Mohawks are not squaws; they will come like the leaves of the forest in number, like the great whirlwind when the voice of Manitou speaks in the clouds, and flashes the light that tears the forest trees and burns the green boughs; they will dig up the root of the poison sapling before it has grown stronger, they will burn the pale-face wigwams, and pull down the strong lodges, they will carry away many pale-faces for the torture, as a sacrifice to the gods of their fathers.

"Wa-ne-no would go to the land where his fathers have gone straight from the battle-ground bearing with him his tough bow, his tomahawk red with the blood of his enemies, their scalps at his belt.

"Wa-ne-no will live and die in the faith of his

ancestors, and be buried with his face toward the setting sun. Wa-ne-no has spoken."

Something of the fire in the heart of the Mohawk communicated in an electric spark with the volcanic flame seething in the breast of the stripling, the Iroquois blood inherited from his mother flowed hot in his veins and flushed his cheek.

"Let the ears of Wa-ne-no be open," he replied in a tense whisper. "Wyancombone, the son of Wyandance does not forget that Wic-chi-tau-bit, a princess of the Iroquois, is his mother; he does not come to his red brother to ask for peace, nor to cry like a sick papoose, but to bid Wa-ne-no, who is a great brave, go tell Sine-rong-ni-rese to dig up the hatchet.

"Listen! A serpent has hissed in the ear of Wyandance and asked for more of the land of his fathers. His tongue was forked, and while he gave the right hand to the great Sachem of the Montauks, he held his left hand behind his back with an open palm to the Narragansetts."

"Ugh!" assented Wa-ne-no.

"Listen!" continued the young Indian. "From the far north where the guide-star rides in the clouds, to the place where the soft south winds whisper in the caves, from away toward the setting sun to the great waters where he rises, the name of Heather Flower has been heard in praise of her beauty."

"Wa-ne-no has heard," assented the Mohawk, almost reverently.

"Listen! When the Sachem, her father, would have given her to go to the lodge of the great warrior To-cus, the White Fox whispered the secret to the enemies of the Montauks that they might come while the Montauks were making merry, and with no weapons of war in their hands. Ninigret brought his warriors, in number like the snow-flakes, and as silent, and cut down our warriors like corn that falls by the hands of the squaws of burden. When the battle was over To-cus lay upon the earth, wet with his blood from many spear thrusts. Heather Flower was gone—carried away a prisoner.

"Listen! When the sun was red in the east the White Fox who had sold the blood of the Montauks to the wolves came and stood by the dead warriors and young squaws, and whispered in the ear of Wyandance, when his heart was soft with grief, a promise that he would bring back Heather Flower to her father's lodge, and the great Sachem promised that when the core of his heart sat again beside his lodge-fire another portion of the land of the Montauks should be given to the pale-face."

"Who is the fox the young brave tells of?" asked Wa-ne-no, a baleful light flaming in his eyes.

Wyancombone whispered the name.

"Ugh! Wa-ne-no has seen the pale-face who came to the land of the Narragansetts, when Wa-ne-no had brought to them the wampum asking them to come to the council fire.

"And does Wa-ne-no remember the pale-face?" asked the youth.

"Wa-ne-no has looked in the face of the fox—the Mohawk warrior's eyes are like the eagle's. He never forgets."

"It is well. Listen! Let Wa-ne-no first swear by the Great Spirit who watches over his red children that his hand shall kill the white fox, then Wyancombone will set him free and tell him where he may find his enemy."

The voices of the twain sank to a low whisper, and when the strange conference was ended Major Gordon's doom was sealed—the fierce Mohawk had sworn to slay the treacherous, grasping, white man whom his tribe had learned to hate and dread.

Wyancombone's sharp knife-blade severed the bonds, and the warrior glided from the prison wigwam. A moment later Wyancombone stole away in the direction of his father's lodge.

At dawn of day five warriors entered the prison wigwam to find it empty; they were the guard chosen to escort the prisoner to Saybrook Fort, where he was to be delivered into the hands of the English. Not a trace of the late occupant could be found, not even the thongs that had bound his powerful limbs remained, but an examination of the stake to which they had been attached bore evidence of a tremendous struggle made by the captive, supposably, to free himself and escape the doom that hung over him —the probability of death by the white man's gibbet. In truth the marks had been made and the thongs taken away that no evidence of the complicity of the Indian youth might remain.

At length the fruitless search was ended. But one mark was found, a single imprint of a Mohawk moccasin in a sodden hollow at a short distance from the village, pointing to the westward, telling that the fugitive had fled in the direction of the Mohawk country. Pursuit was useless, and, chagrined beyond measure, the party returned to the village.

The opinion prevailed that, being of gigantic stature and heroic mould, possessed of immense strength, the wily ambassador had succeeded in breaking the rawhide bonds at the point where they were wrapped about the stake, the deep indentations in the bark warranting the surmise.

For years a desultory warfare had been waged between the powerful Mohawks and the Canarsees, one of the minor tribes inhabiting Sea-wan-ha-ka, occupying a small territory of the western portion; the occasion of the strife being the refusal of the Canarsees to pay the usual tribute to the Mohawks, a measure that had been instigated by the European settlers at Gravesend and the adjoining settlements. Frequent raids had been made by small war parties, whose mode of warfare was, according to the usual practice of that fierce branch of the Five Nations,[1] a swift and sudden descent upon the village of the Canarsees; and at an earlier period the Canarsees had several times attacked the scattered dwellings of the English settlers, but the differences had been adjusted.

When peace was thus declared between the settlers and the Indians near at hand, the animosity existing between the Canarsees (over whom Pennowits ruled) and the Mohawks became proportionately greater, as the friendship of the Long Island tribes for the invaders of the soil elicited the contempt and hatred of these fierce warriors whose hunting grounds extended along the Mohawk and the North River.[2]

The Mohawk Sachem, Sine-rong-ni-rese, a renowned warrior, had conceived the idea of uniting the Five Nations and the Indians of New England and the adjacent islands in a mighty confederation that would destroy every vestige of the European settlements, and capture or slay every white settler; and for this purpose he sent emissaries bearing the pipe of peace and the wampum belt, whereby a treaty might be made binding with the various tribes east of the Long River.[3]

The most dreaded tribe of New England, the Pequots, had been annihilated, almost in a day; their

---

[1] *Five Nations.*—Or Iroquois, Mohawks, Oneidas, Onondagas Cayugas and Senecas.
[2] *North River.*—The Hudson.   [3] *Long River.*—The Connecticut.

villages and forts burned by the English, aided by the Narragansetts, and Mohicans under Uncas, and fearing a like fate at the hands of the usurpers of their lands, the New England tribes refused the treaty with the haughty Mohawk Sachem, and his ambassadors failed of accomplishing their object.

Among those to whom a messenger had been sent was Wyandance, but, as we have seen, the envoy was promptly made a prisoner.

A body of Mohawk warriors had moved down to the southward to within striking distance, where they lay encamped, awaiting the return of their messenger.

Wa-ne-no had made the journey to Sea-wan-ha-ka in a canoe, to a point within five miles of the Montauk village, where he concealed it in an almost impenetrable tangle of black alders and thorn trees so closely matted with vines that there was slight danger of its discovery by even a lynx-eyed savage.

This done, he made the remainder of his journey on foot, thus, with true Indian cunning, securing a means of retreat should those to whom he had come meditate treachery. At short distances he had marked the trail, and under the brilliant moonlight he had no difficulty in making his way directly to the hiding place, where he found his canoe undisturbed, and in a moment he darted out like a sparrow-hawk across the deep, still basin indented in the shore, the paddle dipped noiselessly, the canoe swept sharply around on its westward course.

Keeping well within the fringe of shadow cast by the unbroken forest lining the shore, Wa-ne-no bent to his task, nor paused until the dawn tipped the east, and the first golden spears from the rising sun rent the soft rosy veil of pink and amber mist and gilded the broad expanse of waters, tinting the light waves with undulating rainbows of light and gorgeous colouring.

The musical ripple of the waters broke against the prow of the frail bark, the matin songs of the birds came faintly from the shelter of the forest.

Scanning the shore with an eagle glance, the young Mohawk perceived a dense fringe of hazel bushes, dwarf oaks and miniature pines, laden with clinging vines from which the purple grapes hung in great clusters, with here and there patches of glossy leaves inlaid with plashes of crimson, the foliage and buds of the ripened sumach glowing like fire in the slanting sunbeams.

Turning shoreward, he gained the welcome shelter moored his frail bark to a stout sapling, and peered out from his leafy covert.

Not until nightfall could he resume his journey, and gathering a supply of grapes and a store of hazel-nuts, he crept beneath the umbrageous canopy and stretched himself upon the earth, almost immediately sinking into a profound slumber, from which he did not arouse until the sun was descending in the west and casting long arrows of red flame between the boles of the mighty oaks and feathered pines.

Refreshed and strengthened by the long rest, he again appeased his appetite with both fruit and nuts, quenched his thirst from the waters of a clear spring bubbling in a crystal ribbon from beneath a bristling rock near at hand, and again extended his lithe form upon the earth, waiting patiently until evening trailed her silver grey mantle over earth and sea. The journey must be made by stealth until he should reach the country of the Mohawks, for upon land roamed an enemy who would be proud to take his scalp, and out upon the waters floated the white man's ships.

CHAPTER XXXIII

ON ALL-HALLOW EVE

> "A lonely stillness so like death,
> So touches, terrifies all things,
> That even rooks that fly o'erhead
> Are hush'd, and seem to hold their breath,
> To fly with muffled wings,
> And heavy as if made of lead."

IT was on the evening of the fourth day when, wearied with the tedious voyage, the Mohawk neared his journey's end.

The moon waded up, dim and pallid, amid billows of vaporous clouds that at intervals veiled her face, as the canoe shot into the waters of the North River, and, obedient to the strong strokes of the paddle, moved up the stream. The scenery, at the outset half-pastoral, soon became wilder, as each mile was passed becoming more gloomy; dark hills towered on right and left shore clothed in sombre pine forests bristling against the sky; high barriers of rock lined the stream. The broad paddle glanced with measured sweep, while the light canoe rocked and danced upon the murky waters that crept onward with stealthy flow between the high bluffs and deep forest shadows ere it emptied into the waters of the bay at New Amsterdam.

Darker and darker the night shut down as the little bark glided onward, tossing like a feather, but keeping its course upon the very fringe of the eddies, with which Wa-ne-no appeared familiar.

The wind had risen and swept down the defiles in

gusts, moaning among the tree tops as the Indian guided his frail craft between the jaws of a gloomy defile into a narrow stream cutting the precipice to the base. Here the waters of the tributary lay black and comparatively sluggish, spreading out in a deep basin encircled by precipitous walls a few yards from the entrance, and here the Mohawk secured his canoe and leaped ashore upon a shelf.

A dozen war-canoes lay moored within the cove, quite screened from the view of any voyager up or down the North River.

Upward, along the rocky, dimly-defined trail, Wane-no made his way with the assurance of one accustomed to the route, among the rough crags, along narrow ledges, across sharp, broken rocks and smooth boulders, his scalp-lock tossing in the wind, the whirling autumn leaves, wind-driven, striking his face, until at last he stepped out upon a granite shelf from which a path led down a steep descent into a rock-girdled basin, where a singular scene was presented.

A score of camp-fires blazed up redly, casting a flickering light like witch-flames upon the rough ledges built upon the bottom of a huge bowl scooped by the hand of nature, and softly carpeted with green moss and still succulent grass which had lain protected from the biting frost that had nipped the leaves of the forest and browned the herbage of the upper strata.

Within the natural enclosure three-score swarthy figures were moving about or lying at full length, basking in the warmth and light of the ruddy fires. A hundred feet above, the wind rioted and raved through the waving branches; down in the heart of the basin the tumult was hushed, only a light puff at intervals betokened the strong current of air whistling dirge-like across the bluffs and sweeping down the stream on a level with the base of the rock-bound bowl, its proximity made apparent only by the vibration of the ground at regular intervals as the deep current rolled onward.

The narrow, well-worn path, attesting that the spot was a favourite camping-ground, led in a zig-zag course adown a side of the natural excavation less precipitous than other portions of the wall, and with swift, silent strides Wa-ne-no descended and made his way straight across the encampment to the single lodge reared at the opposite side of the basin.

Not a warrior appeared to notice his advent, although their curiosity must have been excited to the utmost, neither did he pay the slightest attention to any as he strode forward and disappeared within the lodge.

Beside a fire in the centre of the wigwam the great Sachem of the Mohawks was sitting, and at the entrance of his envoy he merely turned his eyes and with the gravity of his race peered again into the glowing coals, remaining silent, while Wa-ne-no stood motionless, awaiting his pleasure.

At length the war-chief demanded an account of the ambassador, and, in the graphic style of the red men, Wa-ne-no related the story, while the chief listened, his fierce eyes kindling with a baleful glare, his fingers toying with the handle of his tomahawk, the only signs of his vindictive rage.

"The Canarsees—they will not give the tribute?" he asked, after a pause, during which Wa-ne-no had stood mutely regarding the fire.

"The pale-faces have said keep wampum," returned Wa-ne-no, sententiously.

With a slight wave of the hand the Sachem dismissed his messenger.

Half-an-hour later a dozen of the chiefs and principal men of the party gathered about the council fire in solemn conclave, and before the midnight hour a plan of attack upon the Canarsees and the English who had instigated them to rebel against the delivery of the customary tribute had been formulated.

The sun, an hour high, shone upon the encampment embosomed in the wild gorge, a deserted spot; not a living thing was in sight, and only the blackened, extinguished embers of the camp fires, lying in masses of white ashes, remained to tell how lately the hidden basin had been thronging with hideously painted savages equipped for the war-path. But down the mighty river two score canoes were floating on the first stage of the long journey before them, freighted with Mohawk warriors, each with bow and arrows slung at his back, tomahawk and scalping-knife in his girdle.

Not a sound save the soft ripple of the waves and the low soughing of the autumn wind broke the stillness of the dull October morning as the war-party glided swiftly with the current, on the mission of death.

On the southern shore of Sea-wan-ha-ka, where the waves of the restless ocean washed the sandy beach, there nestled an embryo town, a tract of territory marked in village farms, or boweries, the grants allotted to each proprietor converging to an angle toward the thick palisade which served the double purpose of an enclosure for cattle and as a stockade within which the settlers might take refuge whenever danger from an Indian outbreak threatened, furnishing a stronghold of no mean quality against the primitive weapons of the savages.

Upon a commanding elevation stood the pride of

the settlement, the substantial mansion where dwelt the Lady Deborah Moody and her son, Sir Henry Moody, Baronet, and, notwithstanding his youth, a man of note in the colony.

Lady Deborah, spare, tall, patrician, with long, slender hands and aristocratically small feet, but with the step and air of a grenadier, was as unlike the typical Quakeress as it is possible to conceive, for in dress and speech alone she conformed to the preconceived model attached to the sect. A drab gown of rich material encased her figure, a kerchief of sheer muslin, worn over her tapering but thin shoulders and pinned in precise folds at her belt, was only rivalled in primness and immaculate whiteness by the plain muslin cap covering her abundant hair and framing in the thin, high-bred face with narrow folds. Through a pair of gold-bowed spectacles bridging a high Roman nose two steel-grey eyes peered with keen glances, a mouth with closely-set lips adding to the shrewd expression characterising this remarkable woman who had fled from England to the wilderness for freedom of speech and the right to worship God according to the peculiar tenets of the sect of which she was a consistent member.

Altogether, Lady Deborah was a most elegant and ladylike person, her manners unexceptional,—and so decided her guest, Major Gordon, as he sat in the capacious chimney-corner beside the cheerful fire blazing on the hearth, on the All-Hallow Eve following the day of his arrival at Gravesend.

Standing before one of the narrow, diamond-paned windows, set at a goodly height from the polished floor, was a tall, dark gentleman, of perhaps thirty years, but looking older from the fixed gravity of his expression, the sternly-set lips and the dark circles beneath his keen, grey eyes. His face was clean shaven, but a mass of dark hair fell over his broad shoulders from beneath the wide-brimmed hat which he had not removed, even when at table, for the Quaker customs were strictly adhered to in Lady Deborah's household.

The room was comfortably, even elegantly, but plainly furnished, the floor polished, the wainscoting and mantel bare of picture or carving; the window draperies of heavy damask, silver-grey in colour, were for use rather than ornament; massive mahogany tables, and heavy oaken chairs cushioned in grey velvet, were ranged primly against the walls; an immense bear-skin mat lay before the wide stone hearth, and grate and irons, of polished brass, glittered in the firelight, matched by the brass-mounted shovel, tongs and poker in the rest beside the chimney; the tall candlesticks were of sterling silver, and the wax candles burned brightly upon the mantel and table. Every article within the room was in strict keeping with the lady and lord of the mansion —all, except the guest, in his knee-breeches, wide-cuffed coat sleeves falling away to display the lace at his wrists, and turned back from a satin waistcoat, embroidered in the style affected by the " royalists," as those who favoured the restoration were termed. The man and his attire offered a striking contrast to his surroundings.

"And so, Lady Moody, you are of the opinion that Stuyvesant will listen favourably to a petition for a grant in this township?" queried the Major.

"Verily, that is uncertain," returned Lady Moody. "Thee can do no more than offer thy petition and await the pleasure and convenience of friend Peter; but, friend, thou hast not yet mentioned the name given by thy sponsors in baptism. Pray, tell me, that I may address thee after the manner most congenial to members of our sect, and, in accordance with the custom of Friends, thee will name me as Deborah, thereby conferring a favour," said Lady Moody, in a smooth, almost caressing tone, quite at variance with her rather austere bearing, as she raised her eyes to the Major's face.

"My sponsors gave me the name of Cornelius," returned the Major, smiling inwardly. "Scarcely a euphonious name, but mine, notwithstanding."

"A goodly name," quoth Lady Deborah, with an approving little nod. "Friend Cornelius, thee may count upon what trifling influence I may have with friend Peter to further thy interests and wishes regarding the grant."

"Many thanks, Lady—Deborah," he replied, hastily correcting his speech and at his mistake Lady Moody smiled.

"By the gods of war, I pray my good angel she may not insist on my ' theeing ' and ' thouing,' else I may chance to find myself in no end of trouble," mused Gordon, whimsically.

"Is it your opinion there is danger of an uprising among the tribes upon the island?" he inquired, after a pause.

"Nay, verily, friend, it is true that vague rumours of a contemplated outbreak have, from time to time, reached the settlement; but in all probability they are but imaginary," returned Lady Deborah, as she smoothed her kerchief placidly. "Thou must recollect that Wyandance is much attached to friend Lyon, and should any disaffection be discovered the Sachem would soon subdue the wicked spirit."

"You have suffered from one attack, have you not?" asked Gordon.

"Yea, verily," returned Deborah, quietly.

"And have you no fear of future depredations

from these Indians?" he asked. "I must confess I have a creeping sensation not altogether comfortable, at times, when I reflect that I am surrounded by these sanguinary warriors, and that the slightest breath may kindle a fire that would be difficult to quench," he concluded with a sudden shiver, as if a draught of ice-cold air had chilled the blood in his veins.

"Nay," returned Lady Deborah, "the God who brought us here is able to protect thee and me."

"Your house is strong, and well secured; I observe you have ponderous shutters barring every window, and that the doors are of tough oak, and thoroughly studded with iron spikes," remarked Gordon, with mild sarcasm, which did not pass unnoticed by the demure Quakeress.

"Yea, my house is well protected and serves as a place of refuge should these red men forget the law which forbids violence and the shedding of blood," she returned.

"I perceive you have a store of weapons at hand in case of such an emergency—a wise precaution," added the Major, as he glanced above the mantel, where two fowling pieces rested upon a pair of buck's antlers, beneath a brace of navy pistols of heavy calibre.

Lady Moody's eyes followed the gaze of her guest, and a half smile dawned upon her lips as she replied:

"Of a truth, friend Cornelius—'the sword of the Lord and of Gideon.' These are troublous days, and it behooves us to be prepared for an emergency. Should these benighted red men come down upon us with carnal weapons in their hands, the spirit might move us to e'en use the means of self-defence."

Sir Henry had taken no part in the conversation, but now he drew the curtains just as the supper bell

ON ALL-HALLOW EVE

pealed a summons, and Lady Deborah, taking the Major's arm, led the way to the dining-room, where a hearty repast was spread, assigning her guest to a chair upon her right hand.

A neat, deft-handed young Quakeress served the coffee in dainty china cups which her mistress had brought from across seas; and, with the massive silver service so strangely out of place in the rude settlement, Major Gordon quite forgot that he was thousands of miles from "Merrie England," and in the heart of an American forest.

An hour was passed at table over the substantial viands, the wine and nuts, and conversation flowed freely concerning the political affairs of the colonies, the relative claims of the English and Dutch, and the aspect should Cromwell declare war upon their Dutch neighbours, the subject being still under discussion after the trio returned to the sitting-room, interrupted only when Miriam, a trim handmaiden, brought the bedroom candles and placed them upon the light stand.

It was Sir Henry who conducted the Major to one of the guest chambers, a pleasant apartment upon the second floor, directly across the hall from the chamber occupied by Lady Moody.

Here, as below stairs, a bright fire glowed, putting to shame the candle-light, and flickering redly upon the ceiling, walls and canopied bed in the corner.

Sir Henry bade him good-night, and the guest was left alone.

The minutes passed, the house was silent as a tomb, and the Major started nervously as the clock standing upon the stair landing, after the English fashion, chimed the hour of eleven, each blow of the brazen hammer echoing hollowly through the halls and mingling with the moaning of the wind and rustle of the withered leaves, the creaking of the dry boughs and the shivering of the vines tapping like skeleton fingers outside the oaken window shutters, sharply as if some spirit from the other world, charged with some mournful message, was seeking admittance.

"All-Hallow E'en! I had absolutely forgotten, and the hour, if the tales of the goodwives are true, when the dead are permitted to come forth. from their graves. Ugh! it is a weird fancy! by the shrieking of the wind, I believe a storm is brewing."

The Major crossed over to a window, raised the sash, unbolted the shutter, and looked out into the night.

The sky had darkened ominously, one by one the stars were extinguished, the moon, low in the west, looked out with a pallid face only at intervals between the drifting cloud-veils, lighting with fitful, ghostly gleam the clearing where a few stately trees standing singly, and a grove from which the undergrowth had been cleared, left the earth in shadow, while, beyond, the depth of the primæval forest surrounding the mansion was wrapped in Tartarean blackness.

"What a beastly place! a horribly dreary outlook," he muttered. "The Isle of Wight is a secluded nook where a Christian may well feel cut off from the outer world, but it is sea-girt, with less opportunity for a lurking Indian to steal upon one unawares. But to pitch one's tent in this solitude, which the imagination can but people with pale ghosts is suicidal! Ugh! I would not consent to remain here for a kingdom—not I, faith! Nevertheless, I'll comply with the requirements, get a big slice, with a clear title, from old Wooden-leg, have a dwelling erected, and get a substitute to take up his abode here."

He had dropped into a great armchair beside the window, and, lost in his speculations, he took no note of the flight of time until midnight tolled from the old clock bell.

Rousing from his reverie, he was in the act of closing the shutter when a hazy object, flitting upon the edge of the forest, attracted his attention, whether human or beast he could not determine.

Wolves were plentiful in the woods. It might be a prowling stray from a pack, it might be a shuffling bear, but while he strained his gaze the dark shadow vanished, and the doleful hoot of an owl from the direction in which the object had disappeared convinced him that it was but the low, heavy flight of the night bird that had deceived him.

CHAPTER XXXIV

THE WAR PARTY

> "Each at the head
> Levell'd his deadly aim; their fatal hands
> No second stroke intend."

AS the shadows of evening were wrapping the dying day in the funereal robes of night, a strange but not unusual sight at the period of which we write might have been witnessed along the banks of the lower Hudson at a point just above Manhattan Island.

From the western bank of the noble river a dense and almost impenetrable forest of cypress, spruce and hemlock stretched away in boundless expanse to the north and west. As the daylight gave place to the gloom of night, and darkness lay over all, save for the glimmering light of the stars, silent witnesses with twinkling eyes, there appeared a horde of tall, sinewy, athletic Indians, dark of visage, with aspect fierce and grim in the hideous war-paint, moving like figures in a ghostly panorama, and bearing upon their shoulders two-score or more birchen canoes.

Silently as the dark waters of the river before them rolled on its course, unvexed, to the sea, they moved, and, unbetrayed by a sound, deposited their buoyant burdens upon the bosom of the placid waters.

When the last canoe was floating in the sedgy waters laving the shore, the group of figures sank down like shadows, to lie in wait in the murky night.

Presently from out the blackness of the opposite shore, at a point some distance below, came the clear, plaintive call of the coluber.[1] Again, and yet again, was the signal repeated, distinctly heard by the crouching figures across the hushed expanse of waters, and from the throat of a prostrate warrior on the western bank, who placed his lips close to the ground, came the answering call, in the same plaintive note.

Within a few moments thereafter a weird and startling phenomenon was seen.

At a point on the east side of the river, from whence the call of the serpent had come, a crescent moon was seen to rise, but casting no beams or illuminating rays, showing only a blue, phosphorescent light.

When it had risen to the height of a man of full stature, it became stationary, quickly grew into a full moon, and then slowly waned and faded from sight.

Instantly upon its disappearance the dusky forms crouched upon the opposite bank rose and stealthily they took their places in the canoes, which, under powerful strokes, sped athwart the waters of the Hudson, and ere long were swallowed up in the shadowless gloom across the river, at the spot where the rayless moon had waxed and waned. Here they were met by two of their clan, advance scouts who, by sundry grunts and guttural gurglings, assured their brethren that the coast was clear.

Without further delay the canoes were once more transferred to the shoulders of the tawny marauders, and the journey to reach the headwaters of Long Island Sound before daybreak was resumed.

This course was taken to avoid the white settle-

[1] *Coluber.*—Black snake.

ments at the southern end of Manhattan Island and the adjacent shores opposite.

It was past the hour of midnight when another pantomime of phantoms was enacted in this wild drama of a night. To a point in the East River known as "Hell-Gate," where the Harlem emptied its hurrying waters into the surging, angry maelstrom of dangerous and rock-ribbed, swirling shallows and seething, eddying whirlpools that gave the wildly picturesque locality the name, the light, silent, phantom fleet swept until the friendly shadows of the overhanging cliffs of Sea-wan-ha-ka were gained, then the prows of the entire number were turned sharply to the eastward and continued their course until they arrived at one of the many small densely wooded islands that dotted the headwaters of the Sound. Here the voyagers disembarked, and lifting their light canoes, strode away with cat-like tread beneath the sheltering trees, and were lost to view amid the fastnesses of the wooded islet, leaving behind but a single trail that might easily have been mistaken for the track of a colony of beavers, and the entire party was safely ensconced before the first grey streaks of dawn shot up in the eastern horizon.

They remained inactive until night fell, but as the shades gathered and blotted out the fatal day, a council of war was held on the tiny islet. The council pipe had been smoked with becoming gravity, but no council fire had been lighted, for they were in an enemy's country, and about to wreak a dire vengeance upon their unsuspecting victims, the Canarsees, for withholding the tribute they were under to their relentless conquerors, and to leave a trail of pillage and murder wherever they could surprise and strike the hated whites.

"The leader of the band arose and harangued his followers—"

THE WAR PARTY

The pipe had passed around the circle of hideous and paint-begrimed warriors, when the leader of the band arose and harangued his followers.

At last the conference was ended. Darkness settled again upon the face of the surrounding waters, and the shore of the little isle was swarming with a horde of bloodthirsty braves in full war array, who were now to re-embark upon their terrible mission of rapine and wholesale murder.

Very soon all were afloat, headed for the low-lying shore of Sea-wan-ha-ka, to the south.

In the darkness and stillness of the midnight hour the belated travellers and settlers who were abroad were petrified with terror when a fierce, long-drawn yell broke startlingly upon the air:

"Whoo-o-o-o-oot-a-loo-o-o-oot!" the warcry of the renowned and dreaded Mohawks.

CHAPTER XXXV.

SINE-RONG-NI-RESE

"Hand to hand, and foot to foot,
Nothing there, save death, was mute;
Stroke, and thrust, and flash, and cry
For quarter, or for victory."

UPON a low-lying strip of territory, almost devoid of hillocks, if we except the bluff that lined the shores, was the country of the Canarsees, comprising a few square miles, situated at the extreme southwestern end of Sea-wan-ha-ka.

They were a small but valiant tribe of red men, who were found here by Hendrick Hudson when that intrepid mariner's *Half-Moon* was first kissed by the waters of the noble river that still bears his name.

Like the Rockaways, their neighbours on the east, the Canarsees were a race of fishermen, or more properly, wampum-makers, as the south and west shores of their domain were washed by the waves of the Atlantic and indented by numerous creeks and inlets that teemed with every variety of shells from which wampum was wrought.

The Canarsees were also cunning hunters, and conducted a not inconsiderable commerce with their red brethren inland, in dried fish and dried clams.

As one of the thirteen confederated tribes of Sea-wan-ha-ka, the Canarsees had long paid tribute to the Grand Sachem of Montauk.

When the Mohawks made the conquest of the Hudson, or North River country, and drove the Mohicans, or River Indians, to the eastward, they descended upon the Canarsees and conquered them.

The unwillingness of the latter to engage in a war with the fierce and warlike people who outnumbered them ten to one was but natural, as such a war would mean the loss of their identity and independence and an exile from their beloved home, by being forced to amalgamate with some other minor tribe of Sea-wan-ha-ka, with the loss of the rich harvest their waters yielded them in the annual run of the myriad shoals of salmon and shad. These considerations, together with the fact that they were free from territorial disturbances on two sides, and immunity from interference by their single neighbours to the eastward, determined them to submission.

On the other hand, while the Mohawks were easily the masters of the situation, they could not profitably or safely colonise the territory, if acquired, for they were neither fishers nor makers of wampum. Hence, we find that at the time of the advent of white settlers the Canarsees were under unwilling tribute to the Mohawks, who demanded it with remorseless exaction.

In course of time the influx of whites from England, Holland and France, and their questionable and unscrupulous methods of dealing with the Indians, not only betrayed their too apparent greed, but alarmed and aroused the entire family of aborigines with whom they had come in contact.

At this period the different tribes were designated as "friendly" or "hostile," and every colony was the theatre of Indian uprisings and attacks, or of massacres by the whites, and this unhappy state of affairs had a depressing effect upon the industries of the Canarsees, whose trade in wampum and dried fish was cut off with the tribes living in the interior.

Encroachments by white settlers upon their small, tribal domain, under one pretext or another, had reduced it to less than one-half its original acreage, and from this small residue the game was rapidly disappearing, which caused apprehension and distrust, and more or less disturbance with the neighbouring whites.

The peace-loving Canarsees accepted the inevitable, and, as a means of livelihood, settled down to planting corn. The moons had waxed and waned until the tribute due the Mohawks was payable, and the Canarsees, who were insolvent, by the advice of the whites refused to pay it. This enraged the revengeful Iroquois and sounded the death-knell of the Canarsees.

Accordingly, Sine-rong-ni-rese, the great war Sachem of the Mohawks, resolved to destroy the hapless Canarsees.

It was at the time when the confederated tribes of the Five Nations, inhabiting the country stretching between the Hudson and Ohio Rivers, constituted the league of the Iroquois who were making the conquest of all the surrounding tribes, east, south, and west of them, whose wise men saw, with prophetic vision, the doom of the entire race if the invasion of their country by the pale-faces was not stopped, and the white man driven out or annihilated.

On the night preceding the contemplated attack, after the war-canoes had shot the rapids of Hell Gate and gained the rocky cliffs of Sea-wan-ha-ka, one of them touched the base of a precipitous bluff long enough for two lithe savages to alight. These were scouts who were to report to the war party on the following night, upon its arrival from the wooded islet, where it was to lie in wait during the day.

Timed with the precision of clockwork, they were on hand when the savage army, with muffled paddle-strokes, glided into the sleepy cove that offered a secure hiding-place for the many canoes to be left under the guard of two of their number, while the band filed away with hurrying feet, shielded by the dark and almost unbroken forest which they knew, and could traverse with instinct of wolves, shaping their course toward the village of the doomed Canarsees.

Very soon these swift-footed, lynx-eyed assassins, led by their unerring scouts, arrived within striking distance of their victims, and, making a detour, they quickly surrounded the village.

Suddenly the mournful howl of a lone wolf was heard to the south, and this was speedily answered by a howl from the north, and shortly after the same lonely cry was echoed and re-echoed to the east and west of the fated village.

Instant with the howling signals the hapless Canarsees had taken the alarm, and although most of them had retired, the entire village was at once astir, the inhabitants exhibiting the utmost consternation at the unwonted, untoward disturbance.

Before the slightest solution could be offered, the war-cry of the fierce and merciless Mohawks rent the air, on this memorable night of All-Hallow E'en.

Simultaneously with the utterance of their resounding war-whoop, the invaders closed in upon the surprised and terrified handful of Canarsees, who, entirely demoralised by the suddenness of the attack, offered no resistance, but sought safety in attempting to flee to some hiding place. Vain hope! The howling Mohawks followed like blood-hounds, leaping upon them with tomahawks and knives; some were pierced with murderous, stone-headed lances, others, upon their knees begging for mercy, fell back with heads crushed by the terrible war-clubs. Regardless of their piteous appeals for mercy, they were dragged from beneath the bushes, from behind fallen logs, from every hiding place, and butchered.

The Mohawks rushed from point to point, bounding and howling like ravenous wolves, cutting off retreat.

Thus, in a few moments, a tribe was annihilated, men, women and children, from the eldest to the youngest, from the aged man and the infirm squaw to the tiny infant who had numbered but a few short hours; all had perished, pierced with spears, shot with arrows, tomahawked, beat down by the war-club and scalped. Weltering upon the earth they lay in awful silence, while the flames from their burning wigwams lit up the horrid carnival of death with lurid light. Not a single prisoner was reserved, even for the torture, the only fate that awaited captives of the Mohawks.

Notwithstanding their ferocious nature, and strange as it may seem, such was their sense of the rights of men that the Iroquois never enslaved their captives, although they sometimes adopted them.

In one short hour naught remained where the village had stood, and naught told the tale of terror save the mutilated remains of the dead, charred saplings and tree trunks, and heaps of grey ashes choking the few glowing coals.

Thus was the devotion of the Canarsees to their white neighbours visited by the fearful retaliation dealt out by Sine-rong-ni-rese, the dreaded war-chief of the Mohawks, who, after descending upon, and destroying the Canarsees, proceeded to carry into effect the design he had mapped out for this night of horrors.

As soon as the last body of the murdered Canarsees was cast into the flames of the burning wigwams, at a given signal the entire band made a hasty retreat in the direction of the home of Lady Moody, the next place fixed upon to be surprised, its inmates murdered, the dwelling sacked and burned. When this was accomplished, they were to swoop down on Lawrence's Neck, several miles distant, and in close proximity to the quiet cove where their canoes were moored awaiting their return to re-cross the Sound and attack the home of Lady Ann Hutchinson, upon Throgg's Neck.

The first portion of the programme had been carried out with fearful accuracy. The three most important plantation houses must be laid in ruins ere they returned to their own country, and all the work of a single night.

But in striking Lady Moody's house they were to learn that they had reckoned without their host; Sine-rong-ni-rese was doomed to disappointment and was totally unprepared for the unwelcome set-back to his murderous campaign.

The surprise and repulse that awaited him was due to the sagacious service of Canady, a friendly Canarsee who had been employed upon Lady Moody's plantation, and to whom the eccentric Quakeress had been uniformly kind and generous, and for whom, in return, the grateful Indian felt a strong and faithful attachment. Both the Moody and Lawrence plantations owed their preservation to the good offices of this wily Canady, whose cunning had saved his own life.

When surrounded, and after every one of his ill-fated people had perished at the hands of the Mohawks, he attempted escape by flight, but received a blow from a tomahawk that had wellnigh spent its force. Feigning to be hard hit, he fell headlong into a thick coppice of hazelnut bushes, and crept rapidly away until outside the danger line, when he rose to his feet and darted away in the direction of the Moody house. Being one of the swiftest runners of his tribe, he was in time to give the alarm, and to tell the awful fate that had overtaken his people.

CHAPTER XXXVI

A CAPTIVE TO THE MOHAWKS

"All that the mind would shrink from of excesses;
  All that the body perpetrates of bad;
All that we read, hear, dream, of man's distresses;
  All that the devil would do, if run stark mad;
All that defies the worst which pen expresses;
  All by which hell is peopled, or is sad
As hell—mere mortals who their power abuse—
Was here (as heretofore and since) let loose."

THE minutes passed slowly, the clock had chimed the half-hour after midnight, and still Major Gordon sat in front of the open window. Within the mansion all was still, a deathly silence reigned in the forest, for the wind had lulled to an ominous calm, the King of the Gale was marshalling his forces for a terrific onslaught.

The watcher at the window saw nothing of the figure crouching in the thick shadow of a coppice of hemlocks like a tiger in the jungle.

Wa-ne-no, *avant courier* of the horde of warriors so near at hand, had reached the scene, outstripping his fellows on the march, and was lying in wait for a fitting opportunity to strike the man who had, thus unexpectedly, been presented for the accomplishment of the fell design.

The night grew more overcast, a strong wind suddenly tossed the fan-like branches of the hemlocks and roared through the leafless branches of oaks and maples, increasing to a shrieking gale, and the roar of the waves dashing high against the beach grew momentarily louder.

For an instant only the Major had descried the assassin as he flitted to a point nearer, and within striking distance of his victim.

Across the park, upon the opposite side of the mansion, and screened from the view of the Major and the skulking Mohawk, a human form dashed at breakneck speed, making straight for the rear entrance—an Indian, his arms outstretched in his mad flight, the soft patter of his moccasined feet lost in the soughing wind, as Canady, the last of his tribe, rushed blindly forward in his fearful race with death, embodied in the red-handed murderers swiftly nearing.

The cold breeze was chilling the Major to the bone, and, rising, he leaned far over the window-sill, his hand outstretched to reach the edge of the heavy shutter that had swung back against the wall.

At that fateful instant the brands upon the hearth fell apart, a strong draught swirled down the wide chimney, the red sparks danced and whirled in a glittering shower of stars, and a bright blaze flared up, illuminating the interior with a red glare against which the figure at the window stood out in bold relief, a fair target.

A rushing sound like the wings of a hawk swooping upon its prey startled the victim. Too late!—an arrow buried itself deep in his shoulder, a keen sense of pain overpowered him, his sight failed as he reeled, threw out his arms, lost his balance, and, clutching at empty air, plunged helplessly, striking the ground beneath the window, with a dull thud.

Like a harpy from the shades of the Inferno, Wa-ne-no darted forward, crouching like a beast of prey, grasped the shoulders of the half-unconscious man, and with Titan strength dragged his captive within the shelter of the black forest line.

Scarcely a moment after the captor and captive had disappeared Sir Henry Moody was roused from a sound slumber by a tattoo of ringing blows upon the rear door.

Ever alert, in those troublous times, and scenting danger in every unwonted sound, the Baronet slipped into his nether garments, and without waistcoat, coat, or dressing-gown, descended to the lower hall, where the imperative knocking continued, the blows falling thick and fast. But too cautious to open the door, Sir Henry called out in a stern voice:

"Who's there?"

"White man, open door—Canady come—Mohawks on war-path, kill all Canarsees—burn all wigwams—Canady hurt much—let Indian in!"

Sir Henry recognised the voice, and certain that the young Indian brought dire intelligence at that uncanny hour, he withdrew the bolts, and admitted the visitor, starting involuntarily as he saw the blood trickling down the young warrior's face from the scalp wound where the tomahawk had glanced. Hastily closing the door and dropping the stout iron bar in its socket, Sir Henry turned to the wounded youth, who had crouched upon a mat and was breathing heavily and in short gasps from his severe exertion.

"The Mohawks upon the war-path, and thou art sent to warn us?" questioned Sir Henry. "Where are they?"

"None sent Canady—all dead—father, mother, brothers, sister—all gone—nobody live to tell.

Canady—he come himself—run fast—keep scalp," replied the youth, in short gasps, and instinctively raising his hand to his crown, as if to assure himself that his scalp was indeed safe.

"All thy kin—all? I do not understand," returned Sir Henry. "And thy people?"

"Canady has no people—all Canarsees gone—Mohawks creep in dark, kill all warriors, squaws, papooses—Canady see brother with tomahawk sticking in head—see mother with spear in side—all dead—then Canady feel tomahawk—fall down dead—crawl like snake in bush—run—Mohawks like leaves in trees falling in great wind—not make noise—now come kill pale-faces!"

The words were more gasped than spoken, and the powerful young brave, little more than a boy in years, allowed his head to sink forward upon the broad settle.

"White brother, get gun—Mohawk come like leaves in north wind," he whispered hoarsely, the knife he had held in his flight dropping to the hearth with a clang.

A draught of brandy revived the wounded youth, and Sir Henry hastily made the rounds of the mansion, rousing his three stout henchmen, the trim housemaid, Miriam, with the cook, Dodo, a negress black as charcoal, with strong arms, huge fists, and a physique which an athlete might have envied, a slave whom Sir Henry had purchased from a slaver direct from the African coast, that he might save her from the horrors of a worse captivity.

A slight tap at the door sufficed to awaken Lady Deborah, who was a light sleeper.

"Wake, mother, the Philistines are upon us!" called Sir Henry. "The Mohawks have come down upon our friends, the Canarsees, and slain all—

men, women and children, and are now on their way hither!"

"Art assured, Henry?" called Lady Deborah, as she arose and quickly attired herself in a dressing gown and slippers. "How didst thou come by the knowledge?"

"Canady is here—the sole survivor of the massacre, as appears by the tale he tells," returned Sir Henry, as his mother appeared upon the threshold. "I'll e'en awaken friend Cornelius," and crossing the hall he knocked loudly for admittance, but there was no reply.

"He sleeps soundly for a soldier, but this is no time to wait upon ceremony," quoth Lady Deborah, "thou must open the door."

Lady Deborah hastened to the lower hall, while her son raised the latch and entered the Major's room. A blaze of firelight greeted his vision, but the Major was nowhere in sight.

The open window and swaying shutter attracted the Baronet's instant attention, and wondering much as to the cause of his guest's absence, he closed both window and shutter, securing the latter in its place by the stout iron hook, and made a hasty examination of the room.

He saw at a glance the Major's side-arms lying upon the table, pistols and a light rapier; his cloak and hat were thrown carelessly upon a chair, a drinking cup, and a flask partially filled with rum, stood upon a small tea-table close beside the arm of the high-backed chair in the chimney corner.

Thoroughly mystified, Sir Henry followed his mother to the lower hall, where he found her ministering to the wounded Indian.

"Mother, dost thou know aught of where friend Cornelius may be?" he inquired, anxiously.

"Nay, didst thou not find him in his bed?"

"I can find naught of him, and thou canst see that he hath not been in his bed."

Lady Moody followed her son to the chamber and made a hasty search in the chambers, even looking in the closets and wardrobes.

"It is passing strange," said Sir Henry.

"He may have returned to the sitting-room, or, perchance, have ventured outside—a most foolhardy action, if so," returned Lady Moody.

There was not a moment to waste, and thoroughly perplexed, but scarcely alarmed, except that the Major, who must have left the house, might fail to return in time to be admitted before the Mohawks made the attack, the mother and son joined the group in the lower hall.

A draught of brandy had revived the wearied, wounded Canady, and with her own hands Lady Moody carefully bathed and bound up the wound, which proved to be more superficial than might be expected from the loss of blood. Refreshed and strengthened, Canady made his story more in detail. His white friends understood the gravity of the situation but too well; that there would be an attack before day-dawn they were certain, and the few preparations necessary to be made at that day were completed.

From a tall cabinet cupboard Lady Deborah produced a dozen muskets and a like number of pistols, and assisted the five men to load, her slender white hands manipulating the pieces with a dexterity that could only have been acquired by frequent practise.

Scarcely had the arrangements been completed when a confused noise, as of shouts, came faintly on the breeze, accented, in a moment, by half-a-dozen musket shots, delivered in quick succession, a warning that dispelled all doubt as to the nature of the commotion.

An interval of silence, and again the crash of musketry broke, nearer, more distinct, mingling with and followed by the dread cry all recognised, the long-drawn, peculiar war-whoop of the Mohawks:

"Whoo-oo-oo-oo-oo-oot-a-loo-oo-oo-oo-oo-oot!"

There was a volume of sound, proving that the Mohawks were in force, and again the sullen crack of musketry reverberated through the forest, now near at hand, and an answering yell of defiance to the savage war-cry told that the settlers had been attacked and were evidently in retreat toward the stronghold, and were making a brave fight as they fell back.

There was a fourth volley, followed by the unmistakable tramp of leather-clad feet, in great bounds, like the rush of charging cavalry, and a shout rang out in stentorian tones:

"Open the door, for the love of God! The Mohawks are at our heels!"

"Whoo-oo-oo-oo-oo-oot-a-loo-oo-oo-oo-oot!"

The terrible whoop mingled with the appeal of the white man, so near at hand that it was clear the pursuing Mohawks were within a few yards of their white foeman, and Lady Moody unhesitatingly drew back the ponderous bolts and raised the stout bar, the oaken, iron-spiked door swung wide, and half-a-score women rushed through the portal, panting with fatigue and terror, one with an infant in her arms, three with children clinging to their hands, while outside, twelve men who had formed a rearguard for their wives and little ones, delivered a Parthian volley into the dark horde leaping forward in swift pursuit.

A shower of arrows hurtled like hailstones against

the strong walls of the mansion as the door closed with a clang behind the white men, the stout bars and bolts shot into their places, and Lady Moody's stronghold was in readiness to stand a seige, with the little garrison to defend it to the last extremity.

The story of the settlers was briefly told. A dozen planters, with their wives and little ones, had gathered at the house of one of their neighbours, William Goulding, to celebrate All-Hallow Eve agreeably to the English custom, and the guests were on their return homeward when the savage war-whoop burst upon their ears from a point directly between them and their little settlement.

There was but one course to pursue—a hasty flight, and that in but one direction, the nearest habitation that could afford them shelter, Lady Deborah's dwelling, and, dropping in the rear, the husbands and fathers urged the women to their utmost speed, while they covered the retreat with their fire-locks.[1]

But while the terrified women fled with the speed of frightened deer, their protectors were forced to follow almost as fleetly, hurried forward by overwhelming numbers of savages, and thus the stout yeomen were but a few paces in the rear of their families when the door of the welcome haven was opened wide to admit them.

The presence of Canady and his story were the first intimations they had of the destruction of the Canarsee village and the massacre of the tribe.

The swivel gun had been wheeled into position, the heavy section of wall masking it was drawn aside, and the brazen throat protruded in readiness to pour a deadly hail upon the advancing savages.

[1] It was usual in those perilous times for the people to carry their firearms to church on the Sabbath, in case of an Indian attack.

"Elizabeth, thou must not remain idle, the tenets of the Friends forbid not the defending of life when assailed by the heathen," admonished Lady Deborah, as she passed a musket to Elizabeth Applegate.

"Of a truth, friend Deborah, I shrink not from taking carnal weapons when duty demands—I may e'en follow thy worthy example in this regard," returned Elizabeth, mildly, "for, verily, those heathen without are but ravening wolves that seek thy life and the lives of the babes God has given."

A few moments of silence followed the first attack. The Mohawks had delivered the shower of arrows and ambushed themselves within the black belt of forest near at hand.

At the loopholes, disclosed by sliding panels along the entire length of wall on all sides of the mansion, and at different heights, men and women took their stations, the deadly muskets protruding to the outer surface of the wall, while every eye was strained in the direction of the black shadows where scores of ferocious savages were lying in wait.

By tacit consent the leadership of the little garrison had been given to Ensign Baxter,[2] he having served with honour in the English army, and, moreover, he was a man of dauntless spirit, a quality which all the teachings of the peaceful sect which he adorned had failed to eradicate.

The opinion of the entire party had been voiced by Lady Moody, in the quietest matter-of-fact tone, and the responsibility of the position was assumed by Ensign Baxter in an equally calm manner.

---

[2] Ensign George Baxter, with Sergeant James Hubbard, came to Gravesend with Lady Moody and others, in 1643. They were named as Sergeant and Ensign in the charter of Gravesend. Both were men of talent and capacity and were generally entrusted with the management of the affairs of the town.

"Friend Deborah, although, at the present time, I am not a man of bloodshed, yet, verily, I will do all in my power to prevent the forcible entrance into thy house of yon heathen, and I fain would have the counsel and support of friend James," was George Baxter's reply, as he turned to James Hubbard.

"Yea, verily," returned Hubbard, laconically.

At the first alarm the candles had been extinguished, save two, and the red fires buried beneath a mass of grey ashes, that not a ray of light might serve to betray the position of the loopholes or the death-dealing tubes that, at the word of command from those placid-browed Quakers, would belch a rain of bullets, each almost certain to find a living mark.

The lull of expectation had fallen. Even the little ones, huddled in a safe corner, hushed their frightened sobbing and remained in a listening attitude.

Canady had regained his strength sufficiently to enable him to take his place among the defenders, and at Baxter's command he took his station at a loophole high upon the wall, an excellent point of observation, overshadowed by the sloping eaves, his keen vision enabling him to discern the first appearance of the wily savages, and to note their movements with a knowledge and accuracy impossible to a white man.

Baxter had been wise in his choice, for presently a guttural exclamation broke the hush.

"Wagh! Mohawk come—hear war-whoop, maybe—maybe crawl like snake."

Not a white man had detected the stealthy approach of the crouching forms moving at almost full length upon the earth, dragging themselves forward by elbows and knees, like huge reptiles, but at the Indian's warning the index finger of each right hand sought the trigger of a firelock. There was an interval of breathless anxiety and uncertainty, then the crouching forms sprang erect, while a fiendish yell pealed in chorus from more than a hundred throats.

Like a demon-howl that fearful war-cry rolled out with blood-curdling echoes through the mist-laden air, and like a herd of infernal spirits the Mohawks broke from their covert, leaping in great bounds until within bow-shot, but at a peculiar cry from their leader every moccasined foot stood in its track, every strong warrior drew an arrow to the head, and the whistling missiles cut the air and were buried deep in the targets at which they were aimed, the thick, wooden shutters, and door, that bristled with darts like the body of an enraged porcupine.

With a yell of triumph the red archers turned, but not in time to escape the reckoning that came.

"Fi-i-i-i-i-ir-r-re!"

They heard and comprehended the single word that rolled from Baxter's throat, and a line of flame-jets flickered along the dark wall, while from the swivel a storm of shot poured, directed by Sir Henry's marksmanship. Half-a-score leaden bullets found targets in the bodies and limbs of the assailants, and the howl of exultation died away in a long, mournful death-wail, while a half-score forms lay huddled upon the earth under the faint, watery moonlight that for a moment struggled through a rift in the murky clouds, only to be swallowed in swift gloom.

Like phantoms, the uninjured disappeared, leaving their line of dead and wounded.

The death-wail of the Mohawks was echoed by a yell, fierce, defiant, almost demoniacal, the pealing war-cry of the Canarsees, uttered by the sole survivor of the tribe:

"Taa-a-har-r-whoo-wah-wah-wah-wah-ah-ah-ah!"

It was an uncanny wail, falling upon the senses of the ambushed Mohawks like a shriek from a ghostly phalanx of the slaughtered, whose bones lay unburied amid the smoking ruins of their homes.

For minutes all was still as the grave, a hush so deep that the sudden rustle of the wind-tossed, dead leaves was distinctly audible to the defenders within the dwelling.

So long was the silence maintained that even Ensign Baxter and stout James Hubbard began to entertain a hope that the assailants had departed, but their false confidence was destroyed by the young warrior stationed at the lookout.

"Have they gone, dost thou think, friend Canady?" questioned Baxter.

"Hide in woods—come back," replied Canady, positively.

His prevision was verified in the most startling manner.

Away to the right of the spot where the savages had entered the forest a red light suddenly gleamed, rising like a meteor from the shelter of a great boulder, and falling upon an open space, a single torch flaming balefully, and illuminating a radius of several yards, flashing redly over a human form standing beneath the arms of a spreading maple.

"God Almighty! it is the Major!" exclaimed Sir Henry.

"Swear not at all, friend Henry," admonished Elizabeth Applegate, mildly.

"Dost thou not consider that thy profanity can do friend Cornelius no good? Verily, my son, thou hast strangely forgotten thy creed, and that it is written 'Thou shalt not take the name of the Lord thy God in vain,' " said Lady Moody, rebukingly.

But in his overwhelming surprise and consternation Sir Henry quite lost sight of his Quaker principles, and their peculiar dialect as well, and in spite of his mother's remonstrances he delivered a volume of oaths that would have done credit to a trooper in Flanders.

Higher streamed the torch, lighting up the features of the prisoner, upon whom all eyes were fixed in a fascinated stare. Their attention thus diverted to another point, they saw nothing of the dark objects crawling towards the spot where the dead and wounded Mohawks lay. Ten brawny warriors had wormed their way over the brown sod and lay prone upon the earth among the wounded and dead. Two of the wounded had been merely stunned, and had regained their senses sufficiently to creep away with the rescuing party, while three others, whose injuries had been more painful than dangerous, were aided by their friends, and thus rescued and rescuers dragged their dark, painted forms across the open space and were presently lost in the woods.

The dead were left as they had fallen, and as the last of the wounded gained the shelter, he rose to his feet and gave a yell of defiance.

Canady's sharp orbs had detected the ruse, but only at the last moment, and thus divined the object of the demonstration from the opposite quarter.

As the yell pealed out, those watching the white prisoner saw him throw up his arms and topple to the ground, as if struck by a bullet, but on the instant he was being dragged at full length across the rough ground, and disappeared from view just as the torch sputtered and went out. Not a Mohawk was in sight, but the young Canarsee knew that the free end of a thong about the captive's waist was grasped by a powerful warrior concealed in the thicket near at hand.

The exhibition of their captive had served the double purpose of bravado and as a ruse by which to remove their wounded.

Anxiously the little band waited, but neither sight nor sound of the savages rewarded their vigil.

"Mohawk gone—not come back!" declared Canady, after an interval of silence. "Big wigwam not burn, Mohawk no get in. Gone burn 'nother wigwam—pale-face sleep, not see Mohawk, go kill, take scalp."

He waved his hand in the direction he believed the band to have taken.

"Lawrence's house?" asked Hubbard.

"Lawrence—big wigwam," assented the Indian.

"If they attack the lion in his stronghold they'll e'en find no easy prey. Art sure, friend Canady?" inquired Ensign Baxter.

"Canady know—find 'em—let pale-face open door—let Canady go!"

It was all in vain that they combated his decision, useless that they pleaded the danger after his fatigue from the already long journey, his weakness from the loss of blood, or the terrible shock he had sustained.

"Pale-face chief much good to Indian—give 'em blanket, give 'em meat—give drink. Canady not forget good pale-face squaw—leg long—run fast!"

Perceiving all protests vain, Sir Henry unbarred the door, and silently the loyal young brave slipped into the darkness and sped away on the trail of the assassins.

CHAPTER XXXVII

VIKING

*"Cease to consult, the time for action calls,
War, horrid war, approaches to your walls."*

"URR-RR-RR-RR-RR! Urr-rr-rr-rr!"
The great Livonian hound that had been the constant companion of Colonel Lawrence since his arrival at his cousin's house gave vent to the threatening growl.

He was lying upon the bearskin mat in front of the hearth, just as he had lain every night since Captain Lawrence, well pleased with the affection the animal had at once evinced for the visitor, had presented the Colonel with the noble brute, who was a recent purchase of the Captain's while on his late visit to Nova Scotia, and the Colonel prized his kinsman's gift far more than he would have valued a present of silver or gold.

Awakened by the warning growl, Lawrence raised himself upon his elbow and looked about the room.

From the edge of a mass of ashes under which the fire was buried a line of red coals cast a smouldering light, just sufficient to reveal the position of the animal, with body raised upon the haunches, his fore feet resting upon the hearth, his massive head turned expectantly toward the window, his ears and back bristling, his nose tilted as if scenting game. And while his master looked, the hound lifted himself and walked lightly to the window, placed his huge paws upon the sill and rubbed his nose against the pane, as if asking that he might be allowed a view of the outer world.

Obeying the mute appeal, Colonel Lawrence raised the sash and allowed the shutter to swing back sufficiently to permit a view of the park to the westward, and adown a vista where the moon gleamed out with pallid face between inky bars of cloud low down in the horizon ere it vanished in the blackness.

"Must be nearly three in the morning," muttered Lawrence. "The moon is nigh to the setting. By Jupiter, what a gale! What ails you, Viking?" he apostrophised, patting the animal's head, as the dog snuffed vigorously, and a deeper growl rumbled in his throat. "What do you see, old fellow, eh?"

Thick darkness had fallen, the trees groaned and writhed, a few particles of hail tapped the windows like a shower of shot, the elemental uproar denoting that the storm so long in gathering was near at hand.

The Colonel was about to close the window when the growl of anger changed to a welcoming whine, and there was the sudden, swift patter of feet, that ceased just beneath the window.

Something, either animal or human was there, but what human being could be prowling about at this abnormally early hour?

"Quotha! I'll see!" muttered the Colonel, and almost like an echo a voice answered, as if the words had been heard by the intruder:

"Ka-har-wee!"

The single word, in the Indian tongue, was uttered in a cautious tone, and answered by a whimper from Viking, and a wag of the tail.

"Who the devil are you?" called the dog's master.

"Sh-h-h-h-h!" came back a sharp whisper. "Me Canady!"

A tall figure, wrapped in an Indian blanket, was standing directly beneath the window, both hands raised, palm outward, the signal of peace among all the tribes; and at the instant the dog leaped through the window, and raising himself upon his hind feet, planted his broad paws upon the Indian's shoulders in the most friendly manner.

"Look, white brother, Viking know Canady. Poor Indian run like deer, say to white brother Mohawk come—burn—kill—scalp! Let Canady in."

"Take care of him, Viking—I'll call the master," returned the Colonel, as he closed the shutter.

It was the work of a moment to rouse the Captain, who, with the alertness so soon acquired by the colonists, stepped from his couch at the first tap upon the door panel.

"Canady, eh? Make haste to let him in. Some grave matter brings him—mayhap a threatened uprising—he's the swiftest runner among the Canarsees."

"I could not take the risk of admitting an Indian," returned the Colonel.

"Assuredly not, but this Canady is one of the friendliest of his friendly tribe, and can be depended upon more than most white men. Do you let him in, and I will at once waken my henchmen."

Henry hastened to open the door, and the visitor sprang within, seized the bar and dropped it in its rest as one thoroughly familiar with the place and the arrangement of the fastenings, and easily shooting the bolts in their places.

"Prithee, good Canady, what the devil is to pay?" called the Captain, as he hurried downstairs, musket in hand, followed by Elizabeth, who was habited only in petticoat and short gown, woollen hose and high-heeled slippers, while in one hand she bore a lighted candle held above her head.

Immediately the party was joined by Richard Smith, who had remained a guest at his daughter's house, and now strode down the staircase with the tread of a grenadier, his nether limbs encased in corduroys and military boots, his hands busy in adjusting a pistol belt.

"Hech! maisters, theer be bluid i' the air?" questioned McGregor, the butler, as he joined the group.

"We have not heard Canady's story," returned William Lawrence. "We only know that the Mohawks are let loose like hell-hounds. Let the young warrior speak," he added, turning to Canady.

In the curt style of his people the young brave told his terrible story, of the massacre of his tribe, his flight, his arrival at Lady Moody's, the advent of the settlers, of the attack and retreat of the Mohawks, and finally of the capture of the Major, and of his own flight to warn his friends.

"Canady run like deer before the hunter—Mohawk come fast—see 'em little minutes."

"But the Major—where is he?" demanded the Colonel, anxiously.

"Canady do' know—mabbe out in woods tomahawk sticking in head; mabbe Mohawk keep 'um—burn bimeby," responded the Indian.

An exclamation of horror escaped Elizabeth's lips.

"William, husband, can nothing be done to rescue the poor man?" she gasped, as she held her husband's arm nervously, her face paling under the candle-light.

"I fear not, Bess," he returned. "How many are there—the Mohawks, I mean?" turning to Canady.

"Like leaves on trees when the sun warms the earth—many more than all Canarsee warriors."

The entire household had gathered in the great hall, and each face blanched as the young Indian replied.

"We can do nothing, at least until a demonstration from the red devils," Lawrence said. "You hear what Canady tells us. At present we can only hope to make a successful defence behind these strong walls when the fiends attack, as it is certain they will. I believe the wholesale slaughter of the settlers is the object of these accursed Iroquois, and by destroying the dwellings one by one."

The candle was placed within a tin lantern and hidden upon the floor of a capacious closet, to be used if necessity required. Then the party repaired to the upper story, which projected three feet beyond the lower wall, the oak flooring pierced with apertures to serve as port-holes should a skulking enemy succeed in gaining a position beside the wall, while a similar line of portholes in the wall commanded the approaches from forest and shore.

Presently the hawk-eyed Indian discovered three prowlers darting from tree to tree, halting at each before making a forward rush in the direction of the mansion.

"Not a shot until I give the word!" commanded Captain Lawrence. "There are but three, and they believe us sleeping. We shall give them a warmer welcome than they dream of."

The moon, wading among black cloud-drifts tossing like piratical banners in the west, appeared at uncertain intervals in the occasional rifts, and at length was totally obscured. So dense was the gloom that even the keen-sighted warrior was unable to mark the movements of the skulking trio, who seized the opportune moment and gained a position beneath the windows, and at the door. Scarcely a moment had they tarried, and before the moon struggled from the black billows and shone out through a narrow rift they had bounded away like greyhounds and rejoined their companions.

The moments dragged slowly, while the watchers kept their eyes fixed upon the dark timber line, every instant looking for some demonstration, which came in a startling form.

A pale gleam flickered upon the brown grass and dead leaves, growing until a broad glow surged athwart the darkness, and pennons of lurid flame streamed upward like demon wings, bringing out the great boles and naked branches of the trees lining the avenue in bold relief. And, while they gazed, a broad sheet of smoky flame swept past the portholes, so near that its hot breath fanned the faces pressed close against the openings, and through the apertures at their feet tiny jets darted like serpent-tongues, quivering and emitting a pungent smoke that was stifling, filling the room with a ghostly light.

"God above us! they have fired the house under our very noses!" exclaimed Richard Smith.

"But, thank God, there is no combustible material except doors and shutters," declared Colonel Lawrence; "we have ample means to put out the blaze! Heavens! the stench is overpowering! What devil's agent have they employed?"

"We are breathing the fumes of the Indian turnip,"[1] growled Smith. "I don't know how they managed it."

The men were rushing down stairs to the lean-to in the rear of the building, where a deep well furnished an unfailing supply of water, the oaken bucket hung upon the sweep, and a dozen milking pails were ranged upon a shelf to their hand.

"Indian turnip?" repeated Colonel Lawrence, inquiringly.

"A plant indigenous to the country, having an unbearably-penetrating, burning effect upon the tongue and palate, and a suffocating smell when burned, as you perceive," explained Smith.

"Mohawk hide fire-balls in blanket—creep in dark—burn hole—let Mohawk in," explained Canady.

Mounting the stairs upon a run, they poured the contents of their buckets through the openings in the floor, an angry hiss rose as the water met the flame, while clouds of steam floated up like the thick vapours from a boiling cauldron.

Chloe, the sable handmaiden, filling an immense brass kettle, mounted the stairs, her giant strength serving her well as she stooped and tilting the vessel to a convenient angle, allowed the water to flow in a steady downpour upon the heart of the flame kindled upon the threshold.

"Chloe fix 'em, mistiss!" she gurgled in a satisfied tone. "Dat dar brass kittle hol' mos' fo' dem milk pails!"

To and fro the line of water-bearers passed between the well and the second story, and an almost continuous stream fell upon the great balls of pitch,

---

[1] *Indian Turnip.*—An American plant, *Arum triphylium*, with a head of red flowers growing on a stem, a root resembling a small turnip, but having an intensely acrid juice.

bear-fat and shredded bark, intermingled with the dry leaves of the pungent turnip stalk piled upon threshold and sill, a highly combustible compound which burned with an intensity that would soon have reduced the wood to a mass of ashes, leaving an unobstructed entrance at different portions of the dwelling, and placing the inmates, whom they believed sleeping, wholly at the mercy of the demon crew. The entire programme might have been carried out successfully had not the noble-hearted young Canarsee warrior risked his life to warn them of the contemplated attack.

The charred wood, indented with clusters of iron spikes, had withstood the flames for the few moments; the last vestige of fire had been quenched; the moon went down, not a star was visible, the darkness was lighted only by the ghostly glimmer of the sleet that began to be driven aslant in fine needle-points.

But presently a brighter gleam flashed athwart the gloom at a short distance adown the avenue, growing brighter as the watchers gazed, the spires of flame rapidly widening and shedding a red glow upon the brown sward and out upon the expanse of water now tossing turbulently in foam-wreathed lines reflecting the red glare in torn banners, and turning the fine particles of hail into a quivering shower of flashing diamonds, while beneath the shelter of the thick cedar and hemlock branches a shadowy group of gnomes swarmed, darting hither and thither like sharks leaping in search of prey.

From the gloom outside the circle of firelight two brawny Mohawks emerged, dragging with them a prisoner.

CHAPTER XXXVIII

AFTER THE MOON WENT DOWN

"Through the leafy halls of the wild, old wood,
 Rang an echo full and free,
To the savage shout of a fearful band,
As they bound the white man foot and hand,
 To the sacrificial tree."

CAPTAIN LAWRENCE looked steadily through the glass that he held in his hand.

"A white prisoner, and they are about to subject him to the torture!" he groaned.

"Let me see his face—it must be the Major! In God's name, let me see!" entreated Colonel Lawrence, his hand shaking nervously as he raised the glass to his eyes.

"God have mercy—it is he!"

The words fell from his whitening lips in a horrified whisper, as the prisoner's features were brought near with terrible distinctness, under the red glare of the fire—the anguished brow, the drawn lips, the imploring eyes, and the ghastly pallor, as with clenched hands the wretched man tugged madly at the thongs that bound him; and at the awful revelation the Colonel groaned.

The figure was visible to all within that chamber, but the two savages had retreated, leaving the nearly nude victim standing alone, the pitiless sleet driving against his flesh.

With bated breath the watchers waited for the next scene in the terrible drama. It came, and strong men turned deadly faint, while a sob choked Elizabeth, and she covered her face with both trembling hands, after the first glance, to shut out the horrid sight.

A shower of arrows, sped by unseen marksmen, rained upon the prisoner, bristling in his arms, his legs, his hands and even his feet, but carefully aimed by skilled archers, so as to avoid a vital spot.

Again naught save still life reigned. Even the tortured man had swayed forward and hung motionless, with bowed head and drooping form, upheld only by the strong ligaments that secured his waist to the tree trunk.

"Heaven be merciful!" exclaimed Colonel Lawrence, the great beads of perspiration starting upon his forehead. "Cousin, can we stand by and look upon this accursed work? In God's name, let us make a sortie and drive back these fiends! The sight is more than I can bear!"

But William Lawrence laid his hand warningly upon his kinsman's shoulder.

"It would be madness, Henry, to attempt a rescue!" he exclaimed, with emphasis; "there are at least a hundred powerful Indians, doubtless picked men, and they are skulking within a few yards of the wretched prisoner. We could not save him, and should be but playing into their hands; they hope, by this very means, to decoy us from behind these walls."

"White Eagle not go—Mohawks like wolf—great many—kill pale-face, then burn wigwam, shoot white squaw, burn papoose—not go!" warned Canady, earnestly.

"The young warrior is right; he knows the danger," counselled Captain Lawrence.

"But, merciful Heaven, William, I cannot remain here idle without raising a hand to aid! Can I allow the father of the girl I—of a tender maiden like Damaris Gordon, to be tortured before my eyes while there is the slightest hope of affording assistance?" still remonstrated Henry.

"There is not a hope. We should be but falling into the snare they are so cunningly baiting. I know their infernal devices, the ingenuity and diabolical cunning of these Iroquois,—the Five Nations, of which the Mohawks are the most dreaded, the most fiendish. They never make prisoners, except for torture. Should we make a dash to the rescue, a hundred yelling monsters would close in upon us; instead of one, my wife, my children, my maids, the entire household, would be forced to witness our torture, and afterwards they would fall into the hands of these fiends. No, cousin, our duty is here; every arm is needed to defend our own lives and the lives of our loved ones, for God alone knows how this thing will end—am I not right, father?"

Receiving no reply, he peered about in the gloom, but Richard Smith was absent.

"Father went down to the rear door to find whether any of the Indians are about the stables," whispered Elizabeth. "He fears they may burn the barn and slaughter the stock."

"Well thought of, wife; in my confusion, I had forgotten the beasts."

A yell pealed out from the edge of the forest, where a swarm of savages thronged about the prisoner, and began circling around him in a wild, grotesque dance, brandishing war-clubs and tomahawks, their fierce cries rising above the moaning of the wind and the continued patter of the sleet.

"War-dance," explained Canady.

Henry Lawrence felt a hand upon his arm, and a low whisper close at his ear warned him to silence.

Richard Smith had entered and stood by his side.

"Come with me. You are a man after my own heart. We will break up that hellish sport outside, or die."

He turned and slipped from the room, following Richard Smith down the back staircase.

"Hist not a word!" admonished Smith. "They will not discover our absence, for a time at least, and I have hope in a little piece of strategy I have on hand. Come!"

The outer door swung slightly ajar and the twain stood outside in the thick darkness. Smith closed and locked the door, thrust the mammoth key in his pocket, and hurried away, followed by his companion.

In the obscurity none had missed the Colonel, or observed the entrance of Richard Smith, save Canady, who made no sign.

"Laird save us, laddie!" exclaimed McGregor, believing he was addressing Colonel Lawrence, "gang ye theer an' ye coom to dool. Aye, laddie, we maun be flathered an' it wad be by the gudeness o' the Laird wad they tak' his life noo——"

The old butler's further speech was cut short by an exclamation from Chloe:

"Marse, look dar—dem g'wine kill um right 'way! Look!"

"Gude Laird gie the puir mon the maircy o' a quick endin' o' a' suffering!" groaned McGregor; "it is a' to wish for noo."

"It would be a mercy indeed if they would end his suffering," gasped Elizabeth.

"Aye, dame, aye!" agreed Captain Lawrence, "it would. If we were but within musket shot I would not hesitate to send a friendly ball, as the kindest office I could perform, and we would be able to send a few of these howling devils out of the world, but the cunning imps have measured the distance accurately enough—— Great Heavens! they are about to inflict some hellish torture!"

"Throw tomahawk!" exclaimed Canady.

A powerful savage stepped back and hurled his tomahawk; over and over, describing circles in its flight, the weapon sped, barely missing the captive's head, and falling at a short distance beyond the trunk of the tree to which the Major was bound.

A tall, cruel-faced savage stood apart from a line drawn up, evidently the master-of-ceremonies, for at his signal, a wave of the arm, a second brave stepped forward, hurled his hatchet and stepped to the rear; he, too, had barely missed the living target.

"Sine-rong-ni-rese!" exclaimed Canady, through his set teeth.

"And is yon monster the dreaded war-chief whose name is a terror to both white and red men?" asked Captain Lawrence, as he looked through his glass.

"That him—that Sine-rong-ni-rese," replied the Indian. "Um kill sister, kill father."

Like automatons, the warriors obeyed the unspoken command of their chief, the imperative gesture. Tomahawk after tomahawk whirled through the air, each missing the captive's head or body by a narrow margin, many by but a hair's breadth, as it seemed, while, roused from the stupor into which he appeared to have fallen, the Major raised his head and stretched his arms toward the dwelling where he believed white men were watching, for with eyes sharpened by despair he had noticed every demonstration, the sudden blaze of the fire at windows and doors, and its as sudden quenching as the streams of water flooded the combustibles.

It was a fearful scene upon which the watchers

gazed adown the broad vista bordered by tall pines fast crystallising in a glittering coat of ice, the long arms crashing and creaking, tossed by the stinging blasts, the glistening sleet whirling in a fantastic dance swallowed by the camp-fire, which threw up great clouds of grey smoke, through which a broad sheet of flame waved, lighting up the ice-paved earth like to a carpet of frosted silver.

Amid the white whirl the red blaze streamed across the pale, set features of the man chained to the tree trunk, looming above his head a pillar of crystal.

"Mohawk make sport—not fling tomahawk to kill."

Scarcely had the words passed Canady's lips when the scene changed. Sine-rong-ni-rese uttered a peculiar cry, and the screeching, dancing horde stood still, as if petrified by an enchanter's wand. The chief raised his hand and appeared to be haranguing his followers, concluding his oration by a sweep of the tomahawk above his head, a signal which Canady recognised as an order for an execution by torture.

A fiendish yell that fairly curdled the blood of the listening white men broke forth, rolling back in hollow echoes, the leaping savages circling in the horrid contortions of the war-dance, brandishing their weapons, threatening the captive at every turn, while to the right and left the head of the wretched man moved instinctively, to avoid the knife and spear thrusts, the demons gloating over the terror of the pale-face, and the spectators within the shelter of the beleaguered dwelling, powerless to aid, gazing in the dumb fascination of horror.

The frightful orgies were brought to a termination in a most unexpected manner.

From the forest on the right two streams of fire burst simultaneously, and two Mohawks, leaped upward with a convulsive shudder and fell upon their faces.

Conspicuous among his warriors loomed up the powerful figure of Sine-rong-ni-rese, his dancing plume and elaborate adornment of necklace, belt and embroidered robe glancing under the red light. And as the warriors fell, almost at his feet, he raised his head and gave utterance to a long-drawn cry, that was taken up by his followers, which Canady interpreted as a signal for retreat. And at that instant a terrific presence issued from the depth of the wood, a monster, black as night, with long tail lashing the air, great hoofs spurning the ice-coated earth at every bound, and bearing upon his back a monstrous figure, a giant in bulk, uncouth in shape as a shade from Tartarus, with four arms outstretched, hydra-headed and hideous, squat as the idols of a Hindoo temple, the two faces corpse-hued, with wide open jaws in each ashen visage, from which issued fitful gleams of fire alternately lighting and fading.

Straight across the fire-lit arena rushed the awful apparition, the monster beast with lowered head, a tremendous hollow bellow rolling out like the rumble of thunder.

The Mohawks heard the thud and crash of the great hoofs upon the ice-bound turf, the storm of icicles and the clash of the frozen underbrush as the behemoth swooped down upon them, and the horrible cry of the rider, discordant, frightful, continuous.

Into the thicket upon the opposite side of the arena plunged the uncanny object, only to wheel and reappear, and at the second sight of the terrible phantom the Mohawks fled at their utmost speed.

"Ho-bam-o-koo! Ho-bam-o-koo!"

The cry of dread floated back as the gigantic

apparition dashed straight to the blazing camp-fire, wheeled sharply, circling about the blaze, tossing its horned head and bellowing defiance, but finally stopping short and tearing up the earth with its thick hoofs, and again rushing round the circle.

Two of the four arms of the rider tugged at the thong which was passed through a ring in the nozzle of the beast, which came to a sudden halt, its broad flanks quivering, a long roar rolling out like the rumble of a volcano on the verge of an eruption, and mingling with the unearthly shriek of the rider.

Then a most singular transformation occurred; the dual figure separated, two forms leaped to the ground, each with the corpse-like visage, and while the stouter of the twain held the rawhide thong and patted the bellowing steed, the second severed the captive's bonds, and raising the limp, senseless Major in its arms, lifted him to the back of the now quiet animal.

Covering the burden with the flowing mantle that had clothed their own forms, the twain moved rapidly up the avenue, disappearing in the rear of the mansion.

The Mohawks had decamped, not a sound was audible save the voice of the storm. The sharp crackle of the frozen twigs under their moccasined feet had died away in the distance. The siege was raised.

CHAPTER XXXIX

AN EFFECTIVE MASQUERADE

"He shuddered, as no doubt the bravest cowers
When he can't tell what 'tis that doth appal.
How odd a single hobgoblin's nonentity
Should cause more fear than a whole host's identity."

. . . . .

"And Hamlet's father from the tomb,
And Faustus from the Devil."

THE awful phantom that had so terrified the superstitious savages as to cause them to beat a precipitate retreat was distinctly visible to the watchers within the mansion, and on the instant William Lawrence, Elizabeth and McGregor recognised the animal as "Whisper," Richard Smith's bovine steed—but the rider, who was he? N'ether Smith nor the Colonel had been missed, for, as we know, the room was dark, and those within spoke only at intervals, and then in whispers or the lowest murmurs.

Even the learned of the European nations were deeply imbued with a belief in the ghostly and uncanny and with all the superstitions of the age, a credulity that held the savage tribes in a thrall and awe more potent than musket ball or edged sword. No wonder, then, that at first sight of the singular spectacle the onlookers shivered, and, believing the animal was bestridden by some terrible spectre, their hands trembled and their knees smote together with a sudden weakness; but their awe gave place to what at any other crisis would have amounted to mirth. As the last savage disappeared and the beast came to a halt, the riders slipped from the folds of the mantle, the prisoner was released and laid upon the back of the phantom steed and was being rapidly borne toward the mansion. They had barely time to collect their scattered senses when the identity of the rescuers dawned upon them, and it was discovered that Richard Smith was still absent and the Colonel was not in the room.

"Heaven preserve us!" exclaimed Captain Lawrence, "what a venture! We should have known that there is none other than father who can handle that vicious brute, and it is our cousin with him. God be praised, Bess! for their ruse has saved the Major, and served to scatter the heathen like chaff before the wind; I make no doubt they think the devil at their heels. I hear Whisper's hoofs in the rear."

Hastening to the back door, he was surprised to find the bolt shot in its place, and the key missing from the iron hook upon the lintel post.

"Aha! our worthy father has secured the means of re-entering, and here he is!" soliloquised the Captain.

The key grated from the outside, the bolt sprang back with a click, and bearing the insensible Major, Smith and the Colonel stepped within and laid their burden upon the broad settle in the chimney-corner.

William Lawrence met his wife at the head of the staircase, the red light he held in his hands sifting through the perforations of the tin lantern, falling in grotesque patterns and circles on the wall.

"Husband, do shut out the light!" exclaimed Elizabeth, nervously; "it is dangerous."

"No fear, Bess," he returned, confidently. "Sine-rong-ni-rese and his cut-throats are at a safe distance at this very moment, I'll dare warrant. Father and cousin are below. They have saved the Major's scalp, happily, but there is little life left in his poor, mutilated frame."

"Praise God that you have saved him from further torture!" breathed Elizabeth, fervently.

"We must attend to his necessities at once. I will close the ports, except one, where our faithful Canady will stand as a lookout. Rest assured his lynx eyes will suffer no motion of an enemy to pass unobserved."

"Mohawk not show white of eye, he show sole of foot—run fast," returned the young warrior, gravely, as he took his station while the Captain closed the remaining port-holes.

The entire household had gathered in the hall where Richard Smith and Colonel Lawrence were bathing and binding up the wounds upon the limbs of the suffering man, while the Captain raked the ashes from the fire and placed fresh wood across the andirons.

"It is well the cruel devils wrenched the arrows from his limbs, else our task would have been wellnigh unbearable," said the Colonel, as he bound up the lacerated shoulder. "My God! but this is terrible!"

"A man takes his life in his hand when he makes his home among the savages," returned the Captain, bending over and examining the pale features of the sufferer.

"I am cold—so cold!" gasped the dying man through chattering teeth. "Brandy, brandy—my limbs are ice, my brain is fire—are you here, Henry Lawrence—are you here?"

He strained his eyes in a glassy stare, striving to

pierce the film with mortal eyes. "It is dark—all blackness. What sound is that?" as a gust of wind swept down the chimney with a roar, and a shower of sleet rattled against the shutters and door. "How the sharp hail beats upon my naked body! Let me take your hand. Hold me from the horrible pit where they would cast me—the painted devils! Save me! save me!"

Henry Lawrence took the hand already chilling in death in his own warm palm, and the cold fingers closed feebly.

"I am beside you, Major. You know me, Henry Lawrence, do you not?"

"My child—Damaris—I would speak—of her I——"

The words were breathed in gasps, and the Colonel held his brandy flask. With difficulty the dying man swallowed a portion, and the fiery draught revived him slightly.

"Promise me that—when I am—gone you will take my body to—her," he whispered, hoarsely.

"I promise," returned Lawrence, solemnly.

"Lay your ear against my lips while—I speak—the words you alone—must—hear," gasped the sinking man, and the Colonel bent his head to catch the message from the dying.

"You love—her—Damaris—my child, but you —cannot wed her—swear to bear to—her my last words—promise—swear!" whispered the fast stiffening lips.

"I swear," murmured the listener, his face whitening.

"Bid her as—she values my—blessing—nay, as she dreads my dying—curse, bid her keep her vow— she must wed—Guy Kingsland,—should she fail I will—come to her from—my bloody grave to—to reproach her for her unfaithfulness. Swear to—me—that you will—take this message from the dying."

"I swear!" moaned Henry Lawrence, the drops of agony standing thick upon his forehead.

"But, listen; should Kingsland wed—another, my wraith shall follow him to curse him. Should he die, then, and only then, you—have my permission to wed—the girl you love—and my blessing shall be—upon your union. Promise that—you will do your duty—that no word shall pass—your—lips that may—cause her to forget—or—set aside the obedience she—owes—the dead!"

"By all I hold sacred I swear to fulfil your commands to the utmost, setting my own deep affection aside, and remembering only that I have a solemn promise to keep!" returned the heartsick lover.

Once more the stiffening lips moved, without sound—the power of speech had departed forever. The glazing eyes turned from side to side, then fixed their unseeing stare upon the face bending near, while Henry Lawrence clasped the cold hand until it stiffened in death and the hard, cruel frown deepened and slowly froze on the stony face.

To Henry Lawrence alone the whispers of the dying had been audible, and Captain Lawrence looked curiously at his kinsman as he rose to his feet, marvelling much at the sudden pallor that crept over the handsome face, but Bessie Lawrence, looking in the anguished eyes, with a woman's quick sympathy divined the secret.

Briefly Richard Smith sketched the circumstances that had prompted the desperate venture resulting in terrorising the ferocious Mohawks, whose superstitious fears were stronger than their thirst for blood.

"I little thought, when I whittled those turnip-faces for the little lads, that my work would prove the salvation of our household. Verily, trifles turn the scale of life and death; I'm sharp o' hearing, and I fancied there was a commotion in the stable, and hurried down to get a peep in that direction, hoping to get in a telling shot or two if they were running off the stock. The dull light from the coals fell upon something white lying upon the settle, and I saw that the lads had left the turnip masks loose and handy; but I forgot their untidiness, for an idea suddenly presented itself, and I regarded the lads as especially directed by Providence. I sketched the plan which we carried out successfully. A pair of skull-caps hanging on a peg served to muffle our heads. We adjusted the masks. The big camlet cloak that was Bessie's mother's was folded in the settle chest, and broad enough to cover both. At the Colonel's suggestion we lighted two bits of walnut wood and gripped the chips between our teeth, the coal just within our jaws, and sallied out to the stables, two hideous spectres breathing fire. I had only to attach the bridle to the ring in the beast's nose, and mounting, we drew the big cloak about our shoulders and were off on our course, making a circuit in order to fall upon the devils in the rear. Had not the clatter of Whisper's hoofs upon the frozen ground warned them, we might have been in time to save the prisoner's life, for up to that moment his wounds had not been of a character to injure him permanently. As it was, at the first alarm they believed a body of white men at hand, and the knives and hatchets did their work. They left him for dead, but the sight of the awful spook set their feet in motion. A prod in the brute's neck caused him to roar in a frightful manner, and the bray of the big dinner horn the Colonel carried, added to the bellow as we dashed round the circle—no wonder the imps believed Satan was after them in bodily form."

"Aweel, maisters, ye lookit lak the de'il. Ye fuffed fire lak auld Clootie [1] hissel," said McGregor, as he took one of the corpse-white masks in his hand, a mere shell hewed from a mammoth turnip, fashioned with cavernous eye-holes, a grinning mouth, a high, hooked nose secured by a peg, and with four stout cords as a convenience in fastening the contrivance to the head of the wearer, who appeared like a moving corpse.

"Hecht, sirs! but it's a fearsome face. It do lookit lak a ghaist [2] a-glowrin' [3] an' a-girnin'.[4] Nigher ane cooms i' the candle-licht the mair awfu' it lookit! The guid-father [5] did weel; it's the luck they tak 'ee for a bogle,[6] else the dwellin' wad noo 'a' been a-reekin' [7] an' the murderers red-wat-shod [8] i' the morn!" croaked the old butler dismally, in the broad Scottish dialect he fell into whenever unduly excited.

"Bear a hand, McGregor, no time to be crooning!" called Captain Lawrence, rather impatiently. "We must take this poor, abused body above stairs and compose his limbs decently."

The morning broke, clear and cold, the sunlight streamed through the narrow chink where, all the dark hours preceding the dawn, the faithful Canarsee had kept his vigil. Not a tufted head had appeared, not an unwonted sound had mingled with

[1] *Clootie.*—The Devil.
[2] *Ghaist.*—Ghost.
[3] *Glowrin'.*—Staring.
[4] *Girnin'.*—Grinning in agony or anger.
[5] *Guid-father.*—Father-in-law.
[6] *Bogle.*—Hobgoblin.
[7] *Reekin'.*—Burning.
[8] *Red-wat-shod.*—Over shoes in blood.

the clash of the falling sleet and the roar of the wind, sounds that died away and were succeeded by a hush as of death ere the day dawned.

The fire was quenched upon the icy earth, leaving naught beside a mass of grey ashes and blackened, charred embers upon which the dancing sunbeams shone aslant, turning the ice-laden branches of the trees to masses of shimmering diamonds, amethysts, topaz and emeralds, in bars and slender wreaths outlined sharply against the opal sky.

"Mohawks gone back to own country, not come back," declared Canady, when, after sunrise, he returned from the examination of the trail he had followed, until satisfied of the direction which the war-party had taken. With the first dawn he had quietly left the house, taken up the broad trail of the retreating Indians, and satisfied himself that they were on their homeward way.

"You think there is no danger of another attack to-night?" questioned the Captain.

"Not come here—mabbe go some wigwam on trail—mabbe go to Mohawk country not stop—do' know."

After a hearty breakfast Captain Lawrence knelt with his household and devoutly thanked God for their providential deliverance from the massacre that had menaced all beneath his roof.

The day passed without alarm, and no sound of war-whoop disturbed the night, but early upon the second morning after the attack the brig *Nautilus* cast anchor at the little landing, the Captain bringing the intelligence that Lady Ann Hutchinson, with her entire household, had been massacred at Throgg's Point, the attack having been made by the Mohawks shortly after ten o'clock on the previous evening. The dwelling had been burned, the outbuildings destroyed, the cattle slaughtered, and after completing their murderous work the savages had beat a retreat, taking with them the spoils they had collected, but not a single prisoner. Every white person was slain—men, women and children lay weltering in their life-blood beneath the pitying stars when the slayers embarked in their canoes on their retreat to their own country.

As on the former occasion, they had lain in wait during the day, to sally forth under cover of darkness on their mission of slaughter.

Colonel Lawrence gladly embraced the opportunity of sailing to the Isle of Wight, and although the seamen, with all the superstition of their calling, and the times, demurred against taking a dead body aboard, Captain Broadbent, willing to accommodate a man in the high standing of Captain Lawrence, put aside his own secret misgiving and consented to receive the mutilated remains.

"Canady has no people—no home, he will go with his white brother, to live in the wigwam of the Montauks, and they shall be his people," declared the bereaved young warrior. "When Mohawks come to kill red brothers, Canady take scalps. Ugh!"

At sunset the rude coffin, fashioned by the carpenter at the little settlement, was borne to the waiting boat, the two passengers stepped in and were rowed to the ship, and with a fair wind the *Nautilus* sailed away.

CHAPTER XL

THE SLAVE SHIP

"Over the roar of the signal gun
  The surging billows swept;
Over the peaceful, dreaming forms
  The treacherous waters crept;
And the midnight sky, like a funeral pall,
  Hung low o'er the sinking ship,
And the cry of terror, 'We're lost, we're lost!'
  Went trembling from lip to lip."

THE green ocean waves, fringed with snow-white foam, rose and fell in measured rhythm, sparkling and shimmering under the rays of the round moon sailing upward in aerial splendour toward the zenith, a disc of burnished gold paling the galaxy of stars in the pearly November sky flecked here and there with fleecy cloud mists, ever changing as they floated softly in the opal arch.

A fair wind filled the canvas of the *Nautilus*, bearing her smoothly onward toward the Isle of Wight, a destination she was swiftly nearing.

Captain Broadbent, her weather-beaten, staunch commander, impatiently paced the quarter-deck, giving an occasional order to the wheelman, as he glanced at the compass within the binnacle, or whenever his keen eye detected, by the drawing of the sails, that the vessel was off her course by a quarter of a point.

Leaning against the taffrail stood Henry Lawrence, his eyes fixed thoughtfully, almost sternly, upon the long lines of spray flashing back the moon's silver in prismatic lustre, while the ship sped over the rippling waters, his thoughts with the maiden he was soon to meet, whose sire, asleep in death, lay in the cabin below.

By his side stood Canady, a picturesque figure, enveloped in a bearskin robe, his arms folded across his chest, an impersonation of manly strength, his head towering above the brawny marines near at hand.

" Big canoe! "

The Indian uttered the brief sentence, and pointed eastward.

Seven bells had just been struck.

" I see nothing. I think for once you must be mistaken, Canady," returned Colonel Lawrence. " Neither the Captain nor the lookout appears to have noticed a sail."

" Indian see 'em in moonshine—pale-face brother see 'um bimeby," answered Canady, and with his eyes fixed intently in the direction he had indicated, he awaited the discovery by the lookout.

" Sail-ho! " shouted the lookout two minutes later, the stentorian shout ringing over the water like a trumpet call.

" Whereaway? " called the Captain, as, glass in hand, he swept the broad expanse.

" About two points off the lee-bow, sir."

" Aye, aye," responded the Captain, as instantly he levelled his glass in the direction given by the lookout, and there, in the moonglade, less than a mile distant, was a long, low-hulled, rakish-looking craft that appeared to be sailing close-hauled, but her behaviour would seem to suggest that her wheelman was but a novice, as one moment she would luff until her sails were all aflap and the next moment she would swing off two or three points free.

Captain Broadbent surveyed her long and steadily through his glass. At length he asked:

"What do you make her out, Sandy?"

"Can't make her out, sir," was the reply from the knight-head. "Something odd about her; looks like mutiny. The crew is rushing about like a swarm of bees. The devil is to pay, or I'm a landsman!"

It was Canady, after gazing long and steadily, who solved the riddle.

"Fire."

"By the beard of Neptune, you're right—the ship is on fire," exclaimed the Captain, and even as the words left his lips a spire of flame, like a devouring sword, streamed upward from the hatchway, illuminating the deck with a red glare and plainly revealing the figures scurrying hither and thither.

"Call all hands!" commanded Captain Broadbent; then turning to the helmsman, he called:

"Port your wheel and run off so as to round to off the windward of the stranger!"

Both orders were obeyed on the instant.

"There goes her signal gun!" exclaimed Lawrence. "Good God! Look at the poor wretches! See them crowd and jostle each other!"

"She's a queer looking craft—shouldn't be in the least surprised if she should prove to be a pirate, though what the devil such a craft can be doing in these waters, I can't make out!" grumbled Captain Broadbent, in a puzzled tone.

All sail was crowded, and as they neared the sharp-prowed, black, dismal-looking ship, the crew could be seen huddling upon the deck, where they appeared to be lowering the boats, and evidently the officers had lost all control, for nothing like order was apparent.

THE SLAVE SHIP

"Who'll volunteer for the rescue?" shouted the Captain of the *Nautilus*.

Colonel Lawrence stepped forward with Canady, and officers and marines followed the example.

"Avast there! I won't spare the entire ship's crew!" bawled the Captain. "Mr. Harrup, clear and man the starboard-quarter and waist boats. You take command of one, and Colonel Lawrence of the other; have everything in readiness to lower away when we heave-to to windward of the burning craft!"

In due time the boats were lowered, and as Lawrence took his place in command of the second boat, Canady stepped in beside him.

"Give way, lads!" he commanded, and the oarsmen bent to their task with a will that sent the boat dancing across the waves like a cockle-shell, the Colonel standing upright with Canady beside him, the attention of both rivetted upon the vessel they were swiftly nearing.

Meanwhile the burning ship's boats, heavily freighted, had put off and were pulling away from the doomed craft; but a little group, who had evidently been left by their companions to perish, were crowding back from the black columns of smoke rolling up from below, mottled with red flames, reaching toward them, darting and lapping like dragon tongues in search of prey.

It was an awful scene. The flames were bursting from the fore and main hatchways, and a volume of sulphurous smoke was pouring from the cabin windows, while the devouring monster, creeping at first stealthily along the rigging, outlining them against the sky in crimson silhouette, suddenly streamed out in broad banners. And as the rescuers gazed with fascinated stare, a port-hole belched flame with a roar and recoil that rocked the dark hull, as a gun, heated by the conflagration, hurled a rain of shot whistling dangerously low over the heads of the boats' crews.

"Ha! an armed vessel; and that is part of her armament—loaded to the muzzle! Harkee, my lads! That she's a pirate, or something like, I'll lay fifty pounds!" shouted Lieutenant Harrup. "Zounds! there's another!"

A second gun roared like a burst of thunder, the sudden flash darting straight through the redder glare of flame bursting from the ship's side like a paler meteoric blaze of lambent light.

"Fortunate for us that we are below range!" called Colonel Lawrence, "else our errand of mercy would cost us dear."

Three human figures were crouching closer and closer together, striving to escape the flames fast rolling toward the spot where they had taken refuge. A sheet of fire swept high in air, revealing the faces of the frightened beings, who, with hands uplifted and clasped above their heads, strove to incite the oarsmen of the fast nearing boats to greater exertion, while a long dismal cry arose, but in a language unintelligible to all save the young Canarsee brave.

"God save us! they are Indians, and manacled! Pull for your lives, lads! Pull!" shouted Lawrence, his dark eyes flashing.

Again and again frantic yells rang out over the waters, in response to the shouts from Canady, in the Delaware tongue, and with straining sinews the oarsmen of both boats pulled, the great beads of perspiration rolling down their weather-bronzed faces and the boats leaped forward like living things.

Two guns roared in quick succession, but the shot hurtled high overhead.

"Tell 'em to jump overboard, Indian!" shouted Harrup; "tell 'em we'll pick 'em up! If the fire reaches the magazine, we shall all be blown to Davy Jones' locker without a minute to say our prayers."

The boats were within a cable-length of the burning vessel, and again Canady raised his voice in a deep, guttural call, heard above the roar of the conflagration, shouting a command in the Indian tongue.

A long, monotonous wail, the mournful death-chant, was the sole reply, swelling on the air like the cry of a lost soul and dying away in a piteous plaint.

"Merciful Saviour! See, they are manacled, hand and foot!" groaned the Colonel, as he gazed with horror-stricken eyes. "God help them!"

Two warriors sprang upright, their lithe figures standing out in horrible relief against the background of flame, their long black hair already crisping in the heat, tossed by the hot air of the raging furnace that was blistering their naked shoulders, while for one brief moment they stood confronting the boats' crews, gazing upon them in horrified amazement. And then, throwing up their arms, they bent forward, balanced their half-nude bodies across the rail, and rolled helplessly into the sea, sinking like lead from the heavy weights of their cruel irons, only a circle of swirling water marking the place where they went down.

One alone stood upon that fire-begirt pyre, a mere youth, slender and straight as a bronze Apollo. Stretching out his hands he held them over a tongue of flame writhing along the rail.

CHAPTER XLI

AN OCEAN GRAVE

"Down on the vale of death with dismal cries
The fated victims shuddering cast their eyes
In wild despair; while yet another stroke,
With strong convulsion rends the solid oak;
Ah Heaven—behold her crashing ribs divide!
She loosens, parts, and spreads in ruin o'er the tide."

PERHAPS the number of manacles on board had been too few, perchance his youth had rendered the use of irons needless in the estimation of the captain. At all events, the bonds confining the limbs of the Indian boy had been of rawhide, and the fire rapidly shrivelled the ligament connecting the wrists.

A lighted splinter applied to the thongs upon his ankles but a moment snapped the bonds. His flesh must have been severely blistered, but with Spartan firmness the lad nerved himself, and as the tough rawhide parted he leaped overboard from the very jaws of the fire-demon as it closed over the spot where he had stood.

A few powerful strokes and Lawrence's boat came alongside the strong swimmer, Canady gripped a shoulder and drew him into the boat, while the Colonel, unclasping the cloak from his own neck, wrapped it about the shivering youth.

The doomed ship stood wrapped in a winding-sheet of flame, fiery serpents entwined her masts, lapped spars and leaped from her sides, sending up volumes of black smoke and evanescent millions of stars glittering for an instant to be swallowed in the green depths below.

"The fire is close to the magazine! Pull, lads, pull for your lives!" shouted Harrup, and with almost superhuman strength the stout oarsmen obeyed, the boats dashing away from the burning wreck as if propelled by Titans.

Barely in time to escape destruction. A roar, as of a volcanic eruption, heaved the ocean and rent the air, a vast sheet of flame and lurid smoke burst heavenward, bearing the splintered masts and stout timbers high in air as if they had been straws at the sport of the wind, the terrific pyrotechnic display flaming over the waters, colouring the heaving billows to floods of blood-red wine far down the vortex that seethed as if heated by a subterranean furnace kindled in the glowing heart of Hades.

Gigantic rockets of burning timbers hurled into the heavens were outlined against the chill blue of the November sky, amid great drifts of blazing sails hovering like the fiery wings of the fabled roc[1] above an army of flying serpents, a figment from an Oriental tale of diablerie and enchantment, fascinating from its very horror.

One moment,—an age it seemed to the beholders,—the display blazed with an intense brilliancy, flickered and flamed, spread, and circled against the blue arch, then suddenly descended, flashing like masses of rubies, garnets and carbuncles, their red lustre quenched forever in the blackness of the maelstrom, while in the pale glow of the moonlight,

---

[1] *Roc.*—A fabled bird of such monstrous proportions as to be enabled to carry away an elephant in its talons. Frequently mentioned in "Arabian Nights' Entertainments."

dimmed by the contrast, the rescuing boats reeled, tossed, and shivered like wounded birds upon the outer circle of the awful whirlpool among the few scattered brands afloat far out upon the waves, glimmering like fireflies—all that was left of the stout ship.

It was a moment of dreadful suspense.

From the most hardened among those hearts of oak, and from their messmates watching with straining gaze from the deck of the *Nautilus*, a silent thanksgiving arose to Almighty God for the miraculous salvation from what had seemed certain death, and each drew a long breath of relief, while tears, that were no shame to their manhood, bedewed many a bronzed cheek when they stood safe upon the deck amid the cowardly officers and crew of the lost ship, seamen who had basely left their fellow-beings, manacled and helpless as they were, to perish miserably.

"Were there others besides this boy and his companions aboard your craft?" asked Captain Broadbent, turning his stern face toward the captain.

"No others," returned the black-browed captain doggedly.

"The pale-face lies!" contradicted the Indian boy, as he boldly confronted the wretch. "Much people—black men down in black hole, under great water! Pale-face bring black brother in big canoe—make 'em work—work—steal Indian—mabbe make 'em work—mabbe no!"

"And was that an accursed slaver?" demanded Colonel Lawrence, his fine eyes kindling wrathfully, his brow contracting. "The truth, sirrah!" he added, as the captain made an indistinct reply in bad English.

"Aye, man, if ye be a man, you miserable villain!" exclaimed Captain Broadbent, with an ugly frown, and laying his hand upon his sword-hilt.

"The *Dragon* was a slaver, and in the employ of those yon in power. Look ye to my masters in New Amsterdam, an' ye have fault to offer!" snarled the captain sullenly. "I'm Captain Butcher."

"Umph! a Dutchman! just the kind of craft to overhaul. Butcher, eh? the *Dragon!* The names suit. The statutes framed by the government we serve provide for such cases as this. We'll e'en look to 't, varlet, and do our bounden duty in seeing that the laws are enforced!" declared Captain Broadbent.

"Your English ships fiddle to the same tune. Had we sailed under the English flag your authorities would 'a' winked at our cargo," retorted Captain Butcher, boldly. "Off the Guinea coast we crossed the forefoot of an English slaver; skipper, mate and crew English, as piratical a craft as ever sailed under the black flag. I doubt me not she will have no trouble in disposing of her cargo. Take me before your cursed courts, an' be damned to ye!"

A thorough catechism of the crew was productive of slight information. It was a motley band, beetle-browed Italians, swarthy Spaniards, fierce-eyed Portuguese, with a fair-haired Norseman and a trio of savage cut-throats from Flanders, as murderous a crew as ever crossed the Spanish Main. Butcher, their captain was undoubtedly of Dutch birth and breeding, but his long companionship with the desperate, lawless herd had increased the inborn savagery of his nature and made him more brutal than even his following. The facts elicited were that the *Dragon* was on her return voyage from the Guinea coast, having on board over one hundred men, women and children, some mere infants, stolen from their native wilds to be sold as slaves in the colonies. A storm having driven the *Dragon* off her course, she had lost her reckoning and went ashore on the New England coast, where the distressed mariners were received by the Indians and kindly treated. When, finally, the ship had been repaired, and was in a condition to put to sea, two warriors and the boy had been decoyed aboard by promises of presents for their people, and ere they were aware the sails were spread and the unfortunates were borne away to become the slaves of the very monsters they had succoured and entertained. The warriors defended themselves bravely, and strove to leap into the sea and swim ashore, but were overpowered by numbers, heavily ironed and confined in the steerage, while the blacks were chained in the hold. Many of the latter had died during the terrible voyage.

The Indian boy, Skong-ga-mong, the son of a chieftain, had learned something of both the English and Dutch languages during the frequent visits of white men to the Indian village and his journeys to the white settlements, but professing a profound ignorance, he had listened to the ribald jests of the captain and some of his crew concerning the unfortunates who had been thrown to the sharks in tropical waters, when too far exhausted or diseased to recuperate, learning that Butcher and his sailors had made a gladiatorial sport of the terrors of their victims. When the fire broke out, the remnant of the living cargo—men, women and babes—were left in their close confinement to perish miserably below the hatches, with not even a possibility of escape.

Like brutes caught in a trap, the crew of the slaver listened to the accusations and anathemas showered upon them, this villainous assortment, from the captain, with his powerful physique and cruel, stony eyes to the slender, tigerish Italian, each replying merely by shrugs.

"Monsters! devils incarnate!" exclaimed Colonel Lawrence. "Mongrel curs that sought your own safety, leaving these helpless human beings a prey to the flames! Cravens! Cowards! Dastards! But one white human soul that stood upon that deck is incased now in a living body, and that the heroic spirit of yon Indian lad. The brave warriors who succoured you in your distress have gone to the depths of the sounding sea, but their spirits will rise in judgment against you, to whom the curse of the Almighty must cling here, and in the great hereafter!"

A laugh of derision from the captain's heavy, sensual lips was the only response, accented by the leers and shrugs of his crew.

"Seize them! see that they are securely ironed!"

In obedience to Captain Broadbent's command the villainous Butcher and his hang-dog faced crew were put under arrest, heavily ironed, and bundled below.

"And the colonists prate of the cruelty of the savages! Little wonder that these abused, insulted people commit acts of atrocity in retaliation upon those whom they have sheltered and fed, who have rewarded their hospitality by treachery that would shame the devil himself!" cried Lawrence. "But the most horrible feature in the case is that the lives of innocent white women and infants must pay the forfeit for the crimes of such as these, when these red sons of the forest avenge their own wrongs for the inhumanities practised upon them."

"Fortunately this Butcher is a Dutchman, his craft was sailing under Dutch colours, and, if afloat, we could have taken her as a prize. These fellows are really worth nothing except as targets for our firelocks," returned Captain Broadbent.

"I fear our skirts are scarcely clean in this matter of slave stealing. Here we have the example of our colonists purchasing and holding slaves, in direct violation of the English law regarding slavery, and had this piratical captain been an Englishman, and sailing under the British flag, it is extremely doubtful, to my mind, whether these law-abiding magistrates would deal out the punishment they will mete to this Dutch slaver skipper and his men," spoke Harrup.

"An' I'll not dispute you there, Mr. Harrup," agreed Captain Broadbent, candidly, "though the tale told by this young savage concerning the cruelties practised during the voyage would bring the Dutchman and his crew under the ban as pirates. They are guilty of murder most foul."

"Wholesale slaughter," commented Lawrence.

"I make no doubt they will get their deserts. It would have been the work of a few minutes to have opened the hatches and set free the human beings, leaving them a chance for their lives. As it is, they went down loaded with fetters,—or rather up, for they must have been blown to atoms," answered Captain Broadbent.

"Even had we known these poor wretches were confined in the depths of that black hold we were powerless to save them," returned Lawrence. "Hanging is far too mild a punishment for such devils as the captain of the *Dragon* and his cursed crew!"

"We've got 'em," rejoined the Captain, grimly. "We are on a war footing with our Dutch neighbours, and it will be no easy matter for these bloody sharks to slip their heads out of the noose—they should be drawn and quartered, after being strung up at the yardarm for a short space. I'll land my passengers, take in a supply, and sail for Saybrook Fort. Once in the hands of the authorities they'll get their deserts, I'll lay five pound."

CHAPTER XLII

A VOW FULFILLED

> "They say the tongues of dying men
> Enforce attention like deep harmony;
> Where words are scarce they're seldom spent in vain,
> For they breathe truth that breathe their words in pain."

DAMARIS GORDON was alone in the wide world, an orphan, the last of her race.

Very tenderly Henry Lawrence had broken the news of her bereavement, for Guy Kingsland, with a selfishness that was part and parcel of his nature, had shrunk from what he termed " a devilish disagreeable task."

"My dear Colonel, I'd a thousand times rather you should do the job. I hate scenes, and these lasses are sure to faint, or something equally absurd and annoying, and it would be deucedly unpleasant, so I'll e'en take myself off for an hour or so, till she has leisure to lament in the most approved manner of her sex. Of course I'm no end of sorry, and all that, and properly shocked, at the Major's sudden taking-off," he added, as he noticed the shadow of contempt and anger on the Colonel's expressive face; "but prithee, man, I fear I am really too sensitive to be the proper person. Besides I'm a deuced poor hand at telling bad news, and above all things I abhor tears—make me cursed uncomfortable, upon honour, so good luck to you!" and with this heartless avowal Guy sauntered away, his pipe between his lips. And strolling beyond the stockade, he took his way to the bluff overhanging the sea, musing upon the strangeness of events in this world in general, and the unpleasantness of the situation in particular evidently considering himself a much injured individual.

"I'm a lucky dog in one respect," he ruminated. "I've no craving to have my neck encircled by the matrimonial noose until it is absolutely unavoidable, and she is sure to demand one year of mourning—a respite which will be by no means distasteful. Yes, I'll observe the proprieties with the utmost pleasure."

It was Henry Lawrence's broad breast that had pillowed the orphan's head; his voice that was, in its modulations, a caress, that whispered words of comfort after the first great shock was over; while Guy kept aloof, answering never a word when he heard Lyon Gardiner shouting his name, as he sought through the grounds and groves in vain quest for the man who should have been the consoler of his promised wife, in this, her hour of greatest need and deepest woe.

It was Henry Lawrence who clasped her hand, pressing it tenderly, when the four who had been detailed as bearers came slowly up the long avenue, and she saw, with pallid cheek, and through blinding tears, the black-draped coffin upon the bier. Her heart had been chill, but now it lay like a marble weight in her bosom while those strangers entered the hall. Not a word was uttered when Lyon Gardiner swung the door wide and led the way, and very reverently those bold marines passed on with slow, measured tread, as if their steps might disturb the sleeper. With careful hands they placed the coffin upon the trestles prepared to receive it, in the chamber the dead soldier had occupied while in life,

It was Henry Lawrence who supported the half-fainting girl when she followed the bearers to the chamber of death, where every item of furnishing, the trifles upon mantel and tables, spoke to the desolate mourner of the father lying in that narrow couch, with ears closed to every mortal sound, and eyes sealed in the last dreamless sleep.

A thrill of anguish shot through her heart like a knife thrust, as her eyes wandered mechanically from one familiar object to another, but even then she could not comprehend the extent of her desolation.

She dimly realised that others entered the chamber, that kind faces were near, pitying voices striving to comfort her, in words that were meaningless to her dull senses, and the speakers but actors or automatons in a tragedy in which she bore no part.

One figure alone was real, the man who stood by her side, her hand clasped fondly in his own warm palm, while he smoothed her hair—oh, so pitifully!—his stern lips quivering, and there was a suspicion of tears in his dark eyes as he closed the lids for an instant, to shut out the scene.

There was a magnetism in his touch, but the spell was rudely broken by the entrance of Guy Kingsland, who came forward with firm step and stood in the place vacated by Colonel Lawrence.

The girl covered her face with her hands, and a half-shudder chilled her as Guy's arm encircled her waist and she heard his murmured commonplaces. that fell icily upon her senses; and mechanically she held out her arms as if to clasp some beloved form, and raised her eyes as if in search of a beloved face. But Henry Lawrence had hurried from the room, the bearers and members of the family had slipped silently away, leaving her alone with the man to whom her father's dying commands had bound her with bonds she could not sever, of which she knew naught, for Henry Lawrence could not speak the words while the first agony of her loss held her in thrall.

In the privacy of his own chamber he was wrestling with the temptation that assailed him. No ear save his own had listened to the whispered words of the dying man, words that burned his heart like a consuming fire, that must condemn an innocent maiden to a lifelong, unavailing regret and fill his own whole future with sorrow.

Had Guy evinced the loyalty and affection due to the poor girl, there would have been not an instant's hesitation in the heart of the noble man as to his duty. But Kingsland's indifference, his coldness, his hollow mockery of a sympathy he was incapable of feeling, roused the noble-minded Lawrence to a pitch of indignation that was well-nigh uncontrollable. He had noted that beside the coffin the Lieutenant was observing the strict amenities, observances that might pass current to outward notice; but to the eyes of love the studied attention but thinly veiled his impatience and heartlessness. Had the dying man known the true character of the being to whom he had given his daughter, would he have exacted such a promise? Yes! Not all the forgetfulness of the errors accorded the dead could blunt the conviction that a prospective coronet outweighed the happiness of a daughter, even in the father's dying hours.

Faint with his own heavy heart-throbs, Henry Lawrence thus pondered: could he blast his own hopes, break the heart of the woman he adored; would not the promise wrung from him be more sacred in the breaking than the keeping?

"Oh, Damaris! my love, my darling, must I give you to another, and that other Guy Kingsland—a man without principle, without heart, selfish, aye, cruel, without honour save such as glosses the surface? O God! in mercy pity and direct me in my sore distress, for the cross is very grievous!" he prayed, falling upon his knees.

There was a depth of agony in that voice that might have won pardon even from the man lying in his coffin could those marble lips have unclosed, as with bowed head Henry Lawrence prayed for strength to fulfil the vow made to the dying.

It was a fearful struggle between love and honour while the strong man wrestled for the victory over his own love and pity for the tender heart that loved him.

To Guy the semblance of grief was irksome, and presently he summoned Mrs. Gardiner, insisting that Damaris should be taken to her own chamber.

With gentle insistence the good lady seconded Guy's entreaties, or rather commands, as with a polite semblance of affection he led the sorrowing girl to her room.

Without a word she shut the door upon his retreating figure, and sinking upon her couch, closed her eyes and strove to compose her mind; but the dull aching of her heart precluded rest, and presently she began pacing up and down the length of the room. She could not weep, for the fountain of tears seemed frozen, and in a numb quiet she drank the cup of steaming coffee Mrs. Gardiner had prepared, but the delicately-browned toast upon the tray was untouched when the goodwife returned.

"Come with me to the library, dear, Guy is there; he will comfort you as none other can. Thank the All-Father he is left to you, my poor, shorn lamb!"

cooed the matron, as she wound her arm about the slender form and strove to lead her from the chamber; but Damaris shrank back with a shiver, begging piteously to be left alone, a sense of the hollowness of the heart she could not trust piercing her soul like a second-sight, an intuitive perception of the character of her betrothed, from whom she shrank with an undefined repulsion.

"I cannot! Oh, I cannot!" she sobbed, when the distressed dame would have led her away. "I am so cold, so weary! Why am I not permitted to sit beside my poor father? Surely it is but mete that his child should keep the vigil beside him while he is —is here! This one night—only one!"

With fond words and motherly caresses her friend strove to soothe her, wondering a little at the perversity of the girl who shrank from the companionship of the handsome Lieutenant she was to wed.

For hours Damaris lay upon her couch just as Mrs. Gardiner had left her, her wide-open eyes fixed drearily upon the glancing arrows cast by the fire, her mind a chaos.

The striking of the clock roused her from the lethargy into which she had fallen—twelve sonorous chimes. The family had long since retired, all save the lone watcher beside the dead, who half-reclined upon the settle within the deep alcove, his head bent upon his hand, his figure a palpable shadow among shadows.

As the brazen alarm rang out Damaris started from her couch, a sensation of choking in her throat. There was something appalling in the remembrance that her father, shrouded for the grave, was pent within that narrow prison-house of the dead, the gruesome coffin, shut out from the world in his dreamless slumber. And scarcely realising what she was doing, she wrapped a heavy mantle about her shoulders, stole softly from her room, crossed the hall and entered the silent chamber.

A candle, half burned, stood upon the mantel, high over the empty, black fireplace, where no fire blazed, the feeble glimmer illuminating but a circumscribed semi-circle about the cold hearth-stone, leaving the corners of the room in gloom and the alcove a square of blackness.

Not once had the sorrowing daughter looked upon the dead face, for careful friends had interposed to save her from the spectacle hidden beneath the black pall, which she drew back, and with a gasp as if she were stifling, she raised the coffin lid, involuntarily drawing a sigh of relief as if the dead might inhale a breath of the pure air that swept across the marble features dimly revealed in the indistinct rays of the candle. Great patches of shade in strange shapes, as it appeared at first to the half-unseeing eyes, lay upon the cheeks, the lips, the brow, almost obscuring the outlines, and with trembling hands she drew back the window shutter, letting in a flood of white moonlight, and disclosing the ghastly marks of knife and tomahawk.

So silently had the girl entered the room, so absorbed was Henry Lawrence in his bitter reflections, that he had heard nothing, saw nothing, until the frightened, gasping cry fell upon his ears, and in another moment he received the fainting form in his arms, which trembled strangely beneath the slight weight.

A passion of grief and terror had unsealed the fountain of tears, and the weeping orphan clung to the breast of the strong man, while her very life seemed ebbing in the paroxysm of lamentation.

He made no effort to restrain her tears, that must

ease the aching heart more surely than could the only words he must speak.

Ah! could he but have folded her to his heart and breathed his love! But no, the words trembling upon his lips must not be uttered; the promise made to the dying must be kept, here and now, beside the lifeless form; and to his overwrought imagination a frown flitted across the cleft brow of the dead, as if in menace, should he fail to fulfil his vow.

The words that broke from his lips were mournful in their tender accent, almost a whisper, as he told her of her father's wishes, of the promise he had made; but all his self-control could not render steady the tones of the man whose enforced utterances were sealing his own fate and probing his heart like the keen edge of the blade a suicide plunges in his breast.

In his wild excitement he was quite unconscious of the overtax upon her strength. She struggled feebly from his clasping arms, smiled faintly, essaying to speak, but the words she would have spoken froze upon her lips, and she fell senseless in the arms outstretched to receive her.

Henry Lawrence drew his breath with a sobbing gasp. The tenderness welling in his heart swept away all barriers; for the moment his firmness gave way—he forgot his vow, forgot all save that he held in his arms the woman who loved him, whom he loved with all the fervency of a deep, abiding passion, while lower and lower his head bowed over that sweet, pale face, as he held her in a close embrace, raining kisses upon the forehead, the lips, the silken hair, while he murmured such words of endearment as had never before passed his lips, his strong frame shivering as if with an ague.

"God forgive me! I am sinful, but how can I

give her up, the idol of my life, when my heart is swelling, aching with the excess of love that has made me a coward? God help me? God pity her, for she loves me! she loves me! and I—merciful Saviour, I am but human! I am but human, and this love has conquered me!"

A rain of tears fell from his proud eyes, his broad breast heaved, his arms closed more closely about the slender figure.

"She is mine! mine! I will not give her up!" he cried, exultingly, almost fiercely, and the cry rang out in strange echoes, breaking the solemn silence. And in spite of his own volition, the speaker turned his gaze upon the face of the dead, framed in by the narrow coffin, and to his distorted vision a spasm of anger appeared to contract the rigid lips, the sunken eyelids seemed to quiver as if about to unclose. The play of the moonbeams had mocked him, but the spell was broken as if dissolved by a voice from the tomb.

A sob choked his utterance, the deep heaving of his chest partially aroused Damaris, and she raised her arms feebly, clasping his neck.

None save God knew the mighty struggle between stern duty and the soul worship he had given. One more embrace, a lingering pressure of the lips—such a kiss as we give the dead ere the beloved face is shut forever from our sight, and the temptation that had nearly overcome him was conquered.

Very gently he unclasped the clinging arms, still holding the soft hands in his warm clasp, while he pleaded the cause of his unworthy rival, a man whom, in his secret heart, he despised.

Dizzy with the pain that shot like needle-points through her throbbing temples, Damaris released her hands, turned, almost coldly, walked to the side

"She is mine! mine! I will not give her up—"

of the coffin, and dropping upon her knees laid her cheek against the pall.

"Father, father!" she wailed, "I will obey, I will be Guy's wife!"

Her vow was registered, and like one in a dream she rose to her feet and glided away, pausing upon the threshold and taking the hand the lover held out in a parting clasp. She was gone, and Henry Lawrence closed the door softly as if he feared a sound might disturb the sleeping dead.

"The vow is fulfilled!" he moaned, "but at what a fearful cost only Thou, the searcher of all hearts, canst know! Cornelius Gordon, dead in your coffin though you are, I could almost find it in my heart to curse your memory for the woe you have wrought!"

It was but fancy, he knew, but it seemed as if a smile of triumph and derision played about the marble lips as the watcher closed the coffin lid and shut out the gruesome spectacle. He reeled to the couch, as one drunken with strong wine. Smothered groans shook his stalwart frame as he lay there, face downward, while the tempest of grief and indignation held sway, until at length even his iron strength succumbed and he fell into a profound slumber, which held his senses benumbed until the grey dawn was stealing through the window panes.

CHAPTER XLIII

CUT-WAS, THE ARROW-MAKER

> "Nor custom, nor example, nor vast numbers
> Of such as do offend, make less the sin;
> For each particular crime a strict account
> Will be exacted; and that comfort which
> The damned pretend, fellows in misery,
> Takes nothing from their torments; every one
> Must suffer in himself the measure of
> His wickedness."

AN indispensable functionary in every Indian tribe is the arrow-maker, the artificer and custodian of the weapons of war and the chase, an artisan on whose skill in the manufacture of his wares so much depends.

His occupaton is the most diversified and distinctively constructive of any among his people. He is the designer and maker of spear-heads, lances, arrow-heads, stone axes or tomahawks in constant use by the warriors and hunters of his tribe, and, as the lapidary of more favoured races is a virtuoso in determining the uses and value of gems or works of art, so is the Indian arrow-maker a connoisseur in selecting, with unerring judgment, from the vast storehouse of nature the materials best suited for the manufacture of the weapons he fashions with wonderful skill.

The trade of the arrow-maker is the oldest known. In prehistoric ages man was an artificer in stone implements, the only art of the primitive period that has not been lost in the turmoil of centuries of evolution. Among the Indian tribes the work of the makers of wampum, so beautifully wrought from various shells, with the rudest appliances, compares favourably with the productions of the Anglo-Saxon silversmith.

The work produced by the deft-handed arrow-maker is the more amazing from the fact that there is no implement used by any craftsman that can be successfully employed in his work except the tools he designed and fashioned from the stones in which he wrought, and with which he produced the many and varied articles that must remain as examples of his wondrous skill and patience for all time.

From the day when Poniute visited the lodge of the medicine-man of the Montauks, Guy Kingsland had been doomed.

It had been a severe blow to the young and ambitious warrior when he learned that the maiden he coveted had been given to To-cus, but with all the cunning of his nature he bided his time, appearing as one of the guests at the festivities, and so dissembling that none suspected the jealous rage filling his breast. Sooner or later To-cus would have fallen by his hand had not the Narragansetts slain the bridegroom and saved him from the crime he meditated, and after the return of Heather Flower to her father's lodge his hopes revived.

From Wyancombone, whose attendant and confidant he was, he learned the price To-cus would have paid for the hand of the princess, and his heart beat high with hope and exultation.

Time passed, and the period when he had been bidden by Wee-gon to seek the assistance of the arrow-maker had arrived.

Stricken and palsied in spirit, no longer reflecting sunshine upon all around her, Heather Flower passed much of her time in the solitude of the forest or upon the bold bluff overlooking the sea, the spot where she had first met Guy Kingsland. And here, one crisp, clear morning in early November, she was standing, dreamily surveying the shores of Man-cho-nock across the vista of blue water.

"Does the Heather Flower await the coming of the white chief?"

The deep voice startled her from her reverie, and she turned to see Poniute standing at her elbow.

Perhaps she divined the intent of his question, for, without reserve, she replied to the interrogatory.

"Heather Flower waits not for the coming of the serpent who has stung her heart—she asks only his scalp!"

"Poniute saw his black heart many moons ago, and would have taken his scalp, but you would not," returned the young warrior.

"Nay, I would not! your blood was hot; but I knew not how false was the heart he told me was all mine—now I know."

"And would Heather Flower have also the life of the white lily?" he asked.

"Nay, the Snowbird has a white heart. She does not know. I believed his forked tongue spoke truly. He is false—that is all. No harm must come to the Snowbird, who is still the sister of Heather Flower."

"Poniute would have taken the Heather Flower to his lodge before the pale-faced stranger came, but she would not."

"I could not; Poniute did not tell me. How could the daughter of the Montauks know?"

"It is not too late yet."

Poniute made the assertion in a questioning tone, his keen eyes searching her face, but her cheek neither paled nor flushed.

"It is not too late. Had To-cus taken Heather Flower to his lodge the scalp of the white dog would have dried in the smoke of her lodge-fire. When his scalp hangs at the belt of Poniute the warriors and maidens shall dance at the wedding feast of Heather Flower, and she will go to the wigwam of Poniute. The silken scalp of the pale-face warrior must be Poniute's wedding offering to his bride."

The strange wooing was over, and she turned abruptly away in the direction of the Montauk village, leaving her bold wooer lost in contemplation of the happiness and gratified ambition offered him as the price of the death of Guy Kingsland.

On the crest of Shag-wan-nock,[1] the bold and rocky cliff overlooking the dangerous reef that also bears the name, and that puts far out into the sea at the eastern extremity of Montauk, sat an aged Indian enjoying his sun bath and complacently smoking his pipe while he contemplated the scene before him.

It was one of wildest confusion. From where he sat to the beach below him, sixty feet, an almost perpendicular wall of solid rock intervened, while up and down along the shore, and far to seaward, great boulders of flint and shale and sandstone were strewn and massed, as if, at the end of creation, they had been hurled out of this out-of-the-way backdoor of nature as refuse.

The sea, at this point, is ever at war with the rocky reef. The ceaseless march of the inrolling billows is tremendous. When fretted to anger, they swoop with resistless power as if to lift the rocky intruders from their briny depths and hurl them in still greater disorder along the strand, and, failing

[1] *Shag-wan-nock.*—The end of the land.

in this, their foaming crests break with sullen roar and recede to give place to those that follow them.

The Indian upon the cliff watched, in turn, the seals that were at play upon and around the wave-washed rocks and the army of fish-hawks that preyed upon the numerous shoals of fish sporting in the rippling eddies around the reef, but turned his eyes with a keener zest as a hungry eagle swooped down upon a hapless hawk, and, hard-pressed, the smaller bird, screaming with terror, released his prey, which the pirate of the air grasped in his cruel talons and sailed away to alight on some isolated rock where he might devour his ill-gotten spoil at leisure.

The venerable student, who studied nature in all her phases from a leafless and pageless open book, was Cut-was, the old arrow-maker of the Montauks.

He was low of stature, and attenuated almost to an anatomy, yet there was that indefinable expression in his clear, deep-set eyes betokening a hidden and unexplored mine of knowledge. In demeanour he was mild to gentleness.

He was recalled from his pastime by the hoarse bark of a dog that came up from the foot of the hill, landward, where, upon the margin of a small and placid lake, hidden among the wind-swept hills, was the old man's wigwam, sheltered by a grove of stunted scrub oak.

With a look of inquiry upon his shrivelled visage he descended into the thicket, where his savage wolf-dog kept guard in his master's absence. There he found the great brute disputing a passage to an Indian brave.

Obedient to a wave of his master's hand, the dog slunk away, his furious barks changed to sullen growls, as he still cast sidelong glances toward the intruder.

"Ugh! What brings Poniute to the lodge of Cut-was?" demanded the arrow-maker. "It is many moons since he came."

Poniute drew up his fine figure as he replied to the curt inquiry:

"I am sent by Wee-gon. Cut-was must give an arrow, long, narrow, sharp—cut deep,—carry poison to kill a pale-face wolf."

"What has the pale-face done, that he must die?" questioned the arrow-maker.

"He would blast the Heather Flower, the pride of the Montauks—he would have made her a reproach among even the women of burden," returned Poniute, grimly. "He must die!"

"Ha! say you so? Who is he?" demanded the old man, his eyes blazing ominously.

"He is the young white chief who wears the red coat, who came to the lodge of Wyandance and stole the heart of Heather Flower. He came to the Sachem's lodge bringing with him the white lily, the maiden whose cheeks are like the heart of the sea-shell."

"How knows the young brave that the pale-face would harm the daughter of Wyandance?" asked Cut-was.

"He has stolen her heart. He will take to his lodge across the big water the white lily, who comes no more to visit her red sister," returned Poniute.

"Can the Heather Flower love one not of her own people?" inquired the old man.

"She listened to his words of love, and when he came by stealth she stole away to meet him unattended."

"How know you this is so?"

"The eyes of a Montauk warrior who loves are like the red eye of a hawk. Poniute was on his trail, he followed him to the meeting-place, and would have slain him but Heather Flower saved him from the vengeance of the red man who loves her."

"Cut-was would know all," returned the old arrow-maker, "then he will give the young warrior the arrow with which to slay his rival. If she loved the white wolf, why did she take To-cus for her mate?"

"That he might kill the white chief when she knew that he had lied. That was the price To-cus would have paid. He has gone to the land of his fathers. Poniute would take to his lodge the daughter of Wyandance."

Then, in the graphic, comprehensive language of his race, Poniute sketched the story, and as he spoke the eyes of the old arrow-maker grew lurid with anger.

"The young brave of the Montauks says well; the pale-face wolf must die!" assented the old man, as he led the way into his wigwam.

The interior was a revelation, a curiosity shop. Lances, spears, and arrow-heads of many sizes, of different shapes, of divers kinds of black, white, and yellow flint stones, fashioned to meet the requirements of warriors and hunters, were ranged systematically within the circular lodge, together with an array of implements used by this queer craftsman.

Bundles of sticks, moulded with the utmost care, for arrow-shafts, hung around the interior, graduated in length and thickness, to which were adjusted arrow-heads of different weights to balance the perfectly moulded shaft to a nicety, such as only a skilled artisan could determine.

Cut-was examined his collection with a critical eye, and after a most careful scrutiny selected one, which he placed in the hand of his visitor.

The young warrior inspected the arrow with a look of satisfaction, and turned to the old man with an approving nod.

"To Wee-gon," Cut-was said, with a wave of the hand signifying that the interview was ended.

After carefully wrapping the arrow in a snake-skin, and placing it securely within the quiver at his back, Poniute departed without even a word of farewell.

The tall trees growing upon the little wooded islet where Wee-gon, the medicine-man, had his home were casting their long shadows eastward. when, from the western shore of the lake that cradled the dream of an island retreat, a canoe put off, in which sat a single occupant, who was shaping his course toward the island, and paddling with swift, strong strokes.

In a few minutes Poniute drew the canoe upon the shore, and for the second time stood within the domain of Wee-gon.

Uttering the plaintive cry of the red fox, he advanced toward the medicine lodge, his call waking the echoes.

As he neared the wigwam, Wee-gon appeared at the entrance, environed as when the visitor saw him upon a former occasion.

"My son, four moons have waxed and waned, and the time has come. Poniute brings the arrow fashioned by the cunning hand of Cut-was?"

Wee-gon spoke in a harsh, croaking voice, with the intonation of an assertion rather than a question, and for reply Poniute placed the arrow in the hand of the sorcerer. After a careful examination the medicine-man spoke again.

"Wee-gon has talked with the spirit that whispers in the leaves, and has listened to the voice of the spirit of the night-wind, to the roll of the thunder that speaks from the storm clouds, sent from the Source of Light, that bids the earth to tremble, or be silent. He has listened when no sound is heard but the ceaseless roar of the waters, he has talked with the many stars that hide behind the sunlight in the day, and that look down upon the red children of the Great Spirit by night. When all is dark the Manitou tells Wee-gon many things.

"I have called up the spirits that live in the dark caverns of night, that wander about unseen, who hear the forked tongues of men speak lies, and who look into their hearts when they are black, who know their thoughts, and who reveal all to Wee-gon. He knows all that Poniute would tell.

"Listen! The pale-face young chief came to Sea-wan-ha-ka; he looked upon the proud daughter of Wyandance with a covetous eye. He would not make her his squaw—he would have made her an outcast from her people; more, he would have the Sachem of the Montauks give all his land to his pale-faced enemies, who called him brother. But Heather Flower listened while his false tongue spoke words of the Snowbird, words that sent the cooing dove from the Indian maiden's breast; the black vulture of hate and revenge came and brooded in her heart, tearing it and eating out her life. When the white serpent knew that the daughter of the Montauks was no longer blind, he sent the Narragansetts, the enemies of the Montauks, to steal her away, and when she was the captive of Ninigret one of his white brothers came to take from Wyandance a promise of the land he would not sell, but gladly gave as a ransom.

"Listen! The Great Spirit is angry and paints the sun with blood. The white dog must die. The spirits of the air have whispered it in the ear of Wee-gon. When the moon is young again the white serpent will come with the redcoats from the great war-canoe of the pale-faces to hunt the deer in the home of the Montauks, and when he shall search for the wounded doe in the brakes of Mah-chon-it-chuge,[1] let Poniute shoot the arrow that shall pierce his thigh, and carry into his blood the poison of the rattlesnake, when there will be none to help him. His bottle for strong water will be empty—he will die the death of torture. But he will be a squaw, and wail like the hungry wolf cub; he will call his brothers, but they will not hear, and when, in his last agony, he bites the dust like the stricken panther, the Manitou will not answer him.

"On the third day of the young moon let Poniute go to the dark swamp and lie in ambush until his enemy comes."

Placing his lean, dark hand within the bosom of his mantle, the wizard drew forth an ugly reptile, which coiled lazily about his withered arm, its wicked head slowly moving from side to side in rhythm with the crooning sound issuing from the sorcerer's lips. As the monotonous drone changed to a drowsy hum the motions of the serpent quickened, and presently it uncoiled and swung to the ground. The hum rose to a sharp hiss that cut the air like a knife, and the reptile glided swiftly away, making straight for a flat stone, at which it struck viciously, with distended jaws, its long, needle-like fangs clicking like steel points upon flint.

Wee-gon stooped and dipped the arrow point in the yellow, viscid poison deposited upon the rock, and the envenomed dart, rapidly drying, assumed a greenish hue. Thrice the operation was repeated,

[1] *Mah-chon-it-chuge.*—A deep swamp in the north neck of Montauk.

until the entire venom had been transferred from the smooth stone to the flinty arrow-head.

Poniute received the poisoned arrow, handling it cautiously as he replaced it within the snakeskin sheath, and returned it to his quiver.

The old sorcerer crouched upon the mat of furs and drew his blanket over his face, thus signifying that he desired his visitor to depart, and with not a glance behind him Poniute left the wigwam, quickening his steps almost to a run, as the sharp hiss of the snake hastened his departure, and, stepping into his canoe, he paddled swiftly away.

CHAPTER XLIV

HONOUR FOR NAUGHT

"No tears for those who win the martyr's crown
    Through some brief hours of bitter tribulation,
Bearing a heavy cross but for a day,
    To win eternity's great compensation.

"Weep for the martyrs walking in your midst,
    Who bear the fire without an outward token,
Who tread the changeless round of daily care,
    Wearing a smile altho' the heart be broken.

"Weep saddest tears for those who make no moaning,
    The river deepens as it nears the sea;
The noisy, brawling brook runs loud and shallow,
    But deepest grief is for eternity."

A MONTH had dragged its slow length since all that was mortal of Major Gordon was laid away in its last sleep beneath the sods of Man-cho-nock, rightly named "the place of many dead," where, for countless moons, the bones of the red sons of the forest had reposed, but a soil that never before had pressed upon a white man's breast.

In accordance with her father's command, Damaris had consented to become Guy's wife without delay, that she might not be allowed time to renounce her pledge, and that the young couple might return to their native land on the next outgoing vessel, the *Goodspeed*, then lying at anchor at Saybrook Fort.

Captain Gardiner and his lady strongly urged that

the marriage was the most fitting, and the lady advocating the expediency on the ground that it would be highly improper for the maiden to make the voyage under the protection of the Lieutenant, except as his wife. The pang with which Damaris had finally consented was keen as a knife thrust.

For Guy, he acquiesced in the measures proposed by the Captain and his lady, with a carelessness that savoured of indifference, in his self-communings voting the whole proceeding " a devilishly unfortunate affair," only stipulating that his friend, the Colonel, should remain as best man. And Henry Lawrence, with a kind of gladiator's endurance, consented to be present at the ceremony, accepting the ordeal as a form of penance, to be borne for what his rigid sense of honour caused him to regard as his treachery to Guy.

Keenly reproaching himself for the misery his love had inflicted upon the being he loved best on earth, he resolved to strive to the utmost to undo the evil, and in accordance with that decision he passed a greater portion of his time in company with the Lieutenant, who rallied him unmercifully upon his distraught manner, which Guy ascribed to be the terrible experience through which the Colonel had recently passed, that were characterised as needless, harrowing memories—deucedly unpleasant, of course, but that should be exorcised, or ignored.

Had his love for the bride he was soon to wed been a tithe deeper, his eyes might have been opened to the truth, but with a total disregard of her sorrow, and with all the carelessness and blindness of his overweening self-esteem, he failed to perceive.

That Damaris spent the greater portion of the time in the solitude of her own chamber was rather a matter for congratulation than regret. It was eminently proper, under the circumstances, he reasoned; besides, it would be no end of trouble to play the part of consoler, a bore he was willing to be rid of, and thus the sorrowing, desolate girl was left to the self-imposed quiet she craved.

Besides, she partially misunderstood the generosity of the man she loved so fervently, and there was a bitterness in her heart that he could thus resign her without a word of protest. How little she dreamed of the fierce struggle in his soul when, for the moment he held her in his arms, an unconscious burden, while love waged a war with honour. No word or look of her own should betray the agony she was enduring, for pride was still strong and upheld her. Surely he had cast aside the love he once felt, else he could not have consented to remain in her presence while she plighted her solemn vows to another—that other the man she could never love, save as a sister.

Very dismal and melancholy was the hall, while outside the November winds were piping in mournful consonance

For days the storm clouds had lowered, the red deer had trooped away to their coverts in the deep forest, the trees writhed their giant arms in the high gale, sea and sky blended in one grey expanse, the inrolling billows tossed back their ghostly manes upon the black valleys of water in their wake, like snow-capped mountains overtopping deep dark gorges.

Each day during the period of his enforced stay upon the island. Henry Lawrence regretted that he had not sailed away in the good ship that had brought him, instead of remaining where, day by day, he was crucifying his own soul, and assailed by a temptation that forced his strong will to waver between honour that was for naught and his unconquerable affection.

Now it was too late; Man-cho-nock was isolated by the storm as entirely as the lone isle upon which Alexander Selkirk dwelt, imprisoned by the waves of the sounding sea, and daily his heart sickened as he realised that the love he had striven to conquer still held possession of his whole being with a strength unconquerable by his iron will. His soul worshipped on.

It was terrible to mingle, hour after hour, day after day, with those whose conversation was most frequently of the coming bridal, to listen to the numerous discussions concerning the future of the bride and groom in their home beyond the sea. He formed a sudden resolution—he would not return to England, but would remain in the colonies, take up the sword and court a soldier's death in some fierce battle with the savages.

Guy's constant levity and careless jests smote heavily, betraying, as they did, his utter disregard for the death of the man so lately consigned to the grave, who, whatever his faults, had been more a father to the gay, young Lieutenant than to the daughter whom he had consigned to the faithless, conscienceless heir of a barren title, and who now displayed his real character in no enviable light.

During the days that followed the funeral Guy yawned dismally, cursing the fate that kept him confined within the narrow space bounded by the grey expanse of water, and longing to cross to Sea-wan-ha-ka in search of recreation.

His fears concerning Heather Flower had been lulled. She had quite forgotten the little episode, else she would not have consented to become the bride of To-cus, reasoned Guy, and on several occasions he had accompanied one of the Montauk warriors upon a hunting expedition.

The long season of storm was over at last, and on the afternoon of the fifth day a rift of blue cleft the leaden bank in the west, the storm-rack floated away in fragments, like torn banners swept piecemeal by the wind, changing to iridescent hues, pale amber, violet, crystal, pink and crimson, as the sun, suddenly flashing out, fell upon a most welcome object, a noble ship, looming in the distance and sharply defined against the gorgeous background of sky and glittering, jewel-tipped waves, her white sails spread to the fair breeze as she gallantly breasted the long swells and came swiftly nearer, her course directed to Man-cho-nock.

Before sunset the ship dropped anchor, and a boat put off for shore, bearing two officers in the uniform of the British navy.

Captain Monckton and his first officer stepped ashore to receive a warm welcome from both Captain Gardiner and Lieutenant Kingsland, whom they greeted as old acquaintances.

"Glad to see you, Monckton!" exclaimed Gardiner, heartily, as he gripped his visitor's hand, "and you, Roswell," turning to the mate, who was shaking hands with the Lieutenant in the most cordial fashion. "What lucky adventure brings you to the Isle of Wight? It warms one's heart to greet old friends after a long exile from Old England!"

"We have had a long and boisterous passage, Captain, and have put in for provisions. The ship's larder is low, and, learning that an old comrade had cast anchor on a lone island in this wild country, I put in here as a matter of choice, hoping to leave some broad pieces of real English gold in exchange for an outfit of provisions. Ship's crew and marines are famishing for fresh rations. We were driven off our course by adverse winds, and experienced rough weather to the northward," explained Captain Monckton.

"'It's an ill wind that blows no one good'" returned Captain Gardiner. "My good dame will be charmed to entertain guests from home, I'll warrant!"

"Tell you what, Tom," chimed in Guy, addressing the mate, "there's big game over yon," pointing across to where the bold Montauk cliffs loomed up. "On the morrow we'll e'en make up a hunting party and betake ourselves to the woods. There's no chance for a scurry across country, riding to hounds, for horse-flesh is scarce in this benighted land, but I will e'en confess that a pair of stout legs serves one's turn better in crossing swamps and dodging about in the tangled undergrowth after the fashion of our redskinned brothers. We'll secure game in plenty to stock the *Highflyer's* larder, never fear, lad. Crew and marines will have no cause to grumble for many a day regarding their diet. I'm dying of the blue-devils, moping here, and it's deuced good luck that sent you to give me a valid excuse for going over to Sea-wan-ha-ka—a golden link in the iron chain of Fate, my lad."

"Agreed!" assented Lieutenant Roswell, eagerly, as the two seafaring men sauntered up the avenue with the easy roll acquired upon the ship's deck. "Nothing could suit us better than to stretch our legs ashore and bring down the game that must be plentiful in this wilderness."

"Plentiful! You may well say that," returned Guy, "but at the rate in which white men are thinning them out the quarries will be cleared ere many years pass, and with their means of subsistence taken, our red brothers will find it convenient to migrate. The same holds good with regard to their fishing."

"Strikes me that it is rather a novel, not to say devilish unjust, proceeding with regard to these savages—the land is their own, man!" remonstrated Roswell.

"A slight error on your part," laughed Guy. "Most of the land, or a goodly portion of it, is already in the possession of the planters, but these Indians have not the least idea of the actual value of these broad acres. A few gewgaws in the shape of blankets of gaudy colouring, hatchets, looking-glasses, a musket or two, a gallon of fire-water, or a dog, will buy up a dukedom——"

"And where, prithee, are they to dwell, how get their subsistence, when their lands are taken from them?" interrupted Roswell, in a tone not unmixed with indignation.

"Oh, as to that, they are allowed to reserve the right to hunt in the forest, fish in the streams, and a certain percentage of the whales that are taken by them—that is, they are allowed the tails and fins," replied Guy.

"Truly a munificent allowance, considering," returned Roswell, as he looked askance at his companion's face.

"There are laws governing these transactions," returned Guy, serenely.

"Who makes the laws?" asked Roswell, a trifle sarcastically.

"We do, of course. You are not such a muff as to suppose these barbarians capable of framing laws, or thoroughly understanding a code, any more than they are of reading Latin!" returned Guy, with a short laugh.

"Or of the trickery of their civilised white

brethren. It strikes me, Guy, that this is a game in which not only the lion's share falls to the European civiliser, but a wholesale theft, or 'stand-and-deliver' sort of proceeding; an English footpad could save his neck under the provisions of such a law! I must confess, that unless you are only joking——"

"Joking!" interrupted Guy, with a smile, "I assure you I speak with a straight tongue, as these red men would put it."

"I'm sorry," exclaimed Roswell, "I must declare most emphatically, that I cannot find it in my heart to censure these poor barbarians should they rise in their righteous indignation and slaughter every European within their borders."

"Bah! Your sentiment does you credit, Tom, but fortunately we have the whip hand in this matter."

"How so?"

"This: that it is getting late in the day for successful resistance, and the wisest of their Sachems—old Wyandance, King of the Montauks, among the rest—recognise the fact. They, with their primitive weapons of warfare, can do little against the disciplined, well-armed soldiers we can send against them. True, they may make attacks upon small settlements, but with little avail in the end. The reign of the aborigines is drawing to a close. When their game and fish are exhausted, starvation will complete the work."

"Rank injustice!" protested Roswell. "For myself I should scarcely care to acquire territory at the expense of every attribute of honour, humanity and gratitude!"

"Tush! If you had been given the opportunity to look upon Major Gordon's remains, hacked out of all semblance to humanity, by these self-same Indians, you might have occasion to change your views," answered Guy, with some warmth. "Why, lad, his legs and arms were as full of holes as a riddle-sieve, the marks of spears, tomahawks and knives, and——"

"Major Gordon! our Major Gordon, did you say?" broke in Roswell. "Is he dead?"

"Dead as Pharaoh and his host, done to death by these gentle savages. Lies yon—first grave made for a white man on the Isle of Wight."

"Eh! Did I hear aright? Gordon—what of him?" called Captain Monckton, turning short in his tracks and halting.

"Killed by the Indians—I quite forgot that you knew the Major," answered Captain Gardiner. "He laid his bones here—more's the pity. Had he died a soldier's death upon the battlefield we could but say it was the fortune of war, but to be captured and tortured by these savages is quite a different thing."

"But I had supposed that you, and the colonists in general, were now upon the most friendly footing with the natives," said Captain Monckton.

"Assuredly, with the Long Island tribes, the Narragansetts, the Mohicans, and, in fact, all the neighbouring tribes; but these Indians of the confederacy, called the Five Nations, often make a descent upon the friendly Indians and upon the colonists. The stamping grounds of the hostiles is upon the North River, and the country westward, and their war-chief, Sine-rong-ni-rese, is a bloody devil. Why, lad, on the night of the attack upon the plantation of Lady Moody, where the Major was taken prisoner, they massacred an entire tribe—the Canarsees, one of the minor tribes of Long Island; but one escaped the slaughter, and their village was laid in ashes.

They were repulsed at Lady Moody's and came down upon the plantation at Lawrence's Neck, for they move with the rapidity of greyhounds. The following night they fell upon Lady Ann Hutchinson's plantation and slaughtered the entire family, and were off in their canoes, safe from pursuit."

"Destroyed a tribe of their own people—how is that?" asked Captain Monckton.

"The tribes of Sea-wan-ha-ka, being friendly, their chief, Wyandance, who is my firm friend, refused to join in a confederacy with the Five Nations against the settlers, and the slaughter of this minor tribe followed."

"Strikes me they paid dearly for their allegiance," returned Monckton.

"Zounds! you are well intrenched here," broke in Roswell, as the quartette passed through the great gate of the stockade, "a regular fortress, egad!"

"An indispensable condition out here," replied Guy. "There might be an uprising at any moment—a man never knows exactly when his scalp is safe on his head."

Mrs. Gardiner welcomed her unexpected guests with the hospitality for which she was famed, and leaving her husband to entertain them went away to superintend the culinary operations necessary to supply the demands of their appetites.

CHAPTER XLV

READING BETWEEN THE LINES

"There's a dainty window over the way,
  Draped with laces and decked with flowers,
Where a golden bird in a fairy cage
  Sings and swings through the daylight hours;
But his voice has ever a mournful note,
  As if he sighed for an absent mate,
Or dreamed of the forest green and free
  Beyond the bars of his golden grate.

"There's a sweet, pale face, with heaven-blue eyes,
  That looks from the window over the way,
With a wishful gaze at the far-off skies,
  And the golden glow of the fading day;
And I know that many an aching heart
  Beats like the bird with prisoned wings;
And I hear the sound of the grieving note
  In many a song that the poet sings."

"WHAT'S to do about sport, eh?" questioned Captain Monckton, who had caught the drift of a remark made by Roswell to Kingsland.

"We were speaking about making up a hunting party and treating the ship's crew to a surfeit of wild game—deer, bear, wild turkey, and the like,—that is with your permission, Captain," replied Guy.

"Which won't be lacking, lad," rejoined the Captain. "I've some crack shots and keen sportsmen among my marines, whose practice has been upon the enemies of Old England, and on the high seas—and so, my lad, we'll e'en not tarry longer than the morrow."

"And we can offer you some prime oysters, clams, fish and seafowl," chimed in Captain Gardiner. "Why, man, ducks are as abundant in these waters as rooks are in the parks at home. Truth to tell, we have a surfeit, but I confess there's not a proper supply of stock here to compensate, for the game suits me not so well as the roast beef at home."

"There should be a large importation of kine and oxen to suit the demand," returned Mockton. "You have swine in plenty, I dare say."

"Scarcely; but bear's flesh fills the gap in a great measure. One can scarcely detect the difference in flavour between a slice from a bear's hind quarter and a rasher of ham."

"Possible? And are there fruits plentiful?"

"Wild fruit in abundance—grapes, apples, blackberries, raspberries, strawberries, and the like, of course an inferior flavour and size to the cultivated article in England," answered Gardiner, "but I have imported pears and peaches, currants and apples, and have thriving young orchards of the choicest—— Ah, here comes Lawrence, and there's the dinner bell."

Colonel Lawrence joined the group gathered about the hickory wood fire, and received the introductions courteously, but rather coldly, so Tom Roswell fancied.

The dinner bell pealed the second time, and the party adjourned to the dining-room, a snug apartment lighted with wax candles, the table aglitter with silver and cut glass, where the butler waited, solemn and dignified as a church magnate, as became a servitor in Captain Gardiner's employ.

Damaris Gordon joined the family at dinner, taking her accustomed seat upon the right of the Colonel, and feeling a painful sense of restraint.

It was certainly difficult to frame a remark to the silent man sitting by her side, but Guy, upon her right, proved himself capable of any amount of small talk, exerting his conversational powers to the utmost to elicit replies from the moody Colonel.

Captain Monckton, not a particularly observant man, saw nothing of the by-play, but Tom Roswell, quick of perception, stole covert glances across the board at the drooping face of the young girl, noticing her silent, preoccupied manner, but attributing it to a grief natural from her recent loss.

The two captains engaged in a lively conversation, reminiscences of the past, while Mrs. Gardiner accented now and then with a pleasant remark.

It was a positive relief to Damaris when dinner was over and the company returned to the sitting-room.

Guy, wondering, in his easy fashion, at the Colonel's taciturnity, attempted to draw him out, but for once the gay Lieutenant was baffled, Lawrence replying courteously, but briefly, to his sallies, and at an early hour excusing himself and going away to his own room.

He did not remain in his chamber, however, but wrapping his cloak about his tall figure he went out into the starlight, taking his way in the direction of the newly made grave beneath the spreading pine near the spot where Wyancombone had entered the grounds.

A single parting glance from the splendid eyes of her hero, an involuntary weakness upon his part, had caused Damaris' heart to flutter like a wounded dove, and Tom Roswell caught that swift gleam and the tell-tale blush mantling the girl's pale cheek with sudden flame, a conscious droop of the white eyelids over the violet eyes. The glance and answering glow were revelations to the mate of the *Highflyer*.

"A key to the Colonel's moodiness—clear case of love on his part, I'll dare swear. How is it with her, I wonder?" mused Tom; "and does Kingsland suspect? I trow not, or he would be on tenter-hooks. Is there, or has there been an understanding between this uplifted Colonel and our demure little puss? I fancy not."

For an instant Tom studied the girl's face as the bright colour faded as swiftly as it had flamed, leaving her cheeks pallid, her lips white.

"I'll wager a pound against a farthing that the Lieutenant is but an indifferent wooer at best, or he would surely note the signs. I don't think his heart was ever touched. Capital fellow with his messmates, and all that, but that he will ever be in love with anything or anybody except Guy Kingsland, I have my doubts. Such natures are incapable of a grand passion, and yet that high-born lassie, with her shining eyes and sweet, proud lips, is a fitting mate for royalty."

"Dreaming, eh, Tom?"

It was Guy's gay tone in his ear, and Roswell started and stared guiltily, as if his thoughts had been an open book for the perusal of the questioner.

"I was thinking of your friend, the Colonel; there is something about him that interests, yet puzzles me. You knew him before you came to the colonies—I gathered as much through your speech."

"Known him for ages. Capital fellow is Lawrence. A bit proud—one of the uplifted ones to whom honour is dearer than life—squeamish, in fact, but a good sort after all. You'll like him after you have time to learn his good points."

"Avast, there! I don't dislike him in the least,

on the contrary, I have taken a prodigious fancy to him. He's a born soldier, eh? I gather that from the cut of his jib and the way he carries sail generally."

"A soldier—yes. Brave as a lion, an incarnate whirlwind in a fight. I suppose he has led more forlorn hopes and cut down more foemen than any man of his years in Old Noll's army. You should see him at his best. To-night—in fact, ever since his exploit in company with Bull Smith, when they rescued the body of the Major from the Mohawks—he has been down in the mouth, as nearly sulky as it is in the nature of a Lawrence to get. I imagine that episode gave even his iron nerves a wrench that it will take some time to cure."

"He is fine-looking, yet there is something in his grave, handsome face and stern lips that gives one the idea of some hidden trouble. Is he married, widowed, or a bachelor?"

"A confirmed bachelor, don't think he ever felt a twinge of the volcanic fire men call love in all his existence. I should imagine that the fair sex is a riddle which he does not care to solve."

"And yet such as he are men most capable of deep love and great sacrifice for one who is fortunate enough to gain their affection," responded Roswell, thoughtfully.

He was adroitly probing the heart of his friend, but started uneasily. Damaris had quietly taken a seat near at hand, quite unobserved by the speakers, and sat, white and still, gazing in Roswell's face with wide, anguished eyes. He felt assured she must have heard their remarks, which certainly he had not intended for her ears.

"Mayhap some damsel has whistled him down the wind," broke in Captain Monckton, in his loud, hearty voice. He, too, had approached and was standing close by Guy's elbow. "It's the Colonel you are speaking of, I suppose. Aye, my lads, a woman is generally at the bottom of all a soldier's troubles. One in every ten the unmarried officers in our ranks are love-lorn—fact, by Jupiter! make the best fighters, the biggest dare-devils, hold life cheaply, and come through without a scratch," concluded the Captain, sagely.

Languidly Damaris arose from her chair, said her good-night briefly, and flitted away, sick at heart with the intuitive sense that Tom Roswell had fathomed her secret.

CHAPTER XLVI

GUY KINGSLAND'S UNDOING

"The owl shrieked at thy birth, an evil sign;
The night-crow cried, aboding luckless time;
Dogs howl'd, and hideous tempests shook down trees;
The raven rook'd her on the chimney's top,
And chattering pies in dismal discords sung."

IT was yet early morning and the stars still held their tiny lamps in the western sky when Captain Gardiner, with Guy Kingsland, joined the captain and mate of the *Highflyer* at the breakfast which the host had ordered for the abnormally early hour of four, that the party might be enabled to get an early start and enjoy a long day's sport.

Colonel Lawrence had declined to accompany the hunters, politely but firmly urging his recent fatigue as an excuse.

Only Xantippe, the cook, an African slave, black as night, and the solemn-visaged butler were astir, sleepy-eyed and hiding dismal yawns as best they might, both as nearly out of temper as was permissible for the servants of an aristocratic family to be.

"Pity Lawrence is not to be along," grumbled Guy. "He's a thorough sportsman and never wastes good powder and ball on mean game. It is absolutely churlish of him to hive himself like old What-dye-call-'em, in his tub. Egad! the Colonel was always quiet, but of late he's been sour—positively sour! Don't see what's come over him!"

"I'm of Monckton's opinion," put in Captain Gardiner, breaking an egg. "Some fair fisher of men has done for him—I noticed he was unusually silent before he went to Lawrence's Neck. My word for it, gentlemen, the Colonel has been jilted and is sore. Some haughty dame has done for him and cast him aside like an old glove, as the best of their sex will do with these dashing, dauntless, magnificent heroes, such as our gallant Colonel. It's a demned outrage!"

"Any idea who the charmer may be?" chimed in Roswell, his keen gaze fixed on Gardiner's face. "A lady of high degree back there in England, or some colonial maiden?"

"Faugh!" broke in Guy, "the fastidious Colonel in love with the linsey-woolsey maids! Ha, ha! A colonial damsel, forsooth! If *he* has ever been trapped, it is by some high-born daughter of an earl at the very least; but, I' faith, I'm not at all of the opinion that their's a woman in the case—in truth, he appears to be a woman-hater."

"Shouldn't be surprised if you are right, lad," assented Captain Gardiner, placidly, and as he spoke Roswell again regarded him curiously. "Now there's our little Damaris, with whom he was on the most friendly footing, and she is of the sort to attract one of your mighty men of war, he should have admired her—though of course he knew of her engagement. I thought at one time he was pleased with her manners. Whatever friendship he may have felt for her has evaporated, and he appears to have quite forgotten her kindness in nursing him through his illness, after that ugly episode of the poisoned arrow—I told you about that, you know. The poor child made a martyr of herself in reading to him and amusing him generally. I can scarcely wonder that he has fallen in her estimation, for she is barely civil to him when they meet, while he acknowledges her presence by a polite bow. Have you noticed it, Kingsland?"

"He mistrusts nothing," thought Roswell.

"I fancied she regarded him in rather the light of a hero, at the time of the accident, but on closer acquaintance she evidently found his society a bore, though she has never spoken of him in that light."

Guy spoke with a nonchalance that was not in the least feigned, betraying the fact that no twinge of jealousy, so far as his affianced was concerned, had ever touched his heart or self-esteem.

"Of all the muffs, or rather self-conceited prigs, I ever chanced to meet, Guy Kingsland tops the pack," mused Roswell. "I'm not skilled in the ways of the fair sex, but, by the great sea-god, I'm positive that demure, little puss he is going to wed is fathoms deep in love with the sedate Colonel, and that accounts for his moody, abstracted air. The big soldier, so much her senior, loves her—adores her, else his eyes belie him; but he is honourable, she pure and faithful, one that would walk over hot ploughshares to perform what she believes her duty. As to Guy, he is too much wrapped up in his self-admiration to fancy for a moment he could have a rival—he's well enough, a deuced companionable fellow, and will make her a passable husband, I dare say. Well, it's none of my concern, and I'll e'en keep my tongue between my teeth."

Thus cogitating, Tom lounged idly at the window while Captain Gardiner and Guy went away to accoutre themselves for the chase, and Monckton stood beside the mantel puffing vigorously at his pipe.

Guy, returning to the breakfast room, came suddenly upon Damaris, who was awaiting his coming in the upper hall. She had wrapped a heavy dressing gown about her, her long hair fell unbound over her shoulders, and even in the dim light of early morning creeping through the leafless branches of the trees outside, and falling greyly through the diamond-paned window at the end of the hall, he noticed that her cheeks were pallid.

"Heyday, little one, up with the lark! Bound to see the last of me, eh? Very good of you, I'm sure," was his greeting, as he pinched her cheek playfully. "We're off for a glorious day's sport. Tell Lawrence to take good care of you while I'm away. Why! what on earth ails the child?"

He wound his arm about her waist, carelessly, as in duty bound, kissing her forehead with a little bird peck.

"I could not sleep, I was disturbed by such frightful dreams, and so I came to bid you good-bye," she whispered. "I wish you were not going away to-day. Do you believe in dreams?"

"Tush, lassie; I believe in the effect of bad digestion, and I advise a morning nap—what you ladies call a beauty sleep—supplemented by a brisk walk in the crisp air. There's nothing like this bracing sea-breeze to set one up. Take my prescription, and good-bye, sweetheart."

He bent, just touched her cheek with his lips, and ran downstairs, leaving her to return to her room with reluctant steps.

With a heavy feeling of unrest, a presentiment of evil, and a strong sense of her lover's indifference, she threw herself upon her bed and presently fell into a deep slumber.

The sun was gilding sea and shore in its luminous sheen when Captain Monckton and Lieutenant Roswell, with a company of officers from the *High-flyer*, under the guidance of Captain Gardiner and Guy, landed at Montauk for a day's hunt in the solemn woods.

The majority of the party were rather clumsy, those florid-faced, ginger-haired, heavy marines, mostly hard-drinkers, hard-swearers, but many of them sons of peers of the realm, a fox-hunting lot, to whom this deer hunt was a rare treat.

A fine doe had been sighted several times during the morning, but had successfully eluded her pursuers, until, at length, in the afternoon, Lieutenant Kingsland observed her line of retreat, and taking advantage of his knowledge, forelaid her, by which means he was enabled to secure a telling shot.

As she was crossing a densely wooded ridge, running to the wind, being hard hit and sorely wounded, she suddenly turned and made straight for a dense swamp encircling a small but deep lake.

Kingsland had quite lost sight of the fact that he was separated from his companions, and that their clumsy crash through the undergrowth had long since died away.

The afternoon was waning, night was coming on, the deathly silence of the forest reigned, but, eager to bag his quarry, he pursued in hot haste, trampling over damp brake and brier with great strides, and plunging recklessly into the green gloom of the interlaced woodland of hemlock and pine.

At every step the way grew more dismal among the tangled brown vines and tall dead spikes of cattails and rushes that rustled like the hiss of serpents in the rising breeze. On and on fled pursued and pursuer.

Kingsland saw nothing of the man-hunter close

upon his trail, a lithe Indian with eyes glaring, teeth clenched like a mastiff's, his black brow bent, his lips set wide in an open parallel, as he flitted in and out among the giant tree trunks with the sinuous movement of a tiger.

With all the persistence of a bloodhound, Poniute moved in the steps of the white man. Guy Kingsland must not live to leave the dismal swamp of Mah-chon-it-chuge; he must die this night and find a tomb in the black ooze where his feet were already miring.

There was no relenting in that savage breast, no dread of the work in hand, except the fear of possible failure, while, all unconscious of his impending doom, Guy plunged on through brake and bramble, sinking in the morass ankle-deep, expectant at every step to get sight of the wounded doe.

Nearer and nearer stole the avenger, and there, at the end of a vista through an arch of naked boughs, gazing intently across the sluggish waters of the forest lake, the victim had halted.

The silence was oppressive, the sun had hidden beneath the encircling ridge; the lake, black with brooding shadows, lay moveless, unruffled as a sheet of lead, sheltered from the wind that rioted beyond the hills, and seen through the twilight that reigned in the rocky bowl Guy's figure loomed up spectrally. Now and again some bird on lagging wing floated overhead, flitting across the leaden lake like an unquiet ghost, the only sign of life except the two human forms visible in the lonely spot far in the depths of the wildwood.

With noiseless movements the lurking savage fitted the envenomed arrow, the bow-string was drawn tense by the dark, sinewy hand until the tough bow was bent to its fullest.

"Swift as the lightning's bolt the arrow sped"

One instant the red man stood, stern as death, terrible as doom.

"Look, white wolf, take a last look at earth and sky—you will never again see the Heather Flower, but your scalp will dry in the smoke of her lodge-fire!"

The horrible words were spoken under his breath, as Poniute poised for the fatal aim.

Swift as the lightning's bolt the arrow sped, true to its mark, piercing the thick portion of the thigh, cleaving its way to the bone. Had the Indian aimed at his heart Guy Kingsland would never have realised his suffering.

With an angry oath he wrenched the deadly missile from the wound, and glared about to discover who the unseen archer might be, never dreaming that the sharp point carried with it, and had implanted enough of deadly virus to slay half-a-score of men.

The small incision made by the slender arrow, and the fact that it gave comparatively little pain, lulled the apprehension concerning the wound. He was no coward physically, and he pluckily set about the task of driving his ambushed enemy from cover, half-believing that it was a chance shot from some Indian hunter at wild game lurking in the morass.

Not a living thing was in sight, neither man nor beast, and after beating about among the leafless brambles, and floundering across the dark bogs and sodden network of roots, he discovered, to his dismay, that he was lost in the jungle, and presently he felt a strange sensation of numbness in his feet, his skin became dry and hot, and soon a chilling ague crept over him.

Sharp pains began to dart through his frame like

the stings of innumerable bees, his limbs became cramped, a sickening nausea possessed him, an intolerable thirst gnawed at his stomach, and his eyes started from their sockets as he began to realise the horrible truth, that he had been pierced by a poisoned arrow.

Raising his brandy flask with trembling hands, he drained the small quantity that it contained, and dashed it upon the earth; but the deadly poison was doing its work, and in a paroxysm of desperation he strove to make his way in the direction he believed his friends to be searching for him. He succeeded in reaching the crest of the low ridge. A storm was gathering blackly, the clouds were scudding wildly athwart the zenith, a strong north wind tore through the ghostly pines tossing the branches that creaked dismally.

It was an eerie scene, the leafless limbs of the oaks, frost-bitten and brown, swaying their skeleton arms outlined against the grey sky, while the twilight was dying, fast driven by the swift darkness of night, and already the fen stretching out at the foot of the ridge upon which he stood and the deep lake were lost in the blackness.

Benumbed by terror and pain, with his blood fast thickening in his veins, Guy sank down, his head drooped, his fowling-piece fell from his nerveless fingers.

CHAPTER XLVII

AN INDIAN TORQUEMADA

*"If heaven have any grievous plague in store,
Exceeding those that I can wish upon thee,
O let them keep it, till thy sins be ripe,
And then hurl down their indignation
On thee, the troubler of the poor world's peace."*

ONCE again he strove to rise from the spot where he had fallen, by clutching at the bushes and lower limbs of a knotted sapling, and at length he staggered to his feet.

"Curse the cowards who have left me to die alone! where are they?" he groaned, in a vague sort of way. "I must seek the Indian village. Old Wyandance will not deny me shelter, and he will know the remedy—Ascassasatic used the tobacco, and sucked the poison——"

His voice died away, he strove to reach the wound with his lips, but tried in vain. Then he clutched eagerly at his pipe, but found it empty—his tobacco pouch he had left with Captain Monckton.

"I must reach the village," he whispered, hoarsely, and grasping at the low-bending limbs he stumbled forward a few yards, then reeling, half crouching, he found himself descending the incline, and ere he could check his steps he was again upon the very brink of the fen. His limbs failed and he sank down in a heap, groaning piteously with the pain that was becoming almost unendurable.

"Wagh! White wolf cry like squaw! red man's medicine strong—white wolf no more talk love to the red flower of the Montauks!"

The groan upon Guy's lips died away in a gasp of horror, as a dark form glided to his side like a crouching tiger, an iron hand grasped his wrist, a scowling face bent low over him, like a hideous phantom seen in a dream, which he recognised, even in the gloom.

"Poniute!"

"Ugh!"

"The Great Spirit has sent you to me in this terrible strait! Help me! For the love of God, give me something to take away this horrible pain! I will give you of the white man's gold. I am sore wounded by an arrow, and I am certain it is poisoned! You know the cure—your people can take away the poison; Ascassasatic saved Lawrence —for the love of God, make haste! Don't you know I am suffering the tortures of the damned?" pleaded the wretched victim, essaying to ignore the bitter hatred the warrior had implied by his speech, and hoping to move the savage heart to pity.

A blaze of exultation swept over the Indian's countenance, a cruel glare flamed in his deep-set eyes.

"Did the white hawk spare the red bird that sung all the long days in the wigwam of the great Sachem of the Montauks? No! he set a poisoned talon in her heart that turned the red blood black, and hot, and thick, and changed all the love which the maiden had given him to hatred and revenge. For love of the pale-face wolf the forest flower turned her face from the warriors of her tribe.

"What would the white wolf do? Would he give her love for love? Would he have taken her to his wigwam before her tribe and his own people? No! he would have made the pride of the Montauks a shame to the women of her tribe. The squaws of burden would have pointed their fingers toward her and bent their eyes to the ground when she passed, until she should be cast forth from her people to die in the forest, where nothing but the wild beasts should look upon her shame! Would the white dog know whose tongue spoke the words that sent him to a death by the poison of the rattlesnake?"

"Merciful Saviour! you cannot tell me that it was—was she?" gasped Guy, as he raised his burning eyes to the face of his tormentor. "A woman, with a woman's tender heart, could not do this!"

"It was Heather Flower who sent Poniute to drive the poisoned arrow through the white man's thigh, to watch his agonies, and take his scalp that will dry in the smoke of her lodge-fire when Poniute takes her to his wigwam. The pale-face wolf promised to make her his squaw. He lied—she would have revenge!"

"I did not lie! I told her I loved her—it is true! Give me the medicine that will take away this cursed poison and I swear by the Great Spirit that I will go to the village and make Heather Flower my wife, before her tribe, and by the customs of her people!"

"What does the white man care for the red man's law?" sneered the Indian. "Wagh! the white man's law calls the custom of the red man nothing! Pouf! to him it is like the breath of wind that comes and goes and cannot be seen."

"I will swear to make Heather Flower my wife before my race. A black-coat shall wed us, and before every white man in the settlements and every warrior of her tribe!" groaned Guy, as he clutched frantically among the rushes where he lay.

There was a depth of scorn and triumph in the Indian's tones as he replied:

"Heather Flower will come to the lodge of Poniute when the scalp of the white warrior who has told her lies hangs at his belt. The Montauk warrior will go when his white enemy has groaned away his breath, and then——"

A savage pantomime of scalping a foe emphasised the unfinished sentence.

"Almighty God! Can the woman who has sworn to love give the man she has loved to such a fate? Have mercy! mercy! mercy! Savage though you are, is there not one spark of pity left?" shrieked the victim, as he struggled to his knees and clutched the Indian's blanket; but the implacable savage met the piteous entreaties with an exultant cry that froze the supplicant to the heart, and wrenching the clinging fingers from his mantle with a force that rattled the wampum ornaments like a fringe of icicles, he stepped back a pace, wrapped his blanket closely and folded his arms across his brawny chest.

"Listen! Shall the red warrior see the bird crushed in the coils of the serpent whose song charmed her while she fluttered nigh to the open jaw? Shall he spare the serpent? Listen! The pale-face has stolen the red man's lands; he has taken from him the right to dig in the ground for the roots to make his medicine; he has driven the fish from the streams; the great fish that the Indian takes from the big water is stolen by the white man who leaves the red man only tails and fins; he is scaring the deer from the forest, and soon he will have all; but he could not take away the red flower Poniute would wear in his bosom!

"Wagh! The white fox is a great brave, let him sing his death-song! Why does he whine like a sick papoose because he is afraid to die like a warrior of the Montauks? Poniute has spoken."

Guy realised but too well that his pleading would be of no avail, and in his desperation he tore the covering from his breast and spread out his arms.

"I can die! Let the red warrior strike! Let him plunge his knife in my heart!"

"Let the white wolf howl his death-song!" returned Poniute, grimly.

With the strength born of frenzy the dying man tottered to his feet, and groped his way a few paces, only to fall in a heap upon the very edge of the fen.

"Help! help! Gordon, come—come nearer! Have you been sent from the world of spirits to take me from the clutches of my tormentor?" he gasped, groping as if to grasp a shadowy form, the phantom he imagined hovering almost within his reach; but the spectral vision floated away as if borne on a current of air, and only the Indian hunter, seated upon a spur of rock near at hand, remained.

Minutes passed, ages of torture, the moans suddenly ceased, a wild, exultant cry pealed out, the watcher sprang to his feet. His enemy lay dead.

Poniute crouched for a moment above his fallen foe, his left hand closed over a lock of the soft, curling hair that had been Guy Kingsland's pride, his right hand clasped the haft of his knife.

The next instant the Indian glided away, a scalp hanging at his girdle. Heather Flower's behest had been accomplished.

The storm burst in its fury, a cold, cutting sleet swept in slanting needle-points as it lashed the face of the dead.

CHAPTER XLVIII

MAH-CHON-IT-CHUGE

"Away to the dismal swamp he speeds,
   His path was rugged and sore,
Through tangled juniper, beds of reeds,
Through many a fen where the serpent feeds,
   And man never trod before;
And when, at night, he sank to sleep,
   If slumber his eyelids knew,
He lay where the deadly vine doth weep
Her venomous tear, and nightly steep
   The flesh with blistering dew."

WEARIED with the day's sport, that had been rewarded but with indifferent success, the hunters gathered upon a little knoll that had been designated as the place of meeting.

"Where the devil is Kingsland?" inquired Tom Roswell, as he shaded his eyes with his hand and peered through the dim greenness of the pines. "Now I bethink, I've not heard the report of his firelock for the deuce of a time. He should be within earshot. Pipe up, Captain, and call him in."

Gardiner raised the bugle horn to his lips and blew a shrill blast that echoed and re-echoed through the forest aisles.

"That will bring him in," quoth Monckton. "That blare was enough to wake the dead."

"Aye, he'll be here presently. He is nimble of foot and strong of limb. Doubtless he was hot on the chase and the quarry took him a good bit of a distance, and, if I mistake not, he intends to bag the biggest game by himself," returned Gardiner.

"The lad has a spice of selfishness in his composition, or I don't read the signs," muttered Monckton, but Captain Gardiner caught the drift.

"Ambitious is the better word, Captain," he corrected. "He's a good sort, is the lad."

"Umph!" commented Monckton, under his breath, "he's a Kingsland, and I never quite liked the stock. Easy-going to laziness, at times, but keen as a brier when self-interest prompts to action—chip of the old block," then aloud, he added, "Is there danger from savage wild beasts in these forests? If I recollect aright, I have been told there are some formidable animals in the colonies."

"Bears are plenty, wolves numerous—both are savage, so much so that a bounty is offered for every wolf's head. They hunt in packs for their prey, and together are bold. It is no joke to find one's self surrounded by a pack of snarling wolves, especially in the night, when they come from their dens; alone the brutes are arrant sneaks. Kingsland is safe enough unless he has got lost in some swamp."

The echoes of the winding horn had died away. It was still—oppressively still, the night was falling swiftly, the sun had sunk and in place of the amber and opal twilight a grey veil was sweeping over forest and sea.

"We improved the only day of pleasant weather, for there's a squall bottled in yon ugly-looking clouds," commented Captain Monckton, uneasily. "If we don't get a hurricane out o' yon black wind-caps, I'm no sailor. 'Twill blow great guns before another hour is gone. Give another blast o' the horn, for there's no time to waste an' we get safely aboard the *Highflyer* before the blow comes."

Gardiner gave a bugle call that reverberated through the dim arcades like a trumpet call to battle, winding in waves of sound and dying away in a long-drawn wail.

"He'll hear that if he is within the radius of miles," remarked Gardiner.

"Aye, man, there's his answering halloa," exclaimed Monckton, cheerily.

The faint, distant cry was repeated, long and melancholy, from the heart of the woods, and Gardiner's face fell.

"Faugh! it is but the hoot of an owl! I wonder what's to do o' the lad—I fear he may be lost. Shall we look about a bit?" he asked.

"Should we be likely to come across him in this bloody tangle?" asked Monckton. "I imagine it is the surer plan to remain here and try to signal him. This is the precise spot where we parted company, or rather he ran away from us, and it is good horse sense that he will look for us where we agreed to meet. Zounds! but he must be daft to loiter, and such a storm brewing!"

"Wind the bugle, an' it please you, Captain," put in Tom Roswell. "If the Lieutenant is lost the sound will guide him."

Blare after blare roared from the brazen-throated horn, with short intervals between the calls, and with heads bowed and palms at their ears the group listened intently, but no answering cry came back.

"What besotted idiots we are," suddenly exclaimed Gardiner, in a relieved tone. "It is all plain. The lad has seen the tempest rising and I make no doubt he scurried to the Indian village for shelter. He is thoroughly at home with the Montauks, and I'll wager a pound he is safely housed with old Wyandance. The old pagan won't turn him out, so

I'll e'en give another blast, and if it don't bring him we'll go aboard and make sail for the Isle o' Wight."

Once more the horn brayed hoarsely, and they waited for a reply, which came not, and thoroughly convinced that Gardiner's theory was correct, they quickened their steps almost to a run on their way shoreward. As they gained their boat a strange and altogether unwonted scene greeted their vision.

It was nearly dark, and from all directions the myriad waterfowls, of every species that frequented the surrounding waters, were flying seaward in the wildest disorder, and great clouds of them could be seen high in air, while dense flocks were scurrying along on swiftest wing just above the bosom of the turbid waters, all shaping their mad flight seaward, as if in terror, to escape the oncoming tempest.

"What's the meaning of all this exodus, Gardiner?" called Monckton. "Looks demned near as if all the ducks in creation were on a migratory passage! Is not this an unusual occurrence at this season of the year?"

"Zounds! you may well ask," responded Captain Gardiner. "In all the years I have spent in the colonies I have never witnessed anything like it; not that it is unusual to see such numbers, but such demoralisation is singular, for, although it is the habit of some of the varieties to go to sea at nightfall, most of them remain in shallow water."

"So I supposed," replied Monckton. "There's method in their madness, or rather their instinct, and if we reach yon island to-night it will be in the teeth of a hurricane. Pull away, lads! the sooner we are alongside the better."

"Aye, aye, sir," was the hearty response, as the hardy sailors gave way at the oars that sent the boat swiftly over the turbid waters, and in an incredibly short time alongside the *Highflyer*.

The wind had risen to a shrieking gale, bearing lance-points of stinging sleet; not a star was visible, the moon was blotted out by a dense bank of clouds, the roar of the sea and the sullen battering of the great breakers against the lofty cliffs to leeward was like the thunderous boom of artillery, the roar of the waves about and below the ship like the bellow of dragons imprisoned far, far below.

In haste the boat was hoisted upon the davits, the orders were given in quick succession, and the ship was under way for the run across to Man-cho-nock.

Scarcely was the anchor broke and the ship filled away, when, butt end first, the hurricane burst upon them in all its fury. The ship was knocked down not two cables' length from the rocky cliff under her lee, but, being a staunch vessel, she righted as she gathered momentum from the terrific force of the wind.

The grave danger that menaced the *Highflyer* at this time, was of being stranded for want of sea-room, before she could gather headway enough to offset the leeway she was making toward the rocky shore, while it would have been sheer madness to attempt to go in stays; but gallantly she held her way, forging to windward, pointing her nose seaward, and gradually, but surely, widening her distance from the dangerous lee-shore.

It was minutes before a word was spoken, as with set teeth and bated breath all waited until the supreme moment of danger was past.

White foam-capped waves rose like mocking, giant spectres, leaping past the flying ship in flashes of pale fire, lighting the darkness with phosphorescent glow, only to reveal the terrors around, and with a crash like the whistle of shot the sleet came surging aslant, sweeping the deck with an icy broadside and encasing the creaking masts and ropes with crystal sheaths encrusted with innumerable diamonds.

The boldest among the brave sailors on that icy deck shuddered; stout hearts and nerves of steel must tremble when the Creator manifests His power upon the face of the mighty deep. Daring and godless indeed is the mortal who refuses to bow in humble supplication when the Almighty reveals Himself in awful majesty and sublimity out upon the angry waters lashed by the hurricane.

Not a soldier or sailor on board the *Highflyer* who did not offer a silent petition while the stout timbers and planks groaned and creaked beneath their feet, as they realised the terrific power of the winds and waves tossing the leviathan ship-o'-war hither and thither, a waif upon the inferno of waters, one moment rising with the fearful impetus upon the shoulder of a monster billow, only to plunge again into a black abyss, while the wind raved and the sleet froze a winding sheet upon the deck.

Captain Monckton was the first to speak, as in a devout voice he cried:

"Thank God, we are safe!"

"Amen!" responded Gardiner, and a low-breathed echo rose from the lips of all on board.

"I am a stranger in these waters," continued Captain Monckton, "and we have escaped the momentary danger possibly to run headlong into greater peril, if greater there can be, with no friendly beacon lights, and no charts pointing out the danger on these coasts. We should still be in sorry plight were it not for your presence on board, Captain. What is to be done?"

"Have no fear, Monckton," returned sturdy Captain Gardiner, cheerfully; "your good ship is staunch and seaworthy, and I feel as safe now upon her deck as I should if we were in Gardiner Hall at this moment. I say this that all may feel assured. It is folly to attempt to reach the Isle of Wight to-night, in the teeth of a tempest of such unwonted fury as this, and when, as you say, we have no guiding-star. But, the alternative is a feasible and safe one—that is, simply to hold on our way seaward until the dangerous reef that is still under our lee, that the Indians call Shag-wan-nock, is passed; we can then run off a few miles to sea, heave-to and ride out the storm, which, from its severity, I am certain will be short-lived. We can make our way back after the gale has broken."

Accordingly a double watch was set, and the ship was put to sea. For hours the noble craft, storm-driven, sped like a thing of life over the dark heaving waters, while the aërial batteries thundered, the storm-spirit held high carnival alow and aloft, and the blinding sleet fast wove icy coats of mail and glittering helmets on the shaggy sou'westers and tarpaulins of the poor fellows exposed to its cruel force.

It was past the midnight hour when the storm ceased, with the suddenness with which it had arisen; the wind had passed, shrieking on its way, and naught was felt of it; but the sullen roar was heard high overhead, as it receded seaward until the sound was lost.

The sea continued boisterous for hours after, as the *Highflyer*, hove-tó under close-reefed topsails, rode in safety leagues away from the perils that had menaced her a few short hours before.

The skies were cleared of the rift that had floated away in ribbons, the moon, sailing a crystal disc high up toward the zenith, lent her opalescent light, the stars came forth like sparkling brilliants in the diadem of night, and under the clear rays the ship rode, hull, spars and sails shrouded in frozen snow and sleet, a barque wrought in frosted silver, weird, white, ghostly.

Presently the wind, that had died out, sprang again to life in the same quarter from whence the storm had come, increasing to a steady breeze, and under a press of sail the *Highflyer* went on her course, traversing her briny pathway back to the friendly shore of the Isle of Wight, from which, so lately and so unceremoniously, she had been forced to fly.

Nothing occurred to interrupt the even tenor of her way, and in the early hours of morning the ship cast anchor in the offing at the Isle of Wight, at about the hour that she had left the same anchorage upon the previous morning, to run over to Montauk for her officers and marines to indulge in a day's hunt.

As soon as the salute was fired a boat left her gangway, bearing Captain Gardiner, Captain Monckton and Lieutenant Roswell, as the two latter had accepted an invitation to breakfast at Gardiner Hall.

CHAPTER XLIX

THE DOPPELGANGER

> "Sometime we see a cloud that's dragonish:
> A vapour, sometime, like a bear or lion,
> A tower'd citadel, a pendant rock,
> A forked mountain, or blue promontory
> With trees upon 't, that nod unto the world,
> And mock our eyes with air; thou hast seen these signs;
> They are black vesper's pageants."

DAMARIS had been restless during the entire day after parting with Guy, why she could scarcely have told, for his presence was, to her, rather depressing than otherwise.

As for Colonel Lawrence, he had isolated himself within his own apartment for hours, as if indeed he were determined to increase the coldness and constraint that had marked his demeanour since his half-enforced sojourn at the hall. The dinner was served at an early hour, and scarcely a word passed between the twain. Immediately after the family rose from the table he excused himself, and wrapping his military cloak about his shoulders he sauntered forth to enjoy his pipe in the frosty air.

The sun had set, and he stood sheltered by a spur of rock, his eyes roving across the broad expanse of water that had begun to ruffle ominously under the rising wind, and anon scanning the scurrying clouds, apprehensively, as they dropped lower and grew blacker and denser with each passing moment.

"I' faith! it is high time that the *Highflyer* should be on her return trip. I see nothing of her lights, and if I don't mistake the signs, there's a black tempest brewing. Monckton is a thorough sailor, but he will have a rough passage, if it is a short one," mused Lawrence, his gaze shifting uneasily from the lowering sky to the murky waters, from which arose a hollow moan, precursor of the hurricane. A few particles of fine sleet rattled through the bare branches of the oaks, striking sharply against his cheek, reminding him that it was time to seek shelter.

Mrs. Gardiner was passing through the hall when he entered the mansion; her face was pallid, her eyes heavy with apprehension.

"I am much concerned about our hunters," she said. "The Captain is never absent from the island after nightfall, except when important business calls him away, and he must have seen the storm gathering. He knows, none better, that these waters are especially dangerous to navigate when a gale is blowing, more particularly at night, seamed as they are with reefs and hidden rocks. I am sorely afraid some accident has detained him."

"Pooh! pooh! Captain Monckton is an old salt, a thorough navigator. I am told Captain Gardiner is acquainted with every rock, shoal and bank. Never fear but they will bring the *Highflyer* through without accident," returned the Colonel, with the purpose of allaying the fears which he secretly shared.

"But something wrong may have occurred ashore," she persisted. "There are rumours of an outbreak of the tribes upon the mainland, and one can never tell at what moment the island tribes may be induced to dig up the hatchet."

"Say you so? I have no idea there is the slightest danger of such a catastrophe, besides, Captain Gardiner, being the close friend of the Montauk Sachem, would be perfectly safe, even should the Long Island Indians take to the war-path. There is nothing serious, depend upon it. I imagine that they got away on a hot chase, and time passed imperceptibly. Quite likely Captain Monckton saw the storm gathering and decided not to risk his vessel in a gale, a wise precaution."

"I am absurd, I dare say, and full of ridiculous fancies," acknowledged Mrs. Gardiner, as she lowered her voice and placed a finger upon her lips. "I think Damaris is yon," with a wave of the hand toward the door of the drawing-room, "and I do not wish her to be alarmed. I have a strange foreboding that something ill has befallen, and that it concerns her more nearly. Last night I dreamed of a wedding—according to old-wives' lore such a dream is an augury of a death, but the peculiarity of my vision points to a calamity. I saw the groom plainly, pallid, and drawn, and blue,—the face of a corpse; and in place of wedding garments he was wrapped in a winding-sheet," shuddered the lady.

"Very Scotch," replied Lawrence, lightly. "I have very small faith in omens. Have no fear, lady, until you have a more tangible foundation for apprehension than an idle dream, which can have no signification."

"I saw the faces of groom and bride—the groom as pale as death."

"And who were the contracting parties?" asked the Colonel, in a strangely constrained voice.

"Who but our little Damaris and Guy—it was his face I saw."

"And what more natural?" queried Lawrence. "Nothing singular when you remember that the coming bridal has been the theme from day to day. Think no more of it, I beseech you, madam."

"But I have not told you all," whispered Mrs. Gardiner, with a glance over her shoulder to the landing at the second story; "but a moment since I saw Guy, face to face——"

"Guy Kingsland? impossible!" exclaimed Lawrence. "Surely you are dreaming!"

"But now, as I came down the upper hall, the door of Guy's chamber swung open noiselessly, Guy came forth, glided past me and passed slowly down yon stairs; his form was clearly outlined, he looked neither to the right nor left, his face was chalky in its pallor, and such a face, such misery in the lines about the lips and eyes I never beheld! But it was Guy—his doppelganger—his spectre! Merciful Saviour! to my dying day I shall never forget that face!"

"Hist! the lassie may overhear!" warned the Colonel. "Dear lady, believe me, the apparition was but the offspring of a disordered fancy, a figment of your dream, at which you will smile when the gay young Lieutenant returns, nearly famished, to make a demand upon your larder quite at variance with the habits of a spook."

"God grant it! Not for the world would I breathe a word to the lass. It would frighten her for naught, mayhap," returned the lady, as the twain entered the drawing-room to find Damaris seated at her tambour frame, plying her needle diligently, but the little fingers trembled nervously as Lawrence took a seat at a respectful distance.

How lovely she looked, her colour rising and fading, her eyes flashing a welcome, spite of her utmost effort to appear indifferent to the man whose presence was mingled rapture and pain for both.

"Of what were you thinking, little one?" he

asked in a whisper audible only to her ear. "Tell me truly, Damaris—were you thinking of him—of Guy?"

The question she might have regarded as impertinent from other lips than his, but the stately little head only drooped a trifle lower over the tambour frame, as she replied in the half-whisper he had used:

"Not of Guy alone—of his companions as well. I wonder what is detaining them. Do you think any accident has happened?"

"Nothing except the storm, I dare say. Listen! how the sleet rattles against the window panes, and the wind is something tremendous. I make no doubt that Captain Monckton would hesitate to cross in the teeth of such a howling gale, and I am quite sure I honour his judgment," answered Lawrence, in a quiet, matter-of-fact tone.

Contrary to their usual custom since the Major's death, neither the Colonel or Damaris retired to their chambers to spend the evening hours, both remaining with Mrs. Gardiner in the pleasant drawing-room.

Never since his return had Henry Lawrence exerted himself so thoroughly to make himself companionable, a matter easy of accomplishment so far as concerned Damaris, who listened to the sound of the loved voice while he talked to Mrs. Gardiner and occasionally addressed a remark to herself. Her fair, sweet face lighted to the sunshine of his presence, the magnetism of his eyes. Her lips grew mobile, while her hands lay idly in her lap, her heart atune in its sudden joyousness, while she was wholly unconscious that her wonderful violet eyes were speaking, so eloquently, the love her lips would not have uttered for the wealth of the Indies. And Colonel Lawrence, watching the play of her emotions, realised with mingled admiration and regret that there existed elements in that guileless, young soul from which the brightest poetry or the saddest destiny of life is wrought, and a moral nature more enchanting than her personal loveliness, and keenly felt that such association as he was indulging was more dangerous to his self-abnegation than words of love from the lips he fain would have pressed. And to the depths of his soul he recognised the peril he had incurred in remaining upon the island. He was a proud man, with an organisation of mind so attuned that the sin of loving, nay, idolising, the affianced bride of another was, to his sensitive conscience, as deep as actual crime.

Haunted though he was by his own misgivings, yet how could he leave those delicate women to endure the suspense, the watching and waiting? He must remain, and promising his own heart that he would flee from temptation the instant the *Highflyer* sailed, he strove to forget, and to converse cheerfully, while the hours wore on.

All through that long night the three watched and waited, hours of blended pain and exquisite joy to the child-woman and the loyal-souled man who so nobly battled against temptation.

A sparkling, wintry morn succeeded the night of tempest. The *Highflyer* lay anchored within a few cables' length of the Isle of Wight, while her captain and mate discussed the excellent breakfast at Gardiner Hall, where Guy's absence caused a slight feeling of uneasiness scarcely amounting to alarm.

"He was heading in the direction of the Indian village, and observing the storm gathering, and near at hand, it was the most natural thing in the world that he should seek shelter in lieu of tramping through brake and brier, where he would be in danger of missing his way, and as a consequence must spend this night in the woods," reasoned Captain Gardiner. An opinion in which all coincided, except Mrs. Gardiner, who had many misgivings.

What was the strange apparition she had seen? Was it in truth a disembodied spirit, or had her senses played her false? She could only wait the course of events, but it was in a most perturbed frame of mind that she did the honours of the board for the guests who were making merry after the rough experience of the preceding night.

CHAPTER L

UNRETURNING

"They sought all that night, and they sought the next day,
And they sought all the time till a week passed away,
In the highest, the lowest, the loneliest spot,
Young Lovell sought wildly, but found her not;
And years flew by, and their grief, at last,
Was told as a sorrowful tale long past."

WHEN, shortly after the breakfast hour, Wyancombone rowed over to the island, and it became known that the Lieutenant had not been seen at the Indian village, uneasiness was changed to keen apprehension, and the *Highflyer* was soon speeding across the bay, bearing the searching party, and guided by those who had accompanied the young officer upon the ill-starred hunt from which he was destined never to return.

The search was begun and prosecuted with unflagging zeal. Aided and piloted by the keenest scouts of the Montauks, parties of white men scoured the island for miles around in a radius from the spot where Kingsland was last seen in life, and among the most zealous of the Indian scouts was Poniute, who chose for his especial ground the low-lying swamp and bog surrounding the dismal lake, where he was accompanied by half a dozen white men.

Captain Gardiner, Colonel Lawrence, the captain, officers and marines of the *Highflyer*, besides planters from the settlements, joined in the hunt in a body, or by turns, but not the slightest trace of the lost one could be found. As mysteriously as if the ocean had engulfed him the Lieutenant had vanished from mortal ken.

The authorities from Easthampton were summoned, and a systematic espionage was kept upon the savages, most prominent among these being Ascassasatic, whose voice had ever been for war, and the minor warriors who had at intervals given token of a disposition to revolt against the encroachments of the whites; but not the slightest sign of treachery or knowledge was discovered.

As we have said, among the foremost and most vigilant in the search was Poniute, who, with Wyancombone, had guided the white men through the intricacies of the forest to the very edge of the quagmire, a point beyond which no human foot might tread lest a life might be lost, Poniute carefully pointing out the various pitfalls, above one of which the stark form of the Lieutenant lay, upheld by the network of frozen roots, and encrusted in the sepulchre of glistening snow and ice piled three feet above his pulseless heart, in the hollow as smoothly and evenly laid as the broad expanse stretching away among the ice-laden tangle of brier, thorn and sedge encircling the frost-bound lake.

Sinking knee-deep in the crusted snow at every stride, four men followed Poniute and Wyancombone, who made their way to the very edge of the growth of hemlocks, where thick, green fans, weighted with snow, drooped low over an embankment, swaying in the sobbing wind, and there Poniute, who was in advance, halted.

The eyes of the grim warrior, resting upon the spot where he had left his victim, scintillated with an unholy light, but neither Captain Gardiner nor Colonel Lawrence noted the fiery gleam that told the youthful Wyancombone where, not ten feet adown the slope from the little ridge upon which they stood, the man they sought slept in death.

Three weeks had been passed in the fruitless search, the wind was blowing sharply, whirling cutting particles of frost from the burdened limbs of the trees in their faces; even the hardy red men, inured as they were to the bitter cold, shivered, and their blue lips closed over their chattering teeth.

Not the faintest clue had been discovered, and weary, discouraged and footsore, the little party made their way back to their waiting boat, fain to give up the quest that had proved so bootless, and trust to time to lift the dark veil of mystery shrouding the fate of the gay young Lieutenant.

"What news? Have you gained a clue?"

Mrs. Gardiner put the stereotyped question, in the hopeless tone she had used of late—she could not frame the words, "Have you found him?" The gloomy brows forbade such an inquiry.

"Not a trace—not a sign, wife. Poor Guy is dead, there's not a doubt. May as well tell our little lass that all hope is at an end—God help her to bear it! Break the news gently, dame, you women-folk having a faculty of doing that sort of thing. It is better that the story should come from your kind lips. Best thing under the circumstances—eh, Colonel?"

The latter portion of the remark was addressed to Lawrence, who paled and flushed, alternately, in spite of his habitual self-control, for the Captain had voiced the conviction for which he had chided himself, fearing that the thought was but a temptation from the Evil One.

In spite of himself, his heart beat with a quicker, joyous throb. Damaris loved him—he knew that, and in his inmost soul he felt the conviction that although the shock of being assured her affianced husband was dead beyond a doubt would unnerve her, yet she would forget, and in time—— Here he checked his musing by a supreme effort, resolutely shutting his eyes to the future which might bring so much of promise.

But to Damaris the universal belief that Guy was dead scarcely came as a shock. From the first she feared the worst, and a tender pity for the youth cut down in the pride and strength of his manhood took the place of the bitter grief she would have felt had she loved him with aught save a sisterly affection—a sorrow that he, so winning, so full of life, and, as she fondly believed, so true, should have been snatched away when life was opening before him with brightest prospects.

Poor child! She strove to prove her loyalty to his memory, for the love she had unconsciously given another she fancied should have been Guy's by unquestionable right, and she still regarded with sisterly affection the man whose wife she would have been.

She mourned for the friend of her childhood, neither weeping nor moaning, but her heart seemed weighted, benumbed by a sense of loneliness. Her father was dead, his grave was beneath the tall pine, within the sound of the restless, moaning sea. Guy—how had he died? A haunting dread assailed her that he had been slain and devoured by wild beasts, else why had he not been found by the keen Indian scouts? How false she had been in her heart to the man who had ever been kind, and who had trusted her so implicitly! She never dreamed, poor, tender child, that the trust was but a lack of affection, a selfishness that blinded him to the truth.

"It grieves me most that I so far forgot his claim

as to listen to words of love from other lips," she whispered, brokenly; "now he is dead, and I can never tell him how deeply I sorrow that I ever wronged him, even in thought; that I only loved him as a friend, I, who was to have been his wife!"

Henry Lawrence, with the keen intuition of one who loves deeply, read the heart of the gentle girl as the pages of an open book. Time alone could heal the wound upon that tender conscience. She invested Kingsland with all the virtues and attributes that were foreign to his nature, while her idol was but potter's clay, a Juggernaut to which she would have sacrificed herself for naught.

Absence of the real object of her love would strengthen her affection. He would go away and leave her to the period of mourning she deemed a sacred duty, but from his lips she must never learn how fickle, how hollow, was the heart she had trusted —better she should not. In after years she would turn to the true love of her heart and be happy.

So reasoned the lover, and when the *Highflyer* sailed away he stood upon her deck, his tall figure towering above the stalwart marines as he waved his adieu to the friends on shore.

CHAPTER LI

TAKING UP THE THREADS OF FATE

> "Pansy, born in the royal purple,
>   Linked by a subtle chain to thought,
> Read me the spell of the mystic meaning
>   Deep in your chalice of gold inwrought."

NEWS had come from far-away England to the Isle of Wight, a letter addressed to Henry Lawrence.

In those days of slow-sailing vessels it was difficult to transmit letters with any certainty, and this particular missive, addressed "Saybrook Fort," had been forwarded to the island, where it awaited the return of the wanderer, whose address was unknown.

Thus it was not until his return from the colony of Virginia, whither his restless spirit had led him, that the Colonel was apprised of the death of a distant relative, the last of his line, and that the estate had passed to the next in succession, no other than himself.

Captain Gardiner was informed upon the subject. A letter addressed to him contained the important information, and he hailed the Colonel as "Sir Henry" with a heartiness that left the latter to doubt the sanity of the speaker.

"You speak in riddles, Captain," he said, very gravely, as he held Gardiner's outstretched hand. "Surely it is rather of a sorry jest."

"No jest, I assure you, Sir Henry," smiled the

Captain. "To be brief, then, I received a letter three days agone, containing the information that by the death of Sir Jonathan you are the heir of his title and estates, which I understand are large."

"I suppose so—at least the title is an old one, but I can scarcely believe but that there is some mistake," returned Lawrence.

"And among the finest estates, if my correspondent is exactly informed," continued the Captain, ignoring the Colonel's protest. "He also states that the accumulations are something substantial. Sir Jonathan was an aged man, and quite incapable of wasting his substance in riotous living, so says Campbell."

"Campbell? and it is he who is your informant? Such being the case, there must be something in it," admitted Lawrence. "I know that Sir Jonathan was an old man, but of the value of his estates or of his mode of living I have never informed myself."

"Campbell, and no other, one of the ablest advocates in the realm; he writes that the rentals are something enormous, and another phase of this stroke of Fortune is to be considered. Your kinsman did not concern himself in politics, else his estates might have been confiscated by the Cromwellians, or the Royalists might have done them a harm. But, lad, as you still appear incredulous, assure yourself by reading that letter, for I make no doubt it will convince you of your good fortune."

The Captain had unlocked a private drawer in his escritoire, and produced a weighty missive, sealed with black, and stamped with a monogram and coat-of-arms.

"Sir Jonathan's private seal," remarked the Colonel, as he took the package in his hand. "Excuse the liberty I am taking."

"Assuredly, Sir Henry," returned the Captain, lighting his pipe, and for five minutes he puffed in silence, watching the play of his friend's countenance as he perused the letter.

"Am I not correct?" queried the Captain, when his guest had read and re-folded the voluminous sheets.

"Quite so, Captain. Sir Jonathan is dead, and, by a freak of fortune, I am his heir—what then? I am quite unconscious of any change in person or mentality," replied Sir Henry, with a grave smile.

"You are the most unaccountable of mortals. I wonder, now, if an earthquake would startle you from the calm repose of manner that appears to be your normal state? I do, by Jupiter! Demme, lad, it's a fine thing to be a peer of the realm! And so, our little Damaris will be 'My Lady,' after all, and the Major will rest in peace. Between us, Sir Henry, Gordon was ambitious—too much so, egad! but it is all in a lifetime, Sir Henry, and his daughter will wear a coronet, for I congratulate you both— quite in advance; I' faith, I was too thick-pated to see through the millstone, but Mary made the discovery, that—— Don't take it ill, but she has seen that you young people are fathoms deep with the madness men call *love*—here, the murder is out!" laughed the Captain.

"I hope to make her my wife when a suitable time has elapsed. I have left her to pass her season of mourning, untrammelled by my presence, as was most proper under the circumstances. Had I remained here, I am free to confess that I should have perhaps been unable to bridle my tongue," returned Lawrence.

"Quite proper," agreed Gardiner, briskly. "But spring is here, and you have no need to serve for

THE THREADS OF FATE

your wife like Jacob. The proprieties have been observed, and after all there is no one here in the colonies to cavil. My advice is to lose no time in wooing."

"I sincerely hope that you have told her nothing concerning this extraordinary change in my fortunes?" said Lawrence, interrogatively.

"Nothing!" returned the Captain. "My good dame cautioned me, else I might have blurted out the whole matter, so I take no credit. Mary advised that we keep the secret from all until you chose to enlighten them."

"Excellent! Your lady deserves credit for her wisdom; for the present, then, let me remain plain Lawrence, or 'Hal' an' it please you."

"With all my heart," returned Gardiner.

"I suppose you have stumbled upon no elucidation of the mystery concerning Kingsland's fate?" asked Lawrence.

"None whatever. But of late I have been revolving the matter, remembering that, as the old adage has it, 'a clean corner is none the worse for being twice swept,' and I have been thinking seriously of making an excursion to the hunting grounds, now that spring has opened, in hopes of making some discovery. The poor lad is dead—of that there cannot be a doubt; but we should feel better satisfied could we come upon the means of knowing how he died."

"Well considered, Captain, and if agreeable to you I will accompany you as soon as a trifle rested after my long voyage, and the tedious land journey. Let the affair be a profound secret, as it is unwise to rehearse the tragedy." An opinion in which the Captain concurred.

The meeting between the lovers was most tender, but their happiness was chastened by the remembrance of the sorrow which had overshadowed, and profound pity for the fate of the young Lieutenant.

On the third day after his arrival, according to agreement, Lawrence, accompanied by the Captain, set out upon an expedition, with but one attendant, Tohemon, the Mohican, whose knowledge of the hunting grounds might aid them in the real object, renewal of the search for the body of Kingsland, if, perchance, it might be above ground.

Not even the wily Indian was informed of their purpose, but with the keen perception of his race he divined the truth, following, rather than guiding, while their way led over a beaten track pursued by the hunters upon that fatal day, months agone, and until they came to the spot where Guy had separated himself from his companions to pursue the game that had led him to his death.

Then Tohemon quietly took the lead, guided by signs that would have escaped the observation of a white man. Broken twigs, the ragged stumps browned by the winter's frosts, reeds withered and bent among the lush, green growth of spring. Step by step, with unerring instinct, the Mohican followed the trail, until at length it was lost upon the edge of the dark swamp.

Viking, the Livonian hound, close at the heels of his master, suddenly rushed forward, his nose in the air, not as if scenting a trail, but rather as if the quarry sought were a bird of the air.

His tawny form was lost to sight among the rank reeds and tangled alders, and in compliance with the Colonel's request the party halted.

"He has struck some quarry, and will give tongue presently. Let us wait and take breath," counselled Lawrence.

Scarcely had the words left his lips when a long-

"The plaintive howl of the hound guided the hunters to the very verge of the fen,—"

drawn howl echoed dismally through the dim arches of the pine forest.

The cry was repeated, and with hurrying feet the hunters sped on, guided by the mournful cry which grew more distinct as they advanced.

Lawrence gave a long, peculiar whistle, which was answered by the sagacious brute, now near at hand.

"God-a-mercy!" groaned Gardiner, as he stumbled across some impediment in his path, "we are upon the right track! Look there!"

He stooped and raised a fire-lock from its lodgment in the thick growth of juniper and bracken; the barrel was rust-eaten, the lock discoloured, the breech sodden, but upon the silver plate tarnished by rain and snow the initials "G. K." were plainly visible. A few feet distant a silver drinking flask lay upon the ground, upon which the same initials were engraved, in monogram.

The plaintive howl of the hound guided the hunters to the very verge of the fen, where at the foot of a high furrow lay the remains of a human being, a skeleton bleaching in the rays of the western sun, falling obliquely between the funereal fronds of hemlock, cedar and pine, half-buried in a drift of decayed leaves and pine needles, and entwined by a spring growth of ground pine and ivy.

Like patches of flame the sleeves of a scarlet coat glowed among the vivid green, and two skeleton hands grasped the laps of the mildewed waistcoat, as if the last moments of the dead had been fraught with unendurable pain.

Their quest was ended. The afternoon was waning, and seeking the proper material they fashioned a rude bier upon which they placed all that remained of the gay Lieutenant, covering the bared skull with a kerchief to shut out the gruesome sight.

"We are not far distant from the Indian village; let us hasten thither and claim the good offices of the old Sachem, who will send some of his warriors with us to the boat," advised Captain Gardiner. "I must confess that bearing such a burden is not to my taste."

CHAPTER LII

AN UNBIDDEN GUEST

"The red-bird warbled as she wrought
Her hanging nest o'erhead,
And careless, near the fatal spot,
Her young the partridge led."

THE trill of the robin mingled with the sharp call of the bluebird, the dandelions and spring violets starred the sward, gleaming gold and blue; from the gnarled apple trees the gentle zephyrs of the fair May day fluttered the pink and white petals of the sweet-scented blossoms, carpeting the velvet grass with a bridal veil.

The air was vocal with drowsy sounds, the low hum of the bee, the twitter of birds, the ripple of brooklets, underlying the deep diapason of the sounding sea as the waves dashed against the base of the cliffs.

Sailing on level wing, a hawk floated with monotonous motion, circling lower and lower, the slanting rays of the descending sun flaming upon his brown plumage, flecking his wings with amber and gold against the azure sky and pearly drifts.

In front of the Montauk Sachem's lodge the green turf spread away, sloping gradually to the forest line, and o'ercanopied by tall, satin-leaved oaks, a sort of dais had been erected, beneath an immense arch of trailing vines, bright-hued spring flowers, violets, cowslips, the royal red of the gay nose-bleed, and the crimson velvet of love-lies-bleeding, lighting the mass of green like jets of flame. There was a preparation for a festival, although the village was unusually quiet. Now and again a grim warrior in elaborate attire, and armed to the teeth, stalked across the arena, or a bright-eyed maiden peeped from a wigwam, the only signs of life in the village.

Slowly the sun retired to his western couch, the changeful hues swept across the drapery of his couch in cloudlets, like magic pictures shifting upon an opal canvas. The round, red moon rose from beneath the wave, and the stars flashed out in masses of jewelled points.

Then, like enchantment, the scene changed. In single file bedecked warriors strode along the broad path leading to the wigwam and ranged themselves in solid cordon about the moss-carpeted lawn, in three ranks. Those of the inner circle bore flaming pine knots that flashed redly upon the canopy and great lodge, and illuminated the dim forest in the background for a depth of many yards.

Each brave was in full dress of gorgeous blanket, gay-coloured plume, gaudily wrought moccasins, and with all the adornment of bear-claw necklace; bright-hued beads and glittering wampum, and each fully armed with his bow and a full complement of arrows in the quiver at his back, and with war-club, spear, tomahawk and scalping-knife, as if marshalling for the war-path.

But the array was for a different occasion. Wyandance was about to give his daughter to the great brave who had earned his reward by a deed which was known to none save the royal family.

The minor tribes had each sent a delegation of their most renowned chiefs, wise men and braves;

even the Canarsees were represented by their sole survivor, Canady, who had taken up his abode with the Montauks.

Presently Poniute, the prospective groom, stalked into the ring, with uplifted head and haughty mien, as if fully conscious of his exalted position, and halting near the door of the lodge, where he stood motionless, the cynosure of all eyes.

He had chosen a costume eminently becoming. A coronet of scarlet and black feathers girded his high, narrow brow, and in place of the gaudy blanket he wore a loose hunting shirt, of softest doeskin, embroidered and fringed, heavy with wampum, but sleeveless and open at the chest, as if to exhibit a livid scar, the mark of a deep wound received in defending his princess at that other wedding festival which had ended so disastrously. A necklace and bracelets of panther's teeth, polished to pearly lustre, completed his attire.

At that other marriage feast the guests had been unarmed—careless; now they stood a living barricade, equipped for battle, while in the numerous paths leading oceanward, and to the depths of the forests, scouts were on the alert, who would give instant alarm at the approach of friend or foe. Yet there was slight probability of an attack, for the intended alliance was known only to a few, and those the chiefs of the minor tribes, until the day preceding the festivities; while from the white settlers, even Lyon Gardiner and his family, the affair was a profound secret.

Presently the spotted catamount skin covering the entrance of the chief's lodge was drawn aside, and Wyandance stepped forth, holding his daughter's hand, followed by Wyancombone, Wic-chi-tau-bit, and a group of merry maidens. From a second lodge a triad of chiefs appeared, Momometou, chieftain of the Corchaigs; Nowedanah, Sagamore of the Shinnecocks, tall, majestic, upright, although the snows of more than fourscore years had bleached their still abundant locks to masses of silver floss, eagle-eyed, and stern of mien as became the brothers of the Great Sachem of the Montauks. With them came Yo-kee, the young chieftain of the Manhansetts, all the native pride inherited from his father apparent in his lofty carriage, his uplifted head, his flashing eyes, as he took his appointed place, beside his kinsmen.

Very little looked Heather Flower like a happy bride as her father placed her hand in the groom's dusky palm, and she stood there with haughty brow and set lips, pledged before the assembled chiefs and braves of Sea-wan-ha-ka as the wife of the warrior at her side, from whose belt a gruesome trophy hung—the waving, silken scalp of a white man. If the savage guests wondered where that tell-tale trophy was secured, none questioned.

A triumphant smile played about the bridegroom's lips as he peered over that assemblage and knew that he was the centre of admiring glances from those sharp, restless eyes, and that as the husband of their princess he must outrank the elder chieftains, for by that marriage he would become a member of the royal family.

Seated beside her lord, beneath the flowery canopy, Heather Flower looked over the sea of waving plumes, with a haughty, rather than an abashed gaze; not a blush suffused her cheek, no love-light filled her eyes, for memory-bells were ringing in her ears, telling of the days when she carolled as sweetly, as blithely as the song birds, as she wandered through the forest in maiden-fancy free, before the false pale-face came with honeyed words and deceitful smile to lure the heart from her bosom. Again she saw the daisy wreath with which her brow was crowned by the delicate, white hand long ago mouldered to dust. Her idol was shattered, her revenge was complete, a life-long servitude was the price she had paid for those silken strands hanging at the girdle of the grim, red-handed warrior to whom she had sold her freedom.

Presently the merry-making began; some engaged in feats of skill in throwing the tomahawk and lance, others exhibited their adroitness as archers, while the younger portion of the guests danced to the monotonous beat of tom-toms and the hollow, droning sounds produced by blowing of conch-shells.

An hour passed, when, in obedience to a signal from their Sachem, the revellers paused.

Obeying a wave of his hand, the band moved away in single file to the open glade where the feast was spread; but scarcely were the guests seated when there was a stir among the warriors, whose quick ears had caught the swift fall of approaching footsteps, and in a moment one of their scouts glided within the circle of light.

As a single man the warriors sprang to their feet and grasped their weapons, but the young Indian raised his hand, palm outward, in token that only friends were at hand, and from a narrow footpath two figures advanced, Captain Gardiner and Henry Lawrence.

The old Sachem and the warriors recognised both at a glance, and met them with open palm of welcome; but even Indian stoicism failed for a brief space, the chief's hand fell to his side and he stopped short in his tracks, when they stooped and deposited their burden upon the earth, a litter upon which rested a skeleton, loosely shrouded in a scarlet hunting-coat, now faded to a dull brown, except for the vivid streaks of scarlet, showing, where the garment had lain in folds. The velvet breeches and hunting boots still clung to the limbs, and the chalky skull was hidden beneath the kerchief. A musket with rusted barrel and water-stained stock, a hunting-knife protected by the sheath, the steel but slightly discoloured, rested upon the skeleton figure of their owner, the only mementoes of the youth who had gone forth on that wintry morning in the vigour of health. The fate that had overtaken Guy Kingsland was plain.

"Poor lad, he lost his way and died miserably in the snowdrifts!" asserted Captain Gardiner, to which the old Sachem answered never a word.

Those nearest the groom noticed that the shining scalp at his girdle was hidden within its folds.

"Chief, we have come to ask your assistance; we were on a hunting expedition, and the chase led us straight to the spot where these poor bones have rested for months. We have borne the burden long and far, and are wearied with the day's hunt, therefore we came asking that you would send some of your warriors with us to the boat. I fear we have interrupted a merry-making—pray, what is the occasion?" continued the Captain, looking with some curiosity at the large assemblage.

"The King of the Montauks has given his daughter to a great brave—the Montauks are making a feast in honour of the marriage," returned Wyandance curtly. "Two of my warriors shall go with my white brothers."

Summoning two powerful savages, he gave a few directions in the Indian tongue, and turned again to the white men.

AN UNBIDDEN GUEST

"Will my pale-faced brothers eat at the feast?" he asked, but both courteously declined, urging the necessity of returning to the Isle of Wight with all speed.

Not a question concerning the gruesome object lying upon the rude bier did the old Sachem ask, much to the surprise of Lawrence, but Captain Gardiner, well versed in Indian taciturnity, laid the omission to the custom prevailing, which forbade any expression of a natural curiosity.

The two warriors lifted the burden as stoically as if it had been a light canoe, and moved away, followed by the white men.

The advent of the unbidden guests made scarcely a ripple in the proceedings. Fast and furious the revels waxed, while among her maidens the haughty, undemonstrative bride sat, as became the daughter of the kingly savage who ruled the tribes of Sea-wan-ha-ka and Manhansett-aha-quash-a-warnuck.

Like a globe of silver the moon was descending the western sky when the lordly Sachem led his daughter to the lodge of the bold warrior who had won her.

CHAPTER LIII

FROZEN

*"Body hides—where?
Ferns of all feather,
Mosses and heather
Yours be the care."*

A STRANGE Providence had ordered that the skeleton of the man who had paid the penalty of his treachery to the daughter of the Montauks should be brought to the wedding feast.

Tohemon had been dispatched to see that the boat was in readiness, and upon the beach he awaited the coming of his master. Without a question he assisted the bearers to deposit their burden in the birch canoe which Wyandance had instructed his warriors to place at the disposal of his white brothers.

Captain Gardiner and Lawrence entered their own boat, Tohemon took the oars, while one of the Montauk warriors silently took his seat in the canoe, the frail vessel keeping abreast the boat. The second brave had been dismissed, with a handsome present for his services.

The moonlight was falling brightly upon the waters, but the shadows of the tamaracks, pines and maples, with their weight of creeping vines, lay darkly across the mouth of the stream flowing between high, mossy banks where the party landed upon a secluded portion of the island, at a goodly distance from the hall, and convenient to a boat-house roughly laid up with stone, within which they laid the body, and closing the door securely made their way to the mansion. Both Mrs. Gardiner and Damaris gave a sigh of relief when the well-known footsteps sounded upon the portico, and Damaris hastened to admit the tardy ones.

A significant glance the Captain gave his wife warned her that he had made a discovery, but the maiden, engaged in the exchange of sweet nothings lovers will indulge after the shortest separation, noticed naught save that her lover was slightly pallid, a circumstance that he attributed to fatigue and disappointment that they had secured but a trivial amount of game which they had left at the Indian encampment.

It was not until after the Captain and his lady had retired to their own apartment that he made explanation.

"What has happened, husband?" she inquired, anxiously, the moment the door closed. "You are pale as a ghost, and your hand trembles—you have discovered something unpleasant, I am sure."

"We have found all that is left of poor Guy—his skeleton is lying in the boat-house below the pine woods."

"At the boat-house—and we have never guessed! How could such a thing happen?" cried Mrs. Gardiner, opening her eyes in horror and amazement.

"Softly, Mollie! He was not found there—we brought him over from Montauk. It was Viking who guided us to the spot, upon the very edge of the fen, Mah-chon-it-chuge, you know. He was lying right under the shadow of a ridge, running like a furrow, upon the twisted roots of a thicket of pines and cedars, just where a hunter's eye would never have discovered it except he had been out upon the sluggish, green-coated water among the tangled dog-lily-pads that cover the lake like a blanket; one might have passed at the distance of five feet and been none the wiser. The ground must have been frozen hard when he ventured there. I stumbled across his flask, knife and firelock some dozen yards from the place where he lay."

"Dreadful!" shuddered the lady. "You will bury the poor boy here, beside the Major?"

"Of course! of course!" assented the Captain.

"Alack! poor lad, poor lad! what a horrible end. He must have been bewildered in that dreadful wood, and probably the night came on and he must have wandered until he was frozen," sighed the lady.

"That is a question, at least to my mind, wife," in a whisper, which surprised her. "In the morn I must e'en inform the authorities, and there will be a commission from Easthampton to examine the remains—a formality of English law that must be complied with. I tell thee, dame, there is some mystery that I hope the sheriff and his fellows will make plain to their own satisfaction, and—mine."

"Why, man alive! what can you mean?"

"Alack, dame! I didn't intend to speak out, even to you, and harkee, wife, not a lisp to mortal being; but I've my suspicions that, like poor Gordon, the lad has fallen a victim to savage hate."

"Husband, your wits must be wool-gathering! There are no hostiles upon the island, and surely none of Wyandance's tribe would murder an Englishman, I'm quite sure of that," objected Mrs. Gardiner, positively.

"Aye, woman, I would be the last to disturb your faith, but you have been quite in the dark—perhaps too much so, though I but held my peace fearing to disquiet you; but there's a whisper abroad that Kingsland has been foolhardy enough to toy with the affection of the red beauty——"

"Surely you cannot mean Wyandance's daughter?" broke in Mrs. Gardiner, incredulously.

"Aye, but I do!" persisted the Captain. "Now, Mollie, I exceedingly dread to censure a man, and he dead and unable to speak up for himself, but I have it from good authority—the officers aboard some of our crafts—that when heated by wine Guy more than once boasted of his conquest of an Indian princess. He could mean no other than Heather Flower."

"Impossible!" exclaimed Mrs. Gardiner. "Surely that proud, beautiful girl, whom even a white man cannot fail to admire, cannot be a light-o'-love?"

"God save you, Mollie, not that," denied the Captain in emphatic tones, "not that! But he boasted that he had won her heart, and fearing further complications should he continue his attentions he quit the field, leaving her to wear the willow."

"Can this be true? is it possible that Guy, betrothed to our little lass, could so far forget his honour as to commit such a crime?" asked Mrs. Gardiner.

"Heyday, wife, one can scarcely call it a crime. The girl has royal blood in her veins, albeit it is the blood of a red Indian, and you will agree that she is handsome enough to attract such a fastidious lad as poor Guy."

"But he had no right to wantonly ignore every principle of justice," exclaimed the lady, indignantly. "I marvel much, husband, that you did not expostulate with him concerning his sinful course!"

"Softly, softly, dame. What's to do when I

learned the truth but yester-e'en, when Captain Travis and his officers told me the tale, vouching that they heard it from the lad's own lips?"

"Alack!" sighed the lady, "I remember that Guy was often at Montauk, and that he suddenly discontinued his visits, although I mind he resumed his calls after a time; the circumstance had no significance to me at the time."

"Nor to me," rejoined the Captain.

"Damaris need never know, poor lass!" said Mrs. Gardiner.

"Marry-come-up! not for a thousand pounds! let the dead rest, say I; it would but harrow her feelings for naught, so we'll e'en rein our tongues between our lips."

"Or Sir—the Colonel, I mean," cried the lady, correcting the title she would have given.

"Prithee, wife, make no more slips o' the tongue, else our lass may chance to read the secret Sir——"

"Aha!" smiled the lady. "If the blind lead the blind both may fall into the ditch. We both have cause for caution, else the title will fall trippingly from the tongue, eh, husband?"

"It is a sweet morsel, I vow," smiled the Captain, "and I own to my mistake."

"I was about to observe that it were best the Colonel should not be informed, it might disturb him——"

"No need for caution in that quarter," broke in the Captain. "He heard it from the lads, and was the first to ask that it might be kept from the lass."

"If such should be the fact, and I am forced to believe, as all circumstances point in that direction, that he was guilty, I can understand what you fear. Revering their princess, as the Montauk warriors do, it is easy to believe that some one of them may have ended the Lieutenant's life in revenge for the insult."

"I will relate the facts, and you may draw your own conclusions—mind, now Mollie, it is but suspicion, but certain it is, that when we set the bier down within the circle of warriors and Heather Flower turned her eyes and beheld the sight, all her Indian nerve—and she has it in an uncommon degree, for a squaw—could not keep the colour from leaving her face, or a quiver of her lips, and as for her groom——"

"Groom!" echoed the mystified lady, "what does the man mean?"

"When we arrived at the Indian village there was a brave wedding in progress, to which not a paleface was bidden—aye, more, a guard was set at every point to prevent surprise. This night Heather Flower has wedded that black-browed, fiery-eyed, vindictive warrior—Poniute."

"Merciful Heaven! it cannot be!" exclaimed Mrs. Gardiner. "If I read him aright, he is cruel, revengeful, ambitious and crafty; who could dream he would be her choice? Although she is an Indian, she is loving, good and true as steel—no mate for such as he."

"Aye, woman, and there's the rub. She is, or was, all you say, but remember she is one of the proudest women in America, and scarce a high-born dame in England can boast a haughtier spirit. Think ye, then, she would allow such an insult to pass?"

"No-o-o!" admitted Mrs. Gardiner, reluctantly.

"What follows? simply this—the savage warrior whom she has wedded was chosen as an instrument through which she might wreak a revenge upon the false lover who stole her heart. I believe her hand was the price she paid in exchange for Guy's life.

But breathe not a suspicion that can do no good, and if bruited abroad would almost certainly result in a bloody war, while it could not bring Guy back. If I am correct in my supposition, he played with edged tools and has suffered the consequences, a warning to our young men not to tamper lightly with these vengeful squaws."

"Well-a-day, we can never know positively, and perhaps it is better so—nay, I am sure it is; but what a pity that Guy should have lost his life for the gratification of a foolhardy pastime."

"Better he should suffer for his fault than that the Indians should have risen and slaughtered the innocent—the hatchet has been dug up for less than such a matter."

"You think there is danger of an outbreak?" asked Mrs. Gardiner, anxiously.

"No—not the slightest, at this length of time, if my surmise is correct, and I regard it as almost a certainty, Heather Flower, weighing the affair in the scales of justice, has destroyed the man who deserved the punishment. Her revenge is complete."

"Let us hope so."

"And now that the body is found our lass must know, but not until after the burial; she must never be enlightened as to our idea—let her believe that he, being lost, perished from cold. As for the rest, she loves Sir—the Colonel, with all her heart, and between us, wife, it was only the wishes of her father that bound her to Guy. He is dead, but truth to tell, in the light of this discovery he would have made her but a sorry mate," concluded the Captain.

Before high noon of the following day a half-dozen officials from the settlement at Easthampton, assembled at the boat-house in response to the summons sent, by Tehemon, who returned with the party.

Not a mark of violence was discovered, the ragged puncture in the thigh of the velvet breeches was easily accounted for as a rent made by the brambles through which the wearer had made his way.

The deliberations lasted but a short time, and the remains were committed to the grave that was hastily hollowed near the last resting-place of Major Gordon.

"Frozen." Such had been the verdict.

CHAPTER LIV

WITH BOOK AND RING

> "Oh, happy, happy, thrice happy state,
> When such a bright planet governs the fate
>   Of a pair of united lovers;
> 'Tis theirs, in spite of the serpent's hiss,
> To enjoy the pure, primeval kiss,
> With as much of the old, original bliss
>   As mortality ever recovers."

LIKE a pleasant dream the time passed to the lovers, but Colonel Lawrence, as he was still known at the Hall, with all a groom-elect's impatience had prevailed upon his affianced to name the happy day.

Invitations were sent to William Lawrence and his stately wife, Lady Moody and her son were bidden. It was Canady, the fleet Indian runner, who had been chosen as a Mercury, his swift journey by land insuring the speedy transmission of the invitations, and the invited guests arrived upon the *Neptune* early on the morning preceding the eve fixed for the ceremony.

Damaris, all unconscious of the dread secret of the manner in which Guy had met his fate, and still retaining the friendship for Heather Flower, insisted that the young Indian wife and her swarthy-browed lord should attend the nuptials as first bridesmaid and groomsman, both to be initiated in the conventional forms by the youthful David Gardiner and his pretty sister, Elizabeth, who were tall and dignified beyond their age.

The grapes were purpling upon the vines, the

thistle-down was drifting lightly upon the soft breeze, the gay golden-rod hung its yellow wreaths in masses, the sumach tossed its blood-red tassels in flaming torches, the forest trees had donned their autumnal robes, the oaks in royal purple, the hickory and elm in brilliant chrome flecked with green, the maples in scarlet, in the moon of ripening fruit and garnered grain, mellow September.

Fain would the good people of Maidstone have witnessed the ceremony, wishing with all their hearts that the marriage might be solemnised within their little sanctuary, a low structure of rough timbers and boards, thatched, like most of the primitive dwellings, and but twenty-six feet square, quite inadequate to accommodate the scores of settlers who would have flocked to witness the ceremony.

The bride-elect insisted that the marriage should take place at the Hall, and in the presence of but a few chosen guests, naming among the first Heather Flower, the stately old Sachem, her father, with Wic-chi-tau-bit and Wyancombone. In her heart she had always held an aversion for the sullen-faced Poniute, but he, as the husband of her friend, could not be ignored, and a messenger was sent, bidding her red friends to the bridal.

This was the message the old Sachem returned:

" Wyandance will go to the marriage feast of the Snowbird, and with him the young warrior who will be the Sachem of the Montauks when a few moons have passed. Wic-chi-tau-bit, the queen of the Montauks, will go with Heather Flower and the great warrior who is her lord. The Sachem of the Montauks would see the Snowbird pledge her vows after the manner of her people. Wyandance is glad for her, but he will mourn in his heart when the Snowbird flies away with her mate, to dwell in his wigwam in the land of the pale-face across the deep water, for Wyandance knows that his aged eyes will look upon her no more until she comes to him in the spirit land after many moons have grown and waned."

It had been arranged that the ceremony should take place at an early hour of the evening, and while the last beams of the day-god wrapped the boles of the mighty forest trees in a mantle of cloth-of-gold, two canoes skimmed over the waters that were scarcely rippled by the light breeze, and seated therein were the Indian guests bidden to the bridal.

As they stepped ashore a third boat approached, occupied by the Reverend Thomas James, who, in the quaint speech of that day, was styled "a painful minister," and who was the first pastor installed over the church, he having become a settler in the year 1650; and with their minister were several solemn-visaged lights of the church and state.

Indians and white having disembarked, the usual saluations were exchanged, and in company they proceeded to the mansion, where they were received by the host and hostess with all the conventional ceremony usual in England upon like occasions.

"I've no patience with the primitive way in which our colonists dispose of such important matters," said Captain Gardiner, confidentially, to the bridegroom-elect. "Why, would you believe it, there was a day when the Puritans came over in the *Mayflower*, that a couple just stood up before the congregation, joined their hands, and solemly promised to live together after God's holy ordinance, with ne'er a clergyman to say amen. Such was the case when the staunch Edward Winslow took White's widow to wife; but it was not so in dear Old England, and I adhere to the good old customs as far as practicable. I mind me of the times when we made merry at a marriage feast over choice vintage and the viands were spread for a goodly company, and though our wedding guests are not numerous, I would have the same hilarity prevail on this auspiciuos occasion. Do you not agree with me, Lawrence?" he added, turning to William, who had entered the room in time to catch the latter portion of the discourse.

"With all my heart, Captain, and if Sir Henry——"

"An' ye would not have me angry in earnest, please forget the title, good cousin, an appendage rather out of place in the colonies. The 'Sir' may be appropriate when I am across seas, but for the present let it be dropped," smiled Henry.

"As you will, good cousin," returned William. "Some are born to fortune, and you are one of the few upon whom the fickle jade has seen fit to shower her favours—wealth, honour, title."

"And last—best gift of all, that priceless jewel, the pure love of a virtuous maiden—ah, William, a gift I prize more than all," replied the Colonel, his fine face flushing. "For her sake I value the bauble that will crown her fair brow, but feeling assured that should an adverse fate strip me of wealth, rob me of title, make me an exile, as in these troublous times so often happens, she will cling to me whatever betide. Thank God, she does not wed me for my title, or for my gold—my accession is as yet a secret from her; she is wedding plain Colonel Lawrence."

"So the Captain told me, warning Bess, also. The news was a surprise to me. Lady Moody knows nothing. In good sooth, cousin, I congratulate you upon the fortune that has given you a bride worthy of a throne."

"A throne in a good man's heart, say rather; I have lived long enough to learn to my cost that kings and their courts are humbugs, the customs of the great a nuisance."

"Here are the remainder of our guests, with the minister, husband!" called Mrs. Gardiner, as she hastened down the staircase accompanied by Lady Moody and Sir Henry Moody.

The guests were coming swiftly up the avenue, the old Sachem and his queen, Wyancombone, with Heather Flower and Poniute, whose sullen features wore a more than usual grimness. Hastening after, and scarcely able to keep pace with the fleet-footed children of the forest, came the Reverend Thomas James, with the coterie of townsmen. Host and hostess met the guests, and the few necessary introductions followed.

According to custom, Poniute remained with the groom and second groomsman, while Heather Flower was conducted to the chamber where the bride and her attendants awaited her coming.

A few whispered words from young David to the grave, attentive savage prepared him for his role, and presently Elizabeth Lawrence appeared and announced the coming of the bride and her maidens.

Always handsome and stately, Colonel Lawrence was even more commanding in form and expressive in feature than usual, and his eyes softened as he drew his bride's hand within his arm and whispered in her ear;

"My love—my life—mine through time and in eternity."

"Yours alone," she breathed softly, raising her eyes in which shone the love-light.

There was a little stir, and the wedding party

entered the drawing-room where the clergyman waited, clothed in the full vestments of his sacred office. It was a picturesque company, like the actors grouped in a masquerade.

Very lovely looked the bride, her bridal veil floating about her slender form like a mist, her cheeks flushing, her white lids veiling the starry eyes; very proud and happy looked the groom in his faultless attire—not the conventional evening costume of the period, but in the scarlet coat and full uniform of a Colonel of light-horse in the British service.

Pretty Elizabeth Gardiner, childish and sweet in her sheer muslin frock, and her brother, the beau-ideal of a best man, were pleasant to see as they drew up their forms to the fullest height. Captain Gardiner and Captain Lawrence were arrayed as became their station, and for the auspicious occasion, while Mrs. Gardiner and Elizabeth Lawrence wore petticoats of satin, with pannier, stomacher and ruffles, identical in fashion, the only difference being in the colour of the garments. Mrs. Gardiner was charming in blue, Elizabeth stately in royal purple. Their brooches, bracelets, lace and rings were fully offset by the knee-buckles, shoe buckles and stock clasps worn by their liege lords.

Remarkable was the attire of the remaining guests. A startling picture Heather Flower presented. Her cheeks, that had been pallid almost to ghastliness, glowed like the bloom on a ripe peach, as she stood motionless, although there was a spirit and fire in the poise of her head, in her whole attitude.

A sleeveless tunic of softest doeskin revealed the contour of her arms, that were encircled by bracelets of purple wampum, matching the girdle about her waist. A robe of russet-brown, edged with a broad band of crimson cloth, embroidered with brilliantly coloured beads and quills, depended from her shoulders; leggings, fringed and beaded, covered her limbs from knee to ankle; her feet were encased in dainty moccasins, elaborately beaded, and laced with crimson cords terminating in heavy tassels.

In grim contrast to his bride Poniute loomed up, clad in a buckskin shirt and wrapped in a mantle of crimson cloth edged with costly fur, its bright hues marred by strange and ugly devices, serpents, insects and turtles. With his tomahawk and scalping knife displayed in his girdle, his unquiet eyes roving restlessly from one object to another, his straight, well-knit physique, he was a picturesque figure.

Near at hand stood Wyandance, tall, majestic, kingly of presence, a single eagle feather rising above the wampum crown girding his brow; his robe of russet and crimson, worn with the grace of a Roman toga, trailed in folds to his feet. In his belt he carried knife and tomahawk. By his side stood Wic-chi-tau-bit, garbed like her daughter, with the exception of colouring. Her dun-coloured robe was edged with silver-grey fur, a crown of soft grey feathers adorned her head; yet her attire was gorgeous in contrast to the Quaker garb worn by Lady Moody, whose drab frock, fashioned to the severest lines, gained even more preciseness from the white kerchief of sheer muslin pinned in snowy folds across her bosom, and the close muslin cap, destitute of bow or lace, that concealed her still abundant hair.

Unconsciously Wyancombone had assumed the pose of a gladiator awaiting the entrance of a contestant within an arena. There was a smouldering fire in his keen eyes, his lips were compressed as if from some hidden pain. His left arm clasped his flame-coloured blanket across his breast, his right hand was clenched and partially outstretched. Canady, standing at his elbow, glanced sharply into the set face, as if he would learn the secret hidden in the heart beating beneath that folded arm.

While in the drawing-room the "goodlie companie" awaited in decorous silence, in the entrance hall a motley gathering of serving men and women were grouped. Conspicuous were the bronzed visages of the Mohicans, the shining black countenance of Xantippe, lighted by two rows of ivory teeth and the whites of the restless eyes. There was the staid, solemn features of the brawny Scot, the ruddy face of the English servitor, the rosy, plump British maids and matrons, making up the sum total of the retainers of the wealthy landholder and magnate of the colony, Captain Lyon Gardiner.

There was a silence so deep that the faint rustle of the leaves was audible as the minister opened the prayer-book at the marriage service. It had been at the especial request of the bride, the use of the prayer book, which had been eschewed by the reigning power. But Major Gordon, as a Royalist at heart, and Guy Kingsland would have insisted upon the form, and Damaris subscribed to their wishes.

With bated breath the children of the forest listened to the impressive service and the solemn benediction, and when the man of God raised his voice in prayer each swarthy forehead was bent low, each dusky hand involuntarily pressed upon the heart, as those untaught souls bowed before the majesty of the God invoked in that earnest appeal.

An expression of awe, almost of fear, stole over the features of Heather Flower's grim lord. Perhaps, at that moment he remembered that, but for his deed, another than the noble, dignified groom might have been standing beside that peerless bride.

CHAPTER LVI

DISSOLVING VIEWS

TWO weeks after their wedding day Sir Henry Lawrence and his bride sailed away for their home in Old England, and the last form that faded from their view as they stood upon the deck of the staunch ship *Triton* was that of Wyancombone, as he watched the fast-receding barque until the sails were but a speck upon the horizon.

From that hour a strange malady seized the young Indian—a wasting of flesh, together with a melancholy for which his people could not account, and which his white friends could not interpret.

"What ails the lad?" Captain Gardiner asked, when Mrs. Gardiner broached the subject. "I fear me much he is in a decline."

"I have a suspicion," returned the lady, oracularly.

"And what is that, dame?"

"In sooth his affliction is like that of one crossed in love. He mopes—loves solitude, and——"

"Tush! You are dreaming, wife. There is not a maiden of his tribe that would not joyfully assume the exalted station among her people that must be accorded the squaw he may elect to share his wigwam."

"I said naught of the squaws of his tribe. Still, I am sure he is the victim of a hopeless love."

"You speak in riddles—prithee, explain your meaning."

"I suspect—nay, I am assured—that he is pining by reason of an unrequited love," persisted the lady.

"For whom?"

"Who but our Damaris," returned Mrs. Gardiner. "Love plays strange pranks. It was his peculiar manner at the wedding that opened my eyes. I marked the glitter in his eyes, the tension of his muscles, and drew my own conclusions."

"I bethink me he did appear a trifle odd—perhaps you are right—if so, from my soul I pity him," returned the Captain.

"Happy for him that the object of his passion is across seas," said Mrs. Gardiner.

"There is Chief Wyandance—he is declining in strength. He has already consulted me relative to the government of his tribe when he shall have passed away, requesting me to become the legal guardian of the 'Sunck-squaw'[1] and of the lad until he shall have reached his majority," said the Captain.

"In view of existing circumstances there is a liability that there will be a great change in the government of the confederated tribes," said Mrs. Gardiner. "Should Wyandance and his son pass hence, the tribe will crown Heather Flower. Have you noted that she comes here but seldom, and only when business calls her hither? She is greatly changed, and not for the better. She is exacting—even arrogant. I believe she would rule with a firm hand."

The prevision of the Captain and his lady was soon to be verified.

Wyandance suddenly sickened with a mortal illness, stricken, not by disease, but by poison secretly administered.

[1] *Sunck-squaw.*—Widow of a chief.

Whose was the hand that had given the death potion? What was the nature of the poison? Even the occult power of the old conjurer Wee-gon failed to probe the mystery, but he unhesitatingly declared that the mortal sickness of the chief was not the result of any animal, reptile or vegetable poison known to any medicine-man. Twice he had made long journeys for the purpose of consulting with the medicine-men of hostile tribes,[2] one to the village of Ninigret, another to the medicine-man of the Mohawks, but their united skill could furnish no antidote against the subtle poison that was sapping the life of the Sachem. Wee-gon averred that the diabolical deed was the work of a pale-face.

Scarcely was the Sachem laid in his grave than the hand of greed, nerved by the tempter of mankind, was outstretched to bring about a sale of Montauk by the Squaw-Sachem and her invalid son.

Tradition tells the story in full. Much persuasion had been brought to bear upon Wic-chi-tau-bit and her unfortunate subjects, who did not take kindly to the sale of their ancestral home.

In the brain of the Indian the events of that day were written in letters of fire, and through the mists of centuries the tradition has come down from father to son, that the Squaw-Sachem, her minor son and three councillors were the only parties to the transaction on the part of the Montauks.

The lords of the soil were disinherited of their domain, and the incident of two-and-a-half centuries ago was closed.

---

[2] Medicine men of all Indian tribes are privileged to visit an enemy's village to consult with those of their own craft. Their persons are held sacred, and they can perform long journeys through the heart of a country inhabited by a tribe at war with their own with perfect safety. Such visits are of frequent occurrence among the tribes.

Wyancombone, upon whose shoulders the mantle of a great Sachem had fallen, had placed his totem to the parchment, through which his people became mere incumbrances, and like a dethroned monarch he wandered, his interest in the chase lost, his ambition blighted, his soul warped by the changes a few short years had wrought.

Ere a twelvemonth passed, heart-stricken and life-weary in the realisation of what her relinquishment had cost her people, Wic-chi-tau-bit was laid beside her husband.

The shadows of a September evening were gathering blackly, heralding a tempestuous night, when the young Sachem glided from his wigwam and took the path to the cove where his canoe lay. Unmooring it, he pushed out upon the ruffled bay with nervous strokes that sent the light bark scudding across the green furrows like a wild bird driven by the tempest, cutting a swift flight for Man-cho-nock.

His forehead was bedewed with a cold perspiration, his lips stained with flecks of crimson, his limbs trembling from exhaustion when he landed upon the island at a secluded spot and moored his light craft.

Great scattering raindrops pattered upon the leaves above his head as he reached the rustic seat reared by Guy Kingsland's hands.

At a little distance two dark mounds, barely discernible in the thickening gloom, marked the spot where rested all that was mortal of the two palefaces whose destinies had so strangely been blended with the life-line of the young Indian.

His voice sounded out in a dirge-like moaning cry:

"Great Spirit, Wyancombone has heard his father calling from the spirit land. Why should he strive to shut out the voice of the dead? The Snowbird will walk beside her white brave, and Wyancombone will forget the wound in his heart that has taken away the life he cared naught for since the Snowbird went away in the white-winged canoe and Wyancombone saw her no more. Snowbird, farewell!"

A roar like the boom of artillery swept across the deep and surged through the forest; the crash of branches torn from the gnarled trunks of mighty oaks mingled with the hoarse voice of the tornado. The hurricane raged on till long past midnight, dying away only when the spectral daylight lifted the veil of night.

Beneath the black pall of cloud and tempest a struggling, human soul had gone forth—a broken heart had ceased to beat.

In the chill, grey morning. the two Mohicans found him, stretched almost beneath the rustic bench.

From the set lips a tiny crimson stream had trickled upon the silken sheen of a creamy white ribbon which the Mohicans recognised as a portion of the adornment in the bridal attire of Damaris Gordon.

They left the mute token in the stiffened fingers that in death had clung so lovingly to the memento of the pale-faced maiden the youth had so passionately loved.

Lyon Gardiner's guardianship was ended, and three days after the burial of the young Sachem Heather Flower was crowned Queen of the Montauks.

While yielding the outward obedience due a husband's supremacy, exacted by the laws of her people, she, in turn, demanded the homage due her rank as his sovereign, and hour by hour her lord felt the coldness of a mere conventional observance of wifely duty, against which not the severest moralist, white man or Indian, could cavil.

Poniute had the shadow for the substance—the heart he craved was dead.

Heather Flower sat alone in the great lodge that Poniute had prepared for her, a structure befitting her station and his added dignity as a member of the royal family. Her husband was absent upon a bear hunt, the warriors were engaged in hunting or fishing, the village was nearly deserted, for most of the squaws had gone into the forest in quest of herbs and nuts.

To outward observation Heather Flower had changed not from the stern haughtiness that had marked her bearing since her marriage, but now, when no eye save that of the Omnipotent was upon her, the mask of pride fell.

Her eyes rested upon the score of scalps suspended from a hoop amid the smoke curling lazily through the opening at the apex of the lodge, and as if charmed by some unseen presence, she placed her hand upon the circlet, selecting one strand of soft, curling hair from the mass of raven scalp-locks, shivering as her fingers caressed it, just as they had many times since the trophy had been placed there.

Ah! spite of the fierce pride inherent in her soul, spite of her Indian birth and the years of repression so much practised by her race, she was but a woman, with only a woman's heart. The absorbing love that had been held in abeyance for the moment asserted itself. A gasping sob rose to her throat, her head sank low as she pressed her lips to the terrible souvenir in a kiss of such tenderness as one gives to the dead, a cold, hopeless sorrow filming her eyes and quenching their light as a fleecy cloud dims the fierce glare of the sun-god.

A piteous invocation broke from her lips:

"Will the Great Spirit look in pity upon Heather Flower? for her heart lies dead and cold within her bosom—buried in the cold grave where they laid her white warrior to sleep.

"Manitou of the red man and the pale-face, listen to Heather Flower when she tells how the shade of the dead comes between her and the brave whose slave she has given herself to be. He paid the price the red maiden asked—for this she hates him.

"Will the Great Spirit bring the white warrior to the happy hunting ground, where, after wandering long in the hot deserts and frozen swamps until she has paid the price of her sinfulness, Heather Flower may meet her white brave whom she has sent to the land of spirits?

"Great Manitou, the soul of the warrior is strong, but Heather Flower has only a woman's heart—the love she gave her white warrior must burn here forever! Great Manitou, call her soon!"

She lifted her hands and pressed the palms against her heart as if to still the agony she was forced to conceal from mortal eyes, and sank fainting upon a couch of furs.

Not for many years was her prayer answered, for she lived long and reigned wisely, but a smile was never seen upon her lips.

Two and a-half centuries have fled into eternity, but men still live who remember the traditions of their ancestors, and the prophecy of Poggatticutt, the Manhansett sage and seer, who, when standing with one foot upon the shore of time and the other foot slipping over the brink of eternity, viewed from Sunset Rock the dying of the last day his mortal eyes would behold, uttered the prediction that has lived in the memory of his descendants, and has been transmitted through their traditions:

"When the Great Spirit is angry with the pale-faced intruders for their injuries to His red children, He will hide His face behind the storm-cloud, and on the wings of the tempest will speak in a voice of thunder and send His lightning to rend this rock that shall be my throne no longer."

The prophecy has been fulfilled. Sunset Rock, known to the ancient Indian tribes as "Poggatticutt's Throne," has been rent in nine fragments by the lightning bolt.

Sir Henry Lawrence and his beautiful wife lived, loving and beloved, to see the third generation of their descendants growing up about them. Side by side they sleep the last sleep in the vaults of a grey old English church, where a tablet is inscribed to their memory.

Only the descendants of the ancient chiefs and warriors of the Montauks know the place of rest, or the shrine, still accounted sacred, where the feet of Poggatticutt pressed the sod during the long march when he was borne to his burial.

Near at hand, where the sun lingers longest, sleeps the royal family of the Montauks, of a dynasty dating back centuries: Wyandance the "Warrior King," Nowedanah, Momometou, Wyancombone and Yo-kee, with Poniute and the Squaw-Sachems, Wic-chi-tau-bit and the Heather Flower, of the Montauks.

> "Their very names are half forgot,
> Their ancient graves unknown,
> And dim oblivion's shadow,
> Around them wide is thrown."

CPSIA information can be obtained
at www.ICGtesting.com
Printed in the USA
LVHW021600310323
743145LV00002B/268